3/1

Praise for the

MORGANVILLE VAMPIRES NOVELS

Date Due

4·12·11			
7·26·11			
9-3-12			
5·1·14			
6·6·15			
11-30-16			
2·19·21			

"Ms. Cai . . . rule, only the strongest . . . hours. Each character . . . nality quirks and a full . . . packed with action, an . . . que Reviews

"Rachel C . . . asy subgenre with her s . . . ller contains plenty of . . . ter driven by the good, . . . — Book Reviews

"The pace . . . chapter on the town o . . .

. . . and Critics

"Bool . . . that the audie . . . ovides a stron . . . Reviews

"A si . . . capture plent . . . ce, and well- . . . Critics

inued . . .

Feast of Fools

"Fast-paced and filled with action. . . . Fans of the series will appreciate *Feast of Fools*."
—Genre Go Round Reviews

"Thrilling. . . . In sharing her well-imagined world, Ms. Caine gives readers the danger-filled supernatural moments they crave while adding friendship, romance, and teen issues to give the story a realistic feel. A fast-moving series where there's always a surprise just around every dark corner."
—Darque Reviews

"Very entertaining. . . . I could not put *Feast of Fools* down. . . . There is a level of tension in the Morganville books that keeps you on the edge of your seat. Even in the background scenes you're waiting for the other shoe to drop. And it always does."
—Flames Rising

"I thoroughly enjoyed reading *Feast of Fools*. . . . It was fantastic. . . . The excitement and suspense . . . [are] thrilling and I was fascinated reading about the town of Morganville. I greatly look forward to reading the next book in this series and catching up with the other books. I highly recommend *Feast of Fools* to paranormal readers for a delightful and fun read that you won't want to put down."
—Fresh Fiction

Midnight Alley

"A fast-paced, page-turning read packed with wonderful characters and surprising plot twists. Rachel Caine is an engaging writer; readers will be completely absorbed in this chilling story, unable to put it down until the last page. . . . For fans of vampire books, this is one that shouldn't be missed!"
—Flamingnet

"Weaves a web of dangerous temptation, dark deceit, and loving friendships. The nonstop vampire action and delightfully sweet relationships will captivate readers and leave them craving more."   —Darque Reviews

The Dead Girls' Dance

"[Glass Houses] left me emotionally spent, in a good way. The intensity is cubed in [The Dead Girls' Dance]. It was hard to put this down for even the slightest break and, forget what happens to the kid with the scar and glasses, I want to know what happens next in Morganville. If you love to read about characters with whom you can get deeply involved, Rachel Caine is so far a one hundred percent sure bet to satisfy that need. I love her Weather Warden stories, and her vampires are even better."   —The Eternal Night

"Throw in a mix of vamps and ghosts and it can't get any better than *Dead Girls' Dance*."   —Dark Angel Reviews

Glass Houses

"Rachel Caine brings her brilliant ability to blend witty dialogue, engaging characters, and an intriguing plot."   —Romance Reviews Today

"A rousing horror thriller that adds a new dimension to the vampire mythos . . . a heroine the audience will admire and root for as she swallows her trepidations to ensure her friend and roomies are safe. The key to this fine tale is her plausible reactions to living in a town run by vampires that make going to college in the Caine universe quite an experience. *Glass Houses* is an electrifying enthralling coming-of-age supernatural tale."

—Midwest Book Review

THE MORGANVILLE VAMPIRES NOVELS

Glass Houses

The Dead Girls' Dance

Midnight Alley

Feast of Fools

Lord of Misrule

Carpe Corpus

Fade Out

Kiss of Death

Ghost Town

THE
MORGANVILLE
VAMPIRES

VOLUME III

Lord of Misrule

and

Carpe Corpus

RACHEL CAINE

 NEW AMERICAN LIBRARY

New American Library
Published by New American Library,
a division of Penguin Group (USA) Inc.,
375 Hudson Street, New York, New York 10014, USA
Penguin Group (Canada), 90 Eglinton Avenue East, Suite 700, Toronto,
Ontario M4P 2Y3, Canada (a division of Pearson Penguin Canada Inc.)
Penguin Books Ltd., 80 Strand, London WC2R 0RL, England
Penguin Ireland, 25 St. Stephen's Green, Dublin 2,
Ireland (a division of Penguin Books Ltd.)
Penguin Group (Australia), 250 Camberwell Road, Camberwell,
Victoria 3124, Australia (a division of Pearson Australia Group Pty. Ltd.)
Penguin Books India Pvt. Ltd., 11 Community Centre,
Panchsheel Park, New Delhi - 110 017, India
Penguin Group (NZ), 67 Apollo Drive, Rosedale, North Shore 0632,
New Zealand (a division of Pearson New Zealand Ltd.)
Penguin Books (South Africa) (Pty.) Ltd., 24 Sturdee Avenue,
Rosebank, Johannesburg 2196, South Africa

Penguin Books Ltd., Registered Offices:
80 Strand, London WC2R 0RL, England

Published by New American Library, a division of Penguin Group (USA) Inc. *Lord of Misrule* and *Carpe Corpus* were previously published in separate Signet and NAL Jam mass market editions.

First New American Library Printing (Double Edition), March 2011
10 9 8 7 6 5 4 3 2 1

Lord of Misrule copyright © Roxanne Longstreet Conrad, 2009
Carpe Corpus copyright © Roxanne Longstreet Conrad, 2009
All rights reserved excerpt from *Bite Club* copyright © Roxanne Longstreet Conrad, 2011

LORD OF MISRULE

To Ter Matthies, Anna Korra'ti, and Shaz Flynn
—courageous fighters, each one.

And to Pat Flynn, who never stopped.

ACKNOWLEDGMENTS

This book wouldn't be here without the support of my husband, Cat, my friends Pat, Jackie, and Sharon, and a host of great online supporters and cheerers-on.

Special thank-you recognition to Sharon Sams, Shaz Flynn, and especially to fearless beta readers Karin and Laura for their excellent input.

Thanks always to Lucienne Diver.

THE STORY SO FAR . . .

Claire Danvers was going to Caltech. Or maybe MIT. She had her pick of great schools, but because she's only sixteen, her parents sent her to a supposedly safe place for a year to mature—Texas Prairie University, a small school in Morganville, Texas.

One problem: Morganville isn't what it seems. It's the last safe place for vampires, and that makes it not very safe at all for the humans who venture in for work or school. The vampires rule the town . . . and everyone who lives in it.

Claire's second problem is that she's gathered both human and vampire enemies. Now she lives with housemates Michael Glass (newly made a vampire), Eve Rosser (always been Goth), and Shane Collins (whose absentee dad is a wannabe vampire killer). Claire's the normal one . . . or she would be, except that she's become an employee of the town Founder, Amelie, and befriended one of the most dangerous, yet most vulnerable, vampires of them all—Myrnin, the alchemist.

Now Amelie's vampire father, Bishop, has come to Morganville and destroyed the fragile peace, turning vampires against one another and creating dangerous new alliances and factions in a town that already had too many.

Morganville's turning in on itself, and Claire and her friends have chosen to stand with the Founder, but it could mean working with their enemies . . . and fighting their friends.

ONE

It was all going wrong, and Morganville was burning—parts of it, anyway.

Claire stood at the windows of the Glass House and watched the flames paint the glass a dull, flickering orange. She could always see the stars out here in the Middle of Nowhere, Texas—but not tonight. Tonight, there was—

"You're thinking it's the end of the world," a cool, quiet voice said behind her.

Claire blinked out of her trance and turned to look. Amelie—the Founder, and the baddest vampire in town, to hear most of the others tell it—looked fragile and pale, even for a vampire. She'd changed out of the costume she'd worn to Bishop's masked ball—not a bad idea, since it had a stake-sized hole in the chest, and she'd bled all over it. If Claire had needed proof that Amelie was tough, she'd certainly gotten it tonight. Surviving an assassination attempt definitely gave you points.

The vampire was wearing gray—a soft gray sweater, and *pants*. Claire had to stare, because Amelie just didn't do pants. Ever. It was beneath her, or something.

Come to think of it, Claire had never seen her in the color gray, either.

Talk about the end of the world.

"I remember when Chicago burned," Amelie said. "And London. And Rome. The world doesn't end, Claire. In the morning, the survivors start to build again. It's the way of things. The human way."

Claire didn't particularly want a pep talk. She wanted to curl up in her warm bed upstairs, pull pillows over her head, and feel Shane's arms around her.

None of that was going to happen. Her bed was currently occupied by Miranda, a freaked-out teenage psychic with dependency issues, and as for Shane . . .

Shane was about to *leave*.

"Why?" she blurted. "Why are you sending him out there? You know what could happen—"

"I know a great deal about Shane Collins that you don't," Amelie interrupted. "He's not a child, and he has survived much in his young life. He'll survive this. And he wishes to make a difference."

She was sending Shane into the predawn darkness with a few chosen fighters, both vampire and human, to take possession of the Bloodmobile: the last reliably accessible blood storage in Morganville.

And it was the last thing Shane wanted to do. It was the last thing Claire wanted for him.

"Bishop isn't going to want the Bloodmobile for himself," Claire said. "He wants it destroyed. Morganville's full of walking blood banks, as far as he's concerned. But it'll hurt *you* if you lose it, so he'll come after it. Right?"

The severe, thin line of Amelie's mouth made it clear that she didn't like being second-guessed. It definitely couldn't be called a smile. "As long as Shane has the book, Bishop will not dare destroy the vehicle for fear of destroying his great treasure along with it."

Translation: Shane was bait. Because of the *book*. Claire hated that damn book. It had brought her nothing but trouble from the time she'd first heard about it. Amelie and Oliver, the two biggest vamps in town, had both been scrambling to find it, and it had dropped into Claire's hands instead. She wished she had the courage to grab it from Shane right now, run outside, and toss it in the nearest burning house to get rid of it once and for all, because as far as she could tell, it hadn't done anybody any good, ever—including Amelie.

Claire said, "He'll kill Shane to get it."

Amelie shrugged. "I gamble that killing Shane is far more difficult than it would appear."

"Yeah, you are gambling. You're betting his life."

Amelie's ice gray eyes were steady on hers. "Be clear on this: I am, in fact, betting all our lives. So be grateful, child, and also be warned. I could concede this fight at any time. My father would allow me to walk away—only me, alone. Defeated. I stay out of duty to you and the others in this town who are loyal to me." Her eyes narrowed. "Don't make me reconsider that."

Claire hoped she didn't look as mutinous as she felt. She pasted on what was supposed to be an agreeable expression, and nodded. Amelie's eyes narrowed even more.

"Get prepared. We leave in ten minutes."

Shane wasn't the only one with a dirty job to do; they were all assigned things they didn't particularly like. Claire was going with Amelie to try to rescue another vampire—Myrnin. And while Claire liked Myrnin, and admired him in a lot of ways, she also wasn't too excited about facing down—again—the vampire holding him prisoner, the dreadful Mr. Bishop.

Eve was off to the coffee shop, Common Grounds, with the just-about-as-awful Oliver, her former boss. Michael was about to head out to the university with Richard Morrell, the mayor's son. How he was supposed to protect a few thousand clueless college students, Claire had no idea; she took a moment to marvel at the fact that the vampires really could lock down the town when they wanted. She'd have thought keeping students on campus in this situation would be impossible—kids phoning home, jumping in cars, getting the hell out of Dodge.

Except the vampires controlled the phone lines, cell phones, the Internet, the TV, and the radio, and cars either died or wrecked on the outskirts of town if the vampires didn't want you to leave. Only a few people had ever gotten out of Morganville successfully without permission. Shane had been one. And then he'd come *back*.

Claire still had no idea what kind of guts that had taken, knowing what was waiting for him.

"Hey," Claire's housemate Eve said. She paused, arms full of clothes—black and red, so they'd almost certainly come out of Eve's own Goth-heavy closet—and gave Claire a quick once-over. She'd changed to what in Eve's world were practical fighting clothes—a pair of tight black jeans, a tight black shirt with red skull patterns all over it, and stompy, thick-soled boots. And a spiked black leather collar around her throat that almost dared the vampires, *Bite that!*

"Hey," Claire said. "Is this really a good time to start laundry?"

Eve rolled her eyes. "Cute. So, some people didn't want to be caught dead in their stupid ball costumes, if you know what I mean. How about you? Ready to take that thing off?"

Claire looked down at herself. She was honestly surprised to realize that she was still wearing the tight, garish bodysuit of her Harlequin costume. "Oh, yes." She sighed. "Got anything without, you know, skulls?"

"What's wrong with skulls? And that would be a no, by the way." Eve dumped the armload of clothing on the floor and rooted through it, pulling out a plain black shirt and a pair of blue jeans. "The jeans are yours. Sorry, but I sort of raided everybody's stash. Hope you like the underwear you have on; I didn't go through your drawers."

"Afraid it might get you all turned on?" Shane asked from over her shoulder. "Please say yes." He grabbed a pair of his own jeans from the pile. "And please stay out of my closet."

Eve gave him the finger. "If you're worried about me finding your porn stash, old news, man. Also, you have really boring taste." She grabbed a blanket from the couch and nodded toward the corner. "No privacy anywhere in this house tonight. Go on, we'll fix up a changing room."

The three of them edged past the people and vampires who packed the Glass House. It had become the unofficial campaign center for their side of the war, which meant there were plenty of people tramping around, getting in their stuff, whom none of them would have let cross the threshold under normal circumstances.

Take Monica Morrell. The mayor's daughter had shed her elaborate Marie Antoinette costume and was back to the blond, slinky, pretty, slimy girl Claire knew and hated.

"Oh my God." Claire gritted her teeth. "Is she wearing my *blouse?*" It was her only good one. Silk. She'd just bought it last week. Now she'd never be able to put it on again. "Remind me to burn that later." Monica saw her staring, fingered the collar of the shirt, and gave her an evil smile. She mouthed, *Thanks.* "Remind me to burn it *twice.* And stomp on the ashes."

Eve grabbed Claire by the arm and hustled her into the empty corner of the room, where she shook out the blanket and held it at arm's length to provide a temporary shelter.

Claire peeled off her sweat-soaked Harlequin costume with a whimper of relief, and shivered as the cool air hit her flushed skin. She felt awkward and anxious, stripped to her underwear with just a blanket held up between her and a dozen strangers, some of whom probably wanted to eat her.

Shane leaned over the top. "You done?"

She squealed and threw the wadded-up costume at him. He caught it and waggled his eyebrows at her as she stepped into the jeans and quickly buttoned up the shirt.

"Done!" she called.

Eve dropped the blanket and smiled poison-sweet at Shane.

"Your turn, leather boy," she said. "Don't worry. I won't accidentally embarrass you."

No, she'd embarrass him completely on purpose, and Shane knew it, from the glare he threw her. He ducked behind the blanket. Claire wasn't tall enough to check him out over the top—not that she wasn't tempted—but when Eve lowered the blanket, bit by bit, Claire grabbed one corner and pulled it back up.

"You're no fun," Eve said.

"Don't mess with him. Not now. He's going out there alone."

Eve's face went still and tight, and for the first time, Claire realized that the shine in her eyes wasn't really humor. It was a tightly controlled kind of panic. "Yeah," she said. "I know. It's just—we're all splitting up, Claire. I wish we didn't have to do that."

On impulse, Claire hugged her. Eve smelled of powder and some kind of darkly floral perfume, with a light undertone of sweat.

"Hey!" Shane's wounded yell was enough to make them both giggle. The blanket had drooped enough to show him zipping up his pants. Fast. "Seriously, girls, *not cool*. A guy could do serious damage."

He looked more like Shane now. The leather pants had made him unsettlingly hot-model gorgeous. In jeans and his old, faded Marilyn Manson T-shirt, he was somebody down-to-earth, somebody Claire could imagine kissing.

And she did imagine, just like that. It was, as usual, heart-racingly delicious.

"Michael's going out, too," Eve said, and now the tension she'd been hiding made her voice tremble. "I have to tell him—"

"Go on," Claire said. "We're right behind you."

Eve dropped the blanket and pushed through the crowd, heading for her boyfriend, and the unofficial head of their strange and screwed-up fraternity.

It was easy to spot Michael in any group—he was tall and blond, with a face like an angel. As he caught sight of Eve heading toward him, he smiled, and Claire thought that was maybe the most complicated smile she'd ever seen, full of relief, welcome, love, and worry.

Eve crashed straight into him, hard enough to rock him back on his heels, and their arms went around each other.

Shane held Claire back with a touch on her shoulder. "Give them a minute," he said. "They've got things to say." She turned to look at him. "And so do we."

She swallowed hard and nodded. Shane's hands were on her shoulders, and his eyes had gone still and intense.

"Don't go out there," Shane said.

It was what she'd been intending to say to *him*. She blinked, surprised.

"You stole my paranoia," she said. "*I* was going to say, *Don't go*. But you're going to, no matter what I say, aren't you?"

That threw him off just a little. "Well, yeah, of course I am, but—"

"But nothing. I'll be with Amelie; I'll be okay. You? You're going off with the cast of *WWE Raw* to fight a cage match or something. It's not the same thing."

"Since when do you ever watch wrestling?"

"Shut up. That's not the point, and you know it. Shane, *don't go*." Claire put everything she had into it.

It wasn't enough.

Shane smoothed her hair and bent down to kiss her. It was the sweetest, gentlest kiss he'd ever given her, and it melted all the tense muscles of her neck, her shoulders, and her back. It was a promise without words, and when he finally pulled back, he passed his thumb across her lips gently, to seal it all in.

"There's something I really ought to tell you," he said. "I was kind of waiting for the right time."

They were in a room full of people, Morganville was in chaos outside, and they probably didn't have a chance of surviving until sunrise, but Claire felt her heart stutter and then race faster. The whole world seemed to go silent around her. *He's going to say it.*

Shane leaned in, so close that she felt his lips brush her ear, and whispered, "My dad's coming back to town."

That *so* wasn't what she was hoping he'd say. Claire jerked back, startled, and Shane put a hand over her mouth. "Don't," he whispered. "Don't say *anything*. We can't talk about this, Claire. I just wanted you to know."

They couldn't talk about it because Shane's father was Morganville's most wanted, public enemy number one, and any conversation they had—at least here—was in danger of being overheard by unfriendly, undead ears.

Not that Claire was a fan of Shane's father; he was a cold, brutal man who'd used and abused Shane, and she couldn't work up a lot of dread for seeing him behind bars . . . only she knew that Amelie and Oliver wouldn't stop at putting him in jail. Shane's father was marked for death if he came back. Death by burning. And while Claire wouldn't necessarily cry any big tears over him, she didn't want to put Shane through that, either.

"We'll talk about it," she said.

Shane snorted. "You mean, you'll yell at me? Trust me, I know what you're going to say. I just wanted you to know, in case—"

In case something happened to him. Claire tried to frame her question in a way that wouldn't tip their hand to any listening ears. "When should I expect him?"

"Next few days, probably. But you know how it is. I'm out of the loop." Shane's smile had a dark, painful edge to it now. He'd defied his dad once, because of Claire, and that meant cutting the ties to his last living family in the world. Claire doubted his dad had forgotten that, or ever would.

"Why now?" she whispered. "The last thing we need is—"

"Help?"

"He's not *help.* He's chaos!"

Shane gestured at the burning town. "Take a good look, Claire. How much worse can it get?"

Lots, she thought. Shane, in some ways, still had a rose-colored view of his father. It had been a while since his dad had blown out of town, and she thought that Shane had probably convinced himself that the guy wasn't all that bad. He was probably thinking now that his dad would come sweeping in to save them.

It wasn't going to happen. Frank Collins was a fanatic, car-bomb variety, and he didn't care who got hurt.

Not even his own son.

"Let's just—" She chewed her lip for a second, staring at him. "Let's just get through the day, okay? Please? Be careful. Call me."

He had his cell phone, and he showed it to her in mute promise. Then he stepped closer, and when his arms closed around her, she felt a sweet, trembling relief.

"Better get ready," he said. "It's going to be a long day."

TWO

Claire wasn't sure if *get ready* meant put on her game face, brush her teeth, or pack up a lot of weapons, but she followed Shane to say good-bye to Michael first.

Michael was standing in the middle of a bunch of hard-looking types—some were vampires, and many she'd never seen before. They didn't look happy about playing defense, and they had that smelling-something-rotten expression that meant they didn't like hanging out with the human help, either.

The non-vamps with Michael were older, postcollege—tough guys with lots of muscles. Even so, the humans mostly looked nervous.

Shane seemed almost small in comparison—not that he let it slow him down as he rushed the defensive line. He pushed a vampire out of his way as he headed for Michael; the vampire flashed fang at him, but Shane didn't even notice.

Michael did. He stepped in the way of the offended vamp as it made a move for Shane's back, and the two of them froze that way, predators facing off. Michael wasn't the one to look down first.

Michael had a strange intensity about him now—something that had always been there, but being a vampire had ramped it up to about eleven, Claire thought. He still looked angelic, but there were moments when his angel was more fallen than flying. But the smile was real, and completely the Michael she knew and loved when he turned it on them.

He held out his hand for a manly kind of shake. Shane batted it aside and hugged him. There were manly backslaps, and if there was a brief flash of red in Michael's eyes, Shane didn't see it.

"You be careful, man," Shane said. "Those college chicks, they're wild. Don't let them drag you into any Jell-O shot parties. Stay strong."

"You too," Michael said. "Be careful."

"Driving around in a big, black, obvious lunch wagon in a town full of starving vampires? Yeah. I'll try to keep it low profile." Shane swallowed. "Seriously—"

"I know. Same here."

They nodded at each other.

Claire and Eve watched them for a moment. The two of them shrugged. "What?" Michael asked.

"That's it? That's your big good-bye?" Eve asked.

"What was wrong with it?"

Claire looked at Eve, mystified. "I think I need guy CliffsNotes."

"Guys aren't deep enough to need CliffsNotes."

"What were you waiting for, flowery poetry?" Shane snorted. "I hugged. I'm done."

Michael's grin didn't last. He looked at Shane, then Claire, and last—and longest—at Eve. "Don't let anything happen to you," he said. "I love you guys."

"Ditto," Shane said, which was, for Shane, positively gushing.

They might have had time to say more, but one of the vampires standing around, looking pissed off and impatient, tapped Michael on the shoulder. His pale lips moved near Michael's ear.

"Time to go," Michael said. He hugged Eve hard, and had to peel her off at the end. "Don't trust Oliver."

"Yeah, like you had to tell me that," Eve said. Her voice was shaking again. "Michael—"

"I love you," he said, and kissed her, fast and hard. "I'll see you soon."

He left in a blur, taking most of the vampires with him. The mayor's

son, Richard Morrell—still in his police uniform, although he was looking wrinkled and smoke stained now—led the humans at a more normal
pace to follow.

Eve stood there with her kiss-smudged lips parted, looking stunned
and astonished. When she regained the power of speech, she said, "Did
he just say—?"

"Yes," Claire said, smiling. "Yes, he did."

"Whoa. Guess I'd better stay alive, then."

The crowd of people—fewer now than there had been just a few
minutes before—parted around them, and Oliver strode through the gap.
The second-most-badass vampire in town had shed his costume and was
dressed in plain black, with a long, black leather coat. His long graying
hair was tied back in a tight knot at the back of his head, and he looked
like he was ready to snap the head off anyone, vampire or human, who
got in the way.

"You," he snapped at Eve. "Come."

He turned on his heel and walked away. This was not the Oliver they'd
known before—certainly not the friendly proprietor of the local coffee shop. Even once he'd been revealed as a vampire, he hadn't been *this*
intense.

Clearly, he was done pretending to like people.

Eve watched him go, and the look in her eyes was boiling with resentment. She finally shrugged and took a deep breath. "Yeah," she said.
"This'll be *so* much fun. See ya, Claire Bear."

"See you," Claire said. They hugged one last time, just for comfort,
and then Eve was leaving, back straight, head high.

She was probably crying, Claire thought. Eve cried at times like these.
Claire didn't seem to be able to cry when it counted, like now. It felt like
pieces of her were being pulled off, and she felt cold and empty inside.
No tears.

And now it was her heart being ripped out, because Shane was being
summoned impatiently by yet another hard-looking bunch of vampires
and humans near the door. He nodded to them, took her hands, and
looked into her eyes.

Say it, she thought.

But he didn't. He just kissed her hands, turned, and walked away, dragging her red, bleeding heart with him—metaphorically, anyway.

"I love you," she whispered. She'd said it before, but he'd hung up the phone before she'd gotten it out. Then she'd said it in the hospital, but he'd been doped up on painkillers. And he didn't hear her now, as he walked away from her.

But at least *she* had the guts to try.

He waved to her from the door, and then he was gone, and she suddenly felt very alone in the world—and very . . . young. Those who were left in the Glass House had jobs of their own, and she was in the way. She found a chair—Michael's armchair, as it turned out—and pulled her feet up under her as humans and vampires moved around, fortifying windows and doors, distributing weapons, talking in low tones.

She might have become a ghost, for all the attention they paid her.

She didn't have to wait long. In just a few minutes, Amelie came sweeping down the stairs. She had a whole scary bunch of vampires behind her, and a few humans, including two in police uniforms.

They were all armed—knives, clubs, swords. Some had stakes, including the policemen; they had them, instead of riot batons, hanging from their utility belts. *Standard-issue equipment for Morganville,* Claire thought, and had to suppress a manic giggle. *Maybe instead of pepper spray, they have garlic spray.*

Amelie handed Claire two things: a thin, silver knife, and a wooden stake. "A wooden stake in the heart will put one of us down," she said. "You must use the silver knife to kill us. No steel, unless you plan to take our heads off with it. The stake alone will not do it, unless you're very lucky or sunlight catches us helpless, and even then, we are slower to die the older we are. Do you understand?"

Claire nodded numbly. *I'm sixteen,* she wanted to say. *I'm not ready for this.* But she kind of had to be, now.

Amelie's fierce, cold expression seemed to soften, just a touch. "I can't entrust Myrnin to anyone else. When we find him, it will be your responsibility to manage him. He may be—" Amelie paused, as if searching for the right word. "Difficult." That probably wasn't it. "I don't want you to fight, but I need you with us."

Claire lifted the stake and the knife. "Then why did you give me these?"

"Because you might need to defend yourself, or him. If you do, I don't want you to hesitate, child. Defend yourself and Myrnin at all costs. Some of those who come against us may be those you know. Don't let that stop you. We are in this to survive now."

Claire nodded numbly. She'd been pretending that all this was some kind of action/adventure video game, like the zombie-fighting one Shane enjoyed so much, but with every one of her friends leaving, she'd lost some of that distance. Now it was right here in front of her: reality. People were dying.

She might be one of them.

"I'll stay close," she said. Amelie's cold fingers touched her chin, very lightly.

"Do that." Amelie turned her attention to the others around them. "Watch for my father, but don't be drawn off to face him. It's what he wants. He will have his own reinforcements, and will be gathering more. Stay together, and watch each other closely. Protect me, and protect the child."

"Um—could you stop calling me that?" Claire asked. Amelie's icy eyes fixed on her in almost-human puzzlement. "Child, I mean? I'm not a child."

It felt like time stopped for about a hundred years while Amelie stared at her. It probably had been at *least* a hundred years since the last time anybody had dared correct Amelie like that in public.

Amelie's lips curved, very slightly. "No," she agreed. "You are not a child, and in any case, by your age, I was a bride and ruled a kingdom. I should know better."

Claire felt heat build in her face. Great, she was blushing, as everybody's attention focused on her. Amelie's smile widened.

"I stand corrected," she said to the rest of them. "Protect this *young woman*."

She really didn't feel like that, either, but Claire wasn't going to push her luck on that one. The other vampires looked mostly annoyed with the distinction, and the humans looked nervous.

"Come," Amelie said, and turned to face the blank far wall of the living room. It shimmered like an asphalt road in the summer, and Claire felt the connection snap open.

Amelie stepped through what looked like blank wall. After a second or two of surprise, the vampires started to follow her.

"Man, I can't believe we're doing this," one of the policemen behind Claire whispered to the other.

"I can," the other whispered back. "My kids are out there. What else is there to do?"

She gripped the wooden stake tight and stepped through the portal, following Amelie.

Myrnin's lab wasn't any more of a wreck than usual. Claire was kind of surprised by that; somehow she'd expected Mr. Bishop to tear through here with torches and clubs, but so far, he'd found better targets.

Or maybe—just maybe—he hadn't been able to get in. Yet.

Claire anxiously surveyed the room, which was lit by just a few flickering lamps, both oil and electric. She'd tried cleaning it up a few times, but Myrnin had snapped at her that he liked things the way they were, so she'd left the stacks of leaning books, the piles of glassware on counters, the disordered piles of curling paper. There was a broken iron cage in the corner—broken because Myrnin had decided to escape from it once, and they'd never gotten around to having it repaired once he'd regained his senses.

The vampires were whispering to one another, in sibilant little hisses that didn't carry even a hint of meaning to Claire's ears. They were nervous, too.

Amelie, by contrast, seemed as casual and self-assured as ever. She snapped her fingers, and two of the vampires—big, strong, strapping men—stepped up, towering over her. She glanced up.

"You will guard the stairs," she said. "You two." She pointed to the uniformed policemen. "I want you here as well. Guard the interior doors. I doubt anything will come through them, but Mr. Bishop has already surprised us. I won't have him surprising us again."

That cut their forces in half. Claire swallowed hard and looked at the two vampires and one human who remained with her and Amelie—she knew the two vampires slightly. They were Amelie's personal bodyguards, and one of them, at least, had treated her kind of decently before.

The remaining human was a tough-looking African American woman with a scar across her face, from her left temple across her nose, and down her right cheek. She saw Claire watching her, and gave her a smile. "Hey," she said, and stuck out a big hand. "Hannah Moses. Moses Garage."

"Hey," Claire said, and shook hands awkwardly. The woman had muscles—not quite Shane-quality biceps, but definitely bigger than most women would have found useful. "You're a mechanic?"

"I'm an everything," Hannah said. "Mechanic included. But I used to be a marine."

"Oh." Claire blinked.

"The garage was my dad's before he passed. I just got back from a couple of tours in Afghanistan—thought I'd take up the quiet life for a while." She shrugged. "Guess trouble's in my blood. Look, if this comes to a fight, stay with me, okay? I'll watch your back."

That was so much of a relief that Claire felt weak enough to melt. "Thanks."

"No problem. You're what, about fifteen?"

"Almost seventeen." Claire thought she needed a T-shirt that said it for her; it would be a great time-saver—that, or some kind of button.

"Huh. So you're about my kid brother's age. His name's Leo. I'll have to introduce you sometime."

Hannah, Claire realized, was talking without really thinking about what she was saying; her eyes were focused on Amelie, who had made her way around piles of books to the doorway on the far wall.

Hannah didn't seem to miss anything.

"Claire," Amelie said. Claire dodged piles of books and came to her side. "Did you lock this door when you left before?"

"No. I thought I'd be coming back this way."

"Interesting. Because someone *has* locked it."

"Myrnin?"

Amelie shook her head. "Bishop has him. He has not returned this way."

Claire decided not to ask how she knew that. "Who else—" And then she knew. "Jason." Eve's brother had known about the doorways that led to different destinations in town—maybe not about how they worked (and Claire wasn't sure she did, either), but he definitely had figured out how to use them. Apart from Claire, Myrnin, and Amelie, only Oliver had the knowledge, and she knew where he'd been since her encounter with Mr. Bishop.

"Yes," Amelie agreed. "The boy is becoming a problem."

"Kind of an understatement, considering he, you know . . ." Claire mimed stabbing with the stake, but not in Amelie's direction—that would be like pointing a loaded gun at Superman. Somebody would get hurt, and it wouldn't be Superman. "Um—I meant to ask, are you—?"

Amelie looked away from her, toward the door. "Am I what?"

"Okay?" Because she'd had a stake in her chest not all that long ago, and besides that, all the vampires in Morganville had a disadvantage, whether they knew it or not: they were sick—really sick—with something Claire could only think of as vampire Alzheimer's.

And it was ultimately fatal.

Most of the town didn't have a clue about that, because Amelie was rightly afraid of what might happen if they did—vampires and humans alike. Amelie had symptoms, but so far they were mild. It took years to progress, so they were safe for a while.

At least, Claire hoped it took years.

"No, I doubt I am all right. Still, this is hardly the time to be coddling myself." Amelie focused on the door. "We will need the key to open it."

That was a problem, because the key wasn't where it was supposed to be. The key ring was gone from where Claire kept it, in a battered, sagging drawer, and the more Claire pawed through debris looking for it, the more alarmed she became. Myrnin kept the weirdest stuff. . . . Books, sure, she loved books; small, deformed dead things in alcohol, not so much. He also kept jars of dirt—at least, she hoped it was dirt. Some of it looked red and flaky, and she was really afraid it might be blood.

The keys were missing. So were a few other things—significant things.

With a sinking feeling, Claire pulled open the half-broken drawer where she'd kept the bag with all the tranquilizer stuff, and Myrnin's drug supplies.

Gone. Only a scrape in the dust to indicate where it had been.

That meant that if—*when*—Myrnin turned violent, she wouldn't have her trusty dart gun to help her. Nor would she have even her trusty injectable pen, so cool, that she'd loaded up for emergencies, because it had been in the bag with the drugs. She'd lost the other supplies she'd had with her.

But even worse, she didn't have any medicine for him, other than the couple of small vials she had with her in her pockets.

In summary: so very screwed.

"Enough," Amelie said, and turned to her bodyguard. "I know this isn't easy, but if you would?"

He gave her a polite sort of nod, stepped forward, and took the lock in his hand.

His hand *burst into flame.*

"Oh my God!" Claire blurted, and clapped her hands over her mouth, because the vampire guy wasn't letting go. His face was contorted with pain, but he held on, somehow, and jerked and twisted the silver-plated lock until, with a scream of metal, it ripped loose. The hasp came with it, right off the door.

He dropped it to the floor. His hand kept burning. Claire grabbed the first thing that came to hand—some kind of ratty old shirt Myrnin had left thrown on the floor—and patted out the fire. The smell of burned flesh made her dry heave, and so did the sight of what was left of his hand. He didn't scream. She almost did it for him.

"A trap," Amelie said. "From my father. Gérard, are you able to continue?"

He nodded as he wrapped the shirt around the ruin of his hand. He was sweating fine pink beads—blood, Claire realized, as a trickle of it ran down his pale face. She realized that as she was standing there right in front of him, frozen in place, and his eyes flashed red.

"Move," he growled at her. "Stay behind us." And then, after a brief pause, he said, "Thank you."

Hannah took her by the arm and pulled her to the spot in the back, out of vampire-grabbing range. "He needs feeding," she said in an undertone. "Gérard's not a bad guy, but you don't want to make yourself too available for snack attacks. Remember, we're vending machines with legs."

Claire nodded. Amelie put her fingers in the hole left by the broken lock and pulled the door open . . . on darkness.

Hannah said nothing. She didn't let go of Claire's arm.

For a long moment, nothing happened, and then the darkness flickered. Shifted. Things came and went in the shadows, and Claire knew that Amelie was shuffling destinations, trying to find the one she wanted. It seemed to take a very long time, and then Amelie took a sudden step back. "Now," she said, and her two bodyguards charged forward into what looked like complete darkness and were gone. Amelie glanced back at Hannah and Claire, and her black pupils were expanding fast, covering all the gray iris of her eyes, preparing for the dark.

"Don't leave my side," she said. "This will be dangerous."

THREE

Amelie grabbed Claire's other arm, and before Claire could so much as grab a breath, she was being pulled through the portal. There was a brief wave of chill, and a feeling that was a little like being pushed from all sides, and then she was stumbling into utter, complete blackness. Her other senses went into overdrive. The air smelled stale and heavy, and felt cold and damp, like a cave. Amelie's icy grip on one arm was going to leave bruises, and Hannah Moses's warmer touch on the other seemed light by contrast, although Claire knew it wasn't.

Claire could hear herself and Hannah breathing, but there was no sound at all from the vampires. When Claire tried to speak, Amelie's ice-cold hand covered her mouth. She nodded convulsively, and concentrated on putting one foot in front of the other as Amelie—she hoped it was still Amelie, anyway—pulled her forward into the dark.

The smells changed from time to time—a whiff of nasty, rotten something, .then something else that smelled weirdly like grapes? Her imagination conjured up a dead man surrounded by broken bottles of wine, and Claire couldn't stop it there; the dead man was moving, squirming toward her, and any second now he'd touch her and she'd scream. . . .

It's just your imagination; stop it.

She swallowed and tried to tamp down the panic. It wasn't helping.

Shane wouldn't panic. Shane would—whatever, Shane wouldn't be caught dead roaming around in the dark with a bunch of vampires like this, and Claire knew it.

It seemed like they went on forever, and then Amelie pulled her to a stop and let go. Losing that support felt as if she were standing on the edge of a cliff, and Claire was really, really grateful for Hannah's grip to tell her there was something else real in the world. *Don't let me fall.*

And then Hannah's hand went away. A fast tightening of her fingers, and she was gone.

Claire was floating in total darkness, disconnected, alone. Her breath sounded loud as a train in her ears, but it was buried under the thunder of her fast heartbeats. *Move,* she told herself. *Do something!*

She whispered, "Hannah?"

Cold hands slapped around her from behind, one pinning her arms to her sides, the other covering her mouth. She was lifted off the ground, and she screamed, a faint buzzing sound like a storm of bees that didn't make it through the muffling gag.

And then she went flying through the air into the darkness . . . and rolled to a stop facedown, on a cold stone floor. There was light here. Faint, but definite, painting the edges of things a pale gray, including the arched mouth of the tunnel at the end of the hall.

She had no idea where she was.

Claire got quickly to her feet and turned to look behind her. Amelie, pale as a pearl, stepped through the portal, and with her came the other two vampires. Gérard had Hannah Moses's arm gripped in his good hand.

Hannah had a bloody gash on her head, and when Gérard let go, she dropped to her knees, breathing hard. Her eyes looked blank and unfocused.

Amelie whirled, something silver in one hand, and stabbed as something came at her from the dark. It screamed, a thin sound that echoed through the tunnel, and a white hand reached out to grab Amelie's shirt.

The invisible portal slammed shut like an iris, and severed the arm just above the elbow.

Amelie plucked the still-grabbing hand from her shirt, dropped the hand to the ground, and kicked it to the side. When she turned back to the others, there was no expression on her face.

Claire felt like throwing up. She couldn't take her eyes away from that wiggling, fish-pale hand.

"It was necessary to come this way," Amelie said. "Dangerous, but necessary."

"Where are we?" Claire asked. Amelie gave her a look and ignored her as she took the lead, heading down the hall. Going through this didn't give her any right to ask questions. Of course. "Hannah? Are you okay?"

Hannah waved her hand vaguely, which really wasn't all that confidence-building. The vampire Gérard answered for her. "She's fine." Sure, he could talk, having one hand burned to the bone. He'd probably classify himself as fine, too. "Take her," Gérard ordered, and pushed Hannah toward Claire as he moved to follow Amelie. The other bodyguard—what was his name?—moved with him, as if they were an old, practiced team.

Hannah was heavy, but she pulled herself back on her own center of gravity after a breath or two. "I'm fine," she said, and gave Claire a reassuring grin. "Damn. That was not a walk in the park."

"You should meet my boyfriend," Claire said. "You two are both masters of understatement."

She thought Hannah wanted to laugh, but instead, she just nodded and patted Claire on the shoulder. "Watch the sides," she said. "We're just starting on this thing."

That was an easy job, because there was nothing to watch on the sides. They were, after all, in a tunnel. Hannah, it appeared, was the rear guard, and she seemed to take it very seriously, although it looked like Amelie had slammed the doorway behind them pretty hard, with prejudice. *I hope we don't have to go back that way,* Claire thought, and shivered at the sight of that pale severed hand behind them. It had finally stopped moving. *I really, really hope we don't have to go back there.*

At the mouth of the tunnel, Amelie seemed to pause for a moment, and then disappeared to the right, around the corner, with her two vampire bodyguards in flying formation behind her. Hannah and Claire hurried to keep up, and emerged into another hallway, this one square instead of arched, and paneled in rich, dark wood. There were paintings on the walls—old ones, Claire thought—of pale people lit by candlelight, dressed in about a thousand pounds of costume and rice white makeup and wigs.

She stopped and backed up, staring at one.

"What?" Hannah growled.

"That's her. Amelie." It definitely was, only instead of the Princess Grace–style clothes she wore now, in the picture she was wearing an elaborate sky blue satin dress, cut way low over her breasts. She was wearing a big white wig, and staring out of the canvas in an eerily familiar way.

"Art appreciation later, Claire. We need to go."

That was true, beyond any argument, but Claire kept throwing glances at the paintings as they passed. One looked like it could have been Oliver, from about four hundred years ago. One more modern one looked almost like Myrnin. *It's the vampire museum,* she realized. *It's their history.* There were glass cases lining the hall ahead, filled with books and papers and jewelry, clothing, and musical instruments. All the fine and fabulous things gathered through their long, long lives.

Ahead, the three vampires came to a sudden, motionless halt, and Hannah grabbed Claire by the arm to pull her out of the way, against the wall. "What's happening?" Claire whispered.

"Sorting credentials."

Claire didn't know what that meant, exactly, but when she risked moving out just a bit to see what was happening, she saw that there were lots of other vampires in here—about a hundred of them, some sitting down and obviously hurt. There were humans, too, mostly standing together and looking nervous, which seemed reasonable.

If these were Bishop's people, their little rescue party was in serious trouble.

Amelie exchanged some quiet words with the vampire who seemed to be in charge, and Gérard and his partner visibly relaxed. That settled the friend-or-foe question, apparently; Amelie turned and nodded to

Claire, and she and Hannah edged out from behind the glass cases to join them.

Amelie made a gesture, and immediately several vampires peeled off from the group and joined her in a distant corner.

"What's going on?" Claire asked, and stared around her. Most of the vampires were still dressed in the costumes they'd worn to Bishop's welcome feast, but a few were in more military dress—black, mostly, but some in camouflage.

"It's a rally point," Hannah said. "She's talking strategy, probably. Those would be her captains. Notice there aren't any humans with her?"

Claire did. It wasn't exactly a pleasant sensation, the doubt that boiled up inside.

Whatever orders Amelie delivered, it didn't take long. One by one, the vampires nodded and peeled off from the meeting, gathered up followers—including humans this time—and departed. By the time Amelie had dispatched the last group, there were only about ten people left Claire didn't know, and they were all standing together.

Amelie came back to them, saw the group of humans and vamps, and nodded toward them.

"Claire, this is Theodosius Goldman," Amelie said. "Theo, he prefers to be called. These are his family."

Family? That was a shock, because there were so many of them. Theo seemed to be kind of middle-aged, with graying, curly hair and a face that, except for its vampiric pallor, seemed kind of . . . nice.

"May I present my wife, Patience?" he said with the kind of old manners Claire had seen only on *Masterpiece Theater.* "Our sons, Virgil and Clarence. Their wives, Ida and Minnie." There were more vampires bowing, or in the case of the one guy down on the floor, with his head held in the lap of a female vamp, waving. "And their children."

Evidently the grandkids didn't merit individual introductions. There were four of them, two boys and two girls, all pale like their relatives. They seemed younger than Claire, at least physically; she guessed the littler girl was probably about twelve, the older boy around fifteen.

The older boy and girl glared at her, as if she were personally responsible for the mess they were in, but Claire was too busy imagining how a whole family—down to grandkids—could all be made vampires like this.

Theo, evidently, could see all that in her expression, because he said, "We were made eternal a long time ago, my girl, by"—he cast a quick look at Amelie, who nodded—"by her father, Bishop. It was a joke of his, you see, that we should all be together for all time." He really did have a kind face, Claire thought, and his smile was kind of tragic. "The joke turned on him, though. We refused to let it destroy us. Amelie showed us we did not have to kill to survive, and so we were able to keep our faith as well as our lives."

"Your faith?"

"It's a very old faith," Theo said. "And today is our Sabbath."

Claire blinked. "Oh. You're Jewish?"

He nodded, eyes fixed on her. "We found a refuge here, in Morganville. A place where we could live in peace, both with our nature and our God."

Amelie said, softly, "But will you fight for it now, Theo? This place that gave you refuge?"

He held out his hand. His wife's cool white fingers closed around it. She was a delicate china doll of a woman, with masses of sleek black hair piled on top of her head. "Not today."

"I'm sure God would understand if you broke the Sabbath under these circumstances."

"I'm sure he would. God is forgiving, or we would not still be walking this world. But to be moral is not to need his divine forgiveness, I think." He shook his head again, very regretfully. "We cannot fight, Amelie. Not today. And I would prefer not to fight at all."

"If you think you can stay neutral in this, you're wrong. I will respect your wishes. My father will not."

Theo's face hardened. "If your father threatens my family again, then we *will* fight. But until he comes for us, until he shows us the sword, we will not take up arms against him."

Gérard snorted, which proved what he thought about it; Claire wasn't much surprised. He seemed like a practical sort of guy. Amelie simply nodded. "I can't force you, and I wouldn't. But be careful. I cannot spare anyone to help you. You should be safe enough here, for a time. If any others come through, send them out to guard the power station and the campus." She allowed her gaze to move beyond Theo, to touch the three humans huddled in the far corner of the room, under another painting, a big one. "Are these under your Protection?"

Theo shrugged. "They asked to join us."

"Theo."

"I will defend them if someone tries to harm them." Theo pitched his voice lower. "Also, we may need them, if we can't get supplies."

Claire went cold. For all his kind face and smile, Theo was talking about using those people as portable blood banks.

"I don't want to do it," Theo continued, "but if things go against us, I have to think of my children. You understand."

"I do," Amelie said. Her face was back to a blank mask that gave away nothing of how she felt about it. "I have never told you what to do, and I will not now. But by the laws of this town, if you place these humans under your Protection, you owe them certain duties. You know that."

Another shrug, and Theo held out his hands to show he was helpless. "Family comes first," he said. "I have always told you so."

"Some of us," Amelie said, "are not so fortunate in our choice of families."

She turned away from Theo without waiting for his response—if he'd been intending to give one—and without so much as a pause, slammed her fist into a glass-fronted wall box labeled EMERGENCY USE ONLY three steps to the right. It shattered in a loud clatter, and Amelie shook shards of glass from her skin.

She reached into the box and took out . . . Claire blinked. "Is that a *paintball* gun?"

Amelie handed it to Hannah, who handled it like a professional. "It fires pellets loaded with silver powder," she said. "Very dangerous to us. Be careful where you aim."

"Always am," Hannah said. "Extra magazines?"

Amelie retrieved them from the case and handed them over. Claire noticed that she protected herself even from a casual touch, with a fold of fabric over her fingers. "There are ten shots per magazine," she said. "There is one already loaded, and six more here."

"Well," Hannah said, "any problem I can't solve with seventy shots is probably going to kill us, anyway."

"Claire," Amelie said, and handed over a small, sealed vial. "Silver powder, packed under pressure. It will explode on impact, so be very careful with it. If you throw it, there is a wide dispersal through the air. It can hurt your friends as much as your enemies."

There were real uses for silver powder, like coating parts in computers; Claire supposed it wasn't exactly restricted, but she was surprised the vampires were progressive enough to lay in a supply. Amelie raised pale eyebrows at her.

"You've been expecting this," Claire said.

"Not in detail. But I've learned through my life that such preparations are never wasted, in the end. Sometime, somewhere, life always comes to a fight, and peace always comes to an end."

Theo said, very quietly, "Amen."

FOUR

They left the museum by way of a side door. It was risky to go out into the night, but since the only other way to exit the museum was to go back into the darkness, nobody argued about the choice.

"Careful," Amelie told them in a very soft voice that hardly reached past the shadows. "I have gathered my forces. My father is doing the same. There will be patrols, especially here."

The flames hadn't reached Founder's Square, which was where they came out—the heart of vamp territory. It didn't look like the calm, orderly place Claire remembered, though; the lights were all out, and the shops and restaurants that bordered it were closed and empty.

It looked afraid.

The only place she could see movement was on the marble steps of the Elders' Council building, where Bishop's welcome feast had been held. Gérard hissed a warning, and they all froze, silent and still in the dark. Hannah's grip on Claire's arm felt like an iron band.

There were three vampires standing there, scanning the area.

Lookouts.

"Go," Amelie said in a whisper so small it was like a ghost. "Move, but be careful."

They reached the edge of the shadows by the corner of the building, but just as Claire was starting to relax a little, Amelie, Gérard, and the other vampires moved in a blur, scattering in all directions.

This left Claire flat-footed for one horrible second, before Hannah tackled her facedown on the grass. Claire gasped, got a mouthful of crunchy dirt and bitter chlorophyll, and fought to get her breath. Hannah's heavy weight held her down, and the older woman braced her elbows on Claire's back.

She's firing the pistol, Claire thought, and tried to raise her head to see where Hannah was shooting.

"Head down!" Hannah snarled, and shoved Claire down with one hand while she continued to fire with the other. From the screams in the dark, she was hitting something. "Get up! Run!"

Claire wasn't quick enough to suit either the marines or the vampires, and before she knew it, she was being half pulled, half dragged at a dead run through the night. It was all a confusing blur of shadows, dark buildings, pale faces, and the surly orange glow of flames in the distance.

"What is it?" she screamed.

"Patrols." Hannah kept on firing behind them. She wasn't firing wildly, not at all; it seemed like she took a second or two between every shot, choosing her target. Most of the shots seemed to hit, from the shouts and snarls and screams. "Amelie! We need an exit, *now!*"

Amelie looked back at them, a pale flash of face in the dark, and nodded.

They charged up the steps of another building on Founder's Square. Claire didn't have time to get more than a vague impression of it—some kind of official building, with columns in front and big stone lions snarling on the stairs—before their little party came to a halt at the top of the stairs, in front of a closed white door with no knob.

Gérard started to throw himself against it. Amelie stopped him with an outstretched hand. "It will do no good," she said. "It can't be opened by force. Let me."

The other vampire, facing away and down the steps, said, "Don't think we have time for sweet talk, ma'am. What you want us to do?" He had a drawling Texas accent, the first one Claire had heard from any vampire. She'd never heard him speak at all before.

He winked at her, which was even more of a shock. Until that moment, he hadn't even looked at her like a real person.

"A moment," Amelie murmured.

The Texan nodded behind them. "Don't think we've got one, ma'am."

There were shadows converging in the dark at the foot of the steps—the patrol that Hannah had been shooting at. There were at least twenty of them. In the lead was Ysandre, the beautiful vampire Claire hated maybe more than she hated any other vampire in the entire world. She was Bishop's girl through and through—Amelie's vampire sister, if they thought in those kinds of terms.

Claire hated Ysandre for Shane's sake. She was glad the vamp was here, and not attacking Shane's Bloodmobile—one, because she wasn't so sure Shane could resist the evil witch, and two, she wanted to stake Ysandre herself.

Personally.

"No," Hannah said, when Claire took a step out from behind her. "Are you crazy? Get back!"

Hannah fired over her shoulder. It was at the outer extreme of the paintball gun's range, but the pellet hit one of the vampires—not Ysandre, Claire was disappointed to see—right in the chest. Silver dust puffed up in a lethal mist, and the close formation scattered. Ysandre might have had a few burns, but nothing that wouldn't heal.

The vampire Hannah had shot in the chest toppled over and hit the marble stairs, smoking and flailing.

Amelie slammed her palm flat against the door and closed her eyes, and deep inside the barrier something groaned and shifted with a scrape of metal. "Inside," Amelie murmured, still wicked controlled, and Claire spun and followed the three vampires across the threshold. Hannah backed in after, grabbed the door, and slammed it shut.

"No locks," she said.

Amelie reached over and pushed Hannah's gun hand into an at-rest position at her side. "None necessary. They won't get in." She sounded sure of it, but from the look Hannah continued to give the door—as if she wished she could weld it shut with the force of her stare—she wasn't so certain. "This way. We'll take the stairs."

It was a library, full of books. Some—on this floor—were new, or at least newish, with colorful spines and crisp titles that Claire could read even in the low light. She slowed down a little, blinking. "You guys have *vampire* stories in here?" None of the vampires answered. Amelie veered to the right, through the two-story-tall shelves, and headed for a set of sweeping marble steps at the end. The books got older, the paper more yellow. Claire caught sight of a sign that read FOLKLORE, CA. 1870–1945, ENGLISH, and then another that identified a *German* section. Then *French.* Then script that might have been Chinese.

So many books, and from what she could tell, every single one of them had to do in some way with vampires. Was it history or fiction to them?

Claire didn't really have time to work it out. They were taking the stairs, moving around the curve up to the second level. Claire's legs burned all along the calf muscles, and her breathing was getting raspy from the constant movement and adrenaline. Hannah flashed her a quick, sympathetic smile. "Yeah," she said. "Consider it basic training. Can you keep up?"

Claire gave her a gasping nod.

More books here, old and crumbling, and the air tasted like dry leather and ancient paper. Toward the back of the room, there were things that looked like wine racks, the fancy X-shaped kind people put in cellars, only these held rolls of paper, each neatly tied with ribbon. They were scrolls, probably very old ones. Claire hoped they'd go that direction, but no, Amelie was turning them down another book aisle, toward a blank white wall.

No, not quite blank. It had a small painting on the wall, in a fussy gilt frame. Some bland-looking nature scene . . . and then, as Amelie stared at it, the painting *changed.*

It grew darker, as though clouds had come across the meadow and the drowsy sheep in the picture.

And then it was dark, just a dark canvas, then some pinpricks of light, like candle flames through smoke. . . .

And then Claire saw Myrnin.

He was in chains, silver-colored chains, kneeling on the floor, and his head was down. He was still wearing the blousy white pantaloons of his Pierrot costume, but no shirt. The wet points of his damp hair clung to his face and his marble-pale shoulders.

Amelie nodded sharply, and put a hand against the wall to the left of the picture, pressing what looked like a nail, and part of the wall swung out silently on oiled hinges.

Hidden doors: vampires sure seemed to love them.

There was darkness on the other side. "Oh, *hell* no," Claire heard Hannah mutter. "Not again."

Amelie sent her a glance, and there was a whisper of amusement in the look. "It's a different darkness," she said. "And the dangers are very different, from this point on. Things may change quickly. You will have to adapt."

Then she stepped through, and the vampires followed, and it was just Claire and Hannah.

Claire held out her hand. Hannah took it, still shaking her head, and the dark closed around them like a damp velvet curtain.

There was the hiss of a match dragging, and a flare of light from the corner. Amelie, her face turned ivory by the licking flame, set the match to a candle and left the light burning as she flicked on a small flashlight and played it around the room. Boxes. It was some kind of storeroom, dusty and disused. "All right," she said. "Gérard, if you please."

He swung another door open a crack, nodded, and widened it enough to slip through.

Another hallway. Claire was getting tired of hallways, and they were all starting to look the same. Where were they now, anyway? It looked like some kind of hotel, with polished heavy doors marked with brass plates, only instead of numbers, each door had one of the vampire markings, like the symbol on Claire's bracelet. Each vampire had one; at least she thought they did. So these would be—what? Rooms? Vaults? Claire thought she heard something behind one of the doors—muffled sounds, thumping, scratching. They didn't stop, though—and she wasn't sure she wanted to know, really.

Amelie brought them to a halt at the T-intersection of the hall. It was deserted in every direction, and disorienting, too; Claire couldn't tell one hallway from another. *Maybe we should drop crumbs,* she thought. *Or M&M's. Or blood.*

"Myrnin is in a room on this hall," Amelie said. "It is quite obviously a trap, and quite obviously meant for me. I will stay behind and ensure your escape route. Claire." Her pale eyes fixed on Claire with merciless intensity. "Whatever else happens, you must bring Myrnin out safely. Do you understand? Do not let Bishop have him."

She meant, *Everybody else is expendable.* That made Claire feel sick, and she couldn't help but look at Hannah, and even at the two vampires. Gérard shrugged, so slightly she thought it might have been her imagination.

"We are soldiers," Gérard said. "Yes?"

Hannah smiled. "Damn straight."

"Excellent. You will follow my orders."

Hannah saluted him, with just a little trace of irony. "Yes sir, squad leader, sir."

Gérard turned his attention to Claire. "You will stay behind us. Do you understand?"

She nodded. She felt cold and hot at the same time, and a little sick, and the wooden stake in her hand didn't seem like a heck of a lot, considering. But she didn't have any time for second thoughts, because Gérard had turned and was already heading down the hall, his wing man flanking him, and Hannah was beckoning Claire to follow.

Amelie's cool fingers brushed her shoulder. "Careful."

Claire nodded and went to rescue a crazy vampire from an evil one.

The door shattered under Gérard's kick. That wasn't an exaggeration; except for the wood around the door hinges, the rest of it broke into hand-sized pieces and splinters. Before that rain of wreckage hit the floor,

Gérard was inside, moving to the left while his colleague went right. Hannah stepped in and swept the room from one side to the other, holding her air pistol ready to fire, then nodded sharply to Claire.

Myrnin was just as she'd seen him in the picture—kneeling in the center of the room, anchored by tight-stretched silvery chains. The chains were double-strength, and threaded through massive steel bolts on the stone floor.

He was shaking all over, and where the chains touched him, he had welts and burns.

Gérard swore softly under his breath and fiercely kicked the eyebolts in the floor. They bent, but didn't break.

Myrnin finally raised his head, and beneath the mass of sweaty dark hair, Claire saw wild dark eyes, and a smile that made her stomach twist.

"I knew you'd come," he whispered. "You fools. Where is she? Where's Amelie?"

"Behind us," Claire said.

"Fools."

"Nice way to talk to your rescuers," Hannah said. She was nervous, Claire could see it, though the woman controlled it very well. "Gérard? I don't like this. It's too easy."

"I know." He crouched down and looked at the chains. "Silver coated. I can't break them."

"What about the bolts in the floor?" Claire asked. In answer, Gérard grabbed the edge of the metal plate and twisted. The steel bent like aluminum foil, and, with a ripping shriek, tore free of the stones. Myrnin wavered as part of his restraints fell loose, and Gérard waved his partner to work on the other two plates while he focused on the second in front.

"Too easy, too easy," Hannah kept on muttering. "What's the point of doing this if Bishop is just going to let him go?"

The eyebolts were all ripped loose, and Gérard grabbed Myrnin's arm and helped him to his feet.

Myrnin's eyes sheeted over with blazing ruby, and he shook Gérard off and went straight for Hannah.

Hannah saw him coming and put the gun between them, but before she could fire, Gérard's partner knocked her hand out of line, and the shot went wild, impacting on the stone at the other side of the room. Silver flakes drifted on the air, igniting tiny burns where they landed on the vampires' skin. The two bodyguards backed off.

Myrnin grabbed Hannah by the neck.

"No!" Claire screamed, and ducked under Gérard's restraining hand. She raised her wooden stake.

Myrnin turned his head and grinned at her with wicked vampire fangs flashing. "I thought you were here to save me, Claire, not kill me," he purred, and whipped back toward his prey. Hannah was fumbling with her gun, trying to get it back into position. He stripped it away from her with contemptuous ease.

"I *am* here to save you," Claire said, and before she could think what she was doing, she buried the stake in Myrnin's back, on the left side, right where she thought his heart would be.

He made a surprised sound, like a cough, and pitched forward into Hannah. His hand slid away from her throat, clutching blindly at her clothes, and then he fell limply to the floor.

Dead, apparently.

Gérard and his partner looked at Claire as if they'd never seen her before, and then Gérard roared, "What do you think you're—"

"Pick him up," Claire said. "We can take the stake out later. He's old. He'll survive."

That sounded cold, and scary, and she hoped it was true. Amelie had survived, after all, and she knew Myrnin was as old, or maybe even older. From the look he gave her, Gérard was reassessing everything he'd thought about the cute, fragile little human he'd been nursemaiding. Too bad. Claire thought one of her strengths was that everybody always underestimated her.

She was cool on the outside, shaking on the inside, because although it *was* the only way to keep Myrnin calm right now without tranquilizers, or without letting him rip Hannah's throat out, she'd just killed her boss.

That didn't seem like a really good career move.

Amelie will help, she thought a bit desperately, and Gérard slung Myrnin over his shoulder in a fireman's carry, and then they were running, moving fast again back down the hall to where Amelie had stayed to secure their escape.

Gérard came to a fast halt, and Hannah and Claire almost skidded into him. "What?" Hannah whispered, and looked past the two vampires in the lead.

Amelie was at the corner ahead of them, but ten feet past her was Mr. Bishop.

They were standing motionless, facing each other. Amelie looked fragile and delicate, compared to her father in his bishop's robes. He looked ancient and angry, and the fire in his eyes was like something out of the story of Joan of Arc.

Neither of them moved. There was some struggle going on, but Claire couldn't tell what it was, or what it meant.

Gérard reached out and grabbed her arm, and Hannah's, and held them in place. "No," he said sharply. "Don't go near them."

"Problem, sir, that's the way out," Hannah said. "And the dude's alone."

Gérard and the Texan sent her a wild look, almost identical in their disbelief. "You think so?" the Texan said. "Humans."

Amelie took a step backward, just a small one, but a shudder went through her body, and Claire knew—just *knew*—it was a bad sign. Really bad.

Whatever confrontation had been going on, it broke.

Amelie whirled to them and screamed, "Go!" There was fury and fear in her voice, and Gérard let go of both girls and dumped Myrnin off his shoulder, into their arms, and he and the Texan pelted not for the exit, but to Amelie's side.

They got there just in time to stop Bishop from ripping out her throat. They slammed the old man up against the wall, but then there were others coming out into the hall. Bishop's troops, Claire guessed.

There were a lot of them.

Amelie intercepted the first of Bishop's vampires to run in her direction. Claire recognized him, vaguely—one of the Morganville vamps, but he'd obviously switched sides, and he came for Amelie, fangs out.

She put him down on the floor with one twisting move, fast as a snake, and looked back at Hannah and Claire, with Myrnin's body sagging between them. "Get him *out!*" she shouted. "I'll hold the way!"

"Come on," Hannah said, and shouldered the bulk of Myrnin's limp weight. "We're leaving."

Myrnin felt cold and heavy, like the dead man he was, and Claire swallowed a surge of nausea as she struggled to support his limp weight. Claire gritted her teeth and helped Hannah half carry, half drag Myrnin's staked body down the corridor. Behind them, the sounds of fighting continued—mainly bodies hitting the floor. No screaming, no shouting.

Vampires fought in silence.

"Right," Hannah gasped. "We're on our own."

That really wasn't good news—two humans stuck God knew where, with a crazy vampire with a stake in his heart in the middle of a war zone.

"Let's get back to the door," Claire said.

"How are we going to get through it?"

"I can do it."

Hannah threw her a look. "You?"

It was no time to get annoyed; hadn't she just been thinking that being underestimated was a gift? Yeah, not so much, sometimes. "Yes, really. I can do it. But we'd better hurry." The odds weren't in Amelie's favor. She might be able to hang on and cover their retreat, but Claire didn't think she could win.

She and Hannah dragged Myrnin past the symbol-marked doorways. Hannah counted off, and nodded to the one where they'd entered.

Not too surprisingly, it was marked with the Founder's Symbol, the same one Claire wore on the bracelet on her wrist.

Hannah tried to open it. "Dammit! Locked."

Not when Claire tried the knob. It opened at a twist, and the single candle in the corner illuminated very little. Claire caught her breath and rested her trembling muscles for a few seconds as Hannah checked the room and pronounced it safe before they entered.

Claire let Myrnin slide in a heap to the floor. "I'm sorry," she whispered to him. "It was the only way. I hope it doesn't hurt too much."

She had no idea if he could hear her when he was like this. She wanted to grab the stake and pull it out, but she remembered that with Amelie, and with Sam, it had been the other vampires who'd done it. Maybe they knew things she didn't. Besides, the disease weakened them—even Myrnin.

She couldn't take the risk. And besides, having him wake up wounded and crazy would be even worse, now that they didn't have any vampires who could help control him.

Hannah returned to her side. "So," she said, as she checked the clip on her paintball gun, frowned, and exchanged it for a new one, "how do we do this? We got to go back to that museum first, right?"

Did they? Claire wasn't sure. She stepped up to the door, which currently featured nothing but darkness, and concentrated hard on Myrnin's lab, with all its clutter and debris. Light swam, flickered, shivered, and snapped into focus.

No problem at all.

"Guess it's only roundabout getting here," Claire said. "Maybe that's on purpose, to keep people out who shouldn't be here. But it makes sense that once Amelie got here, she'd want to take the express out." She turned back. "Shouldn't we wait?"

Hannah opened the door and looked out into the hall. Whatever she saw, it couldn't have been good news. She shook her head. "We bug out, right now."

With a grunt of effort, Hannah braced Myrnin's deadweight on one side and dragged him forward. Claire took his other arm.

"Did he just twitch?" Hannah asked. " 'Cause if he twitches, I'm going to shoot him."

"No! No, he didn't; he's fine," Claire said, practically tripping over the words. "Ready? One, two . . ."

And *three*, they were in Myrnin's lab. Claire twisted out from under Myrnin's cold body, slammed the door shut, and stared wildly at the broken lock. "I need to fix that," she said. But what about Amelie? No, she'd know all the exits. She didn't have to come here.

"Girl, you need to get us the hell out of here, is what you need to do," Hannah said. "You dial up the nearest Fort Knox or something on that thing. Damn, how'd you learn this, anyway?"

"I had a good teacher." Claire didn't look at Myrnin. She couldn't. For all intents and purposes, she'd just killed him, after all. "This way."

There were two ways out of Myrnin's lab, besides the usually-secured dimensional doorway: steps leading up to street level, which were probably the absolute worst idea ever right now, and a second, an even more hidden dimensional portal in a small room off to the side. That was the one Amelie had used to get them in.

But the problem was, Claire couldn't get it to work. She had the memories clear in her head—the Glass House, the portal to the university, the hospital, even the museum they'd visited on the way here. But nothing *worked.*

It just felt . . . dead, as if the whole system had been cut off.

They were lucky to have made it this far.

Amelie's trapped, Claire realized. *Back there. With Bishop. And she's outnumbered.*

Claire double-checked the other door, too, the one she'd blocked.

Nothing. It wasn't just a malfunctioning portal; the whole network was down.

"Well?" Hannah asked.

Claire couldn't worry about Amelie right now. She had a job to do— get Myrnin to safety. And that meant getting him to the only vampire she knew offhand who could help him: Oliver. "I think we're walking," she said.

"The hell we are," Hannah said. "I'm not hauling a dead vampire through the streets of Morganville. We'll get ourselves killed by just about *everybody.*"

"We can't leave him!"

"We can't take him, either!"

Claire felt her jaw lock into stubborn position. "Well, fine, you go ahead. Because I'm not leaving him. I can't."

She could tell that Hannah wanted to grab her by the hair and yank her out of there, but finally, the older woman nodded and stepped back. "Third option," she said. "Call in the cavalry."

FIVE

It wasn't quite the Third Armored Division, but after about a dozen phone calls, they did manage to get a ride.

"I'm turning on the street—nobody in sight so far," Eve's voice said from the speaker of Claire's cell phone. She'd been giving Claire a turn-by-turn description of her drive, and Claire had to admit, it sounded pretty frightening. "Yeah, I can see the Day House. You're in the alley next to it?"

"We're on our way," Claire said breathlessly. She was drenched with sweat, aching all over, from the effort of helping drag Myrnin out of the lab, up the steps, and down the narrow, seemingly endless dark alley. Next door, the Founder House belonging to Katherine Day and her granddaughter—a virtual copy of the house where Claire and her friends lived—was dark and closed, but Claire saw curtains moving at the up-stairs windows.

"That's my great-aunt's house, Great-Aunt Kathy," Hannah panted. "Everybody calls her Gramma, though. Always have, as far back as I can remember."

Claire could see how Hannah was related to the Days; partly her features, but her attitude for sure. That was a family full of tough, smart, get-it-done women.

Eve's big, black car was idling at the end of the alley, and the back door kicked open as the two of them—three? Did Myrnin still count?—approached. Eve took a look at Myrnin, and the stake in his back, sent Claire a you've-got-to-be-kidding-me look, and reached out to drag him inside, facedown, on the backseat. "Hurry!" she said, and slammed the back door on the way to the driver's side. "Damn, he'd better not bleed all over the place. Claire, I thought you were supposed to—"

"I know," Claire said, and climbed into the middle of the big, front bench seat. Hannah crammed in on the outside. "Don't remind me. I was supposed to keep him safe."

Eve put the car in gear and did a ponderous tank-heavy turn. "So, who staked him?"

"I did."

Eve blinked. "Okay, that's an interesting interpretation of *safe.* Weren't you with Amelie?" Eve actually did a quick check of the backseat, as if she were afraid Amelie might have magically popped in back there, seated like a barbarian queen on top of Myrnin's prone body.

"Yeah. We were," Hannah said.

"Do I have to ask? No, wait, do I *want* to ask?"

"We left her," Claire said, miserable. "Bishop set a trap. She was fighting when we had to go."

"What about the other guys? I thought you went with a whole entourage!"

"We left most of them. . . ." Her brain caught up with her, and she looked at Hannah, who looked back with the same thought in her expression. "Oh, crap. The other guys. They were in Myrnin's lab, but not when we came back. . . ."

"Gone," Hannah said. "Taken out."

"Super. So, we're winning, then." Eve's tone was wicked cynical, but her dark eyes looked scared. "I talked to Michael. He's okay. They're at the university. Things are quiet there so far."

"And Shane?" Claire realized, with a pure bolt of guilt, that she hadn't called him. If he'd called her, she wouldn't have known; she'd turned off the ringer, afraid of the noise when creeping around on a rescue mission.

But as she dug out her phone, she saw that she hadn't missed any calls after all.

"Yeah, he's okay," Eve said, and steered the car at semihigh speed around a corner. The town was dark, very dark, with a few houses lit up by lanterns or candles or flashlights. Most people were waiting in the dark, scared to death. "They had some vamps try to board the bus, probably looking for a snack, but it wasn't even a real fight. So far they're cruising without too much trouble. He's fine, Claire." She reached over and took Claire's hand to squeeze it. "You, not so much. You look awful."

"Thanks. I think I earned it."

Eve took back her hand to haul the big wheel of the car around for a turn. Headlights swept over a group on the sidewalk—unnaturally pale. Unnaturally still. "Oh, crap, we've got bogeys. Hang on, I'm going to floor it."

That was, Claire thought, a pretty fantastic idea, because the vampires on the curb were now in the street, and following. There was a kind of manic glee to how they pursued the car, but not even a vamp could keep up with Eve's driving for long; they fell back into the dark, one by one. The last one was the fastest, and he nearly caught hold of the back bumper before he stumbled and was left behind in a black cloud of exhaust.

"Damn freaks," Eve said, trying to sound tough but not quite making it. "Hey, Hannah. How's business?"

"Right now?" Hannah laughed softly. "Not so fantastic, but I'm not bothered about it. Let's see if we can make it to the morning. Then I'll worry about making ends meet at the shop."

"Oh, we'll make it," Eve said, with a confidence Claire personally didn't feel. "Look, it's already four a.m. Another couple of hours, and we're fine."

Claire didn't say, *In a couple of hours, we could all be dead*, but she was thinking it. What about Amelie? What were they going to do to rescue her?

If she's even still alive.

Claire's head hurt, her eyes felt grainy from lack of sleep, and she just wanted to curl up in a warm bed, pull the pillow over her head, and not be *so responsible*.

Fat chance.

She wasn't paying attention to where Eve was going, and it was so dark and strange outside she wasn't sure she'd recognize things anyway. Eve pulled to a halt at the curb, in front of a row of plate-glass windows lit by candles and lanterns inside.

Just like that, they were at Common Grounds.

Eve jumped out of the driver's side, opened the back door, and grabbed Myrnin under the arms, all the while muttering, "Ick, ick, ick!" Claire slid out to join her, and Hannah grabbed Myrnin's feet when they hit the pavement, and the three of them carried him into the coffee shop.

Claire found herself shoved immediately out of the way by two vampires: Oliver and some woman she didn't know. Oliver looked grim, but then, that wasn't new, either. "Put him down," Oliver said. "No, not there, idiots, over there, on the sofa. You. Off." That last was directed at the frightened humans who were seated on the indicated couch, and they scattered like quail. Eve continued her *ick* mantra as she and Hannah hauled Myrnin's deadweight over and settled him facedown on the couch cushions. He was about the color of a fluorescent lightbulb now, blue-white and cold.

Oliver crouched next to him, looking at the stake in Myrnin's back. He steepled his fingers for a moment, and then looked up at Claire. "What happened?"

She supposed he could tell, somehow, that it was *her* stake. Wonderful. "I didn't have a choice. He came after us." The *us* part might have been an exaggeration; he'd come after Hannah, really. But eventually he would have come after Claire, too; she knew that.

Oliver gave her a moment to squirm while he stared at her, and then looked back at Myrnin's still, very corpselike body. The area where the stake had gone in looked even paler than the surrounding tissue, like the edge of a whirlpool draining all the color out of him. "Do you have any of the drugs you have been giving him?" Oliver asked. Claire nodded, and fumbled in her pocket. She had some of the powder form of the drug, and some of the liquid, but she hadn't felt confident at all that she'd be able to get it into Myrnin's mouth without a fight she was bound to lose.

When Myrnin was like this, you were going to lose fingers, at the very least, if you got anywhere near his mouth.

Not so much an issue now, she supposed. She handed over the vials to Oliver, who turned them over in his fingers, considering, and then handed back the powder. "The liquid absorbs into the body more quickly, I expect."

"Yes." It also had some unpredictable side effects, but this probably wasn't the time to worry about that.

"And Amelie?" Oliver continued turning the bottle over and over in his fingers.

"She's—we had to leave her. She was fighting Bishop. I don't know where she is now."

A deep silence filled the room, and Claire saw the vampires all look at one another—all except Oliver, who continued to stare down at Myrnin, no change in his expression at all. "All right, then. Helen, Karl, watch the windows and doors. I doubt Bishop's patrols will try storming the place, but they might, while I'm distracted. The rest of you"—he looked at the humans and shook his head—"try to stay out of our way."

He thumbed the top off the vial of clear liquid and held it in his right hand. "Get ready to turn him faceup," he said to Hannah and Claire. Claire took hold of Myrnin's shoulders, and Hannah his feet.

Oliver took the stake in his left hand and, in one smooth motion, pulled it out. It clattered to the floor, and he nodded sharply. "Now."

Once Myrnin was lying on his back, Oliver motioned her away and pried open Myrnin's bloodless lips. He poured the liquid into the other vampire's mouth, shut it, and placed a hand on his high forehead.

Myrnin's dark eyes were open. Wide-open. Claire shuddered, because they looked completely dead—like windows into a dark, dark room . . . and then he blinked.

He sucked in a very deep breath, and his back arched in silent agony. Oliver held his hand steady on Myrnin's forehead. His eyes were squeezed shut in concentration, and Myrnin writhed weakly, trying without much success to twist free. He collapsed limply back on the cushions, chest rising and falling. His skin still looked like polished marble, veined with cold blue, but his eyes were alive again.

And crazy. And hungry.

He swallowed, coughed, swallowed again, and gradually, the insane pilot light in his eyes went out. He looked tired and confused and in pain.

Oliver let out a long, moaning sigh, and tried to stand up. He couldn't. He made it about halfway up, then wavered and fell to his knees, one hand braced on the arm of the couch for support. His head went down, and his shoulders heaved, almost as if he were gasping or crying. Claire couldn't imagine Oliver—*Oliver*—doing either one of those things, really.

Nobody moved. Nobody touched him, although some of the other vampires exchanged unreadable glances.

He's sick, Claire thought. It was the disease. It made it harder and harder for them to concentrate, to do the things they'd always taken for granted, like make other vampires. Or revive them. Even Oliver, who hadn't believed anything about the sickness . . . even he was starting to fail.

And he knew it.

"Help me up," Oliver finally whispered. His voice sounded faint and tattered. Claire grabbed his arm and helped him climb slowly, painfully up; he moved as if he were a thousand years old, and felt every year of it. One of the other vampires silently provided a chair, and Claire helped him into it.

Oliver braced his elbows on his thighs and hid his pale face in his hands. When she started to speak, he said, softly, "Leave me."

It didn't seem a good idea to argue. Claire backed off and returned to where Myrnin was, on the couch.

He blinked, still staring at the ceiling. He folded his hands slowly across his stomach, but didn't otherwise move.

"Myrnin?"

"Present," he said, from what seemed like a very great distance away. He chuckled very softly, then winced. "Hurts when I laugh."

"Yeah, um—I'm sorry."

"Sorry?" A very slight frown worked its way between Myrnin's eyebrows, made a slow V, and then went on its way. "Ah. Staked me."

"I . . . uh . . . yeah." She knew what Oliver's reaction would have been, if she'd done that kind of thing to him, and the outcome wouldn't have been pretty. She wasn't sure what Myrnin might do. Just to be sure, she stayed out of easy-grabbing distance.

Myrnin simply closed his eyes for a moment and nodded. He looked old now, exhausted, like Oliver. "I'm sure it was for the best," he said. "Perhaps you should have left the wood in place. Better for everyone, in the end. I would have just—faded away. It's not very painful, not comparatively."

"No!" She took a step closer, then another. He just looked so— defeated. "Myrnin, don't. We need you."

He didn't open his eyes, but there was a tiny, tired smile curving his lips. "I'm sure you think you do, but you have what you need now. I found the cure for you, Claire. Bishop's blood. It's time to let me go. It's too late for me to get better."

"I don't believe that."

This time, his great dark eyes opened and studied her with cool intensity. "I see you don't," he said. "Whether or not that assumption is reasonable, that's another question entirely. Where is she?"

He was asking about Amelie. Claire glanced at Oliver, still hunched over, clearly in pain. No help. She bent closer to Myrnin. No way she wouldn't be overheard by the other vampires, though, she knew that. "She's—I don't know. We got separated. The last I saw, she and Bishop were fighting it out."

Myrnin sat up. It wasn't the kind of smooth, controlled motion vampires usually had, as though they'd been practicing it for three or four human lifetimes; he had to pull himself up, slowly and painfully, and it hurt Claire to watch. She put her hand against his shoulder blade to brace him. His skin still felt marble-cold, but not *dead*. It was hard to figure out what the difference was—maybe it was the muscles, underneath, tensed and alive again.

"We have to find her," he said. "Bishop will stop at nothing to get her, if he hasn't already. Once you were safely away, she'd have retreated. Amelie is a guerrilla fighter. It's not like her to fight in the open, not against her father."

"We're not going anywhere," Oliver said, without taking his head out of his hands. "And neither are you, Myrnin."

"You owe her your fealty."

"I owe nothing to the dead," Oliver said. "And until I see proof of her survival, I will not sacrifice my life, or anyone else's, in a futile attempt at rescue."

Myrnin's face twisted in contempt. "You haven't changed," he said.

"Neither have you, fool," Oliver murmured. "Now shut up. My head aches."

Eve was pulling shots behind the counter, wearing a formal black apron that went below her knees. Claire slid wearily onto a barstool on the other side. "Wow," she said. "Flashback to the good times, huh?"

Eve made a sour face as she thumped a mocha down in front of her friend. "Yeah, don't remind me," she said. "Although I have to say, I missed the Monster."

"The Monster?"

Eve patted the giant, shiny espresso machine beside her affectionately. "Monster, meet Claire. Claire, meet the Monster. He's a sweetie, really, but you have to know his moods."

Claire reached out and patted the machine, too. "Nice to meet you, Monster."

"Hey." Eve caught her wrist when she tried to pull back. "Bruises? What gives?"

Amelie's grip on her really had raised a crop of faint blue smudges on her upper arm, like a primitive tattoo. "Don't freak. I don't have any bite marks or anything."

"I'll freak if I wanna. As long as Michael isn't here, I'm kind of—"

"What, my mom?" Claire snapped, and was instantly sorry. And guilty, for an entirely different reason. "I didn't mean—"

Eve waved it away. "Hey, if you can't spark a 'tude on a day like this, when can you? Your mother's okay, by the way, because I know that's your next question. So far, Bishop's freaks haven't managed to shut down the cell network, so I've been keeping in touch, since nothing's happening here except for some serious caffeine production. Landlines are dead, though. So is the Internet. Radio and TV are both off the air, too."

Claire looked at the clock. Five a.m. Two hours until dawn, more or less—probably less. It felt like an eternity.

"What are we going to do in the morning?" she asked.

"Good question." Eve wiped down the counter. Claire sipped the sweet, chocolatey comfort of the mocha. "When you think of something, let us know, because right now, I don't think anybody's got a clue."

"You'd be wrong, thankfully," Oliver said. He seemed to come out of nowhere—*God*, didn't Claire hate that!—as he settled on the stool next to her. He seemed almost back to normal now, but very tired. There was a shadow in his eyes that Claire didn't remember seeing before. "There is a plan in place. Amelie's removal from the field of battle is a blow, but not a defeat. We continue as she would want."

"Yeah? You want to tell us?" Eve asked. That earned her a cool stare. "Yeah, I didn't think so. Vampires really aren't all about the sharing, unless it benefits them first."

"I will tell you what you need to know, when you need to know it," Oliver said. "Get me one of the bags from the walk-in refrigerator."

Eve looked down at the top of her apron. "Oh, I'm sorry, where does it say *servant* on here? Because I'm so very not."

For a second, Claire held her breath, because the expression on Oliver's face was murderous, and she saw a red light, like the embers of a banked fire, glowing in the back of his eyes.

Then he blinked and said, simply, "Please, Eve."

Eve hadn't been expecting that. She blinked, stared back at him for a second, then silently nodded and walked away, behind a curtained doorway.

"You're wondering if that hurt," Oliver said, not looking at Claire at all, but staring after Eve. "It did, most assuredly."

"Good," she said. "I hear suffering's good for the soul, or something."

"Then we shall all be right with our God by morning." Oliver swiveled on the stool to look her full in the face. "I should kill you for what you did."

"Staking Myrnin?" She sighed. "I know. I didn't think I had a choice. He'd have bitten my hand off if I'd tried to give him the medicine, and by the time it took effect, me and Hannah would have been dog food, anyway. It seemed like the quickest, quietest way to get him out."

"Even so," Oliver said, his voice low in his throat, "as an Elder, I have the power to sentence you, right now, to death, for attempted murder of a vampire. You do understand?"

Claire held up her hand and pointed to the gold bracelet on her wrist—the symbol of the Founder. Amelie's symbol. "What about this?"

"I would pay reparations," he said. "I imagine I could afford it. Amelie would be tolerably upset with me, for a while, always assuming she is still alive. We'd reach an accommodation. We always do."

Claire didn't say anything else in her defense, just waited. And after a moment, he nodded. "All right," he said. "You were right to take the action you did. You have been right about a good deal that I was unwilling to admit, including the fact that some of us are"—he cast a quick look around, and dropped his voice so low she could make out the word only from the shape his lips gave it—"unwell."

Unwell. Yeah, that was one way to put it. She resisted an urge to roll her eyes. *How about dying? Ever heard the word* pandemic?

Oliver continued without waiting for her response. "Myrnin's mind was . . . very disordered," he said. "I didn't think I could get him back. I wouldn't have, without that dose of medication."

"Does that mean you believe us now?" She meant, *about the vampire disease*, but she couldn't say that out loud. Even the roundabout way they were speaking was dangerous; too many vampire ears with too little to do, and once they knew about the sickness, there was no predicting what they might do. Run, probably. Go off to rampage through the human world, sicken, and die alone, very slowly. It'd take years, maybe decades, but eventually, they'd all fall, one by one. Oliver's case was less advanced than many of the others, but age seemed to slow down the disease's progress; he might last for a long time, losing himself slowly.

Becoming nothing more than a hungry shell.

Oliver said, "It means what it means," and he said it with an impatient edge to it, but Claire wondered if he really did know. "I am talking about Myrnin. Your drugs may not be enough to hold him for long, and that means we will need to take precautions."

Eve emerged from the curtain carrying a plastic blood bag, filled with dark cherry syrup. That was what Claire told herself, anyway. Dark cherry syrup. Eve looked shaken, and she dumped the bag on the counter in front of Oliver like a dead rat. "You've been planning this," she said. "Planning for a siege."

Oliver smiled slowly. "Have I?"

"You've got enough blood in there to feed half the vampires in town for a month, *and* enough of those heat-and-eat meals campers use to feed the rest of us even longer. Medicines, too. Pretty much anything we'd need to hold out here, including generators, batteries, bottled water. . . ."

"Let's say I am cautious," he said. "It's a trait many of us have picked up during our travels." He took the blood bag and motioned for a cup; when Eve set it in front of him, he punctured the bag with a fingernail, very neatly, and squeezed part of the contents into the cup. "Save the rest," he said, and handed it back to Eve, who looked even queasier than before. "Don't look so disgusted. Blood in bags means none taken unwillingly from your veins, after all."

Eve held it at arm's length, opened the smaller refrigerator behind the bar, and put it in an empty spot on the door rack inside. "Ugh," she said. "Why am I behind the bar again?"

"Because you put on the apron."

"Oh, you're just *loving* this, aren't you?"

"Guys," Claire said, drawing both of their stares. "Myrnin. Where are we going to put him?"

Before Oliver could answer, Myrnin pushed through the crowd in the table-and-chairs area of Common Grounds and walked toward them. He *seemed* normal again, or as normal as Myrnin ever got, anyway. He'd begged, borrowed, or outright stolen a long, black velvet coat, and under it he was still wearing the poofy white Pierrot pants from his costume, dark boots, and no shirt. Long, black, glossy hair and decadently shining eyes.

Oliver took in the outfit, and raised a brow. "You look like you escaped from a Victorian brothel," he said. "One that . . . specialized."

In answer, Myrnin skinned up the sleeves of the coat. The wound in his back might have healed—or might be healing, anyway—but the burns on his wrists and hands were still livid red, with an unhealthy silver tint to them. "Not the sort of brothel I'd normally frequent, by choice," he said, "though of course you might be more adventurous, Oliver." Their gazes locked, and Claire resisted the urge to take a step back. She thought, just for a second, that they were going to bare fangs at each other . . . and then Myrnin smiled. "I suppose I should say thank you."

"It would be customary," Oliver agreed.

Myrnin turned to Claire. "Thank you."

Somehow, she guessed that wasn't what Oliver had expected; she certainly hadn't. It was the kind of snub that got most people hurt in Morganville, but then again, she guessed Myrnin wasn't most people, even to Oliver.

Oliver didn't react. If there was a small red glow in the depths of his eyes, it could have been a reflection from the lights.

"Um—for what?" Claire asked.

"I remember what you did." Myrnin shrugged. "It was the right choice at the moment. I couldn't control myself. The pain . . . the pain was extremely difficult to contain."

She cast a nervous glance at his wrists. "How is it now?"

"Tolerable." His tone dismissed any further discussion. "We need to get to a portal and locate Amelie. The closest is at the university. We will need a car, I suppose, and a driver. Some sturdy escorts wouldn't go amiss." Myrnin sounded casual, but utterly certain that his slightest wish would be obeyed, and again, she felt that flare of tension between him and Oliver.

"Perhaps you've missed the announcement," Oliver said. "You're no longer a king, or a prince, or whatever you were before you disappeared into your filthy hole. You're Amelie's exotic pet alchemist, and you don't give me orders. Not in *my* town."

"Your town," Myrnin repeated, staring at him intently. His face had set into pleasant, rigid lines, but those eyes—not pleasant at all. Claire moved herself prudently out of the way. "What a surprise! I thought it was the Founder's town."

Oliver looked around. "Oddly, she seems unavailable, and that makes it my town, little man. So go and sit down. You're not going anywhere. If she's in trouble—which I do not yet believe—and if there's rescuing to be done, we will consider all the risks."

"And the benefits of not acting at all?" Myrnin asked. His voice was wound as tight as a clock spring. "Tell me, Old Ironsides, how you plan to win this campaign. I do hope you don't plan to reenact Drogheda."

Claire had no idea what that meant, but it meant something to Oliver, something bitter and deep, and his whole face twisted for a moment.

"We're not fighting the Irish campaigns, and whatever errors I made once, I'll not be making them again," Oliver said. "And I don't need advice from a blue-faced hedge witch."

"There's the old Puritan spirit!"

Eve slapped the bar hard. "Hey! Whatever musty old prejudices the two of you have rattling around in your heads, *stop*. We're here, twenty-first century, USA, and we've got problems that don't include your ancient history!"

Myrnin blinked, looked at Eve, and smiled. It was his seductive smile, and it came with a lowering of his thick eyelashes. "Sweet lady," he said, "could you get me one of those delicious drinks you prepared for my friend, here?" He gracefully indicated Oliver, who remembered the cup of blood still sitting in front of him, and angrily choked it down. "Perhaps warm the bag a bit in hot water first? It's a bit disgusting, cold."

"Yeah, sure," Eve sighed. "Want a shot of espresso with that?"

Myrnin seemed to be honestly considering it. Claire urgently shook her head *no*. The last thing she—any of them—needed just now was Myrnin on caffeine.

As Eve walked away to prepare Myrnin's drink, Oliver shook himself out of his anger with a physical twitch, took a deep breath, and said, "It's less than two hours to dawn. Even if something has happened to Amelie—which again, I dispute—it's too risky to launch a search just now. If Bishop has Amelie, he'll have her some place that'll hold against an assault in any case. Two hours isn't enough time, and I won't risk our people in the dawn."

Myrnin flicked a glance toward Claire. "Some of those here aren't affected by the dawn."

"Some of them are also highly vulnerable," Oliver said. "I wouldn't send a human out after Bishop. I wouldn't send a human *army* out after Bishop, unless you're planning to deduce his location from the corpses he leaves behind."

For a horrified second, Myrnin actually mulled that over, and then he shook his head. "He'd hide the bodies," he said regretfully. "A useful suggestion, though."

Claire couldn't tell if he was mocking Oliver, or if he really meant it. Oliver couldn't tell, either, from the long, considering look he gave him.

Oliver turned his attention to her. "Tell me everything."

SIX

In an hour, the blush of dawn was already on the horizon, bringing an eerie blue glow to the night world. Somewhere out there, vampires all over town would be getting ready for it, finding secure places to stay the day—whatever side they were fighting on.

The ones in Common Grounds seemed content to stay on, which made sense; it was kind of a secured location anyway, from what Oliver and Amelie had said before—one of the key places in town to hold if they intended to keep control of Morganville.

But Claire wasn't entirely happy with the way some of those vampires—strangers, mostly, though all from Morganville, according to Eve—seemed to be whispering in the corners. "How do we know they're on our side?" she asked Eve, in a whisper she hoped would escape vampire notice.

No such luck. "You don't," Oliver said, from several feet away. "Nor is that your concern, but I will reassure you in any case. They are all loyal to me, and through me, to Amelie. If any of them 'turn coats,' you may be assured that they'll regret it." He said it in a normal tone of voice, to carry to all parts of the room.

The vampires stopped whispering.

"All right," Oliver said to Claire and Eve. "The light of dawn was creeping up like a warning outside the windows. "You understand what I want you to do?"

Eve nodded and gave him a sloppy, insolent kind of salute. "Sir, yes *sir*, General sir!"

"Eve." His patience, what little there was, was worn to the bone. "Repeat my instructions."

Eve didn't like taking orders under the best of circumstances, which these weren't. Claire quickly said, "We take these walkie-talkies to each of the Founder Houses, to the university, and to anybody else on the list. We tell them all strategic orders come through these, not through cell phone or police band."

"Be sure to give them the code," he said. Each one of the tiny little radios had a keypad, like a cell phone, but the difference was that you had to enter the code into it to access the emergency communication channel he'd established. Pretty high tech, but then, Oliver didn't really seem the type to lag much behind on the latest cool stuff. "All right. I'm sending Hannah with you as your escort. I'd send one of my own, but—"

"Dawn, yeah, I know," Eve said. She offered a high five to Hannah, who took it. "Damn, girl, love the Rambo look."

"Rambo was a Green Beret," Hannah said. "Please. We eat those army boys for breakfast."

Which was maybe not such a comfortable thing to say in a room full of maybe-hungry vampires. Claire cleared her throat. "We should—"

Hannah nodded, picked up the backpack (Claire's, now filled with handheld radios instead of books), and handed it to her. "I need both hands free," she said. "Eve's driving. You're the supply master. There's a checklist inside, so you can mark off deliveries as we go."

Myrnin was sitting off to the side, ominously quiet. His eyes still looked sane, but Claire had warned Oliver in the strongest possible terms that he couldn't trust him. Not really.

As if I would, Oliver had said with a snort. *I've known the man for many human lifetimes, and I've never trusted him yet.*

The vampires in the coffee shop had mostly retreated out of the big, front area, into the better-protected, light-proofed interior. Outside of the plate-glass windows, there was little to be seen. The fires had gone out, or been extinguished. They'd seen some cars speeding about, mostly official police or fire, but the few figures they'd spotted had been quick and kept to the shadows.

"What are they doing?" Claire asked as she hitched her backpack to a more comfortable position on her shoulder. She didn't really expect Oliver to reply; he wasn't much on the sharing.

He surprised her. "They're consolidating positions," he said. "This is not a war that will be fought in daylight, Claire. Or in the open. We have our positions; they have theirs. They may send patrols of humans they've recruited, but they won't come themselves. Not after dawn."

"Recruited," Hannah repeated. "Don't you mean strong-armed? Most folks just want to be left alone."

"Not necessarily. Morganville is full of humans who don't love us, or the system under which they labor," Oliver replied. "Some will believe Bishop is the answer. Some will act out of fear, to protect their loved ones. He will know how to appeal to them, and how to pressure. He'll find his human cannon fodder."

"Like you've found yours," Hannah said.

They locked stares for a few seconds, and then Oliver inclined his head just a bit. "If you like."

"I don't," she said, "but I'm used to the front lines. You got to know, others won't be."

Claire couldn't tell anything from Oliver's expression. "Perhaps not," he said. "But for now, we can count on our enemies regrouping. We should do the same."

Hannah nodded. "I'm out first, then you, Eve. Have your keys in your hand. Don't hesitate, run like hell for the car, and get it unlocked. I'll get Claire to the passenger side."

Eve nodded, clearly jittery. She took the car keys out of her pocket and held them in her hand, sorting through until she had the right key pointing out.

"One more thing," Hannah said. "You got a flashlight?"

Eve fumbled in her other pocket and came up with a tiny little penlight. When she twisted it, it gave a surprisingly bright glow.

"Good." Hannah nodded. "Before you get in the car, you shine that in the front seats and backseats. Make sure you can see all the way down to the carpet. I'll cover you from the door."

The three of them moved to the exit, and Hannah put her left hand on the knob.

"Be careful," Oliver said from the back of the room, which was kind of warmly surprising. He spoiled it by continuing, "We need those radios delivered."

Should have known it wasn't personal. Claire resisted the urge to flip him off.

Eve didn't bother to resist hers.

Then Hannah was swinging open the door and stepping outside. She didn't do it like in the movies; no drama, she just stepped right out, turned in a slow half circle as she scanned the street with the paintball gun held at rest. She finally motioned for Eve. Eve darted out and headed around the hood of the big black car. Claire saw the glow of her penlight as she checked the inside, and then Eve was in the driver's seat and the car growled to a start, and Hannah pushed her toward the passenger door.

Behind them, the Common Grounds door slammed shut and locked. When she looked back, Claire saw that they were pulling down some kind of steel shutters inside the glass.

Locking up for dawn.

Claire and Hannah made it to the car without any problems. Even so, Claire was breathing hard, her heart racing.

"You okay?" Eve asked her. Claire nodded, still gasping. "Yeah, I know. Terror Aerobics. Just wait until they get it at the gym. It'll be bigger than Pilates."

Claire choked on her fear, laughed, and felt better.

"That's my girl. Locks," Eve said. "Also, seat belts, please. We may be making some sudden stops along the way. Don't want anybody saying hello to Mr. Windshield at speed."

The drive through predawn Morganville was eerie. It was very . . .

quiet. They'd mapped out a route, planning to avoid the most dangerous areas, but they almost had to divert immediately, because of a couple of cars parked in the middle of the street.

The doors were hanging open, interior lights were still shining.

Eve slowed down and crawled past on the right side, two wheels up on the curb. "See anything?" she asked anxiously. "Any bodies or anything?"

The cars were completely empty. They were still running, and the keys were in the ignition. One strange thing nagged at Claire, but she couldn't think what it was. . . .

"Those are vampire cars," Hannah said. "Why would they leave them here like that?" Oh. That was the odd thing. The tinting on the windows.

"They needed to pee?" Eve asked. "When you've gotta go . . ."

Hannah said nothing. She was watching out the windows with even more focus than before.

"Yeah, that is weird," Eve said more quietly. "Maybe they went to help somebody." Or hunt somebody. Claire shivered.

They made their first radio delivery to one of the Founder Houses; Claire didn't know the people who answered the door, but Eve did, of course. She quickly explained about the radio and the code, and they were back in the car and rolling in about two minutes flat. "Outstanding," Hannah said. "You girls could give some of my buddies in the marines a run for their money."

"Hey, you know how it is, Hannah: living in Morganville really is combat training." Eve and Hannah awkwardly slapped palms—awkwardly, because Eve kept facing front, and Hannah didn't turn away from her post at the car's back window. She had the window rolled down halfway, and the paintball gun at the ready, but so far she hadn't fired a single shot.

"More cars," Claire said softly. "You see?"

It wasn't just a couple of cars, it was a bunch of them, scattered on both sides of the street now, engines running, lights on, doors open.

Empty.

They cruised past slowly, and Claire took note of the heavy tinting on the windows. They were all the same type of car, the same type Michael had been issued on his official conversion to vampire.

"What the hell is going on?" Eve asked. She sounded tense and anxious, and Claire couldn't blame her. She felt pretty tense herself. "This close to dawn, they wouldn't be doing this. They shouldn't even be outside. He said both sides would regroup, but this looks like some kind of full-on panic."

Claire had to agree, but she also had no explanation. She dug one of the radios out of her backpack, typed in the code that Oliver had given her, and pressed the TALK button. "Oliver? Come in."

After a short delay, his voice came back. "Go."

"Something strange is happening. We're seeing lots of vampire cars, but they're all abandoned. Empty. Still running." Static on the other end. "Oliver?"

"Keep me informed," he finally said. "Count the number of cars. Make a list of license numbers, if you can."

"Er—anything else? Should we come back?"

"No. Deliver the radios."

That was it. Claire tried again, but he'd shut off or he was ignoring her. She pressed the RESET button to scramble the code, and looked at Eve, who shrugged. They pulled to a halt in front of the second Founder House. "Let's just get it done," Eve said. "Let the vamps worry about the vamps."

It seemed reasonable, but Claire was afraid that somehow . . . it wasn't.

Three of the Founder Houses were piles of smoking wood and ash, and the Morganville Fire Department was still pouring water on one of them. Eve cruised by, but didn't stop. The horizon was getting lighter and lighter, and they still had a couple of stops to make.

"You okay back there?" Eve asked Hannah, as they turned another corner, heading into an area Claire actually recognized.

"Fine," Hannah said. "We going to the Day House?"

"Yeah, next on my list."

"Good. I want to talk to Cousin Lisa."

Eve pulled up outside of the big Founder House; it was lit up in every window, a stark contrast to its dark, shuttered neighboring residences.

As she put the car in park, the front door opened and spilled a wedge of lemon-colored light across the immaculately kept front porch. Gramma Day's rocker was empty, nodding in the slight wind.

The person at the door was Lisa Day—tall, strong, with more than a slight resemblance to Hannah. She watched them get out of the car. Upstairs windows opened, and gun barrels came out.

"They're all right," she called, but she didn't step outside. "Claire, right? And Eve? Hey, Hannah."

"Hey." Hannah nodded. "Let's get in. I don't like this quiet out here."

As soon as they were in the front door, in a familiar-looking hallway, Lisa slammed down locks and bolts, including a recently installed iron bar that slotted into place on either side of the frame. Hannah watched this with bemused approval. "You knew this was coming?" she asked.

"I figured it'd come sooner or later," Lisa said. "Had the hardware in the basement. All we had to do was put it in. Gramma didn't like it, but I did it, anyway. She keeps yelling about me putting holes in the wood."

"Yeah, that's Gramma." Hannah grinned. "God forbid we should mess up her house while the war's going on."

"Speaking of that," Lisa said, "y'all need to stay here, if you want to stay safe."

Eve exchanged a quick glance with Claire. "Yeah, well, we can't, really. But thanks."

"You sure?" Lisa's eyes were very bright, very focused. "Because we're thinking maybe these vamps will kill each other off this time, and maybe we should all stick together. All the humans. Never mind the bracelets and the contracts."

Eve blinked. "Seriously? Just let them fight it out on their own?"

"Why not? What's it to us, anyway, who wins?" Lisa's smile was bitter and brief. "We get screwed no matter what. Maybe it's time to put a human in charge of this town, and let the vampires find someplace else to live."

Dangerous, Claire thought. Really dangerous. Hannah stared at her cousin, her expression tight and controlled, and then nodded. "Okay," she said. "You do what you want, Lisa, but you be careful, all right?"

"We're being real damn careful," Lisa said. "You'll see."

They came to the end of the hallway, where the area opened up into the big living room, and Eve and Claire both stopped cold.

"Oh, *shit*," Eve muttered.

The humans were all armed—guns, knives, stakes, blunt objects. The vampires who'd been assigned to guard the house were all sitting tied to chairs with so many turns of rope it reminded Claire of hangman's loops. She supposed if you were going to restrain vamps, it made sense, but—

"What the hell are you doing?" Eve blurted. At least some of the vampires sitting there, tied and gagged, were ones who'd been at Michael's house, or who'd fought on Amelie's side at the banquet. Some of them were struggling, but most seemed quiet.

Some looked *unconscious*.

"They're not hurt," Lisa said. "I just want 'em out of the way, in case things go bad."

"You're making one hell of a move, Lisa," Hannah said. "I hope you know what the hell you're about."

"I'm about protecting my own. You ought to be, too."

Hannah nodded slowly. "Let's go," she said to Claire and Eve.

"What about—"

"No," Hannah said. "No radio. Not here."

Lisa moved into their path, a shotgun cradled in her arms. "Going so soon?"

Claire forgot to breathe. There was a feeling here, a darkness in the air. The vampires, those who were still awake, were staring at them. Expecting rescue, maybe?

"You don't want to do this," Hannah said. "We're not your enemies."

"You're standing with the vamps, aren't you?"

There it was, out in the open. Claire swallowed hard. "We're trying to get everybody out of this alive," she said. "Humans and vampires."

Lisa didn't look away from her cousin's face. "Not going to happen," she said. "So you'd better pick a side."

Hannah stepped right up into her face. After a cold second, Lisa moved aside. "Already have," Hannah said. She jerked her head at Claire and Eve. "Let's move."

Outside in the car, they all sat in silence for a few seconds. Hannah's face was grim and closed off, not inviting any conversation.

Eve finally said, "You'd better tell Oliver. He needs to know about this."

Claire plugged in the code and tried. "Oliver, come in. Oliver, it's Claire. I have an update. Oliver!"

Static hissed. There was no response.

"Maybe he's ignoring you," Eve said. "He seemed pretty annoyed before."

"You try." Claire handed it over, but it was no use. Oliver wasn't responding. They tried calling for anyone at Common Grounds instead, and got another voice, one Claire didn't recognize.

"Hello?"

Eve squeezed her eyes shut in relief. "Excellent. Who's this?"

"Quentin Barnes."

"Tin-Tin! Hey man, how are you?"

"Ah—good, I guess." Tin-Tin, whoever he was, sounded nervous. "Oliver's kind of busy right now. He's trying to keep some people from taking off."

"Taking off?" Eve's eyes widened. "What do you mean?"

"Some of the vamps, they're just trying to leave. It's too close to dawn. He's had to lock some of them up."

Things were getting weird all over. Eve keyed the mike and said, "There's trouble at the Day House. Lisa's tied up the vamps. She's going to sit this thing out. I think—I think maybe she's working with some other people, trying to put together a third side. All humans."

"Dude," Tin-Tin sighed, "that's just what we need, getting the vampire slayers all in the mix. Okay, I'll tell Oliver. Anything else?"

"More empty vampire cars. You think they're like those guys who were trying to leave? Maybe, I don't know, getting drawn off somewhere?"

"Probably. Look, just watch yourself, okay?"

"Will do. Eve out."

Hannah stirred in the back. "Let's move out to the next location."

"I'm sorry," Claire said. "I know they're your family and all."

"Lisa always was preaching about how we could take the town if we stuck together. Maybe she's thinking it's the right time to make a move." Hannah shook her head. "She's an idiot. All she's going to do is get people killed."

Claire was no general, but she knew that fighting a war on two fronts and dividing their forces wasn't a great idea. "We have to find Amelie."

"Wherever she's gotten herself off to," Eve snorted. "If she's even still—"

"Don't," Claire whispered. She restlessly rubbed the gold bracelet on her wrist until it dug into her skin. "We need her."

More than ever, she was guessing.

By the time they'd dropped off the next to last radio, at their own home, which was currently inhabited by a bunch of freaked-out humans and a few vampires who hadn't yet felt whatever was pulling some of them off, the dawn was starting to really set in. The horizon was Caribbean blue, with touches of gold and red just flaring up like footlights at a show. Claire delivered the radio, the code, and a warning to the humans and vampires alike. "You have to watch the vamps," she pleaded. "Don't let them leave. Not in the daylight."

Monica Morrell, who was clutching the walkie-talkie in her red-taloned fingers, frowned at her. "How are we supposed to do that, freak? Give them a written warning and scold them really hard? Come on!"

"If you let them go, they may not get wherever it is they're being called before sunrise," Hannah said. She shrugged, a fluid flow that emphasized her muscles, and smiled. "Hey, no skin off my nose or anything, but we may need 'em later. And you could get blamed for not stepping up."

Monica kept on frowning, but she didn't seem inclined to argue with Hannah. Nobody did, Claire noticed. The former marine had an air about her, a confidence that somehow didn't come off at all like arrogance.

"Great," Monica finally said. "Wonderful. Like I needed another problem. By the way, Claire, your house really sucks ass. I hate it here."

It was Claire's turn to smile this time. "It probably hates you right back. I'm sure you'll figure it out," she said. "You're a natural leader, right?"

"Oh, bite it. Someday, your boyfriend won't be around to—" Monica widened her eyes. "Oh, snap! He's *isn't* around, is he? Won't be back, ever. Remind me to send flowers for the funeral."

Eve grabbed the back of Claire's shirt. "Whoa, Mini-Me, chill out. We've got to get moving. Much as I'd like to see the cage match, we're kind of on a schedule."

The hot crimson haze disappeared from Claire's eyes, and she took in a breath and nodded. Her muscles were aching. She realized she'd managed to clench just about every muscle, iron-hard, and tried to relax. Her hands twinged when she stretched them out of fists.

"See you soon," Monica said, and shut the door on them. "Wait, probably not, loser. And your clothes are pathetic, by the way!"

That last part came muffled, but clear—as clear as the sound of the locks snapping into place.

"Let's go," Hannah said, and herded them off the porch and down the walk toward the white picket fence.

Walking on the street, heading vaguely north, was a vampire. "Oh, crap," Eve said, alarmed, but the vamp didn't seem to care about them, or even know they were there. He was wearing a police uniform, and Claire remembered him; he'd been riding with Richard Morrell, from time to time. Didn't seem like a bad guy, apart from the whole vampire thing. "That's Officer O'Malley. Hey! Hey, Officer! Wait up!"

He ignored them and kept walking.

Claire looked east. The sun's golden glow was heating up the sky, fast. It wasn't over the horizon yet, but it would be in a matter of seconds, minutes at most. "We've got to get him," she said. "Get him inside somewhere."

"And do what, babysit him the rest of the day? O'Malley's not like Myrnin," Eve said. "You can't stake him. He's not that old. Seventy, eighty, something like that. He's only a little older than Sam."

"We could run him over," Hannah said. "It wouldn't kill him."

Eve sent her a wide-eyed look. "Excuse me? With my *car*?"

"You're asking for something nonlethal. That's all I've got right now. The three of us aren't any kind of match for a vampire who wants to get somewhere, if he fights us."

Claire took off running toward the vampire, ignoring their shouts. She looked back. Hannah was after her, and gaining.

She still got to Officer O'Malley first, and skidded into his path.

He paused for a second, his green eyes focusing on her, and then he reached out and moved her aside. Gently, but firmly.

And he kept on walking.

"You have to get inside!" Claire yelled, and got in front of him again. "Sir, you have to! Right now! Please!"

He moved her again, this time without as much care. He didn't say a word.

"Oh, God," Hannah said. "Too late."

The sun came up in a fiery burst, and the first rays of sunlight hit the parked cars, Eve's standing figure, the houses . . . and Officer O'Malley's back.

"Get a blanket!" Claire screamed. She could see the smoke curling off him, like morning mist. "Do something!"

Eve ran to get something from the car. Hannah grabbed Claire and pulled her out of his way.

Officer O'Malley kept walking. The sun kept rising, brighter and brighter, and within three or four steps, the smoke rising up from him turned to flames.

In ten more steps, he fell down.

Eve ran up breathlessly, a blanket clutched in both hands. "Help me get it over him!"

They threw the fabric over Officer O'Malley, but instead of smothering the flames, it just caught fire, too.

Hannah pulled Claire back as she tried to pat out the flames. "Don't," she said. "It's too late."

Claire turned toward Hannah in a raw fury, struggling to get free. "We can still—"

"No, we can't," Hannah said. "There's not a damn thing we can do for him. He's dying, Claire. You tried your best, but he's dying. And he's not going to take our help. Look, he's still trying to crawl. He's not stopping."

She was right, but it hurt, and in the end, Claire wrapped her arms around Hannah for comfort and turned away.

When she finally looked back, Officer O'Malley was a pile of ash and smoke and burned blanket.

"Michael," Claire whispered. She looked at the sun. "We have to find Michael!"

Hannah went very still for a second, and then nodded. "Let's go."

SEVEN

The gates of the university were shut, locked, and there were paramilitary-style men posted at the gates, all in black. Armed. Eve coasted the big car slowly up to them and rolled down the window.

"Delivery for Michael Glass," she called. "Or Richard Morrell."

The guard who leaned in was huge, tough, and intimidating—until he saw Hannah in the backseat, and then he grinned like a kid with a new puppy. "Hannah Montana!"

She looked deeply pained. "Don't *ever* call me that again, Jessup, or I *will* gut you."

"Get out and make me stop, Smiley. Yeah, I heard you were back. How were the marines?"

"Better than the damn rangers."

"Don't you just wish?" He lost the smile and got serious again. "Sorry, H, orders are orders. Who sent you? Who's with you?"

"Oliver sent me. You probably know Eve Rosser—that's Claire Danvers."

"Really? Huh. Thought she'd be bigger. Hey, Eve. Sorry, didn't recognize you right off. Long time, no see." Jessup nodded to the other guard, who slung his rifle and pressed in a key code at the panel on the stone fence. The big iron gates slowly parted. "You be careful, Hannah. This town's the Af-Pak border all over again right now."

Inside, except for the guards patrolling the fence, Texas Prairie University seemed eerily normal. The birds sang to the rising sun, and there were students out—*students!*—heading to class as if there were nothing wrong at all. They were chatting, laughing, running to make the cross-campus early-morning bell.

"What the *hell?*" Eve said. Claire was glad she wasn't the only one freaked out by it. "I know they had orders to keep things low profile, but damn, this is ridiculous. Where's the dean's office?"

Claire pointed. Eve steered the car around the winding curves, past dorms and lecture halls, and pulled it to a stop on the nearly deserted lot in front of the Administration Building. There were two police cruisers there, and a bunch of black Jeeps. Not a lot of civilian cars in the lot.

As they walked up the steps to the building, Claire realized there were two more guards outside of the main door. Hannah didn't know these guys, but she repeated their names and credentials, and after a brief, impersonal search, they were allowed inside.

The last time Claire had been here she'd been adding and dropping classes, and the building had been full of grumpy bureaucrats and anxious students, all moving at a hectic pace. Now it was very quiet. A few people were at their desks, but there were no students Claire could see, and the TPU employees looked either bored or nervous. Most of the activity seemed centered down the carpeted hall, which was hung with formal portraits of the former university deans and notables.

One or two of the former deans, Claire was just now realizing, might have been vampires, from the pallor of their skins. Or maybe they were just old white guys. Hard to say.

At the end of the hallway they found not a guard, but a secretary—just as tough as any of the armed men outside, though. She sat behind an expensive-looking antique desk that had not a speck of dust on it, and nothing else except a piece of paper centered exactly in the middle, a pen at right angles to it, and a fancy, black multiline telephone. No computer that Claire could spot—no, there it was, hidden away in a roll-out credenza to the side.

The room was lushly carpeted, so much so that Claire's feet sank into the depth at least an inch; it was like walking on foam. Solid, dark wood paneling. Paintings and dim lights. The windows were covered with fancy velvet curtains, and there was music playing—classical, of course. Claire couldn't imagine anybody would ever switch the station to rock. Not here.

"I'm Ms. Nance," the woman said, and stood to offer her hand to each of them in turn; she didn't even hesitate with Eve, who intimidated most people. She was a tall, thin, gray woman dressed in a tailored gray suit with a lighter gray blouse under the jacket. Gray hair curled into exact waves. Claire couldn't see her shoes, but she bet they were fashionable, gray, and yet somehow sensible. "I'm the secretary to Dean Wallace. Do you have an appointment?"

Eve said, "I need to see Michael."

"I'm sorry? I don't think I know that person."

Eve's expression froze, and Claire could see the horrible dread in her eyes.

Hannah, seeing it too, said, "Let's cut the crap, Ms. Nance. Where's Michael Glass?"

Ms. Nance's eyes narrowed. They were pale blue, not as pale as Amelie's, but kind of faded, like jeans left in the sun. "Mr. Glass is in conference with the dean," she said. "I'm afraid you'll have to—"

The door at the far end of her office opened, and Michael came out. Claire's heart practically melted with relief. *He's okay. Michael's okay.*

Except that he closed the door and walked straight past them, a man on a mission.

He walked right past Eve, who stood there flat-footed, mouth open, fear dawning in her expression.

"Michael!" Claire yelped. He didn't even pause. "We have to stop him!"

"Great," Hannah said, and the three of them took off in pursuit.

It helped that Michael wasn't actually *running*, just moving with a purpose. Claire and Eve edged by him in the hall and blocked his path.

His blue eyes were wide-open, but he just didn't *see* them. He sensed an obstacle, at least, and paused.

"Michael," Claire said. *Dammit, why couldn't I have tranquilizers? Why?* "Michael, you can't go out there. It's already morning. You'll die."

"He's not listening," Hannah said. And she was right; he wasn't. He tried to push between them, but Eve put a hand in the center of his chest and held him back.

"Michael? It's me. You know me, don't you? Please?"

He stared at her with utterly blank eyes, and then shoved her out of his way. Hard.

Hannah sent Claire a quick, commanding look. "Get help. *Now.* I'll try to hold him."

Claire hesitated, but Hannah was without any doubt better equipped to handle a potentially hostile Michael than she was. She turned and ran, past startled desk jockeys and coffee-bearing civil servants, and slid to a stop in front of one of the black-uniformed soldiers. "Richard Morrell," she blurted. "I need him. Right *now.*"

The soldier didn't hesitate. He grabbed the radio clipped to his shoulder and said, "Admin to Morrell."

"Morrell, go."

The soldier unclipped the radio and silently offered it to Claire. She took it—it was heavier than the walkie-talkies—and pressed the button to talk. "Richard? It's Claire. We have a big problem. We need to stop Michael and anybody else . . ." How could she say *vampire* without actually saying it? "Anybody else with a sun allergy from going outside."

"Why the hell would they be—"

"I don't know! They just *are!*" The image of Officer O'Malley on fire leaped into her mind, and she caught her breath on a sob. "Help us. They're going out in the sun."

"Give the radio back," he ordered. She handed it to the black-uniformed man. "I need you to go with this girl and help her. No questions."

"Yes sir." He clicked off the radio and looked down at Claire. "After you."

She led the way back toward the hallway. As they reached it, there was a crash of glass, and Hannah came flying out to land flat on her back, blinking.

Michael walked over to her. Eve was hauling on his arm, trying to hold him back, but he shook her off.

"We can't let him get outside!" Claire said. She tried to grab him, but it was like grabbing a freight train. She'd forgotten how strong he was now.

"Out of the way," the soldier said, and pulled a handgun from a holster at his side.

"No, don't—"

The bureaucrats scattered, hiding under their desks, dropping their coffee to hug the carpet.

The soldier sighted on Michael's chest, and fired three times in quick succession. Instead of the loud bangs Claire had been expecting, there were soft compressed-air coughs.

And three darts feathered Michael's chest, clustered above his heart.

He *still* took three steps toward the soldier before collapsing in slow motion to his knees, and then onto his face.

"All clear," the soldier said. He took hold of Michael, turned him over, and yanked out the darts. "He'll be under for about an hour, probably no longer than that. Let's get him to the dean's office."

Hannah wiped a trickle of blood from her mouth, coughed, and rolled to her feet. She and Eve helped Claire grab Michael's shoulders and feet, and they carried him down the hallway, past paintings that were going to need some major repair and reframing, past splintered panels and broken glass, into Ms. Nance's office.

Ms. Nance took one look at them and moved smartly to the door marked with a discreet brass plaque that said DEAN WALLACE. She rapped and opened the door for them to carry Michael through.

Dean Wallace was a woman, which was kind of a surprise to Claire. She'd been expecting a pudgy, middle-aged man; *this* Dean Wallace was tall, graceful, thin, and a whole lot younger than Claire would have imagined. She had straight brown hair worn long around her shoulders, and a simple black suit that was almost the negative image of Ms. Nance's, only somehow less formal. It looked . . . lived in.

Dean Wallace's lips parted, but she didn't ask a question. She checked herself, then nodded at the leather couch on the far side of the room, across from her massive desk. "Right, put him there." She had a British accent, too. Definitely not a Texas girl. "What happened?"

"Whatever it is, it's happening all over," Hannah said as they arranged Michael's unconscious body on the sofa. "They're just taking off. It's like they don't even know or care the sun's up. Some kind of homing signal just gets switched on."

Dean Wallace thought for a second, then pressed a button on her desk. "Ms. Nance? I need a bulletin to go out through the emergency communication system. All vampires on campus should be immediately restrained or tranquilized. No exceptions. This is priority one." She frowned as she got the acknowledgment, and looked up at their little group. "Michael seemed very rational, and there was no warning this would happen. I just thought he had somewhere to go. He didn't seem odd, at least at first."

"How many other vampires on campus?" Hannah asked.

"Some professors, of course, but they're mostly not here at the moment, since they teach at night. No students, obviously. Apart from the ones Michael and Richard brought in, we have perhaps five in total on the grounds. More were here earlier, but they headed for shelter before sunrise, off campus." Dean Wallace seemed calm, even in the face of all this. "You're Claire Danvers?"

"Yes, ma'am," she said, and shook the hand Dean Wallace offered her.

"I had a talk with your Patron recently regarding your progress. Despite your—challenges, you have done excellent course work."

It was stupid to feel pleased about that, but Claire couldn't help it. She felt herself blush, and shook her head. "I don't think that matters very much right now."

"On the contrary, it matters a great deal, I believe."

Eve settled herself down next to the sofa, holding Michael's limp hand. She looked shattered. Hannah leaned against the wall and nodded to the soldier as he exited the office. "So," she said, "want to explain to me how you can have half the U.S. Army walking the perimeter and not have massive student panic?"

"We've told all students and their parents that the university is cooperating in a government emergency drill, and of course that all weapons are nonlethal. Which is quite true, so far as it goes. The issue of keeping students on campus is a bit trickier, but we've managed so far by linking it to the emergency drills. Can't go on for long, though. The local kids are already well informed, and it's only a matter of time before the out-of-town students begin to realize that we're having them on when they can't get word out to their friends and relatives. We're filtering all Internet and phone access, of course." Dean Wallace shook her head. "But that's my problem, not yours, and yours is much more pressing. We can't knock out every vampire in town, and we can't *keep* them knocked out in any case."

"Not enough happy juice in the world," Hannah agreed. "We need to either stop this at its source, or get the heck out of their way."

There was a soft knock on the door, and Ms. Nance stepped in. "Richard Morrell," she announced, and moved aside for him.

Claire stared. Monica's brother looked like about fifty miles of bad road—exhausted, red-eyed, pale, running on caffeine and adrenaline. Just like the rest of them, she supposed. As Ms. Nance quietly closed the door behind him, Richard strode forward, staring at Michael's limp body. "Is he out?" His voice sounded rough, too, as if he'd been yelling. A *lot.*

"Sleeping the sleep of the just," Hannah said. "Or the just drugged, anyway. Claire. Radio."

Oh. She'd forgotten about the backpack still slung over her shoulder. She quickly took out the last radio and handed it over, explaining what it was for. Richard nodded.

"I think this calls for a strategy meeting," he said, and pulled up a chair next to the couch. Hannah and Claire took seats as well, but Eve stayed where she was, by Michael, as if she didn't want to leave him even for a moment.

Dean Wallace sat behind her desk, fingers steepled, watching with interested calm.

"I put in the code, right?" He was already doing it, so Claire just nodded. A signal bleeped to show he was logged on the network. "Richard Morrell, University, checking in."

After a few seconds, a voice answered. "Check, Richard, you're the last station to report. Stand by for a bulletin."

There were a few clicks, and then another voice came over the radio.

This is Oliver. I am broadcasting to all on the network with emergency orders. Restrain every vampire allied to us that you can find, by whatever means necessary. Locked rooms, chains, tranquilizers, cells, use what you have. Until we know how and why this is happening, we must take every precaution during the day. It seems that some of us have resistance to the call, and others have immunity, but this could change at any time. Be on your guard. From this point forward, we will conduct hourly calls, and each location will report status. University station, report.

Richard clicked the TALK button. "Michael Glass and all the other vampires in our group are being restrained. We've got student containment here, but it won't last. We'll have to open the gates no later than tomorrow morning, if we can keep it together until then. Even with the phone and Internet blackout, somebody's going to get word out."

"We're following the plan," Oliver said. "We're taking the cell towers down in ten minutes, until further notice. Phone lines are already cut. The only communication from this point forward will be strategic, using the radios. What else do you need?"

"Whip and a chair? Nothing. We're fine here for now. I don't think anybody will try a daylight assault, not with as many guards as we have here." Richard hesitated, then keyed the mike again. "Oliver, I've been hearing things. I think there are some factions out there forming. Human factions. Could complicate things."

Oliver was silent for a moment, then said, "Yes, I understand. We'll deal with that as it arises."

Oliver moved on to the next station on his list, which was the Glass House. Monica reported in, which was annoying. Claire resisted the urge to grind her teeth. It was a quick summary, at least, and as more Founder Houses reported in, the situation seemed the same: some vampires were responding to the homing signal, and some weren't. At least, not yet.

Richard Morrell was staring thoughtfully into the distance, and finally, when all the reports were finished, he clicked the button again. "Oliver, it's Richard. What happens if *you* start going zombie on us?"

"I won't," Oliver said.

"If you do. Humor me. Who takes over?"

Oliver obviously didn't want to think about this, and Claire could hear the barely suppressed fury in his voice when he replied. "You do," he said. "I don't care how you organize it. If we have to hand the defense of Morganville over to mere humans, we've already lost. Oliver signing out. Next check-in, one hour from now."

The walkie-talkie clicked off.

"That went well," Dean Wallace observed. "He's named you heir apparent to the Apocalypse. Congratulations."

"Yeah, it's one hell of a field promotion." Richard stood up. "Let's find a place for Michael."

"We have some storage areas in the basement—steel doors, no windows. That's where they'll take the others."

"That'll do for now. I want to move him to the jail as soon as we can, centralize the containment."

Claire looked at Eve, and then at Michael's sleeping face, and thought about him alone in a cell—because what else could you call it? Locked away like Myrnin.

Myrnin. She wondered if he'd felt this weird pull, too, and if he had, whether or not they'd been able to stop him from taking off. Probably not, if he'd been determined to go running off. Myrnin was one of those unstoppable forces, and unless he met an immovable object . . .

She sighed and helped carry Michael down the hall, past the stunned bureaucrats, to his temporary holding cell.

. . .

Life went on, weirdly enough—human life, anyway. People began to venture out, clean up the streets, retrieve things from burned and trashed
houses. The police began to establish order again.

But there were things happening. People gathering in groups on street
corners. Talking. Arguing.

Claire didn't like what she saw, and she could tell that Hannah and
Eve didn't, either.

Hours passed. They cruised around for a while, and passed bulletins
back to Oliver on the groups they saw. The largest one was almost a hundred people, forming up in the park. Some guy Claire didn't know had a
loudspeaker.

"Sal Manetti," Hannah said. "Always was a troublemaker. I think he
was one of Captain Obvious's guys for a while, but they had a falling-out.
Sal wanted a lot more killing and a lot less talking."

That wasn't good. It really wasn't good how many people were out
there listening to him.

Eve went back to Common Grounds to report in, and that was just
when things started to go wrong.

Hannah was driving Claire back home, after dropping off a trunk full
of blood bags from the university storage vaults, when the radio Claire
had in her pocket began to chime for attention. She logged in with the
code. As soon as she did, a blast of noise tumbled out of the speaker.

She thought she heard something about Oliver, but she wasn't sure.
Her shouted questions weren't answered. It was as if someone had pressed
the button by accident, in the middle of a fight, and everybody was too
busy to answer.

Then the broadcast went dead.

Claire exchanged a look with Hannah. "Better—"

"Go to Common Grounds? Yeah. Copy that."

When they arrived, the first thing Claire saw was the broken glass.
The shutters were up, and two front windows had been shattered out, not
in; there were sprays of broken pieces all the way to the curb.

It seemed very, very quiet.

"Eve?" Claire blurted, and bailed before Hannah could tell her to stay put. She hit the front door of the coffee shop at a run, but it didn't open, and she banged into it hard enough to bruise.

Locked.

"Will you *wait?*" Hannah snapped, and grabbed her arm as she tried to duck in through one of the broken windows. "You're going to get yourself cut. Hang on."

She used the paintball gun she carried to break out some of the hanging sharp edges, and before Claire could dart ahead, she blocked the path and stepped over the low wooden sill. Claire followed. Hannah didn't try to stop her, probably because she knew better.

"Oh man," Hannah said. As Claire climbed in after her, she saw that most of the tables and chairs were overturned or shoved out of place. Broken crockery littered the floor.

And people were down, lying motionless among the wreckage. Hannah went from one to the other, quickly assessing their conditions. There were five down that Claire could see. Two of them made Hannah shake her head in regret; the other three were still alive, though wounded.

There were no vampires in the coffee bar, and there was no sign of Eve.

Claire ducked behind the curtain. More signs of a struggle. Nobody left behind, alive or dead. She sucked in a deep breath and opened up the giant commercial refrigerator.

It was full of blood bags, but no bodies.

"Anything?" Hannah asked at the curtain.

"Nobody here," Claire said. "They left the blood, though."

"Huh. Weird. You'd think they'd need that more than anything. Why attack the place if you're not taking the good stuff?" Hannah stared out into the coffee shop, her expression blank and distant. "Glass is broken out, not in. No sign anybody got in the doors, either front or back. I don't think anybody attacked from the outside, Claire."

With a black, heavy feeling gathering in her stomach, Claire swung the refrigerator door shut. "You think the vampires fought to get *out.*"

"Yeah. Yeah, I do."

"Oliver, too."

"Oliver, Myrnin, all of them. Whatever bat signal was calling them got turned up to eleven, I think."

"Then where's Eve?" Claire asked.

Hannah shook her head. "We don't know anything. It's all guesswork. Let's get some boots on the ground and figure this thing out." She continued to stare outside. "If they went out there, most of them could make it for a while in the sun, but they'd be hurt. Some couldn't make it far at all."

Some, like the policeman Claire had seen burn up in front of her, would already be gone. "You think it's Mr. Bishop?" she asked, in a very small voice.

"I hope so."

Claire blinked. "Why?"

"Because if it's not, that's got to be a whole lot worse."

EIGHT

Three hours later, they didn't know much more, except that nothing they tried to do to keep the vampires from leaving seemed to work, apart from tranquilizing them and locking them up in sturdy cells. Tracking those who did leave wasn't much good, either. Claire and Hannah ended up at the Glass House, which seemed like the best place to gather—central to most things, and close to City Hall in an emergency.

Richard Morrell arrived, along with a few others, and set up shop in the kitchen. Claire was trying to figure out what to do to feed everybody, when there was another knock at the door.

It was Gramma Day. The old woman, straight-backed and proud, leaned on her cane and stared at Claire from age-faded eyes. "I ain't staying with my daughter," she said. "I don't want any part of that."

Claire quickly moved aside to let her in, and the old lady shuffled inside. As Claire locked the door behind her, she asked, "How did you get here?"

"Walked," Gramma said. "I know how to use my feet just fine. Nobody bothered me." Nobody would dare, Claire thought. "Young Mr. Richard! Are you in here?"

"Ma'am?" Richard Morrell came out of the kitchen, looking very

much younger than Claire had ever seen him. Gramma Day had that effect on people. "What are you doing here?"

"My fool daughter's off her head," Gramma said. "I'm not having any
of it. Move out of the way, boy. I'm making you some lunch." And she
tapped her cane right past him, into the kitchen, and clucked and fretted
over the state of the kitchen while Claire stood by, caught between giggles
and horror. She was just a pair of hands, getting ordered around, but at
the end of it there was a plate full of sandwiches and a big jug of iced tea,
and everybody was seated around the kitchen table, except for Gramma,
who'd gone off into the other room to rest. Claire had hesitantly taken
a chair, at Richard's nod. Detectives Joe Hess and Travis Lowe were also
present, and they were gratefully scarfing down food and drink. Claire felt
exhausted, but they looked a whole lot worse. Tall, thin Joe Hess had his
left arm in a sling—broken, apparently, from the brace on it—and both
he and his rounder, heavier partner had cuts and bruises to prove they'd
been in a fight or two.

"So," Hess said, "any word on where the vampires are heading when
they take off?"

"Not so far," Richard said. "Once we started tracking them, we could
keep up only for a while, and then they lost us."

"Aren't they hurt by the sun?" Claire asked. "I mean—"

"They start smoking, not in the Marlboro way, and then they start
crisping," Travis Lowe said around a mouthful of turkey and Swiss. "The
older ones, they can handle it okay, and anyway, they're not just charging
out there anymore. They're putting on hats and coats and blankets. I saw
one wrapped up in a SpongeBob rug from some kid's bedroom, if you
can believe that. It's the younger vamps that are in trouble. Some of them
won't make it to the shade if they're not careful."

Claire thought about Michael, and her stomach lurched. Before she
even formed the question, Richard saw her expression and shook his
head. "Michael's okay," he said. "Saw to it myself. He's got himself a
nice, secure jail cell, along with the other vampires we could catch before
it was too late. He's not as strong as some of the others. He can't bend
steel with his bare hands. Yet, anyway."

"Any word on—" Claire was wearing out the question, and Richard didn't even let her finish it.

"No sign of Eve," he said. "No word from her. I'd try to put a GPS track on her phone, but we'd have to bring the cell network up, and that's too dangerous right now. I've asked the guys on the street to keep an eye out for her, but we've got a lot of things going on, Claire."

"I know. But—" She couldn't put it into words, exactly. She just knew that somewhere, somehow, Eve was in trouble, and they needed to find her.

"So," Joe Hess said, and stood up to look at a blown-up map of Morganville taped to the wall. "This still accurate?" The map was covered in colored dots: blue for locations held by those loyal to Amelie; red for those loyal to Bishop; black for those burned or otherwise put out of commission, which accounted for three Founder Houses, the hospital, and the blood bank.

"Pretty much," Richard said. "We don't know if the vampires are leaving Bishop's locations, but we know they're digging in, just like Amelie's folks. We can verify locations only where Amelie's people were supposed to be, and they're gone from just about every location we've got up in blue."

"Where were they last seen?"

Richard consulted notes, and began to add yellow dots to the map. Claire saw the pattern almost immediately. "It's the portals," she said. "Myrnin got the portals working again, somehow. That's what they're using."

Hess and Lowe looked blank, but Richard nodded. "Yeah, I know about that. Makes sense. But where are they *going*?"

She shrugged helplessly. "Could be anywhere. I don't know all the places the portals go; maybe Myrnin and Amelie do, but I don't think anybody else does." But she felt unreasonably cheered by the idea that the vampires weren't out wandering out in the daylight, spontaneously combusting all over the place. She didn't want to see that happen to them . . . not even to Oliver.

Well, maybe to Oliver, sometimes. But not today.

The three men stared at her for a few seconds, then went back to studying the map, talking about perimeters and strategies for patrols, all kinds of things that Claire didn't figure really involved her. She finished her sandwich and walked into the living room, where tiny, wizened little Gramma Day was sitting in an overstuffed wing chair with her feet up, talking to Hannah. "Hey, little girl," Gramma Day said. "Sit yourself."

Claire perched, looking around the room. Most of the vampires were gone, either confined to cells or locked away for safety; some, they hadn't been able to stop. She couldn't seem to stop anxiously rubbing her hands together. *Shane.* Shane was supposed to be here. Richard Morrell had said that they'd arranged for the Bloodmobile to switch drivers, and that meant Shane would be coming soon for his rest period.

She needed him right now.

Gramma Day was looking at her with distant sympathy in her faded eyes. "You worried?" she asked, and smiled. "You got cause, I expect."

"I do?" Claire was surprised. Most adults tried to pretend it was all going to be okay.

"Sure thing, sugar. Morganville's been ruled by the vampires a long time, and they ain't always been the gentlest of folks. Been people hurt, people killed without reason. Builds up some resentment." Gramma nodded toward the bookcase. "Fetch me that red book right there, the one that starts with *N.*"

It was an encyclopedia. Claire got it and set it in her lap. Gramma's weathered, sinewy fingers opened it and flipped pages, then handed it back. The heading said, *New York Draft Riots, 1863.*

The pictures showed chaos—mobs, buildings on fire. And worse things. Much, much worse.

"People forget," Gramma said. "They forget what can happen, if anger builds up. Those New York folks, they were angry because their men were being drafted to fight the Civil War. Who you think they took it out on? Mostly black folks, of all things. Folks who couldn't fight back. They even burned up an orphanage, and they'd have killed every one of those children if they'd caught them." She shook her head, clicking her tongue in disgust. "Same thing happened in Tulsa in 1921. Called it the Greenwood Riot, said black folks were taking away their business and jobs. Back in France, they had a revolution where they took all those fancy aristocrat folks and cut their heads off. Maybe it was their fault, and maybe not. It's all the same thing: you get angry, you blame it on some folks, and you make them pay, guilty or not. Happens all the time."

Claire felt a chill. "What do you mean?"

"I mean, you think about France, girl. Vampires been holding us all down a long time, just like those aristocrats, or that's how people around here think of it. Now, you think about all those folks out there with generations of grudges, and nobody really in charge right now. You think it won't go bad on us?"

There weren't enough shudders in the world. Claire remembered Shane's father, the fanatical light in his eyes. He'd be one of those leading a riot, she thought. One of those pulling people out of their houses as collaborators and turncoats and hanging them up from lampposts.

Hannah patted the shotgun in her lap. She'd put the paintball gun aside—honestly, it wasn't much use now, with the vampires missing in action. "They're not getting in here, Gramma. We won't be having any Greenwood in Morganville."

"I ain't so much worried about you and me," Gramma said. "But I'd be worried for the Morrells. They're gonna be coming for them, sooner or later. That family's the poster children for the old guard."

Claire wondered if Richard knew that. She thought about Monica, too. Not that she liked Monica—God, no—but still.

She thanked Gramma Day and walked back into the kitchen, where the policemen were still talking. "Gramma Day thinks there's going to be trouble," she said. "Not the vampires. Regular people, like those people in the park. Maybe Lisa Day, too. And she thinks you ought to look after your family, Richard."

Richard nodded. "Already done," he said. "My mom and dad are at City Hall. Monica's headed there, too." He paused, thinking about it. "You're right. I should make sure she gets there all right, before she becomes another statistic." His face had tightened, and there was a look in his eyes that didn't match the way he said it. He was worried.

Given what Claire had just heard from Gramma Day, she thought he probably ought to be. Joe Hess and Travis Lowe sent each other looks, too, and she thought they were probably thinking the same thing. *She deserves it,* Claire told herself. *Whatever happens to Monica Morrell, she earned it.*

Except the pictures from Gramma Day's book kept coming back to haunt her.

The front door banged shut, and she heard Hannah's voice—not an alarm, just a welcome. She spun around and went to the door of the kitchen . . . and ran directly into Shane, who grabbed her and folded his arms around her.

"You're here," he said, and hugged her so tightly that she felt ribs creak. "Man, you don't make it easy, Claire. I've been freaking out all damn day. First I hear you're off in the middle of Vamptown; then you're running around like bait with Eve—"

"You're one to talk about bait," Claire said, and pushed back to look up into his face. "You okay?"

"Not a scratch," he said, and grinned. "Ironic, because I'm usually the one with the battle scars, right? The worst thing that happened to me was that I had to pull over and let a bunch of vampires off the bus, or they'd have ripped right through the walls. You'd be proud. I even let them off in the shade." His smile faded, but not the warmth in his eyes. "You look tired."

"Yeah, you think?" She caught herself on a yawn. "Sorry."

"We should get you home and catch some rest while we can." He looked around. "Where's Eve?"

Nobody had told him. Claire opened her mouth and found her throat clenching tight around the words. Her eyes filled with tears. *She's gone,* she wanted to say. *She's missing. Nobody knows where she is.*

But saying it out loud, saying it to Shane, that would make it real, somehow.

"Hey," he said, and smoothed her hair. "Hey, what's wrong? Where is she?"

"She was at Common Grounds," Claire finally choked out. "She—"

His hands went still, and his eyes widened.

"She's missing," Claire finally said, and a wave of utter misery broke over her. "She's out there somewhere. That's all I know."

"Her car's outside."

"We drove it here." Claire nodded at Hannah, who'd come in behind Shane and was silently watching. He acknowledged her with a glance; that was all.

"Okay," Shane said. "Michael's safe, you're safe, I'm safe. Now we're going to go find Eve."

Richard Morrell stirred. "That's not a good idea."

Shane spun on him, and the look on his face was hard enough to scare a vampire. "Want to try and stop me, *Dick*?"

Richard stared at him for a moment, then turned back to the map. "You want to go, go. We've got things to do. There's a whole town of people out there to serve and protect. Eve's one girl."

"Yeah, well, she's our girl," Shane said. He took Claire's hand. "Let's go."

Hannah leaned against the wall. "Mind if I call shotgun?"

"Since you're carrying one? Feel free."

Outside, things were odd—quiet, but with a suppressed feeling of excitement in the air. People were still outside, talking in groups on the streets. The stores were shut down, for the most part, but Claire noticed with a stir of unease that the bars were open, and so was Morganville's gun shop.

Not good.

The gates of the university had opened, and they were issuing some kind of passes to people to leave—still sticking to the emergency drill story, Claire assumed.

"Oh, man," Shane muttered, as they turned down one of the streets that led to the heart of town, and Founder's Square—Vamptown.

There were more people here, more groups. "I don't like this. There's Sal Manetti up there. He was one of my dad's drinking buddies, back in the day."

"The cops don't like it much, either," Hannah said, and pointed at the police cars ahead. They were blocking off access at the end of the street, and when Claire squinted, she could see they were out of their cruisers and arranged in a line, ready for anything. "This could turn bad, any time. All they need is somebody to strike a match out there, and we're all on fire."

Claire thought about Shane saying his father was coming to town, and she knew he was thinking about that, too. He shook his head. "We've got to figure out where Eve might be. Ideas?"

"Maybe she left us some clues," Claire said. "Back at Common Grounds. We should probably start there."

Common Grounds, however, was deserted, and the steel shutters were down. The front door was locked. They drove around back, to the alley. Nothing was there but trash cans, and—

"What the hell is that?" Shane asked. He hit the brakes and put the car in park, then jumped out and picked up something small on the ground. He got back in and showed it to Claire.

It was a small white candy in the shape of a skull. Claire blinked at it, then looked down the alley. "She left a trail of breath mints?"

"Looks like. We'll have to go on foot to follow it."

Hannah didn't seem to like that idea much, but Shane wasn't taking votes. They parked and locked Eve's car in the alley behind Common Grounds and began hunting for skull candies.

"Over here!" Hannah yelled, at the end of the alley. "Looks like she's dropping them when she makes a turn. Smart. She went this way."

After that, they went faster. The skull candies were in plain sight, easy to spot. Claire noticed that they were mostly in the shadows, which would have made sense, if Eve was with Myrnin or the other vampires. *Why didn't she stay?* Maybe she hadn't had a choice.

They ran out of candy trail after a few blocks. It led them into an area where Claire hadn't really been before—abandoned old buildings, mostly,

falling to pieces under the relentless pressure of years and sun. It looked
and felt deserted.

"Where now?" Claire asked, looking around. She didn't see anything
obvious, but then she spotted something shiny, tucked in behind a tipped-
over rusty trash can. She reached behind and came up with a black leather
collar, studded with silver spikes.

The same collar Eve had been wearing. She wordlessly showed it to
Shane, who turned in a slow circle, looking at the blank buildings. "Come
on, Eve," he said. "Give us something. Anything." He froze. "You hear
that?"

Hannah cocked her head. She was standing at the end of the alley,
shotgun held in her arms in a way that was both casual and scarily com-
petent. "What?"

"You don't hear it?"

Claire did. Somebody's phone was ringing. A cell phone, with an
ultrasonic ringtone—she'd heard that older people couldn't hear those
frequencies, and kids in school had used them all the time to sneak
phone calls and texts in class. It was faint, but it was definitely there.
"I thought the networks were down," she said, and pulled her own
phone out.

Nope. The network was back up. She wondered if Richard had done
it, or they'd lost control of the cell phone towers. Either one was possible.

They found the phone before the ringing stopped. It was Eve's—a
red phone, with silver skull cell phone charms on it—discarded in the
shadow of a broken, leaning doorway. "Who was calling?" Claire asked,
and Shane paged through the menu.

"Richard," he said. "I guess he really was looking for her after all."

Claire's phone buzzed—just once. A text message. She opened it and
checked.

It was from Eve, and it had been sent hours ago; the backlog of mes-
sages was just now being delivered, apparently.

It read, 911 @ GERMANS. Claire showed it to Shane. "What is this?"

"Nine one one. Emergency message. German's—" He looked over at
Hannah, who pushed away from the wall and came toward them.

"German's Tire Plant," she said. "Damn, I don't like that; it's the size of a couple of football fields, at least."

"We should let Richard know," Claire said. She dialed, but the network was busy, and then the bars failed again.

"I'm not waiting," Shane said. "Let's get the car."

NINE

The tire plant was near the old hospital, which made Claire shudder; she remembered the deserted building way too well. It had been incredibly creepy, and then of course it had also nearly gotten her and Shane killed, too, so again, not fond.

She was mildly shocked to see the hulking old edifice still standing, as Shane turned the car down the street.

"Didn't they tear that place down?" It had been scheduled for demolition, and boy, if any place had ever needed it . . .

"I heard it was delayed," Shane said. He didn't seem any happier about it than Claire was. "Something about historic preservation. Although anybody wanting to preserve that thing has never been inside it running for their life, I'll bet."

Claire stared out the window. On her side of the car was the brooding monstrosity of a hospital. The cracked stones and tilted columns in front made it look like something straight out of one of Shane's favorite zombie-killing video games. "Don't be hiding in there," she whispered. "Please don't be hiding in there." Because if Eve and Myrnin *had* taken refuge there, she wasn't sure she'd have the courage to go charging in after them.

"There's German's," Hannah said, and nodded toward the other side of the street. Claire hadn't really noticed it the last time she'd been out here—preoccupied with the whole not-dying issue—but there it was, a four-story square building in that faded tan color that everybody had used back in the sixties. Even the windows—those that weren't broken out—were painted over. It was plain, big, and blocky, and there was absolutely nothing special about it except its size—it covered at least three city blocks, all blind windows and blank concrete.

"You ever been inside there?" Shane asked Hannah, who was studying the building carefully.

"Not for a whole lot of years," she said. "Yeah, we used to hide up in there sometimes, when we cut class or something. I guess everybody did, once in a while. It's a mess in there, a real junkyard. Stuff everywhere, walls falling apart, ceilings none too stable, either. If you go up to the second level, you watch yourself. Make sure you don't trust the floors, and watch those iron stairs. They were shaky even back then."

"Are we going in there?" Claire asked.

"No," Shane said. "*You're* not going anywhere. You're staying here and getting Richard on the phone and telling him where we are. Me and Hannah will check it out."

There didn't seem to be much room for argument, because Shane didn't give her time; he and Hannah bailed out of the car, made lock-the-door motions, and sprinted toward a gap in the rusted, sagging fence.

Claire watched until they disappeared around the corner of the building, and realized her fingers were going numb from clutching her cell phone. She took a deep breath and flipped it open to try Richard Morrell again.

Nothing. No signal again. The network was going up and down like a yo-yo.

The walkie-talkie signal was low, but she tried it anyway. There was some kind of response, but it was swallowed by static. She gave their position, on the off chance that someone on the network would be able to hear her over the noise.

She screamed and dropped the device when the light at the car window was suddenly blocked out, and someone battered frantically on the glass.

Claire recognized the silk shirt—*her* silk shirt—before she recognized Monica Morrell, because Monica definitely didn't look like herself. She was out of breath, sweating, her hair was tangled, and what makeup she had on was smeared and running.

She'd been crying. There was a cut on her right cheek, and a forming bruise, and dirt on the silk blouse as well as bloodstains. She was holding her left arm as though it was hurt.

"Open the door!" she screamed, and pounded on the glass again. "Let me in!"

Claire looked behind the car.

There was a mob coming down the street: thirty, forty people, some running, some following at a walk. Some were waving baseball bats, boards, pipes.

They saw Monica and let out a yell. Claire gasped, because that sound didn't seem human at all—more the roar of a beast, something mindless and hungry.

Monica's expression was, for the first time, absolutely open and vulnerable. She put her palm flat against the window glass. "Please help me," she said.

But even as Claire clawed at the lock to open it, Monica flinched, turned, and ran on, limping.

Claire slid over the front seat and dropped into the driver's seat. Shane had left the keys in the ignition. She started it up and put the big car in gear, gave it too much gas, and nearly wrecked it on the curb before she straightened the wheel. She rapidly gained on Monica. She passed her, squealed to a stop, and reached over to throw open the passenger door.

"Get in!" she yelled. Monica slid inside and banged the door shut, and Claire hit the gas as something impacted loudly against the back of the car—a brick, maybe. A hail of smaller stones hit a second later. Claire swerved wildly again, then straightened the wheel and got the car moving more smoothly. Her heart pounded hard, and her hands felt sweaty on the steering wheel. "You all right?"

Monica was panting, and she threw Claire a filthy look. "No, of *course* I'm not all right!" she snapped, and tried to fix her hair with trembling hands. "Unbelievable. What a stupid question. I guess I shouldn't expect much more from someone like you, though——"

Claire stopped the car and stared at her.

Monica shut up.

"Here's how this is going to go," Claire said. "You're going to act like an actual human being for a change, or else you're on your own. Clear?"

Monica glanced behind them. "They're coming!"

"Yes, they are. So, are we clear?"

"Okay, okay, yes! Fine, whatever!" Monica cast a clearly terrified look at the approaching mob. More stones peppered the paint job, and one hit the back glass with enough force to make Claire wince. "Get me out of here! Please!"

"Hold on, I'm not a very good driver."

That was kind of an understatement. Eve's car was huge and heavy and had a mind of its own, and Claire hadn't taken the time to readjust the bench seat to make it possible for her to reach the pedals easily. The only good thing about her driving, as they pulled away from the mob and the falling bricks, was that it was approximately straight, and pretty fast.

She scraped the curb only twice.

Once the fittest of their pursuers had fallen behind, obviously discouraged, Claire finally remembered to breathe, and pulled the car around the next right turn. This section of town seemed deserted, but then, so had the other street, before Monica and her fan club had shown up. The big, imposing hulk of the tire plant glided by on the passenger side—it seemed like miles of featureless brick and blank windows.

Claire braked the car on the other side of the street, in front of a deserted, rusting warehouse complex. "Come on," she said.

"What?" Monica watched her get out of the car and take the keys with uncomprehending shock. "Where are you going? We have to get out of here! They were going to *kill* me!"

"They probably still are," Claire said. "So you should probably get out of the car now, unless you want to wait around for them."

Monica said something Claire pretended not to hear—it wasn't exactly complimentary—and limped her way out of the passenger side.

Claire locked the car. She hoped it wouldn't get banged up, but that mob had looked pretty excitable, and just the fact that Monica *had* been in it might be enough to ensure its destruction.

With any luck, though, they'd assume the girls had run into the warehouse complex, which was what Claire wanted.

Claire led them in the opposite direction, to the fence around German's Tire. There was a split in the wire by one of the posts, an ancient curling gap half hidden by a tangle of tumbleweeds. She pushed through and held the steel aside for Monica. "Coming?" she asked when Monica hesitated. "Because, you know what? Don't really care all that much. Just so you know."

Monica came through without any comment. The fence snapped back into place. Unless someone was looking for an entrance, it ought to do.

The plant threw a large, black shadow on the weed-choked parking lot. There were a few rusted-out trucks still parked here and there; Claire used them for cover from the street as they approached the main building, though she didn't think the mob was close enough to really spot them at this point. Monica seemed to get the point without much in the way of instruction; Claire supposed that running for her life had humbled her a little. Maybe.

"Wait," Monica said, as Claire prepared to bolt for a broken-out bottom-floor window into the tire plant. "What are you doing?"

"Looking for my friends," she said. "They're inside."

"Well, *I'm* not going in there," Monica declared, and tried to look haughty. It would have been more effective if she hadn't been so frazzled and sweaty. "I was on my way to City Hall, but those losers got in my way. They slashed my tires. I need to get to my parents'." She said it as though she expected Claire to salute and hop like a toad.

Claire raised her eyebrows. "Better start walking, I guess. It's kind of a long way."

"But—but—"

Claire didn't wait for the sputtering to die; she turned and ran for the building. The window opened into total darkness, as far as she could tell,

but at least it was accessible. She pulled herself up on the sash and started
to swing her legs inside.

"Wait!" Monica dashed across to join her. "You can't leave me here
alone! You saw those jerks out there!"

"Absolutely."

"Oh, you're just loving this, aren't you?"

"Kinda." Claire hopped down inside the building, and her shoes
slapped bare concrete floor. It was bare except for a layer of dirt,
anyway—undisturbed for as far as the light penetrated, which wasn't very
far. "Coming?"

Monica stared through the window at her, just boiling with fury;
Claire smiled at her and started to walk into the dark.

Monica, cursing, climbed inside.

"I'm not a bad person," Monica was saying—whining, actually. Claire
wished she could find a two-by-four to whack her with, but the tire plant,
although full of wreckage and trash, didn't seem to be big on wooden
planks. Some nice pipes, though. She might use one of those.

Except she really didn't want to hit anybody, deep down. Claire supposed that was a character flaw, or something.

"Yes, you really are a bad person," she told Monica, and ducked
underneath a low-hanging loop of wire that looked horror-movie ready,
the sort of thing that dropped around your neck and hauled you up
to be dispatched by the psycho-killer villain. Speaking of which, this
whole place was decorated in Early Psycho-Killer Villain, from the
vast soaring darkness overhead to the lumpy, skeletal shapes of rusting
equipment and abandoned junk. The spray painting—decades of it, in
layered styles from Early Tagger to cutting-edge gang sign—gleamed
in the random shafts of light like blood. Some particularly unpleasant
spray-paint artist had done an enormous, terrifying clown face, with
windows for the eyes and a giant, open doorway for a mouth. *Yeah, really
not going in there,* Claire thought. Although the way these things went, she
probably would have to.

"Why do you say that?"

"Say what?" Claire asked absently. She was listening for any sound of movement, but this place was enormous and confusing—just as Hannah had warned.

"Say that I'm a bad person!"

"Oh, I don't know—you tried to kill me? *And* get me raped at a party? Not to mention—"

"That was payback," Monica said. "And I didn't mean it or anything."

"Which makes it all so much better. Look, can we not bond? I'm busy. Seriously. *Shhhh.*" That last was to forestall Monica from blurting out yet another injured defense of her character. Claire squeezed past a barricade of piled-up boxes and metal, into another shaft of light that arrowed down from a high-up broken window. The clown painting felt like it was watching her, which was beyond creepy. She tried not to look too closely at what was on the floor. Some of it was animal carcasses, birds, and things that had gotten inside and died over the years. Some of it was old cans, plastic wrappers, all kinds of junk left behind by adventurous kids looking for a hideout. She didn't imagine any of them stayed for long.

This place just felt . . . haunted.

Monica's hand grabbed her arm, just on the bruise that Amelie's grip had given her earlier. Claire winced.

"Did you hear that?" Monica's whisper was fierce and hushed. She needed mouthwash, and she smelled like sweat more than powder and perfume. "Oh my *God.* Something's in here with us!"

"Could be a vampire," Claire said. Monica sniffed.

"Not afraid of those," she said, and dangled her fancy, silver Protection bracelet in front of Claire's face. "Nobody's going to cross Oliver."

"You want to tell that to the mob of people chasing you back there? I don't think they got the memo or something."

"I mean, no vampire would. I'm Protected." Monica said it like there was simply no possibility anything else could be true. The earth was round, the sun was hot, and a vampire would never hurt her because she'd sold herself to Oliver, body and soul.

Yeah, right.

"News flash," Claire whispered. "Oliver's missing in action from Common Grounds. Amelie's disappeared. In fact, most of the vampires all over town have dropped out of sight, which makes these bracelets cute fashion accessories, but not exactly bulletproof vests or anything."

Monica started to speak, but Claire frowned angrily at her and pointed off into the darkness, where she'd heard the noise. It had sounded odd—kind of a sigh, echoing from the steel and concrete, bouncing and amplifying.

It sounded as if it had come out of the clown's dark mouth.

Of course.

Claire reached into her pocket. She still had the vial of silver powder that Amelie had given her, but she was well aware that it might not do her any good. If her friend-vampires were mixed in with enemy-vamps, she was out of luck. Likewise, if what was waiting for her out there was trouble of a human variety, instead of bloodsuckers . . .

Shane and Hannah were in here. Somewhere. And so—hopefully—was Eve.

Claire eased around a tattered sofa that smelled like old cats and mold, and sidestepped a truly impressive rat that didn't bother to move out of her way. It sat there watching her with weird, alert eyes.

Monica looked down, saw it, and shrieked, stumbling backward. She fell into a stack of ancient cartons that collapsed on her, raining down random junk. Claire grabbed her and pulled her to her feet, but Monica kept on whimpering and squirming, slapping at her hair and upper body.

"Oh my *God*, are they on me? Spiders? Are there spiders?"

If there were, Claire hoped they bit her. "No," she said shortly. Well, there were, but they were little ones. She brushed them off Monica's back. "Shut *up* already!"

"Are you kidding me? Did you see that rat? It was the size of freaking Godzilla!"

That was it, Claire decided. Monica could just wander around on her own, screaming about rats and spiders, until someone came and ate her. What. *Ever.*

She got only about ten feet away when Monica's very small whisper stopped her dead in her tracks.

"Please don't leave me." That didn't sound like Monica, not at all. It sounded scared, and very young. "Claire, please."

It was probably too late for being quiet, anyway, and if there were vampires hiding in German's Tire Plant, they all knew exactly where they were, and for that matter, could tell what blood type they were. So stealth didn't seem a priority.

Claire cupped her hands over her mouth and yelled, very loudly, "Shane! Eve! Hannah! Anybody!"

The echoes woke invisible birds or bats high overhead, which flapped madly around; her voice rang from every flat surface, mocking Claire with her own ghost.

In the whispering silence afterward, Monica murmured, "Wow, I thought we were being subtle or something. My mistake."

Claire was about to hiss something really unpleasant at her, but froze as another voice came bouncing through the vast room—Shane's voice. "Claire?"

"Here!"

"Stay there! And shut up!"

He sounded frantic enough to make Claire wish she'd stuck with the whole quiet-time policy, and then Monica stopped breathing and went very, very still next to her. Her hands closed around Claire's arm, squeezing bruises again.

Claire froze, too, because something was coming out of the mouth of that painted clown—something white, ghostly, drifting like smoke. . . .

It had a face. Several faces, because it was a group of what looked like vampires, all very pale, all very quiet, all heading their way.

Staying put was not such a great plan, Claire decided. She was going to go with *run away.*

Which, grabbing Monica's wrist, she did.

The vampires did make sounds then, as their quarry started to flee—little whispering laughs, strange hisses, all kinds of creepy noises that made the skin on the back of Claire's neck tighten up. She held the glass vial in one hand, running faster, leaping over junk when she could see it coming and stumbling across it when she couldn't. Monica kept up, somehow, although Claire could hear the tortured, steady moaning of her breath. Whatever she'd done to her right leg must have hurt pretty badly.

Something pale landed ahead of her, with a silent leap like a spider pouncing. Claire had a wild impression of a white face, red eyes, a wide-open mouth, and gleaming fangs. She drew back to throw the vial . . . and realized it was Myrnin facing her.

The hesitation cost her. Something hit her from the back, sending her stumbling forward across a fallen iron beam. She dropped the vial as she fell, trying to catch herself, and heard the glass break on the edge of the girder. Silver dust puffed out. Monica shrieked, a wild cry that made the birds panic again high up in heaven; Claire saw her stumble away, trying to put distance between herself and Myrnin.

Myrnin was just outside of the range of the drifting silver powder, but it wasn't Myrnin who was the problem. The other vampires, the ones who'd come out of the clown's mouth, leaped over stacks of trash, running for the smell of fresh, flowing blood.

They were coming up behind them, fast.

Claire raked her hand across the ground and came up with a palm full of silver powder and glass shards as she rolled up to her knees. She turned and threw the powder into the air between her, Monica, and the rest of the vampires. It dispersed into a fine, glittering mist, and when the vampires hit it, every tiny grain of silver caught fire.

It was beautiful, and horrible, and Claire flinched at the sound of their cries. There was so much silver, and it clung to their skin, eating in. Claire didn't know if it would kill them, but it definitely stopped them cold.

She grabbed Monica's arm and pulled her close.

Myrnin was still in front of them, crouched on top of a stack of wooden pallets. He didn't look at all human, not at all.

And then he blinked, and the red light went out in his eyes. His fangs folded neatly backward, and he ran his tongue over pale lips before he said, puzzled, "Claire?"

She felt a sense of relief so strong it was like falling. "Yeah, it's me."

"Oh." He slithered down off the stacked wood, and she realized he was still dressed the way she'd seen him back at Common Grounds—a long, black velvet coat, no shirt, white pantaloons left over from his costume. He should have looked ridiculous, but somehow, he looked . . . right. "You shouldn't be here, Claire. It's very dangerous."

"I know—"

Something cold brushed the back of her neck, and she heard Monica make a muffled sound like a choked cry. Claire whirled and found herself face-to-face with a red-eyed, angry vampire with part of his skin still smoking from the silver she'd thrown.

Myrnin let out a roar that ripped the air, full of menace and fury, and the vampire stumbled backward, clearly shocked.

Then the five who'd chased them silently withdrew into the darkness.

Claire turned to face Myrnin. He was staring thoughtfully at the departing vamps.

"Thanks," she said. He shrugged.

"I was raised to believe in the concept of noblesse oblige," he said. "And I do owe you, you know. Do you have any more of my medication?"

She handed him her last dose of the drug that kept him sane—mostly sane, anyway. It was the older version, red crystals rather than clear liquid, and he poured out a dollop into his palm and licked the crystals up, then sighed in deep satisfaction.

"Much better," he said, and pocketed the rest of the bottle. "Now. Why are you here?"

Claire licked her lips. She could hear Shane—or someone—coming toward them through the darkness, and she saw someone in the shadows behind Myrnin. Not vampires, she thought, so it was probably Hannah, flanking Shane. "We're looking for my friend Eve. You remember her, right?"

"Eve," Myrnin repeated, and slowly smiled. "Ah. The girl who followed me. Yes, of course."

Claire felt a flush of excitement, quickly damped by dread. "What happened to her?"

"Nothing. She's asleep," he said. "It was too dangerous out here for her. I put her in a safe place, for now."

Shane pushed through the last of the barriers and stepped into a shaft of light about fifty feet away. He paused at the sight of Myrnin, but he didn't look alarmed.

"This is your friend as well," Myrnin said, glancing back at Shane. "The one you care so much for." She'd never discussed Shane with Myrnin—not in detail, anyway. The question must have shown in her face, because his smile broadened. "You carry his scent on your clothes," he said. "And he carries yours."

"Ewww," Monica sighed.

Myrnin's eyes focused in on her like laser sights. "And who is this lovely child?"

Claire almost rolled her eyes. "Monica. The mayor's daughter."

"Monica Morrell." She offered her hand, which Myrnin accepted and bent over in an old-fashioned way. Claire assumed he was also inspecting the bracelet on her wrist.

"Oliver's," he said, straightening. "I see. I am charmed, my dear, simply charmed." He hadn't let go of her hand. "I don't suppose you would be willing to donate a pint for a poor, starving stranger?"

Monica's smile froze in place. "I—well, I—"

He pulled her into his arms with one quick jerk. Monica yelped and tried to pull away, but for all his relatively small size, Myrnin had strength to burn.

Claire pulled in a deep breath. "Myrnin. Please."

He looked annoyed. "Please *what?*"

"She's not free range or anything. You can't just munch her. Let go." He didn't look convinced. "Seriously. *Let go.*"

"Fine." He opened his arms, and Monica retreated as she clapped both hands around her neck. She sat down on a nearby girder, breathing hard. "You know, in my youth, women lined up to grant me their favors. I believe I'm a bit offended."

"It's a strange day for everybody," Claire said. "Shane, Hannah, this is Myrnin. He's sort of my boss."

Shane moved closer, but his expression stayed cool and distant. "Yeah? This the guy who took you to the ball? The one who dumped you and left you to die?"

"Well . . . uh . . . yes."

"Thought so."

Shane punched him right in the face. Myrnin, surprised, stumbled back against the tower of crates, and snarled; Shane took a stake from his back pocket and held it at the ready.

"No!" Claire jumped between them, waving her hands. "No, honest, it's not like that. Calm down, everybody, please."

"Yes," Myrnin said. "I've been staked quite enough today, thank you. I respect your need to avenge her, boy, but Claire remains quite capable of defending her own honor."

"Couldn't have said it better myself," she said. "Please, Shane. Don't. We need him."

"Yeah? Why?"

"Because he may know what's going on with the vampires."

"Oh, that," Myrnin said, in a tone that implied they were all idiots for not knowing already. "They're being called. It's a signal that draws all vampires who have sworn allegiance to you with a blood exchange—it's the way wars were fought, once upon a time. It's how you gather your army."

"Oh," Claire said. "So . . . why not you? Or the rest of the vampires here?"

"It seems as though your serum offers me some portion of immunity against it. Oh, I feel the draw, most certainly, but in an entirely academic way. Rather curious. I remember how it felt before, like an overwhelming panic. As for those others, well. They're not of the blood."

"They're not?"

"No. Lesser creatures. Failed experiments, if you will." He looked away, and Claire had a horrible suspicion.

"Are they *people*? I mean, regular humans?"

"A failed experiment," he repeated. "You're a scientist, Claire. Not all experiments work the way they're intended."

Myrnin had done this to them, in his search for the cure to the vampire disease. He had turned them into something that wasn't vampire, wasn't human, wasn't—well, wasn't anything, exactly. They didn't fit in either society.

No wonder they were hiding here.

"Don't look at me that way," Myrnin said. "It's not my fault the process was imperfect, you know. I'm not a monster."

Claire shook her head.

"Sometimes, you really are."

Eve was fine—tired, shaking, and tear streaked, but okay. "He didn't, you know," she said, and made two-finger pointy motions toward her throat. "He's kind of sweet, actually, once you get past all the crazy. Although there's a lot of the crazy."

There was, as Claire well knew, no way of getting past the crazy. Not really. But she had to admit that at least Myrnin had behaved more like a gentleman than expected.

Noblesse oblige. Maybe he'd felt obligated.

The place he'd kept Eve had once been some kind of storage locker within the plant, all solid walls and a single door that he'd locked off with a bent pipe. Shane hadn't been all that happy about it. "What if something had happened to you?" he'd asked, as Myrnin untwisted the metal as though it were solder instead of iron. "She'd have been locked in there, all alone, no way out. She'd have starved."

"Actually," Myrnin had answered, "that's not very likely. Thirst would have killed her within four days, I imagine. She'd never have had a chance to starve." Claire stared at him. He raised his eyebrows. "What?"

She just shook her head. "I think you missed the point."

Monica tagged along with Claire, which was annoying; she kept casting Shane nervous glances, and she was now outright terrified of Myrnin, which was probably how it should have been, really. At the very least, she'd shut up, and even the sight of another rat, this one big and kind of albino, hadn't set off her screams this time.

Eve, however, was less than thrilled to see Monica. "You're kidding," she said flatly, staring first at her, then at Shane. "You're okay with this?"

"Okay would be a stretch. Resigned, that's closer," Shane said. Hannah, standing next to him with her shotgun at port arms, snorted out a laugh. "As long as she doesn't talk, I can pretend she isn't here."

"Yeah? Well, *I* can't," Eve said. She glared at Monica, who glared right back. "Claire, you have to stop picking up strays. You don't know where they've been."

"You're one to talk about diseases," Monica shot back, "seeing as how you're one big, walking social one."

"That's not pot, kettle—that's more like cauldron, kettle. Witch."

"Whore!"

"You want to go play with your new friends back there?" Shane snapped. "The really pale ones with the taste for plasma? Because believe me, I'll drop your skanky butt right in their nest if you don't shut up, Monica."

"You don't scare me, Collins!"

Hannah rolled her eyes and racked her shotgun. "How about me?"

That ended the entire argument.

Myrnin, leaning against the wall with his arms folded over his chest, watched the proceedings with great interest. "Your friends," he said to Claire. "They're quite . . . colorful. So full of energy."

"Hands off my friends." Not that that statement exactly included Monica, but whatever.

"Oh, absolutely. I would never." Hand to his heart, Myrnin managed to look angelic, which was a bit of a trick considering his Lord-Byron-on-a-bender outfit. "I've just been away from normal human society for so long. Tell me, is it usually this . . . spirited?"

"Not usually," she sighed. "Monica's special." Yeah, in the short-bus sense, because Monica was a head case. Not that Claire had time or inclination to explain all the dynamics of the Monica-Shane-Eve relationship to Myrnin right now. "When you said that someone was calling the vampires together for some kind of fight—was that Bishop?"

"Bishop?" Myrnin looked startled. "No, of course not. It's Amelie. Amelie is sending the call. She's consolidating her forces, putting up lines of defense. Things are rapidly moving toward a confrontation, I believe."

That was exactly what Claire was afraid he was going to say. "Do you know who answered?"

"Anyone in Morganville with a blood tie to her," he said. "Except me, of course. But that would include almost every vampire in town, save those who were sworn through Oliver. Even then, Oliver's tie would bind them in some sense, because he swore fealty to her when he came to live here. They might feel the pull less strongly, but they would still feel it."

"Then how is Bishop getting an army? Isn't everybody in town, you know, Amelie's?"

"He bit those he wished to keep on his side." Myrnin shrugged. "Claimed them from her, in a sense. Some of them went willingly, some not, but all owe him allegiance now. All those he was able to turn, which is a considerable number, I believe." He looked sharply at her. "The call continued in the daytime. Michael?"

"Michael's fine. They put him in a cell."

"And Sam?"

Claire shook her head in response. Next to Michael, his grandfather Sam was the youngest vampire in town, and Claire hadn't seen him at all, not since he'd left the Glass House, well before any of the other vamps. He'd gone off on some mission for Amelie; she trusted him more than most of the others, even those she'd known for hundreds of years. That was, Claire thought, because Amelie knew how Sam felt about her. It was the storybook kind of love, the kind that ignored things like practicality and danger, and never changed or died.

She found herself looking at Shane. He turned his head and smiled back.

The storybook kind of love.

She was probably too young to have that, but this felt so strong, so real. . . .

And Shane wouldn't even man up and tell her he loved her.

She took a deep breath and forced her mind off that. "What do we do now?" Claire asked. "Myrnin?"

He was silent for a long moment, then moved to one of the painted-over first-floor windows and pulled it open. The sun was setting again. It would be down completely soon.

"You should get home," he said. "The humans are in charge for now, at least, but there are factions out there. There will be power struggles tonight, and not just between the two vampire sides."

Shane glanced at Monica—whose bruises were living proof that trouble was already under way—and then back at Myrnin. "What are you going to do?"

"Stay here," Myrnin said. "With my friends."

"*Friends?* Who, the—uh—failed experiments?"

"Exactly so." Myrnin shrugged. "They look upon me as a kind of father figure. Besides, their blood is as good as anyone else's, in a pinch."

"So much more than I wanted to know," Shane said, and nodded to Hannah. "Let's go."

"Got your back, Shane."

"Watch Claire's and Eve's. I'll take the lead."

"What about me?" Monica whined.

"Do you really want to know?" Shane gave her a glare that should have scorched her hair off. "Be grateful I'm not leaving you as an after-dinner mint on his pillow."

Myrnin leaned close to Claire's ear and said, "I think I like your young man." When she reacted in pure confusion, he held up his hands, smiling. "Not in that way, my dear. He just seems quite trustworthy."

She swallowed and put all that aside. "Are you going to be okay here? Really?"

"Really?" He locked gazes with her. "For now, yes. But we have work to do, Claire. Much work, and very little time. I can't hide for long. You do realize that stress accelerates the disease, and this is a great deal of stress for us all. More will fall ill, become confused. It's vital we begin work on the serum as quickly as possible."

"I'll try to get you back to the lab tomorrow."

They left him standing in a fading shaft of sunlight, next to a giant rusting crane that lifted its head three stories into the dark, with pale birds flitting and diving overhead.

And wounded, angry failed experiments lurking in the shadows, maybe waiting to attack their vampire creator.

Claire felt sorry for them, if they did.

The mobs were gone, but they'd given Eve's car a good battering while they were at it. She choked when she saw the dents and cracked glass, but at least it was still on all four tires, and the damage was cosmetic. The engine started right up.

"Poor baby," Eve said, and patted the big steering wheel affectionately as she settled into the driver's seat. "We'll get you all fixed up. Right, Hannah?"

"And here I was wondering what I was going to do tomorrow," Hannah said, taking—of course—the shotgun seat. "Guess now I know. I'll be hammering dents out of the Queen Mary and putting in new safety glass."

In the backseat, Claire was the human equivalent of Switzerland between the warring nations of Shane and Monica, who sat next to the windows. It was tense, but nobody spoke.

The sun was going down in a blaze of glory in the west, which normally would have made Morganville a vampire-friendly place. Not so much tonight, as became evident when Eve left the dilapidated warehouse district and cruised closer to Vamptown.

There were people out on the streets, *at sunset.*

And they were angry, too.

"Shouty," Eve said, as they passed a big group clustered around a guy standing on a wooden box, yelling at the crowd. He had a pile of wooden stakes, and people were picking them up. "Okay, this is looking less than great."

"You think?" Monica slumped down in her seat, trying not to be noticed. "They tried to kill me! And I'm not even a vampire!"

"Yeah, but you're you, so there's that explained." Eve slowed down. "Traffic."

Traffic? In Morganville? Claire leaned forward and saw that there were about six cars in the street ahead. The first one was turned sideways, blocking the second—a big van, which was trying to back up but was handicapped by the third car.

The trapped passenger van was vampire-dark. The two cars blocking it in were old, battered sedans, the kind humans drove.

"That's Lex Perry's car, the one turned sideways," Hannah said. "I think that's the Nunally brothers in the third one. They're drinking buddies with Sal Manetti."

"Sal, as in, the guy out there rabble-rousing?"

"You got it."

And now people were closing in around the van, pushing against it, rocking it on its tires.

Nobody in their car spoke a word.

The van rocked harder. The tires spun, trying to pull away, but it tipped and slammed over on its side, helpless. With a roar, the crowd climbed on top of it and started battering the windows.

"We should do something," Claire finally said.

"Yeah?" Hannah's voice was very soft. "What, exactly?"

"Call the police?" Only the police were already here. There were two cars of them, and they couldn't stop what was happening. In fact, they didn't even look inclined to try.

"Let's go," Shane said quietly. "There's nothing we can do here."

Eve silently put the car in reverse and burned rubber backing up.

Claire broke out of her trance. "What are you doing? We can't just leave—"

"Take a good look," Eve said grimly. "If anybody out there sees Princess Morrell in this car, we've all had it. We're all collaborators if we're protecting her, and *you're* wearing the Founder bracelet. We can't risk it."

Claire sank back in her seat as Eve shifted gears again and turned the wheel. They took a different street, this one unblocked so far.

"What's happening?" Monica asked. "What's happening to our town?"

"France," Claire said, thinking about Gramma Day. "Welcome to the revolution."

Eve drove through a maze of streets. Lights were flickering on in houses, and the few streetlamps were coming on as well. Cars—and there were a lot of them out now—turned on their headlights and honked, as if the local high school had just won a big football game.

As if it were one big, loud party.

"I want to go home," Monica said. Her voice sounded muffled. "Please."

Eve looked at her in the rearview mirror, and finally nodded.

But when they turned down the street where the Morrell family home was located, Eve slammed on the brakes and put the car into reverse, instantly.

The Morrell home looked like the site of another of Monica's infamous, unsupervised parties . . . only this one really was unsupervised, and those uninvited guests, they weren't just there for the free booze.

"What are they doing?" Monica asked, and let out a strangled yell as a couple of guys carried a big plasma television out the front door. "They're stealing it! They're stealing our stuff!"

Pretty much everything was being looted—mattresses, furniture, art. Claire even saw people upstairs tossing linens and clothing out the windows to people waiting on the ground.

And then, somebody ran up with a bottle full of liquid, stuffed with a burning rag, and threw it into the front window.

The flames flickered, caught, and gained strength.

"No!" Monica panted and clawed at the door handle, but Eve had locked it up. Claire grabbed Monica's arms and held them down.

"Get us out of here!" she yelled.

"My parents could be in there!"

"No, they're not. Richard told me they're at City Hall."

Monica kept fighting, even as Eve steered the car away from the burning house, and then suddenly just . . . stopped.

Claire heard her crying. She wanted to think, *Good, you deserve it*, but somehow she just couldn't force herself to be that cold.

Shane, however, could. "Hey, look on the bright side," he said. "At least your little sister isn't inside."

Monica caught her breath, then kept crying.

By the time they'd turned on Lot Street, Monica seemed to be pulling herself together, wiping her face with trembling hands and asking for a tissue, which Eve provided out of the glove box in the front.

"What do you think?" Eve asked Shane. Their street seemed quiet. Most of the houses had lights on, including the Glass House, and although there were some folks outside, talking, it didn't look like mobs were forming. Not here, anyway.

"Looks good. Let's get inside."

They agreed that Monica needed to go in the middle, covered by Hannah. Eve went first, racing up the walk to the front door and using her keys to open it up.

They made it in without attracting too much attention or anybody pointing fingers at Monica—but then, Claire thought, Monica definitely didn't look much like herself right now. More like a bad Monica impersonator. Maybe even one who was a guy.

Shane would laugh himself sick over that if she mentioned it. After seeing the puffy redness around Monica's eyes, and the shattered expression, Claire kept it to herself.

As Shane slammed, locked, and dead bolted the front door, Claire felt the house come alive around them, almost tingling with warmth and welcome. She heard people in the living room exclaim at the same time, so it wasn't just her; the house really had reacted, and reacted strongly, to three out of four of its residents coming home.

Claire stretched out against the wall and kissed it. "Glad to see you, too," she whispered, and pressed her cheek against the smooth surface.

It almost felt like it hugged her back.

"Dude, it's a *house*," Shane said from behind her. "Hug somebody who cares."

She did, throwing herself into his arms. It felt like he'd never let her go, not even for a second, and he lifted her completely off the ground and rested his head on her shoulder for a long, precious moment before setting her gently back on her feet.

"Better see who's here," he said, and kissed her very lightly. "Down payment for later, okay?"

Claire let go, but held his hand as they walked down the hallway and into the living room of the Glass House, which was filled with people.

Not vampires.

Just people.

Some of them were familiar, at least by sight—people from town: the owner of the music store where Michael worked; a couple of nurses she'd seen at the hospital, who still wore brightly colored medical scrubs and comfortable shoes. The rest, Claire barely knew at all, but they had one thing in common—they were all scared.

An older, hard-looking woman grabbed Claire by the shoulders. "Thank God you're home," she said, and hugged her. Claire, rigid with surprise, cast Shane a what-the-hell look, and he shrugged helplessly. "This damn house won't do *anything* for us. The lights keep going out, the doors won't open, food goes bad in the fridge—it's as if it doesn't want us here!"

And it probably didn't. The house could have ejected them at any time, but obviously it had been a bit uncertain about exactly what its residents might want, so it had just made life uncomfortable for the intruders instead.

Claire could now feel the air-conditioning switching on to cool the overheated air, hear doors swinging open upstairs, see lights coming on in darkened areas.

"Hey, Celia," Shane said, as the woman let go of Claire at last. "So, what brings you here? I figured the Barfly would be doing good business tonight."

"Well, it would be, except that some jerks came in and said that because I was wearing a bracelet I had to serve them for free, on account of being some kind of sympathizer. What kind of sympathizer, I said, and one of them tried to hit me."

Shane lifted his eyebrows. Celia wasn't a young woman. "What did you do?"

"Used the Regulator." Celia lifted a baseball bat propped against the wall. It was old hardwood, lovingly polished. "Got myself a couple of home runs, too. But I decided maybe I wouldn't stay for the extra innings, if you know what I mean. I figure they're drinking me dry over there right now. Makes me want to rip my bracelet off, I'll tell ya. Where are the damn vampires when you need them, after all that?"

"You didn't take your bracelet off? Even when they gave you the chance?" Shane seemed surprised. Celia gave him a glare.

"No, I didn't. I ain't breaking my word, not unless I have to. Right now, I don't have to."

"If you take it off now, you may never need to put it on again."

Celia leveled a wrinkled finger at him. "Look, Collins, I know all about you and your dad. I don't hold with any of that. Morganville's an all-right place. You follow the rules and stay out of trouble—about like anyplace, I guess. You people wanted chaos. Well, this is what it looks like—people getting beaten, shops looted, houses burned. Sure, it'll settle down sometime, but into what? Maybe no place I'd want to live."

She turned away from him, shouldered her baseball bat, and marched away to talk with a group of adults her own age.

Shane caught Claire looking at him, and shrugged. "Yeah," he sighed. "I know. She's got a point. But how do we know it won't be better if the vamps just—"

"Just what, Shane? *Die?* What about Michael, have you thought about him? Or Sam?" She stomped off.

"Where are you going?"

"To get a Coke!"

"Would you—"

"No!"

She twisted the cap off the Coke she'd retrieved from the fridge—which was stocked up again, although she knew it hadn't been when they'd left. Another favor from the house, she guessed, although how it went shopping on its own she had no idea.

The cold syrupy goodness hit her like a brick wall, but instead of energizing her, it made her feel weak and a little sick. Claire sank down in a chair at the kitchen table and put her head in her hands, suddenly overwhelmed.

It was all falling apart.

Amelie was calling the vampires, probably going to fight Bishop to the death. Morganville was ripping itself in pieces. And there was nothing she could *do*.

Well, there was one thing.

She retrieved and opened four more bottles of Coke, and delivered them to Hannah, Eve, Shane, and—because it felt mean to leave her out at a time like this—Monica.

Monica stared at the sweating bottle as if she suspected Claire had put rat poison in it. "What's this?"

"What does it look like? Take or don't, I don't really care." Claire put it down on the table next to where Monica sat, and went to curl up on the couch next to Shane. She checked her cell phone. The network was back up again, at least for the moment, and she had a ton of voice mails. Most were from Shane, so she saved them to listen to later; two more were from Eve, which she deleted, since they were instructions on where to find her.

The last one was from her mother. Claire caught her breath, tears pricking in her eyes at the sound of Mom's voice. Her mother sounded calm, at least—mostly, anyway.

Claire, sweetie, I know I shouldn't be worrying but I am. Honey, call us. I've been hearing some terrible things about what's happening out there. Some of the people with us here are talking about fights and looting. If I don't hear from you soon—well, I don't know what we'll do, but your father's going crazy. So please, call us. We love you, honey. Bye.

Claire got her breathing back under control, mainly by sternly telling herself that she needed to sound together and completely in control to keep her parents from charging out there into the craziness. She had it more or less managed by the time the phone rang on the other end, and when her mother picked it up, she was able to say, "Hi, Mom," without making it sound like she was about to burst into tears. "I got your message. Is everything okay there?"

"Here? Claire, don't you be worrying about us! We're just fine! Oh, honey, are you okay? Really?"

"Honestly, yes, I'm okay. Everything's——" She couldn't say that everything was okay, because of course it wasn't. It was, at best, kind of temporarily stable. "It's quiet here. Shane's here, and Eve." Claire remembered that Mom had liked Monica Morrell, and rolled her eyes. Anything to calm her fears. "That girl from the dorm, Monica, she's here, too."

"Oh, yes, Monica. I liked her." It really did seem to help, which was not exactly an endorsement of Mom's character-judging ability. "Her brother came by here to check on us about an hour ago. He's a nice boy."

Claire couldn't quite imagine referring to Richard Morrell as a *boy*, but she let it go. "He's kind of in charge of the town right now," she said. "You have the radio, right? The one we dropped off earlier?"

"Yes. We've been doing everything they say, of course. But honey, I'd really like it if you could come here. We want to have you home, with us."

"I know. I know, Mom. But I think I'd better stay here. It's important. I'll try to come by tomorrow, okay?"

They talked a little more, about nothing much, just chatter to make life seem kind of normal for a change. Mom was holding it together, but only barely; Claire could hear the manic quaver in her voice, could almost see the bright tears in her eyes. She was going on about how they'd had to move most of the boxes into the basement to make room for all the company—*company?*—and how she was afraid that Claire's stuff would get damp, and then she talked about all the toys in the boxes and how much Claire had enjoyed them when she was younger.

Normal Mom stuff.

Claire didn't interrupt, except to make soothing noises and acknowledgments when Mom paused. It helped, hearing Mom's voice, and she knew it was helping her to talk. But finally, when her mother ran down like a spring-wound clock, Claire agreed to all the parental requirements to be careful and watch out and wear warm clothes.

Good-bye seemed very final, and once Claire hung up, she sat in silence for a few minutes, staring at the screen of her cell phone.

On impulse, she tried to call Amelie. It rang and rang. No voice mail.

In the living room, Shane was organizing some kind of sentry duty. A lot of people had already crashed out in piles of pillows, blankets, sometimes just on a spare rug. Claire edged around the prone bodies and motioned to Shane that she was going upstairs. He nodded and kept talking to the two guys he was with, but his gaze followed her all the way.

Eve was in her bedroom, and there was a note on the door that said DO NOT KNOCK OR I WILL KILL YOU. THIS MEANS YOU, SHANE. Claire considered knocking, but she was too tired to run away.

Her bedroom was dark. When she'd left in the morning, Eve's kind-of-friend Miranda had been sleeping here, but she was gone, and the bed was neatly made again. Claire sat down on the edge, staring out the windows, and then pulled out clean underwear and her last pair of blue jeans from the closet, plus a tight black shirt Eve had lent her last week.

The shower felt like heaven. There was even enough hot water for a change. Claire dried off, fussed with her hair a bit, and got dressed. When she came out, she listened at the stairs, but didn't hear Shane talking anymore. Either he was being quiet, or he'd gone to bed. She paused next to his door, wishing she had the guts to knock, but she went on to her own room instead.

Shane was inside, sitting on her bed. He looked up when she opened the door, and his lips parted, but he was silent for a long few seconds.

"I should go," he finally said, but he didn't get up.

Claire settled in next to him. It was all perfectly correct, the two of them sitting fully dressed like this, but somehow she felt like they were on the edge of a cliff, both in danger of falling off.

It was exciting, and terrifying, and all kinds of wrong.

"So what happened to you today?" she asked. "In the Bloodmobile, I mean?"

"Nothing really. We drove to the edge of town and parked outside the border, where we'd be able to see anybody coming. A couple of vamps showed, trying to make a withdrawal, but we sent them packing. Bishop never made an appearance. Once we lost contact with the vampires, we figured we'd cruise around and see what was going on. We nearly got boxed in by a bunch of drunk idiots in pickup trucks, and then the vampires in the Bloodmobile went nuts—that call thing going off, I guess. I dropped them at the grain elevator—that was the biggest, darkest place I could find, and it casts a lot of shadows. I handed off the driving to Cesar Mercado. He's supposed to drive it all the way to Midland tonight, provided the barriers are down. Best we can do."

"What about the book? Did you leave it on board?"

In answer, Shane reached into his waistband and pulled out the small leather-bound volume. Amelie had added a lock on it, like a diary lock. Claire tried pressing the small, metal catch. It didn't open, of course.

"You think you should be fooling with that thing?" Shane asked.

"Probably not." She tried prying a couple of pages apart to peek at the script. All she could tell was that it was handwritten, and the paper looked relatively old. Oddly, when she sniffed it, the paper smelled like chemicals.

"What are you doing?" Shane looked like he couldn't decide whether to be repulsed or fascinated.

"I think somebody restored the paper," she said. "Like they do with really expensive old books and stuff. Comics, sometimes. They put chemicals on the paper to slow down the aging process, make the paper whiter again."

"Fascinating," Shane lied. "Gimme." He plucked the book from her hands and put it aside, on the other side of the bed. When she grabbed for it, he got in her way; they tangled, and somehow, he was lying prone on the bed and she was stretched awkwardly on top of him. His hands steadied her when she started to slide off.

"Oh," she murmured. "We shouldn't—"

"Definitely not."

"Then you should—"

"Yeah, I should."

But he didn't move, and neither did she. They just looked at each other, and then, very slowly, she lowered her lips to his.

It was a warm, sweet, wonderful kiss, and it seemed to go on forever. It also felt like it didn't last nearly long enough. Shane's hands skimmed up her sides, up her back, and cupped her damp hair as he kissed her more deeply. There were promises in that kiss.

"Okay, red flag," he said. He hadn't let her go, but there was about a half an inch of air between their lips. Claire's whole body felt alive and tingling, pulse pounding in her wrists and temples, warmth pooling like light in the center of her body.

"It's okay," she said. "I swear. Trust me."

"Hey, isn't that my line?"

"Not now."

Kissing Shane was the reward for surviving a long, hard, terrifying day. Being enfolded in his warmth felt like going to heaven on moonbeams. She kicked off her shoes, and, still fully dressed, crawled under the blankets. Shane hesitated.

"Trust me," she said again. "And you can keep your clothes on if you don't."

They'd done this before, but somehow it hadn't felt so . . . intimate. Claire pressed against him, back to front under the covers, and his arms went around her. Instant heat.

She swallowed and tried to remember all those good intentions she'd had as she felt Shane's breath whisper on the back of her neck, and then his lips brushed her skin. "So wrong," he murmured. "You're killing me, you know."

"Am not."

"On this, you'll have to trust *me*." His sigh made her shiver all the way to her bones. "I can't believe you brought Monica back here."

"Oh, come on. You wouldn't have left her out there, all alone. I know you better than that, Shane. Even as bad as she is—"

"The satanic incarnation of evil?"

"Maybe so, but I can't see you letting them get her and . . . hurt her." Claire turned around to face him, a squirming motion that made them wrestle for the covers. "What's going to happen? Do you know?"

"What am I, Miranda the teen screwed-up psychic? No, I don't know.

All I know is that when we get up tomorrow, either the vampires will be back, or they won't. And then we'll have to make a choice about how we're going to go forward."

"Maybe we don't go forward. Maybe we wait."

"One thing I do know, Claire: you can't stay in the same place, not even for a day. You keep on moving. Maybe it's the right direction, maybe not, but you still move. Every second things change, like it or not."

She studied his face intently. "Is your dad here? Now?"

He grimaced. "Truthfully? No idea. I wouldn't be surprised. He'd know that it was time to move in and take command, if he could. And Manetti's a running buddy from way back. This kind of feels like Dad's behind it."

"But if he does take over, what happens to Michael? To Myrnin? To any other vampire out there?"

"Do you really need me to tell you?"

Claire shook her head. "He'll tell people they have to kill all the vampires, and then, he'll come after the Morrells, and anybody else he thinks is responsible for what happened to your family. Right?"

"Probably," Shane sighed.

"And you're going to let all that happen."

"I didn't say that."

"You didn't say you weren't, either. Don't tell me it's complicated, because it isn't. Either you stand up for something, or you lie down for it. You said that to me one time, and you were right." Claire burrowed closer into his arms. "Shane, you were *right* then. Be right now."

He touched her face. His fingers traced down her cheek, across her lips, and his eyes—she'd never seen that look in his eyes. In anyone's, really.

"In this whole screwed-up town, you're the only thing that's always been right to me," he whispered. "I love you, Claire." She saw something that might have been just a flash of panic go across his expression, but then he steadied again. "I can't believe I'm saying this, but I do. I love you."

He said something else, but the world had narrowed around her.

Shane's lips kept moving, but all she heard were the same words echoing over and over inside her head like the tolling of a giant brass bell: *I love you.*

He sounded like it had taken him completely by surprise—not in a bad way, but more as if he hadn't really understood what he was feeling until that instant.

She blinked. It was as if she'd never really seen him before, and he was *beautiful.* More beautiful than any man she'd ever seen in her entire life, ever.

Whatever he was saying, she stopped it by kissing him. A lot. And for a very long time. When he finally backed up, he didn't go far, and this look in his eyes, this intense and overwhelming *need*—that was new, too.

And she liked it.

"I love you," he said, and kissed her so hard he took her breath away. There was more to it than before—more passion, more urgency, more . . . everything. It was as if she were caught in a tide, carried away, and she thought that if she never touched the shore again, it would be good to drown like this, just swim forever in all this richness.

Red flag, some part of her screamed, *come on, red flag. What are you doing?*

She wished it would just shut up.

"I love you, too," she whispered to him. Her voice was shaking, and so were her hands where they rested on his chest. Under the soft T-shirt, his muscles were tensed, and she could feel every deep breath he took. "I'd do anything for you."

She meant it to be an invitation, but that was the thing that shocked sense back into him. He blinked. "Anything," he repeated, and squeezed his eyes shut. "Yeah. I'm getting that. Bad idea, Claire. Very, very bad."

"Today?" She laughed a little wildly. "Everything's crazy today. Why can't we be? Just once?"

"Because I made promises," he said. He wrapped his arms around her and pulled her close, and she felt a groan shake his whole body. "To your parents, to myself, to Michael. To you, Claire. I can't break my word. It's pretty much all I've got these days."

"But . . . what if—"

"Don't," he whispered in her ear. "Please don't. This is tough enough already."

He kissed her again, long and sweetly, and somehow, it tasted like tears this time. Like some kind of good-bye.

"I really do love you," he said, and smoothed away the damp streaks on her cheeks. "But I can't do this. Not now."

Before she could stop him, he slid out of bed, put on his shoes, and walked quickly to the door. She sat up, holding the covers close as if she were naked underneath, instead of fully clothed, and he hesitated there, one hand gripping the doorknob.

"Please stay," she said. "Shane—"

He shook his head. "If I stay, things are going to happen. You know it, and I know it, and we just can't do this. I know things are falling apart, but—" He hitched in a deep, painful breath. "No."

The sound of the door softly closing behind him went through her like a knife.

Claire rolled over, wretchedly hugging the pillow that smelled of his hair, sharing the warm place in the bed where his body had been, and thought about crying herself to sleep.

And then she thought of the dawning wonder in his eyes when he'd said, *I love you.*

No. It was no time to be crying.

When she did finally sleep, she felt safe.

TEN

The next day, there was no sign of the vampires, none at all. Claire checked the portal networks, but as far as she could tell, they were down. With nothing concrete to do, she helped around the house—cleaning, straightening, running errands. Richard Morrell came around to check on them. He looked a little better for having slept, which didn't mean he looked good, exactly.

When Eve wandered down, she looked almost as bad. She hadn't bothered with her Goth makeup, and her black hair was down in a lank, uncombed mess. She poured Richard some coffee from the ever-brewing pot, handed it over, and said, "How's Michael?"

Richard blew on the hot surface in the cup without looking at her. "He's at City Hall. We moved all the vampires we still had into the jail, for safekeeping."

Eve's face crumpled in anguish. Shane put a hand on her shoulder, and she pulled in a damp breath and got control of herself.

"Right," she said. "That's probably for the best, you're right." She sipped from her own battered coffee mug. "What's it like out there?" *Out there* meant beyond Lot Street, which remained eerily quiet.

"Not so good," Richard said. His voice sounded hoarse and dull, as if he'd yelled all the edges off it. "About half the stores are shut down, and some of those are burned or looted. We don't have enough police and volunteers to be everywhere. Some of the store owners armed up and are guarding their own places—I don't like it, but it's probably the best option until everybody settles down and sobers up. The problem isn't everybody, but it's a good portion of the town who's been down and angry a long time. You heard they raided the Barfly?"

"Yeah, we heard," Shane said.

"Well, that was just the beginning. Dolores Thompson's place got broken into, and then they went to the warehouses and found the bonded liquor storage. Those who were inclined to deal with all this by getting drunk and mean have had a real holiday."

"We saw the mobs," Eve said, and glanced at Claire. "Um, about your sister—"

"Yeah, thanks for taking care of her. Trust my idiot sister to go running around in her red convertible during a riot. She's damn lucky they didn't kill her."

They would have, Claire was certain of that. "I guess you're taking her with you . . . ?"

Richard gave her a thin smile. "Not the greatest houseguest?"

Actually, Monica had been very quiet. Claire had found her curled up on the couch, wrapped in a blanket, sound asleep. She'd looked pale and tired and bruised, and much younger than Claire had ever seen her. "She's been okay." She shrugged. "But I'll bet she'd rather be with her family."

"Her *family's* under protective custody downtown. My dad nearly got dragged off by a bunch of yahoos yelling about taxes or something. My mom—" Richard shook his head, as if he wanted to drive the pictures right out of his mind. "Anyway. Unless she likes four walls and a locked door, I don't think she's going to be very happy. And you know Monica: if she's not happy—"

"Nobody is," Shane finished for him. "Well, I want her out of our house. Sorry, man, but we did our duty and all. Past this point, she'd have to be a friend to keep crashing here. Which, you know, she isn't. Ever."

"Then I'll take her off your hands." Richard set the cup down and stood. "Thanks for the coffee. Seems like that's all that's keeping me going right now."

"Richard . . ." Eve rose, too. "Seriously, what's it like out there? What's going to happen?"

"With any luck, the drunks will sober up or pass out, and those who've been running around looking for people to punish will get sore feet and aching muscles and go home to get some sleep."

"Not like we've had a lot of luck so far, though," Shane said.

"No," Richard agreed. "That we haven't. But I have to say, we can't keep things locked down. People have to work, the schools have to open, and for that, we need something like normal life around here. So we're working on that. Power and water's on, phone lines are back up. TV and radio are broadcasting. I'm hoping that calms people down. We've got police patrols overlapping all through town, and we can be anywhere in under two minutes. One thing, though: we're getting word that there's bad weather in the forecast. Some kind of real big front heading toward us tonight. I'm not too happy about that, but maybe it'll keep the crazies off the streets for a while. Even riots don't like rain."

"What about the university?" Claire asked. "Are they open?"

"Open and classes are running, believe it or not. We passed off some of the disturbances as role-playing in the disaster drill, and said that the looting and burning was part of the exercise. Some of them believed us."

"But . . . no word about the vampires?"

Richard was silent for a moment, and then he said, "No. Not exactly."

"Then what?"

"We found some bodies, before dawn," he said. "All vamps. All killed with silver or decapitation. Some of them—I knew some of them. Thing is, I don't think they were killed by Bishop. From the looks of things, they were caught by a mob."

Claire caught her breath. Eve covered her mouth. "Who—?"

"Bernard Temple, Sally Christien, Tien Ma, and Charles Effords."

Eve lowered her hand to say, "Charles Effords? Like, Miranda's Charles? Her Protector?"

"Yeah. From the state of the bodies, I'd guess he was the primary target. Nobody loves a pedophile."

"Nobody except Miranda," Eve said. "She's going to be really scared now."

"Yeah, about that . . ." Richard hesitated, then plunged forward. "Miranda's gone."

"Gone?"

"Disappeared. We've been looking for her. Her parents reported her missing early last night. I'm hoping she wasn't with Charles when the mob caught up to him. You see her, you call me, okay?"

Eve's lips shaped the agreement, but no sound came out.

Richard checked his watch. "Got to go," he said. "Usual drill: lock the doors, check IDs on anybody you're not expecting who shows up. If you hear from any vampire, or hear anything *about* the vampires, you call immediately. Use the coded radios, not the phone lines. And be careful."

Eve swallowed hard, and nodded. "Can I see Michael?"

He paused, as if that hadn't occurred to him, then shrugged. "Come on."

"We're all going," Shane said.

It was an uncomfortable ride to City Hall, where the jail was located, mainly because although the police cruiser was large, it wasn't big enough to have Richard, Monica, Eve, Shane, and Claire all sharing the ride. Monica had taken the front seat, sliding close to her brother, and Claire had squeezed in with her friends in the back.

They didn't talk, not even when they cruised past burned-out, broken hulks of homes and stores. There weren't any fires today, or any mobs that Claire spotted. It all seemed quiet.

Richard drove past a police barricade around City Hall and parked in the underground garage. "I'm taking Monica to my parents'," he said. "You guys go on down to the cells. I'll be there in a minute."

It took a lot more than a minute for them to gain access to Michael; the vampires—all five of those the humans still had in custody—were housed in a special section, away from daylight and in reinforced cells. It reminded Claire, with an unpleasant lurch, of the vampires in the cells where Myrnin was usually locked up, for his own protection. Had anyone fed them? Had anyone even tried?

She didn't know three of the vampires, but she knew the last two. "Sam!" she blurted, and rushed to the bars. Michael's grandfather was lying on the bunk, one pale hand over his eyes, but he sat up when she called his name. Claire could definitely see the resemblance between Michael and Sam—the same basic bone structure, only Michael's hair was a bright gold, and Sam's was red.

"Get me out," Sam said, and lunged for the door. He rattled the cage with unexpected violence. Claire fell back, openmouthed. "Open the door and get me out, Claire! *Now!*"

"Don't listen to him," Michael said. He was standing at the bars of his own cell, leaning against them, and he looked tired. "Hey, guys. Did you bring me a lockpick in a cupcake or something?"

"I had the cupcake, but I ate it. Hard times, man." Shane extended his hand. Michael reached through the bars and took it, shook solemnly, and then Eve threw herself against the metal to try to hug him. It was awkward, but Claire saw the relief spread over Michael, no matter how odd it was with the bars between the two of them. He kissed Eve, and Claire had to look away from that, because it seemed like such a private kind of moment.

Sam rattled his cage again. "Claire, open the door! I need to get to Amelie!"

The policeman who'd escorted them down to the cells pushed off from the wall and said, "Calm down, Mr. Glass. You're not going anywhere; you know that." He shifted his attention to Shane and Claire. "He's been like that since the beginning. We had to trank him twice; he was hurting himself trying to get out. He's worse than all the others. They seem to have calmed down. Not him."

No, Sam definitely hadn't calmed down. As Claire watched, he tensed his muscles and tried to force the lock, but subsided in panting frustration and stumbled back to his bunk. "I have to go," he muttered. "Please, I need to go. She needs me. Amelie—"

Claire looked at Michael, who didn't seem to be nearly as distressed. "Um . . . sorry to ask, but . . . are you feeling like that? Like Sam?"

"No," Michael said. His eyes were still closed. "For a while there was this . . . call, but it stopped about three hours ago."

"Then why is Sam—"

"It's not the call," Michael said. "It's Sam. It's killing him, knowing she's out there in trouble and he can't help her."

Sam put his head in his hands, the picture of misery. Claire exchanged a look with Shane. "Sam," she said. "What's happening? Do you know?"

"People are dying, that's what's happening," he said. "Amelie's in trouble. I need to go to her. I can't just sit here!"

He threw himself at the bars again, kicking hard enough to make the metal ring like a bell.

"Well, that's where you're going to stay," the policeman said, not exactly unsympathetically. "The way you're acting, you'd go running out into the sunlight, and that wouldn't do her or you a bit of good, now, would it?"

"I could have gone hours ago before sunrise," Sam snapped. *"Hours ago."*

"And now you have to wait for dark."

That earned the policeman a full-out vicious snarl, and Sam's eyes flared into bright crimson. Everybody stayed back, and when Sam subsided this time, it seemed to be for good. He withdrew to his bunk, lay down, and turned his back to them.

"Man," Shane breathed softly. "He's a little intense, huh?"

From what the policeman told them—and Richard, when he rejoined them—all the captured vampires had been at about the same level of violence, at first. Now it was just Sam, and as Michael said, it didn't seem to be Amelie's summons that was driving him. . . . It was fear for Amelie herself.

It was love.

"Step back, please," the policeman said to Eve. She looked over her shoulder at him, then at Michael. He kissed her, and let go.

She did take a step back, but it was a tiny one. "So—are you okay? Really?"

"Sure. It's not exactly the Ritz, but it's not bad. They're not keeping us here to hurt us, I know that." Michael stretched out a finger and touched her lips. "I'll be back soon."

"Better be," Eve said. She mock-bit at his finger. "I could totally date somebody else, you know."

"And I could rent out your room."

"And I could put your game console on eBay."

"Hey," Shane protested. "Now you're just being mean."

"See what I mean? You need to come home, or it's total chaos. Dogs and cats, living together." Eve's voice dropped, but not quite to a whisper. "And I miss you. I miss seeing you. I miss you all the time."

"I miss you, too," Michael murmured, then blinked and looked at Claire and Shane. "I mean, I miss all of you."

"Sure you do," Shane agreed. "But not in that way, I hope."

"Shut up, dude. Don't make me come out there."

Shane turned to the policeman. "See? He's fine."

"I was more worried about you guys," Michael confessed. "Everything okay at the house?"

"I have to burn a blouse Monica borrowed," Claire said. "Otherwise, we're good."

They tried to talk a while longer, but somehow, Sam's silent, rigid back turned toward them made conversation seem more desperate than fun. He was really hurting, and Claire didn't know—short of letting him go for a jog in the noontime sun—how to make it any better. She didn't know where Amelie was, and with the portals shut, she doubted she could even know where to start looking.

Amelie had gathered up an army—whatever Bishop hadn't grabbed first—but what she was doing with it was anybody's guess. Claire didn't have a clue.

So in the end, she hugged Michael and told Sam it would all be okay, and they left.

"If they stay calm through the day, I'll let them out tonight," Richard said. "But I'm worried about letting them roam around on their own. What happened to Charles and the others could keep on happening. Captain Obvious used to be our biggest threat, but now we don't know who's out there, or what they're planning. And we can't count on the vampires to be able to protect themselves right now."

"My dad would say that it's about time the tables turned," Shane said.

Richard fixed him with a long stare. "Is that what you say, too?"

Shane looked at Michael, and at Sam. "No," he said. "Not anymore."

The day went on quietly. Claire got out her books and spent part of the day trying to study, but she couldn't get her brain to stop spinning. Every few minutes, she checked her e-mail and her phone, hoping for something, anything, from Amelie. *You can't just leave us like this. We don't know what to do.*

Except keep moving forward. Like Shane had said, they couldn't stay still. The world kept on turning.

Eve drove Claire to her parents' house in the afternoon, where she had cake and iced tea and listened to her mother's frantic flow of good cheer. Her dad looked sallow and unwell, and she worried about his heart, as always. But he seemed okay when he told her he loved her, and that he worried, and that he wanted her to move back home.

Just when she thought they'd gotten past that . . .

Claire exchanged a quick look with Eve. "Maybe we should talk about that when things get back to normal?" As if they ever were normal in Morganville. "Next week?"

Dad nodded. "Fine, but I'm not going to change my mind, Claire. You're better off here, at home." Whatever spell Mr. Bishop had cast over her father, it was still working great; he was single-minded about wanting her out of the Glass House. And maybe it hadn't been a spell at all; maybe it was just normal parental instinct.

Claire crammed her mouth with cake and pretended not to hear, and asked her mom about the new curtains. That filled another twenty minutes, and then Eve was able to make excuses about needing to get home, and then they were in the car.

"Wow," Eve said, and started the engine. "So. Are you going to do it? Move in with them?"

Claire shrugged helplessly. "I don't know. I don't know if we're going to get through the day! It's kind of hard to make plans." She wasn't going to say anything, truly, she wasn't, but the words had been boiling and bubbling inside her all day, and as Eve put the car in drive, Claire said, "Shane said he loved me."

Eve hit the brakes, hard enough to make their seat belts click in place. "Shane *what*? Said *what*?"

"Shane said he loved me."

"Okay, first impressions—fantastic, good, that's what I was hoping you'd said." Eve took a deep breath and let up on the brake, steering out into the deserted street. "Second impressions, well, I hope that you two . . . um . . . how can I put this? Watch yourselves?"

"You mean, don't have sex? We won't." Claire said it with a little bit of an edge. "Even if we wanted to. I mean, he promised, and he's not going to break that promise, not even if I say it's okay."

"Oh. *Oh*." Eve stared at her, wide-eyed, for way too long for road safety. "You're kidding! Wait, you're not. He said he loved you, and then he said—"

"No," Claire said. "He said no."

"Oh." Funny, how many meanings that word could have. This time it was full of sympathy. "You know, that makes him—"

"Great? Superbly awesome? Yeah, I know. I just—" Claire threw up her hands. "I just *want* him, okay?"

"He'll still be there in a couple of months, Claire. At seventeen, you're not a kid, at least in Texas."

"You've put some thought into this."

"Not me," Eve said, and gave her an apologetic look.

"*Shane?* You mean—you mean you talked about this? With Shane?"

"He needed some girl guidance. I mean, he's taking this really seriously—a lot more seriously than I expected. He wants to do the right thing. That's cool, right? I think that's cool. Most guys, it's just, whatever."

Claire clenched her jaw so hard she felt her teeth grinding. "I can't believe he talked to you about it!"

"Well, you're talking to me about it."

"He's a guy!"

"Guys occasionally talk, believe it or not. Something more than *pass the beer* or *where's the porn?*" Eve turned the corner, and they cruised past a couple of slow blocks of houses, some people out walking, an elementary school with a TEMPORARILY CLOSED sign out front. "You didn't exactly ask for advice, but I'm going to give it: don't rush this. You may think you're good to go, but give it some time. It's not like you have a sell-by date or anything."

Despite her annoyance, Claire had to laugh. "Feels like it right now."

"Well, duh. Hormones!"

"So how old were you when—"

"Too young. I speak from experience, grasshopper." Eve's expression went distant for a second. "I wish I'd waited for Michael."

That was, for some reason, kind of a shock, and Claire blinked. She remembered some things, and felt deeply uncomfortable. "Uh . . . did Brandon . . . ?" Because Brandon had been her family's Protector vampire, and he'd been a complete creep. She couldn't imagine much worse than having Brandon be your first.

"No. Not that he didn't want to, but no, it wasn't Brandon."

"Who?"

"Sorry. Off-limits."

Claire blinked. There wasn't much Eve considered off-limits. "Really?"

"Really." Eve pulled the car up to the curb. "Bottom line? If Shane says he loves you, he does, full stop. He wouldn't say it if he didn't mean it, all the way. He's not the kind of guy to tell you what you want to hear. That makes you really, really lucky. You should remember that."

Claire was trying, really, but from time to time that moment came back to her, that blinding, searing moment when he'd looked into her face and said those words, and she'd seen that amazing light in his eyes. She'd wanted to see it again, over and over. Instead, she'd seen him walk away.

It felt romantic. It also felt frustrating, on some level she didn't even remember feeling before. And now there was something new: doubt. *Maybe that was my fault. Maybe I was supposed to do something I didn't do. Some signal I didn't give him.*

Eve read her expression just fine. "You'll be okay," she said, and laughed just a little. "Give the guy a break. He's the second actual gentleman I've ever met. It doesn't mean he doesn't want to throw you on the bed and go. Just means he won't, right now. Which you have to admit: kinda hot."

Put in those terms, it kind of was.

As it got closer to nightfall, Richard called to say he was letting Michael go. For the second time, the three of them piled into the car and went racing to City Hall. The barricades had mostly come down. According to the radio and television, it had been a very quiet day, with no reports of violence. Store owners—the human ones, anyway—were planning on reopening in the morning. Schools would be in session.

Life was going on, and Mayor Morrell was expected to come out with some kind of a speech. Not that anybody would listen.

"Are they letting Sam out, too?" Claire asked, as Eve parked in the underground lot.

"Apparently. Richard doesn't think he can really keep anybody much longer. Some kind of town ordinance, which means law and order really is back in fashion. Plus, I think he's really afraid Sam's going to hurt himself if this goes on. And also, maybe he thinks he can follow Sam to find Amelie." Eve scanned the dark structure—there were a few dark-tinted cars in the lot, but then, there always were. The rest of the vehicles looked like they were human owned. "You guys see anything?"

"Like what? A big sign saying This Is a Trap?" Shane opened his door and got out, taking Claire's hand to help her. He didn't drop it once she was standing beside him. "Not that I wouldn't put it past some of our finer citizens. But no, I don't see anything."

Michael was being let out of his cell when they arrived, and there were hugs and handshakes. The other vampires didn't have anyone to help them, and looked a little confused about what they were supposed to do.

Not Sam.

"Sam, wait!" Michael grabbed his arm on the way past, dragging his grandfather to a stop. Looking at them standing together, Claire was struck again by how alike they were. And always would be, she supposed, given that neither one of them was going to age any more. "You can't go charging off by yourself. You don't even know where she is. Running around town on your white horse will get you really, truly killed."

"Doing nothing will get *her* killed. I can't have that, Michael. None of this means anything to me if she dies." Sam shook Michael's hand away. "I'm not asking you to come with me. I'm just telling you not to get in my way."

"Grandpa—"

"Exactly. Do as you're told." Sam could move vampire-quick when he wanted to, and he was gone almost before the words hit Claire's ears—a blur, heading for the exit.

"So much for trying to figure out where she is from where he goes," Shane said. "Unless you've got light speed under the hood of that car, Eve."

Michael looked after him with a strange expression on his face—anger, regret, sorrow. Then he hugged Eve closer and kissed the top of her head.

"Well, I guess my family's no more screwed up than anybody else's," he said.

Eve nodded. "Let's recap. My dad was an abusive jerk—"

"Mine, too." Shane raised his hand.

"Thank you. My brother's a psycho backstabber—"

Shane said, "You don't even want to talk about my dad."

"Point. So, in short, Michael, your family is *awesome* by comparison. Bloodsucking, maybe. But kind of awesome."

Michael sighed. "Doesn't really feel like it at the moment."

"It will." Eve was suddenly very serious. "But Shane and I don't have that to look forward to, you know. You're our only real family now."

"I know," Michael said. "Let's go home."

ELEVEN

Home was theirs again. The refugees were all out now, leaving a house that badly needed picking up and cleaning—not that anybody had gone out of their way to trash the place, but with that many people coming and going, things happened. Claire grabbed a trash bag and began clearing away paper plates, old Styrofoam cups half full of stale coffee, crumpled wrappers, and papers. Shane fired up the video game, apparently back in the mood to kill zombies. Michael took his guitar out of its case and tuned it, but he kept getting up to stare out the windows, restless and worried.

"What?" Eve asked. She'd heated up leftover spaghetti out of the refrigerator, and tried to hand Michael a plate first. "Do you see something?"

"Nothing," he said, and gave her a quick, strained smile as he waved away the food. "Not really hungry, though. Sorry."

"More for me," Shane said, and grabbed the plate. He propped it on his lap and forked spaghetti into his mouth. "Seriously. You all right? Because you never turn down food."

Michael didn't answer. He stared out into the dark.

"You're worried," Eve said. "About Sam?"

"Sam and everybody else. This is nuts. What's going on here—" Michael checked the locks on the window, but as a kind of automatic motion, as though his mind wasn't really on it. "Why hasn't Bishop taken over? What's he *doing* out there? Why aren't we seeing the fight?"

"Maybe Amelie's kicking his ass out there in the shadows somewhere." Shane shoveled in more spaghetti.

"No. She's not. I can feel that. I think—I think she's in hiding. With the rest of her followers, the vampires, anyway."

Shane stopped chewing. "You know where they are?"

"Not really. I just feel—" Michael shook his head. "It's gone. Sorry. But I feel like things are changing. Coming to a head."

Claire had just taken a plate of warm pasta when they all heard the thump of footsteps overhead. They looked up, and then at each other, in silence. Michael pointed to himself and the stairs, and they all nodded. Eve opened a drawer in the end table and took out three sharpened stakes; she tossed one to Shane, one to Claire, and kept one in a white-knuckled grip.

Michael ascended the stairs without a sound, and disappeared.

He didn't come back down. Instead, there was a swirl of black coat and stained white balloon pants tucked into black boots; then Myrnin leaned over the railing to say, "Upstairs, all of you. I need you."

"Um . . ." Eve looked at Shane. Shane looked at Claire.

Claire followed Myrnin. "Trust me," she said. "It won't do any good to say no."

Michael was waiting in the hallway, next to the open, secret door. He led the way up.

Whatever Claire had been expecting to see, it wasn't a *crowd*, but that was what was waiting upstairs in the hidden room on the third floor. She stared in confusion at the room full of people, then moved out of the way for Shane and Eve to join her and Michael.

Myrnin came last. "Claire, I believe you know Theo Goldman and his family."

The faces came into focus. She *had* met them—in that museum thing, when they'd been on the way to rescue Myrnin. Theo Goldman had spoken to Amelie. He'd said they wouldn't fight.

But it looked to Claire like they'd been in a fight anyway. Vampires didn't bruise, exactly, but she could see torn clothes and smears of blood, and they all looked exhausted and somehow—hollow. Theo was worst of all. His kind face seemed made of nothing but lines and wrinkles now, as if he'd aged a hundred years in a couple of days.

"I'm sorry," he said, "but we had no other place to go. Amelie—I hoped that she was here, that she would give us refuge. We've been everywhere else."

Claire remembered there being more of them, somehow—yes, there were at least two people missing. One human, one vampire. "What happened? I thought you were safe where you were!"

"We were," Theo said. "Then we weren't. That's what wars are like. The safe places don't stay safe. Someone knew where we were, or suspected. Around dawn yesterday, a mob broke in the doors looking for us. Jochen—" He looked at his wife, and she bowed her head. "Our son Jochen, he gave his life to delay them. So did our human friend William. We've been hiding, moving from place to place, trying not to be driven out in the sun."

"How did you get here?" Michael asked. He seemed wary. Claire didn't blame him.

"I brought them," Myrnin said. "I've been trying to find those who are left." He crouched down next to one of the young vampire girls and stroked her hair. She smiled at him, but it was a fragile, frightened smile. "They can stay here for now. This room isn't common knowledge. I've left open the portal in the attic in case they have to flee, but it's one way only, leading out. It's a last resort."

"Are there others? Out there?" Claire asked.

"Very few on their own. Most are either with Bishop, with Amelie, or"—Myrnin spread his hands—"gone."

"What are they doing? Amelie and Bishop?"

"Moving their forces. They're trying to find an advantage, pick the most favorable ground. It won't last." Myrnin shrugged. "Sooner or later, sometime tonight, they'll clash, and then they'll fight. Someone will win, and someone will lose. And in the morning, Morganville will know its fate."

That was creepy. *Really* creepy. Claire shivered and looked at the others, but nobody seemed to have anything to say.

"Claire. Attend me," Myrnin said, and walked with her to one corner of the room. "Have you spoken with your doctor friend?"

"I tried. I couldn't get through to him. Myrnin, are you . . . okay?"

"Not for much longer," he said, in that clinical way he had right before the drugs wore off. "I won't be safe to be around without another dose of some sort. Can you get it for me?"

"There's none in your lab—"

"I've been there. Bishop got there first. I shall need a good bit of glassware, and a completely new library." He said it lightly, but Claire could see the tension in his face and the shadow in his dark, gleaming eyes. "He tried to destroy the portals, cut off Amelie's movements. I managed to patch things together, but I shall need to instruct you in how it's done. Soon. In case—"

He didn't need to finish. Claire nodded slowly. "You should go," she said. "Is the prison safe? The one where you keep the sickest ones?"

"Bishop finds nothing to interest him there, so yes. He will ignore it awhile longer. I'll lock myself in for a while, until you come with the drug." Myrnin bent over her, suddenly very focused and very intent. "We *must* refine the serum, Claire. We *must* distribute it. The stress, the fighting—it's accelerating the disease. I've seen signs of it in Theo, even in Sam. If we don't act soon, I'm afraid we may begin to lose more to confusion and fear. They won't even be able to defend themselves."

Claire swallowed. "I'll get on it."

He took her hand and kissed it lightly. His lips felt dry as dust, but it still left a tingle in her fingers. "I know you will, my girl. Now, let's rejoin your friends."

"How long do they need to be here?" Eve asked, as they moved closer. She asked not unkindly, but she seemed nervous, too. There were, Claire thought, an awful lot of near-stranger vampire guests. "I mean, we don't have a lot of blood in the house. . . ."

Theo smiled. Claire remembered, with a sharp feeling of alarm, what he'd said to Amelie back at the museum, and she didn't like that smile at all, not even when he said, "We won't require much. We can provide for ourselves."

"He means, they can munch on their human friends, like takeout," Claire said. "No. Not in our house."

Myrnin frowned. "This is hardly the time to be—"

"This is *exactly* the time, and you know it. Did anybody ask *them* if they wanted to be snack packs?" The two remaining humans, both women, looked horrified. "I didn't think so."

Theo's expression didn't change. "What we do is our own affair. We won't hurt them, you know."

"Unless you're getting your plasma by osmosis, I don't really know how you can promise that."

Theo's eyes flared with banked fire. "What do you want us to do? Starve? Even the youngest of us?"

Eve cleared her throat. "Actually, I know where there's a big supply of blood. If somebody will go with me to get it."

"Oh, hell no," Shane said. "Not out in the dark. Besides, the place is locked up."

Eve reached in her pocket and took out her key ring. She flipped until she found one key in particular, and held it up. "I never turned in my key," she said. "I used to open and close, you know."

Myrnin gazed at her thoughtfully. "There's no portal to Common Grounds. It's off the network. That means any vampire in it will be trapped in daylight."

"No. There's underground access to the tunnels; I've seen it. Oliver sent some people out using it while I was there." Eve gave him a bright, brittle smile. "I say we move your friends there. Also, there's coffee. You guys like coffee, right? Everybody likes coffee."

Theo ignored her, and looked to Myrnin for an answer. "Is it better?"

"It's more defensible," Myrnin said. "Steel shutters. If there's underground access—yes. It would make a good base of operations." He turned to Eve. "We'll require your services to drive."

He said it as if Eve were the help, and Claire felt her face flame hot.

"Excuse me? How about a *please* in there somewhere, since you're asking for a favor?"

Myrnin's eyes turned dark and very cold. "You seem to have forgotten that I employ you, Claire. That I *own* you, in some sense. I am not required to say please and thank you to you, your friends, or *any* human walking the streets." He blinked, and was back to the Myrnin she normally saw. "However, I do take your point. Yes. *Please* drive us to Common Grounds, dear lady. I would be extravagantly, embarrassingly grateful."

He did all but kiss her hand. Eve, not surprisingly, could say nothing but yes.

Claire settled for an eye roll big enough to make her head hurt. "You can't all fit," she pointed out. "In Eve's car, I mean."

"And she's not taking you alone, anyway," Michael said. "My car's in the garage. I can take the rest of you. Shane, Claire——"

"Staying here, since you'll need the space," Shane said. "Sounds like a plan. Look, if there are people looking for them, you ought to get them moving. I'll call Richard. He can assign a couple of cops to guard Common Grounds."

"No," Myrnin said. "No police. We can't trust them."

"We can't?"

"Some of them have been working with Bishop, and with the human mobs. I have proof of that. We can't take the risk."

"But Richard——" Claire said, and subsided when she got Myrnin's glare. "Right. Okay. On your own, got it."

Eve didn't want to be dragged into it, but she went without much of a protest—the number of fangs in the room might have had something to do with it. As the Goldmans and Myrnin, Eve and Michael walked downstairs, Shane held Claire back to say, "We've got to figure out how to lock this place up. In case."

"You mean, against——" She gestured vaguely at the vampires. He nodded. "But if Michael lives here, and we live here, the house can't just bar a whole group of people from entry. It has to be done one at a time—at least that's what I understood. And no, before you ask me, I don't know how it works. Or how to fool it. I think only Amelie has the keys to that."

He looked disappointed. "How about closing off these weird doors Myrnin and Amelie are popping through?"

"I can work them. That doesn't mean I can turn them on and off."

"Great." He looked around the room, then took a seat on the old Victorian couch. "So we're like Undead Grand Central Station. Not really loving that so much. Can Bishop come through?"

It was a question that Claire had been thinking about, and it creeped her out to have to say, "I don't know. Maybe. But from what Myrnin said, he set the doorway to exit-only. So maybe we just . . . wait."

Robbed of doing anything heroic, or for that matter even useful, she warmed up the spaghetti again, and she and Shane ate it and watched some mindless TV show while jumping at every noise and creak, with weapons handy. When the kitchen door banged open nearly an hour later, Claire almost needed a heart transplant—until she heard Eve yell, "We're home! Ooooooh, spaghetti. I'm starved." Eve came in holding a plate and shoveling pasta into her mouth as she walked. Michael was right behind her.

"No problems?" Shane asked. Eve shook her head, chewing a mouthful of spaghetti.

"They should be fine there. Nobody saw us get them inside, and until Oliver turns up, nobody is going to need to get in there for a while."

"What about Myrnin?"

Eve swallowed, almost choked, and Michael patted her kindly on the back. She beamed at him. "Myrnin? Oh yeah. He did a Batman and took off into the night. What is *with* that guy, Claire? If he was a superhero, he'd be Bipolar Man."

The drugs were the problem. Claire needed to get more, and she needed to work on that cure Myrnin had found. That was just as important as anything else . . . providing there were any vampires left, anyway.

They had dinner, and at least it was the four of them again, sitting around the table, talking as if the world were normal, even if all of them knew it wasn't. Shane seemed especially jumpy, which wasn't like him at all.

For her part, Claire was just tired to the bone of being scared, and when she went upstairs, she was asleep the minute she crawled between the covers.

But sleep didn't mean it was restful, or peaceful.

She dreamed that somewhere, Amelie was playing chess, moving her pieces at lightning speed across a black-and-white board. Bishop sat across from her, grinning with too many teeth, and when he took her rook, it turned into a miniature version of Claire, and suddenly both the vampires were huge and she was so small, so small, stranded out in the open.

Bishop picked her up and squeezed her in his white hand, and blood drops fell onto the white squares of the chessboard.

Amelie frowned, watching Bishop squeeze her, and put out a delicate fingertip to touch the drops of blood. Claire struggled and screamed.

Amelie tasted her blood, and smiled.

Claire woke up with a convulsive shudder, huddled in her blankets. It was still dark outside the windows, though the sky was getting lighter, and the house was very, very quiet.

Her phone was buzzing in vibrate mode on the bedside table. She picked it up and found a text message from the university's alert system.

CLASSES RETURN TO NORMAL SCHEDULE EFFECTIVE 7 A.M. TODAY.

School seemed like a million miles away, another world that didn't mean anything to her anymore, but it would get her on campus, and there were things she needed there. Claire scrolled down her phone list and found Dr. Robert Mills, but there was no immediate answer on his cell. She checked the clock, winced at the early hour, but slid out of bed and began grabbing things out of drawers. That didn't take a lot of time. She was down to the last of everything. Laundry was starting to be a genuine priority.

She dialed his phone again after she'd dressed.

"Hello?" Dr. Mills sounded as if she'd dragged him out of a deep, probably happy sleep. *He* probably hadn't been dreaming about being squeezed dry by Mr. Bishop.

"It's Claire," she said. "I'm sorry to call so early—"

"Is it early? Oh. Been up all night, just fell asleep." He yawned. "Glad you're all right, Claire."

"Are you at the hospital?"

"No. The hospital's going to need a lot of work before it's even half-way ready for the kind of work I need to do." Another jaw-cracking yawn. "Sorry. I'm on campus, in the Life Sciences Building. Lab Seventeen. We have some roll-away beds here."

"We?"

"My wife and kids are with me. I didn't want to leave them on their own out there."

Claire didn't blame him. "I've got something for you to do, and I need some of the drug," she said. "It could be really important. I'll be at school in about twenty minutes, okay?"

"Okay. Don't come here. My kids are asleep right now. Let's meet somewhere else."

"The on-campus coffee bar," she said. "It's in the University Center."

"Trust me, I know where it is. Twenty minutes."

She was already heading for the door.

With no sounds coming from any of the other rooms, Claire figured her housemates were all crashed out, exhausted. She didn't know why she wasn't, except for a suppressed, vibrating fear inside her that if she slept any more, something bad was going to happen.

Showered, dressed in her last not-very-good clothes, she grabbed up her backpack and repacked it. Her dart gun was out of darts anyway, so she left it behind. The samples Myrnin had prepared of Bishop's blood went into a sturdy padded box, and on impulse, she added a couple of stakes and the silver knife Amelie had given her.

And books.

It was the first time Claire had been on foot in Morganville since the rioting had started, and it was eerie. The town was quiet again, but stores had broken windows, some boarded over; there were some buildings reduced to burned-out hulks, with blind, open doorways. Broken bottles were on the sidewalks and spots of what looked like blood on the concrete—and, in places, dark splashes.

Claire hurried past it all, even past Common Grounds, where the steel shutters were down inside the windows. There was no sign of anyone within. She imagined Theo Goldman standing there watching her from cover, and waved a little, just a waggle of fingers.

She didn't really expect a response.

The gates of the university were open, and the guards were gone. Claire jogged along the sidewalk, going up the hill and around the curve, and began to see students up and moving, even so early in the morning. As she got closer to the central cluster of buildings, the foot traffic intensified, and here and there she saw alert campus police walking in pairs, watching for trouble.

The students didn't seem to notice anything at all. Not for the first time, Claire wondered if Amelie's semipsychic network that cut Morganville off from the world also kept people on campus clueless.

She didn't like to think they were just naturally that stupid. Then again, she'd been to some of the parties.

The University Center had opened its doors only a few minutes before, and the coffee barista was just taking the chairs down from the tables. Usually it would have been Eve on duty, but instead, it was one of the university staffers, on loan from the food service most likely. He didn't exactly look happy to be there. Claire tried to be nice, and finally got a smile from him as he handed her a mocha and took her cash.

"I wouldn't be here," he confessed, "except that they're paying us triple to be here the rest of the week."

"Really? Wow. I'll tell Eve. She could use the money."

"Yeah, get her in here. I'm not good at this coffee stuff. Give me the plain stuff. Water, beans—can't really screw that up. This espresso is hard."

Claire decided, after tasting the mocha, that he was right. He really wasn't cut out for it. She sipped it anyway, and took a seat where she could watch the majority of the UC entrances for Dr. Mills.

She almost didn't recognize him. He'd shed his white doctor's coat, of course, but somehow she'd never expected to see someone like him wearing a zip-up hoodie, sweatpants, and sneakers. He was more the suit-and-tie type. He ordered plain coffee—good choice—and came to join her at the table.

Dr. Mills was medium everything, and he blended in at the university just as easily as he had at the hospital. He'd have made a good spy, Claire thought. He had one of those faces—young from one angle, older from another, with nothing you could really remember later about it.

But he had a nice, comforting smile. She supposed that would be a real asset in a doctor.

"Morning," he said, and gulped coffee. His eyes were bloodshot and red rimmed. "I'm going back to the hospital later today. Damage assessments, and we've already reopened the trauma units and CCU. I'm going to catch some sleep as soon as we're done, in case any crash cases come in. Nothing worse than an exhausted trauma surgeon."

She felt even more guilty about waking him up. "I'll make this quick," she promised. Claire opened her backpack, took out the padded box, and slid it across the table to him. "Blood samples, from Myrnin."

Mills frowned. "I've already got a hundred blood samples from Myrnin. Why—"

"These are different," Claire said. "Trust me. There's one labeled *B* that's important."

"Important, how?"

"I don't want to say. I'd rather you took a look first." In science, Claire knew, it was better to come to an analysis cold, without too many expectations. Dr. Mills knew that, too, and he nodded as he took possession of the samples. "Um—if you want to sleep, maybe you shouldn't drink that stuff."

Dr. Mills smiled and threw back the rest of his coffee. "You get to be a doctor by developing immunity to all kinds of things, including caffeine," he said. "Trust me. The second my head touches the pillow, I'm asleep, even if I've got a coffee IV drip."

"I know people who'd pay good money for that. The IV drip, I mean."

He shook his head, grinning, but then got serious. "You seem okay. I was worried about you. You're just so . . . young, to be involved in all this stuff."

"I'm all right. And I'm really—"

"Not that young. Yes, I know. But still. Let an old man fret a little. I've got two daughters." He tossed his coffee cup at the trash—two points—and stood. "Here's all I could get together of the drug. Sorry, it's not a lot, but I've got a new batch in the works. It'll take a couple of days to finish."

He handed her a bag that clinked with small glass bottles. She peeked inside. "This should be plenty." Unless, of course, she had to start dosing all over Morganville, in which case, they were done, anyway.

"Sorry to make this a gulp-and-run, but . . ."

"You should go," Claire agreed. "Thanks, Dr. Mills." She offered her hand. He shook it gravely.

Around his wrist, there was a silver bracelet, with Amelie's symbol on it. He looked down at it, then at her gold one, and shrugged.

"I don't think it's time to take it off," he said. "Not yet."

At least yours does come off, Claire thought, but didn't say. Dr. Mills had signed agreements, contracts, and those things were binding in Morganville, but the contract she'd signed had made her Amelie's property, body and soul. And her bracelet didn't have a catch on it, which made it more like a slave collar.

From time to time, that still creeped her out.

It was getting close to time for her first class, and as Claire hefted her backpack, she wondered how many people would show up. Lots, probably. Knowing most of the professors, they'd think today was a good day for a quiz.

She wasn't disappointed. She also wasn't panicked, unlike some of her classmates during her first class, and her third. Claire didn't panic on tests, not unless it was in a dream where she also had to clog dance and twirl batons to get a good grade. And the quizzes weren't so hard anyway, not even the physics tests.

One thing she noticed, more and more, as she went around campus: fewer people had on bracelets. Morganville natives got used to wearing them twenty-four/seven, so she could clearly see the tan lines where the bracelets had been . . . and weren't anymore. It was almost like a reverse tattoo.

Around noon, she saw Monica Morrell, Gina, and Jennifer.

The three girls were walking fast, heads down, books in their arms. There was a whole lot different about them; Claire was used to seeing those three stalking the campus like tigers, confident and cruel. They'd stare down anyone, and whether you liked them or not, they were wicked fashion queens, always showing themselves off to best advantage.

Not today.

Monica, who usually was the centerpiece, looked awful. Her shiny, flirty hair was dull and fuzzy, as if she had barely bothered to brush it, much less condition or curl. What little Claire could see of her face looked makeup free. She was wearing a shapeless sweater in an unflatteringly ugly pattern, and sloppy blue jeans, the kind Claire imagined she might keep around to clean house in, if Monica ever did that kind of thing.

Gina and Jennifer didn't look much better, and they all looked defeated.

Claire still felt a little, tiny, unworthy tingle of satisfaction . . . until she saw the looks they were getting. Morganville natives who'd taken off their bracelets were outright glaring at Monica and her entourage, and a few of them did worse than just give them dirty looks. As Claire watched, a big, tough jock wearing a TPU jacket bumped into Jennifer and sent her books flying. She didn't look at him. She just bent over to pick them up.

"Hey, you clumsy whore, what the hell?" He shoved her onto her butt as she tried to get up, but she wasn't his real target; she was just standing between him and Monica. "Hey. Morrell. How's your daddy?"

"Fine," Monica said, and looked him in the eyes. "I'd ask about yours, but since you don't know who he was—"

The jock stepped very close to her. She didn't flinch, but Claire could tell that she wanted to. There were tight lines around her eyes and mouth, and her knuckles were white where she gripped her books.

"You've been Princess Queen Bitch your whole life," he said. "You remember Annie? Annie McFarlane? You used to call her a fat cow. You laughed at her in school. You took pictures of her in the bathroom and posted them on the Internet. Remember?"

Monica didn't answer.

The jock smiled. "Yeah, you remember Annie. She was a good kid, and I liked her."

"You didn't like her enough to stand up for her," Monica said. "Right, Clark? You wanted to get in my pants more than you wanted me to be kind to your little fat friend. Not my fault she ended up wrecking that stupid car at the town border. Maybe it's your fault, though. Maybe she couldn't stand being in town with you anymore after you dumped her."

Clark knocked the books out of her hand and shoved her up against a nearby tree trunk. Hard.

"I've got something for you, bitch." He dug in his pocket and came up with something square, about four inches across. It was a sticky label like a name tag, only with a picture on it of an awkward but sweet-looking teenage girl trying bravely to smile for the camera.

Clark slapped it on Monica's chest and rubbed it so it stuck to the sweater.

"You wear that," he said. "You wear Annie's picture. If I see you take it off today, I swear, what you did to Annie back in high school's going to seem like a Cancún vacation."

Under Annie's picture were the words KILLED BY MONICA MORRELL.

Monica looked down at it, swallowed, and turned bright red, then pale. She jerked her chin up again, sharply, and stared at Clark. "Are you done?"

"So far. Remember, you take it off—"

"Yeah, Clark, you weren't exactly subtle. I get it. You think I care?"

Clark's grin widened. "No, you don't. Not yet. Have a nice day, Queenie."

He walked away and did a high five with two other guys.

As Monica stared down at the label on her chest in utter disgust, another girl approached—another Morganville native who'd taken off the bracelet. Monica didn't notice her until the girl was right in her face.

This one didn't talk. She just ripped the backing off another label and stuck it on Monica's chest next to Annie McFarlane's photo.

This one just said KILLER in big red letters.

She kept on walking.

Monica started to rip it off, but Clark was watching her.

"Suits you," he said, and pointed to his eyes, then to her. "We'll be watching you all day. There are a lot more labels coming."

Clark was right. It was going to be a really long, bad day to be Monica Morrell. Even Gina and Jennifer were fading back now, heading out in a different direction and leaving her to face the music.

Monica's gaze fell on Claire. There was a flash of fear in her eyes, and shame, and genuine pain.

And then she armored up and snapped, "What are you looking at, freak?"

Claire shrugged. "Justice, I guess." She frowned. "How come you didn't stay with your parents?"

"None of your business." Monica's fierce stare wavered. "Dad wanted us all to go back to normal. So people could see we're not afraid."

"How's that going?"

Monica took a step toward her, then hugged her books to her chest to cover up most of the labels, and hurried on.

She hadn't gotten ten feet before a stranger ran up and slapped a label across her back that had a picture of a slender young girl and an older boy of maybe fifteen on it. The words beneath said KILLER OF ALYSSA.

With a shock, Claire realized that the boy in that picture was *Shane*. And that was his sister, Alyssa, the one who'd died in the fire that Monica had set.

"Justice," Claire repeated softly. She felt a little sick, actually. Justice wasn't the same thing as mercy.

Her phone rang as she was trying to decide what to do. "Better come home," Michael Glass said. "We've got an emergency signal from Richard at City Hall."

TWELVE

The signal had come over the coded strategy network, which Claire had just assumed was dead, considering that Oliver had been the one running it. But Richard had found a use for it, and as she burst in the front door, breathless, she heard Michael and Eve talking in the living room. Claire closed and locked the door, dumped her backpack, and hurried to join them.

"What did I miss?"

"Shhh," they both said. Michael, Eve, and Shane were all seated at the table, staring intently at the small walkie-talkie sitting upright in the middle. Michael pulled out a chair for Claire, and she sat, trying to be as quiet as possible.

Richard was talking.

—No telling whether or not this storm will hit us full on, but right now, the Weather Service shows the radar track going right over the top of us. It'll be here in the next few hours, probably right around dark. It's late in the year for tornado activity, but they're telling us there's a strong possibility of some real trouble. On top of all the other things we have going on, this isn't good news. I'm putting all emergency services and citizen patrols on full alert. If we get a tornado, get to your designated shelters.

Designated shelters? Claire mouthed to Michael, who shrugged.

If you're closer to City Hall, come here; we've got a shelter in the basement. Those of you who are Civil Defense wardens, go door-to-door in your area, tell people we've got a storm coming and what to do. We're putting it on TV and radio, and the university's going to get ready as well.

"Richard, this is Hector," said a new voice. "Miller House. You got any news about this takeover people are talking about?"

"We've got rumors, but nothing concrete," Richard said. "We hear there's a lot of talk going around town about taking back City Hall, but we've got no specific word about when these people are meeting, or where, or even who they are. All I can tell you is that we've fortified the building, and the barricades remain up around Founder's Square, for all the good that does. I need everybody in a security-designated location to be on the alert today and tonight. Report in if you see any sign of an attack, any sign at all. We'll try to get to you in support."

Michael exchanged a look with the rest of them, and then picked up the radio. He pressed the button. "Michael Glass. You think Bishop's behind this?"

"I think Bishop's willing to let humans do his dirty work for him, and then sweep in to make himself lord and master on the ashes," Richard said. "Seems like his style. Put Shane on."

Michael held out the radio. Shane looked at it like it might bite, then took it and pressed TALK. "Yeah, this is Shane."

"I have two unconfirmed sightings of your father in town. I know this isn't easy for you, but I need to know: is Frank Collins back in Morganville?"

Shane looked into Claire's eyes and said, "If he is, he hasn't talked to me about it."

He *lied.* Claire's lips parted, and she almost blurted something out, but she just couldn't think what to say. "Shane," she whispered. He shook his head.

"Tell you what, Richard, you catch my dad, you've got my personal endorsement for tossing him in the deepest pit you've got around here," Shane said. "If he's in Morganville, he's got a plan, but he won't be working for or with the vamps. Not that he knows, anyway."

"Fair enough. You hear from him—"

"You're on speed dial. Got it." Shane set the radio back in the center of the table. Claire kept staring at him, willing him to speak, to say *something*, but he didn't.

"Don't do this," she said. "Don't put me in the middle."

"I'm not," Shane said. "Nothing I said was a lie. My dad told me he was coming, not that he's here. I haven't seen him, and I don't want to. I meant what I said. If he's here, Dick and his brownshirts are welcome to him. I've got nothing to do with him, not anymore."

Claire wasn't sure she believed that, but she didn't think he was intentionally lying now. He probably did mean it. She just thought that no matter how much he thought he was done with his dad, all it would take would be a snap of Frank Collins's fingers to bring him running.

Not good.

Richard was answering questions from others on the radio, but Michael was no longer listening. He was fixed on Shane. "You knew? You knew he was coming back here, and you didn't warn me?"

Shane stirred uneasily. "Look—"

"No, *you* look. I'm the one who got knifed and decapitated and buried in the *backyard*, among other things! Good thing I was a ghost!"

Shane looked down. "Who was I supposed to tell? The vamps? Come on."

"You could have told me!"

"You're a vamp," Shane said. "In case you haven't checked the mirror lately."

Michael stood up. His chair slid about two feet across the floor and skidded to an uneven stop; he leaned his hands on the table and loomed over Shane. "Oh, I do," he said. "I check it every day. How about you? You taken a good look recently, Shane? Because I'm not so sure I know you anymore."

Shane looked up at that, and there was a flash of pain in his face. "I didn't mean—"

"I could be just about the last vampire around here," Michael interrupted. "Maybe the others are dead. Maybe they will be soon. Between the mobs out there willing to rip our heads off and Bishop waiting to take over, having your dad stalking me is all I need."

"He wouldn't—"

"He killed me once, or tried to. He'd do it again in a second, and he wouldn't blink, and you know that, Shane. You know it! He thinks I'm some kind of a traitor to the human race. He'll come after me in particular."

Shane didn't say anything this time. Michael retrieved the radio from the table and clipped it to the pocket of his jeans. He shone, all blazing gold and hard, white angles, and Shane couldn't meet his stare.

"You decide you want to help your dad kill some vampires, Shane, you know where to find me."

Michael went upstairs. It was as if the room had lost all its air, and Claire found herself breathing very hard, trying not to tremble.

Eve's dark eyes were very wide, and fixed on Shane as well. She slowly got up from the table.

"Eve—" he said, and reached out toward her. She stepped out of reach.

"I can't believe you," she said. "You see me running over to suck up to my mom? No. And she's not even a murderer."

"Morganville needs to change."

"Wake up, Shane, it *has*! It started months ago. It's been changing right in front of you! Vampires and humans working together. Trusting one another. They're *trying*. Sure, it's hard, but they've got reason to be afraid of us, good reason. And now you want to throw all that away and help your dad set up a guillotine in Founder's Square or something?" Eve's eyes turned bitter black. "Screw you."

"I didn't—"

She clomped away toward the stairs, leaving Shane and Claire together.

Shane swallowed, then tried to make it a joke. "That could have gone better." Claire slipped out of her chair. "Claire? Oh, come on, not you, too. Don't go. Please."

"You should have told him. I can't believe you didn't. He's your friend, or at least I thought he was."

"Where are you going?"

She pulled in a deep breath. "I'm packing. I've decided to move in with my parents."

She didn't pack, though. She went upstairs, closed the door to her room, and pulled out her pitifully few possessions. Most of it was dirty laundry. She sat there on the bed, staring at it, feeling lost and alone and a little sick, and wondered if she was making a point or just running like a little girl. She felt pretty stupid now that she had everything piled on the floor.

It looked utterly pathetic.

When the knock came on her door, she didn't immediately answer it. She knew it was Shane, even though he didn't speak. *Go away,* she thought at him, but he still wasn't much of a mind reader. He knocked again.

"It's not locked," she said.

"It's also not open," Shane said quietly, through the wood. "I'm not a complete ass."

"Yes, you are."

"Okay, sometimes I am." He hesitated, and she heard the floor creak as he shifted his weight. "Claire."

"Come in."

He froze when he saw the stuff piled in front of her, waiting to be put in bags and her one suitcase. "You're serious."

"Yes."

"You're just going to pick up and leave."

"You know my parents want me to come home."

He didn't say anything for a long moment, then reached into his back pocket and took out a black case, about the size of his hand. "Here, then. I was going to give it to you later, but I guess I'd better do it now, before you take off on us."

His voice sounded offhand and normal, but his fingers felt cold when she touched them in taking the case, and there was an expression on his face she didn't know—fear, maybe; bracing himself for something painful.

It was a hard, leather-wrapped case, on spring hinges. She hesitated for a breath, then pried up one end. It snapped open.

Oh.

The cross was beautiful—delicate silver, traceries of leaves wrapped around it. It was on a silver chain so thin it looked like a breath would melt it. When Claire picked up the necklace, it felt like air in her hand.

"I—" She had no idea what to say, what to feel. Her whole body seemed to have gone into shock. "It's beautiful."

"I know it doesn't work against the vamps," Shane said. "Okay, well, I didn't know that when I got it for you. But it's still silver, and silver works, so I hope that's okay."

This wasn't a small present. Shane didn't have a lot of money; he picked up odd jobs here and there, and spent very little. This wasn't some cheap costume jewelry; it was real silver, and really beautiful.

"I can't—it's too expensive." Claire's heart was pounding again, and she wished she could *think.* She wished she knew what she was supposed to feel, supposed to do. On impulse, she put the necklace back in the box and snapped it shut, and held it out to him. "Shane, I can't."

He gave her a broken sort of smile. "It's not a ring or anything. Keep it. Besides, it doesn't match my eyes."

He stuck his hands in his pockets, rounded his shoulders, and walked out of the room.

Claire clutched the leather box in one sweaty hand, eyes wide, and then opened it again. The cross gleamed on black velvet, clean and beautiful and shining, and it blurred as her eyes filled with tears.

Now she felt something, something big and overwhelming and far too much to fit inside her small, fragile body.

"Oh," she whispered. "Oh *God.*" This hadn't been just any gift. He'd put a lot of time and effort into getting it. There was love in it, real love.

She took the cross, put it around her neck, and fastened the clasp with shaking fingers. It took her two tries. Then she went down the hall and, without knocking, opened Shane's door. He was standing at the window, staring outside. He looked different to her. Older. Sadder.

He turned toward her, and his gaze fixed on the silver cross in the hollow of her throat.

"You're an idiot," Claire said.

Shane considered that, and nodded. "I really am, mostly."

"And then you have to go and do these awesome things—"

"I know. I did say I was *mostly* an idiot."

"You kind of have your good moments."

He didn't quite smile. "So you like it?"

She put her hand up to stroke the cross's warm silver lines. "I'm wearing it, aren't I?"

"Not that it means we're—"

"You said you loved me," Claire said. "You did say that."

He shut his mouth and studied her, then nodded. There was a flush building high in his cheeks.

"Well, I love you, too, and you're still an idiot. Mostly."

"No argument." He folded his arms across his chest, and she tried not to notice the way his muscles tensed, or the vulnerable light in his eyes. "So, you moving out?"

"I should," she said softly. "The other night—"

"Claire. Please be straight with me. Are you moving out?"

She was holding the cross now, cradling it, and it felt warm as the sun against her fingers. "I can't," she said. "I have to do laundry first, and that might take a month. You saw the pile."

He laughed, and it was as if all the strength went out of him. He sat down on his unmade bed, hard, and after a moment, she walked around the end and sat next to him. He put his arm around her.

"Life is a work in progress," Shane said. "My mom used to say that. I'm kind of a fixer-upper. I know that."

Claire sighed and allowed herself to relax against his warmth. "Good thing I like high-maintenance guys."

He was about to kiss her—finally—when they both heard a sound from overhead.

Only there was nothing overhead. Nothing but the attic.

"Did you hear that?" Shane asked.

"Yeah. It sounded like footsteps."

"Oh, well, that's fantastic. I thought it was supposed to be exit-only or something." Shane reached under his bed and came up with a stake. "Go get Michael and Eve. Here." He handed her another stake. This one had a silver tip. "It's the Cadillac of vampire killers. Don't dent it."

"You are so weird." But she took it, and then dashed to her room to grab the thin silver knife Amelie had given her. No place to put it, but she poked a hole in the pocket of her jeans just big enough for the blade. The jeans were tight enough to keep the blade in place against her leg, but not so much it looked obvious, and besides, it was pretty flexible.

She hurried down the hall, listening for any other movement. Eve's room was empty, but when she knocked on Michael's door, she heard a startled yelp that sounded very Eve-like. "What?" Michael asked.

"Trouble," Claire said. "Um, maybe? Attic. Now."

Michael didn't sound any happier about it than Shane had been. "Great. Be there in a second."

Muffled conversation, and the sound of fabric moving. Claire wondered if he was getting dressed, and quickly tried to reject that image, not because it wasn't awesomely hot, but because, well, it was *Michael*, and besides, there were other things to think about.

Such as what was upstairs in the attic.

Or who.

The door banged open, and Eve rushed out, flushed and mussed and still buttoning her shirt. "It's not what you think," she said. "It was just—oh, okay, whatever, it was exactly what you think. Now, *what?*"

Something dropped and rolled across the attic floor directly above their heads. Claire silently pointed up, and Eve followed the motion, staring as if she could see through the wood and plaster. She jumped when Michael, who'd thrown on an unbuttoned shirt, put a hand on her shoulder. He put a finger to his lips.

Shane stepped out of his room, holding a stake in either hand. He pitched one underhand to Michael.

Where's mine? Eve mouthed.

Get your own, Shane mouthed back. Eve rolled her eyes and dashed into her own room, coming back with a black bag slung across her chest, bandolier-style. It was, Claire assumed, full of weapons. Eve fished around in it and came up with a stake of her very own. It even had her initials carved in it.

"Shop class," she whispered. "See? I *did* learn something in school."

Michael pressed the button to release the hidden door, and it opened without a sound. There were no lights upstairs that Claire could see. The stairs were pitch-black.

Michael, by common consent, went first, vampire eyes, and all. Shane followed, then Eve; Claire brought up the rear, and tried to move as silently as possible, although not really all that silently, because the stairs creaked beneath the weight of four people. At the top, Claire ran into Eve's back, and whispered, "What?"

Eve, in answer, reached back to grip her hand. "Michael smells blood," she whispered. "Hush."

Michael flicked on a light at the other end of the small, silent room. There was nothing unusual, just the furniture that was always here. There were no signs anybody had been here since the Goldmans and Myrnin had departed.

"How do we get into the attic?" Shane asked. Michael pressed hidden studs, and another door, barely visible at that end of the room, clicked open. Claire remembered it well; Myrnin had shown it to her, when they'd been getting stuff together to go to Bishop's welcome feast.

"Stay here," Michael said, and stepped through into the dim, open space.

"Yeah, sure," Shane said, and followed. He popped his head back in to say, "No, not you two. Stay here."

"Does he just not get how unfair and sexist that is?" Eve asked. "Men."

"You really want to go first?"

"Of course not. But I'd like the chance to *refuse* to go first."

They waited tensely, listening for any sign of trouble. Claire heard Shane's footsteps moving through the attic, but nothing else for a long time.

Then she heard him say, "Michael. Oh man . . . over here." There was tension in his voice, but it didn't sound like he was about to jump into hand-to-hand combat.

Eve and Claire exchanged looks, and Eve said, "Oh, screw it," and dived into the attic after them.

Claire followed, gripping the Cadillac of stakes and hoping she wasn't going to be forced to try to use it.

Shane was crouched down behind some stacked, dusty suitcases, and Michael was there, too. Eve pulled in a sharp breath when she saw what it was they were bending over, and put out a hand to stop Claire in her tracks.

Not that Claire stopped, until she saw who was lying on the wooden floor. She hardly recognized him, really. If it hadn't been for the gray ponytail and the leather coat . . .

"It's Oliver," she whispered. Eve was biting her lip until it was almost white, staring at her former boss. "What *happened?*"

"Silver," Michael said. "Lots of it. It eats vampire skin like acid, but he shouldn't be this bad. Not unless—" He stopped as the pale, burned eyelids fluttered. "He's still alive."

"Vampires are hard to kill," Oliver whispered. His voice was barely a creak of sound, and it broke at the end on what sounded almost like a sob. "*Jesu.* Hurts."

Michael exchanged a look with Shane, then said, "Let's get him downstairs. Claire. Go get some blood from the fridge. There should be some."

"No," Oliver grated, and sat up. There was blood leaking through his white shirt, as if all his skin were gone underneath. "No time. Attack on

City Hall, coming tonight—Bishop. Using it as a—diversion—to—"
His eyes opened wider, and went blank, then rolled up into his head.

He collapsed. Michael caught him under the shoulders.

He and Shane carried Oliver out to the couch, while Eve anxiously followed along, making little shooing motions.

Claire started to follow, then heard something scrape across the wood behind her, in the shadows.

Oliver hadn't come here alone.

A black shadow lunged out, grabbed her, and something hard hit her head.

She must have made some sound, knocked something over, because she heard Shane call her name sharply, and saw his shadow in the doorway before darkness took all of it away.

Then she was falling away.

Then she was gone.

THIRTEEN

Claire came awake feeling sick, wretched, and cold. Someone was pounding on the back of her head with a croquet mallet, or at least that was how it felt, and when she tried to move, the whole world spun around.

"Shut up and stop moaning," somebody said from a few feet away. "Don't you dare throw up or I'll make you eat it."

It sounded like Jason Rosser, Eve's crazy brother. Claire swallowed hard and squinted, trying to make out the shadow next to her. Yeah, it looked like Jason—skanky, greasy, and insane. She tried to squirm away from him, but ran into a wall at her back. It felt like wood, but she didn't think it was the Glass House attic.

He'd taken her somewhere, probably using the portal. And now none of her friends could follow, because none of them knew how.

Her hands and feet were tied. Claire blinked, trying to clear her head. That was a little unfortunate, because with clarity came the awareness of just how bad this was. Jason Rosser really *was* crazy. He'd stalked Eve. He'd—at least allegedly—killed girls in town. He'd definitely stabbed Shane, and he'd staked Amelie at the feast when she'd tried to help him.

And none of her friends back at the Glass House would know how to find her. To their eyes, she would have just . . . vanished.

"What do you want?" she asked. Her voice sounded rusty and scared. Jason reached out and moved hair back from her face, which creeped her out. She didn't like him touching her.

"Relax, shortcake, you're not my type," he said. "I do what I'm told, that's all. You were wanted. So I brought you."

"Wanted?"

A low, silky laugh floated on the silence, dark as smoke, and Jason looked over his shoulder as the hidden observer rose and stepped into what little light there was.

Ysandre, Bishop's pale little girlfriend. Beautiful, sure. Delicate as jasmine flowers, with big, liquid eyes and a sweetly rounded face.

She was poison in a pretty bottle.

"Well," she said, and crouched down next to Claire. "Look at what the cat dragged in. Meeow." Her sharp nail dragged over Claire's cheek, and judging from the sting, it drew blood. "Where's your pretty boyfriend, Miss Claire? I really wasn't done with him, you know. I hadn't even properly *started*."

Claire felt an ugly lurch of anger mix with the fear already churning her stomach. "He's probably not done with you, either," she said, and managed to smile. She hoped it was a cold kind of smile, the sort that Amelie used—or Oliver. "Maybe you should go looking. I'll bet he'd be *so* happy to see you."

"I'll show that boy a real good time, when we do meet up again," Ysandre purred, and put her face very close to Claire's. "Now, then, let's talk, just us girls. Won't that be fun?"

Not. Claire was struggling against the ropes, but Jason had done his job pretty well; she was hurting herself more than accomplishing anything else. Ysandre grabbed Claire's shoulder and wrenched her upright against the wooden wall, hard enough to bang Claire's injured head. For a dazed second, it looked like Ysandre's ripe, red smile floated in midair, like some undead Cheshire cat.

"Now," Ysandre said, "ain't this nice, sweetie? It's too bad we couldn't get Mr. Shane to join us, but my little helper here, he's a bit worried about tackling Shane. Bad blood and all." She laughed softly. "Well, we'll make do. Amelie likes you, I hear, and you've got on that pretty little gold bracelet. So you'll do just fine."

"For what?"

"I ain't telling you, sweetie." Ysandre's smile was truly scary. "This town's going to have a wild night, though. Real wild. And you're going to get to see the whole thing, up close. You must be all atingle."

Eve would have had a quip at the ready. Claire just glared, and wished her head would stop aching and spinning. What had he hit her with? It felt like the front end of a bus. She hadn't thought Jason could hit that hard, truthfully.

Don't try to find me, Shane. Don't. The last thing she wanted was Shane racing to the rescue and taking on a guy who'd stabbed him, and a vampire who'd led him around by a leash.

No, she had to find her own way out of this.

Step one: figure out where she was. Claire let Ysandre ramble on, describing all kinds of lurid things that Claire thought it was better not to imagine, considering they were things Ysandre was thinking of doing to *her.* Instead, she tried to identify her surroundings. It didn't look familiar, but that was no help; she was still relatively new to Morganville. Plenty of places she'd never been.

Wait.

Claire focused on the crate that Jason was sitting on. There was stenciling on it. It was hard to make it out in the dim light, but she thought it said BRICKS BULK COFFEE. And now that she thought about it, it smelled like coffee in here, too. A warm, morning kind of smell, floating over dust and damp wood.

And she remembered Eve laughing about how Oliver bought his coffee from a place called Bricks. *As in, tastes like ground-up bricks,* Eve had said. *If you order flavored, they add in the mortar.*

There were only two coffee shops in town: Oliver's place, and the University Center coffee bar. This didn't look like the UC, which wasn't that old and was mostly built of concrete, not wood.

That meant . . . she was at Common Grounds? But Common Grounds didn't make any sense; there wasn't any kind of portal leading to it.

Maybe Oliver has a warehouse. That sounded right, because the vampires seemed to own a lot of the warehouse district that bordered Founder's Square. Brandon, Oliver's second-in-vampire-command, had been found dead in a warehouse.

Maybe she was close to Founder's Square.

Ysandre's cold fingers closed around Claire's chin and jerked it up. "Are you listening, honey?"

"Truthfully, no," Claire said. "You're kind of boring."

Jason actually laughed, and turned it into a fake cough. "I'm going outside," he said. "Since this is going to get all personal now." Claire wanted to yell to him not to go, but she bit her tongue and turned it into a subsonic whine in the back of her throat as she watched him walk away. His footsteps receded into the dark, and then finally a small square of light opened a long way off.

It was a door, too far for her to reach—way too far.

"I thought he'd never leave," Ysandre said, and put her cold, cold lips on Claire's neck, then yelled in shock and pulled away, covering her mouth with one pale hand. "You *bitch!*"

Ysandre hadn't seen the silver chain Claire was wearing in the dim light, as whisper-thin as it was. Now there were welts forming on the vampire's full lips—forming, breaking, and bleeding.

Fury sparked in Ysandre's eyes. Playtime was over.

As Claire squirmed away, the vampire followed at a lazy stroll. She wiped her burned lips and looked at the thin, leaking blood in distaste. "Tastes like silver. Disgusting. You've just ruined my good mood, little girl."

As she rolled, Claire felt something sharp dig into her leg. *The knife.* They'd found the stake, but she guessed their search hadn't exactly been thorough; Jason was too crazy, and Ysandre too careless and arrogant.

But the knife wasn't going to do her any good at all where it was, unless . . .

Ysandre lunged for her, a blur of white in the darkness, and Claire twisted and jammed her hip down at an awkward angle.

The knife slipped and tore through the fabric of her jeans—not much of it, just a couple of inches, but enough to slice open Ysandre's hand and arm as it reached for her, all the way to the bone.

Ysandre shrieked in real pain, and spun away. She didn't look so pretty now, and when she turned toward Claire again, from a respectful distance this time, she hissed at her with full cobra fangs extended. Her eyes were wild and bloodred, glowing like rubies.

Claire twisted, nearly yanking her elbow out of its joint, and managed to get the ropes around her wrist against the knife. She didn't have long; the shock wouldn't keep Ysandre at bay for more than a few seconds.

But getting a silver knife to cut through synthetic rope? That was going to take a while—a while she didn't have.

Claire sawed desperately, and got a little bit of give on the bonds— enough to *almost* get her hand into her pocket.

But not.

Ysandre grabbed her by the hair. "I'm going to destroy you for that."

The pain in her head was blinding. It felt like her scalp was being ripped off, and on top of that, the massive headache roared back to a new, sickening pulse.

Claire loosened the rope enough to plunge her aching hand into her pocket and grab the handle of the knife. She yanked it out of the tangle of fabric and held it at a trembling, handicapped *en garde*—still tied up, but whatever, she wasn't going to stop fighting, not *ever.*

Ysandre shrieked and let her go, which made no sense to Claire's con-fused, pain-shocked mind. *I didn't stab her yet. Did I?* Not that she wanted to stab anybody, even Ysandre. She just wanted—

What was going on?

Ysandre's body slammed down hard on the wooden floor, and Claire gasped and flinched away . . . but the vampire had fallen facedown, limp, and weirdly broken.

A small woman dressed in gray, her pale hair falling wild around her shoulders, dropped silently from overhead and put one impeccably lovely gray pump in the center of Ysandre's back, holding her down as she tried to move.

"Claire?" The woman's face turned toward her, and Claire blinked twice before she realized whom she was looking at.

Amelie. But not Amelie. Not the cool, remote Founder—this woman had a wild, furious energy to her that Claire had never seen before. And she looked *young.*

"I'm okay," she said faintly, and tried to decide whether this version of Amelie was really here, or a function of her smacked-around brain. She decided it would be a good idea to get her hands and feet untied before figuring anything else out.

That took long minutes, during which Amelie (really?) dragged Ysandre, whimpering, into the corner and fastened her wrists to a massive crossbeam with chains. The chains, Claire registered, had been there all along. Lovely. This was some kind of vamp playpen/storage locker—probably Oliver's. And she felt sick again, thinking about it. Claire sawed grimly at the ropes binding her and finally parted one complete twist around her hands. As she struggled out of the loops of rope, she saw deep white imprints in her skin, and realized that her hands were red and swollen. She could still feel them, at least, and the burn of circulation returning felt as if she were holding them over an open flame.

She focused on slicing the increasingly dulled knife through the rope on her feet, but it was no use.

"Here," Amelie said, and bent down to snap the rope with one twist of her fingers. It was *so* frustrating, after all that hard work, to see just how easy it was for her. Claire stripped the ties away and sat for a moment breathing hard, starting to feel every cut, bump, and bruise on her body.

Amelie's cool fingers cupped Claire's chin and forced her head up, and the vampire's gray eyes searched hers. "You have a head injury," Amelie said. "I don't think it's too serious. A headache and some dizziness, perhaps." She let go. "I expected to find you. I did not expect to find you *here,* I confess."

Amelie looked *fine.* Not a prisoner. Not a scratch on her, in fact. Claire had lots more damage, and she hadn't been dragged off as Bishop's prisoner. . . .

Wait. "You—we thought Bishop might have gotten you. But he didn't, did he?"

Amelie cocked an eyebrow at her. "Apparently not."

"Then where did you go?" Claire felt a completely useless urge to lash out at her, crack that extreme cool. "Why did you *do this*? You left us alone! And you called the vampires out of hiding—" Her voice failed her for a second as she thought about Officer O'Malley, and the others she'd heard about. "You got some of them killed."

Amelie didn't respond to that. She simply stared back, as calm as an ice sculpture—calmer, because she wasn't melting.

"Tell me why," Claire said. "Tell me why you did that."

"Because plans change," Amelie replied. "As Bishop changes his moves, I must change mine. The stakes are too high now, Claire. I've lost half the vampires of Morganville to him. He's taking away my advantage, and I needed to draw them to me, for their own safety."

"You got *vampires* killed, not just humans. I know humans don't mean anything to you. But I thought the whole point of this was to save *your* people!"

"And so it is," Amelie said. "As many as can be saved. As for the call, there is a thing in chess known as a blitz attack, you see—a distraction, to cover the movement of more important pieces. You retrieved Myrnin and set him in play again; this was most important. I need my most powerful pieces on the board."

"Like Oliver?" Claire rubbed her hands together, trying to get the annoying tingle out of them. "He's hurt, you know. Maybe dying."

"He's served his purpose." Amelie turned her attention toward Ysandre, who was starting to stir. "It's time to take Bishop's rook, I believe."

Claire clutched the silver knife hard in her fist. "Is that all I am, too? Some kind of sacrifice pawn?"

That got Amelie's attention again. "No," she said in surprise. "Not entirely. I do care, Claire. But in war, you can't care too much. It paralyzes your ability to act." Those luminous eyes turned toward Ysandre again. "It's time for you to go, because I doubt you would enjoy seeing this. You won't be able to return here. I'm closing down nodes on the network. When I'm finished, there will be only two destinations: to me, or to Bishop."

"Where is he?"

"You don't know?" Amelie raised her eyebrows again. "He is where it is most secure, of course. At City Hall. And at nightfall, I will come against him. That's why I came looking for you, Claire. I need you to tell Richard. Tell him to get all those who can't fight for me out of the building."

"But—he *can't*. It's a storm shelter. There are supposed to be torna-does coming."

"Claire," Amelie said. "Listen to me. If innocents take refuge in that building, they will be killed, because I can't protect them anymore. We're at endgame now. There's no room for mercy." She looked again at Ysan-dre, who had gone very still, listening.

"Y'all wouldn't be saying this in front of me if I was going to walk out of here, would you?" Ysandre asked. She sounded calm now. Very still.

"No," Amelie said. "Very perceptive. I wouldn't." She took Claire by the arm and helped her to her feet. "I am relying on you, Claire. Go now. Tell Richard these are my orders."

Before Claire could utter another word, she felt the air shimmer in front of her, in the middle of the big warehouse room, and she fell . . . out over the dusty trunk in the Glass House attic, where Oliver had been. She sprawled ungracefully on top of it, then rolled off and got to her feet with a thump.

When she waved her hand through the air, looking for that strange heat shimmer of an open portal, she felt nothing at all.

I'm closing the portals, Amelie had said.

She'd closed this one, for sure.

"Claire?" Shane's voice came from the far end of the attic. He shoved aside boxes and jumped over jumbled furniture to reach her. "What hap-pened to you? Where did you go?"

"I'll tell you later," she said, and realized she was still holding the bloody silver knife. She carefully put it back in her pocket, in the make-shift holster against her leg. It was so dull she didn't think it would cut anything again, but it made her feel better. "Oliver?"

"Bad." Shane put his hands around her head and tilted it up, looking her over. "Is everything okay?"

"Define *everything*. No, define *okay*." She shook her head in frustration. "I need to get the radio. I have to talk to Richard."

Richard wasn't on the radio. "He's meeting with the mayor," said the man who answered. Sullivan, Claire thought his name was, but she hadn't really paid attention. "You got a problem there?"

"No, Officer, you've got a problem *there*," she said. "I need to talk to Richard. It's really important!"

"Everybody needs to talk to Richard," Sullivan said. "He'll get back to you. He's busy right now. If it's not an emergency response—"

"Yes, okay! It's an emergency!"

"Then I'll send units out to you. Glass House, right?"

"No, it's not—" Claire wanted to slam the radio down in frustration. "It's not an emergency *here*. Look, just tell Richard that he needs to clear everybody out of City Hall, as soon as possible."

"Can't do that," Sullivan said. "It's our center of operations. It's the main storm shelter, and we've got one heck of a storm coming tonight. You're going to have to give me a reason, miss."

"All right, it's because—"

Michael took the radio away from her and shut it off. Claire gaped, stuttered, and finally demanded, "Why?"

"Because if Amelie says Bishop's got himself installed in City Hall, somebody there has to know. We don't know who's on his team," Michael said. "I don't know Sullivan that well, but I know he never was happy with the way things ran in town. I wouldn't put it past him to be buying Bishop's crap about giving the city back to the people, home rule, all that stuff. Same goes for anybody else there, except maybe Joe Hess and Travis Lowe. We have to know who we're talking to before we say anything else."

Shane nodded. "I'm thinking that Sullivan's keeping Richard out of the loop for a reason."

They were downstairs, the four of them. Eve, Shane, and Claire were at the kitchen table, and Michael was pacing the floor and casting looks at the couch, where Oliver was. The older vampire was asleep, Claire guessed, or unconscious; they'd done what they could, washed him off and wrapped him in clean blankets. He was healing, according to Michael, but he wasn't doing it very fast.

When he'd woken up, he'd seemed distant. Confused.

Afraid.

Claire had given him one of the doses she'd gotten from Dr. Mills, and so far, it seemed to be helping, but if Oliver was sick, Myrnin's fears were becoming real.

Soon, it'd be Amelie, too. And then where would they be?

"So what do we do?" Claire asked. "Amelie said we have to tell Richard. We have to get noncombatants out of City Hall, as soon as possible."

"Problem is, you heard him giving instructions to the Civil Defense guys earlier—they're out telling everybody in town to *go* to City Hall if they can't make it to another shelter. Radio and TV, too. Hell, half the town is probably there already."

"Maybe she won't do it," Eve said. "I mean, she wouldn't kill *everybody* in there, would she? Not even if she thinks they're working for Bishop."

"I think it's gone past that," Claire said. "I don't know if she has any choice."

"There's always a choice."   ·

"Not in chess," Claire replied. "Unless your choice is to lie down and die."

In the end, the only way to be sure they got to the right person was to get in the car and drive there. Claire was a little shocked at the color of the sky outside—a solid gray, with clouds moving so fast it was like time-lapse on the Weather Channel. The edges looked faintly green, and in this part of the country, that was never a good sign.

The only good thing about it was that Michael didn't have to worry about getting scorched by sunlight. He brought a hoodie and a blanket to throw over his head, just in case, but it was dark outside, and getting darker fast. Premature sunset.

Drops of rain were smacking the sidewalk, the size of half-dollars. Where they hit Claire's skin, they felt like paintball pellets. As she looked up at the clouds, a horizontal flash of lightning peeled the sky in half, and thunder rumbled so loudly she felt it through the soles of her shoes.

"Come on!" Eve yelled, and started the car. Claire ran to open the backseat door and piled in beside Shane. Eve was already accelerating before she could fasten her seat belt. "Michael, get the radio."

He turned it on. Static. As he scanned stations, they got ghosts of signals from other towns, but nothing came through clearly in Morganville—probably because the vampires jammed it.

Then one came in, loud and clear, broadcasting on a loop.

Attention Morganville residents: this is an urgent public service announcement. The National Weather Service has identified an extremely dangerous storm tracking toward Morganville, which will reach our borders at six twenty-seven this evening at its present speed. This storm has already been responsible for devastation in several areas in its path, and there has been significant loss of life due to tornadic activity. Morganville and the surrounding areas are on tornado watch through ten p.m. this evening. If you hear an alert siren, go immediately to a designated Safe Shelter location, or to the safest area of your home if you cannot reach a Safe Shelter. Attention Morganville residents—

Michael clicked it off. There was no point in listening to the repeat; it wasn't going to get any better.

"How many Safe Shelters are there?" Shane asked. "University dorms have them, the UC—"

"Founder's Square has two," Michael said, "but nobody can get to them right now. They're locked up."

"Library."

"And the church. Father Joe would open up the basements, so that'll fit a couple of hundred people."

Everybody else would head to City Hall, if they didn't stay in their houses.

The rain started to fall in earnest, slapping the windshield at first, and then pounding it in fierce waves. The ancient windshield wipers really weren't up to it, even at high speed. Claire was glad she wasn't trying to drive. Even in clear visibility she wasn't very good, and she had no idea how Eve was seeing a thing.

If she was, of course. Maybe this was faith-based driving.

Other cars were on the road, and most of them were heading the same way they were. Claire looked at the clock on her cell phone.

Five thirty p.m.

The storm was less than an hour away.

"Uh-oh," Eve said, and braked as they turned the last corner. It was a sea of red taillights. Over the roll of thunder and pounding rain, Claire heard horns honking. Traffic moved, but slowly, one car at a time inching forward. "They're checking cars at the barricade. I can't believe—"

Something happened up there, and the brake lights began flicking off in steady rows. Cars moved. Eve fell into line, and the big, black sedan rolled past two police cars still flashing their lights. In the red/blue/red glow, Claire saw that they'd moved the barricades aside and were just waving everyone through.

"This is crazy," she said. "We can't get people out. Not fast enough! We'd have to stop everybody from coming in first, and then give them somewhere to go. . . ."

"I'm getting out of the car here," Michael said. "I can run faster than you can drive in this. I'll get to Richard. They won't dare stop me."

That was probably true, but Eve still said, "Michael, don't—"

Not that it stopped him from bailing out into the rain. A flash of lightning streaked by overhead and showed him splashing through thick puddles, weaving around cars.

He was right; he was faster.

Eve muttered something about "Stupid, stubborn, bloodsucking boyfriends," and followed the traffic toward City Hall.

Out of nowhere, a truck pulled out in front of them from a side street and stopped directly in their path. Eve yelled and hit the brakes, but they were mushy and wet, and not great at the best of times, and Claire felt the car slip and then slide, gathering speed as it went.

Glad I put on my seat belt, she thought, which was a weird thing to think, as Eve's car hydroplaned right into the truck. Shane stretched out his arm to hold her in place, anyway—instinct, Claire guessed—and then they all got thrown forward hard as physics took over.

Physics hurt.

Claire rested her aching head against the cool window—it was cracked, but still intact—and tried to shake it off. Shane was unhooking himself from the seat belt and asking her if she was okay. She made some kind of gesture and mumbled something, which she hoped would be good enough. She wasn't up to real reassurances at the moment.

Eve's door opened, and she got dragged out of the car.

"Hey!" Shane yelled, and threw himself out his own door. Claire fumbled at the latch, but hers seemed stuck; she navigated the push button on her seat belt and opted for Shane's side of the car instead.

As she stumbled out into the shockingly warm rain, she knew they were really in trouble now, because the man holding a knife to Eve's throat was Frank Collins, Shane's father and all-around badass, crazy vampire hater. He looked exactly like she remembered—tough, biker-hard, dressed in leather and tattoos.

He was yelling something at Eve, something Claire couldn't hear over the crash of thunder. Shane threw himself into a slide over the trunk of the car and grabbed at his dad's knife hand.

Dad elbowed him in the face and sent him staggering. Claire grabbed for the silver knife in her jeans, but it was gone—she'd dropped it somewhere. Before she could look for it, Shane was back in the fight, struggling with his dad. He moved the knife enough that Eve slid free and ran to grab on to Claire.

Frank shoved his son down on the hood of the car and raised the knife. He froze there, with rain pouring from his chin like a thin silver beard, and off the point of the knife.

"No!" Claire screamed. "No, don't hurt him!"

"Where's the vampire?" Frank yelled back. "Where is Michael Glass?"

"Gone," Shane said. He coughed away pounding rain. "Dad, he's gone. He's not here. *Dad.*"

Frank seemed to focus on his son for the first time. "Shane?"

"Yeah, Dad, it's me. Let me up, okay?" Shane was careful to keep his hands up, palms out in surrender. "Peace."

It worked. Frank stepped back and lowered the knife. "Good," he said. "I've been looking for you, boy." And then he hugged him. Shane still had his hands up, and froze in place without touching his father. Claire shivered at the look on his face.

"Yeah, good to see you, too," he said. "Back off, man. We're not close, in case you forgot."

"You're still my son. Blood is blood." Frank pushed him toward the truck, only lightly crushed where Eve's car had smacked it. "Get in."

"Why?"

"Because I said so!" Frank shouted. Shane just looked at him. "Dammit, boy, for once in your life, do what I tell you!"

"I spent most of my life doing what you told me," Shane said. "Including selling out my friends. Not happening anymore."

Frank's lips parted, temporarily amazed. He laughed.

"Done drunk the suicide cola, didn't you?" When he shook his head, drops flew in all directions, and were immediately lost in the silver downpour. "Just get in. I'm trying to save your life. You don't want to be where you're trying to go."

Strangely enough, Frank Collins was making sense. Probably for all the wrong reasons, though.

"We have to get through," Claire shouted over the pounding rain. She was shivering, soaked through every layer of clothing. "It's important. People could die if we don't!"

"People are going to die," Collins agreed. "Omelets and eggs. You know the old saying."

Or chess, Claire thought. Though she didn't know whose side Frank Collins was playing on, or even if he knew he was being manipulated at all.

"There's a plan," Frank was saying to his son. "In all this crap, no-body's checking faces. Metal detectors are off. We seize control of the building and make things right. We shuffle these bastards off, once and for all. We can *do it!*"

"Dad," Shane said, "everybody in that building tonight is going to be killed. We have to get people *out*, not get them *in*. If you care any-thing about those idiots who buy your revolutionary crap, you'll call this off."

"Call it off?" Frank repeated, as uncomprehending as if Shane were speaking another language. "When we're this close? When we can *win*? Dammit, Shane, you used to believe in this. You used to—"

"Yeah. Used to. Look it up!" Shane shoved his father away from him, and walked over to Eve and Claire. "I've warned you, Dad. Don't do this. Not today. I won't turn you in, but I'm telling you, if you don't back off, you're dead."

"I don't take threats," Frank said. "Not from you."

"You're an idiot," Shane said. "And I tried."

He got back in the car, on the passenger-side front seat where Michael had been. Eve scrambled behind the wheel, and Claire in the back.

Eve reversed.

Frank stepped out into the road ahead of them, a scary-looking man in black leather with his straggling hair plastered around his face. Add in the big hunting knife, and cue the scary music.

Eve let up on the gas. "No," Shane said, and moved his left foot over to jam it on top of hers. "Go. He wants you to stop."

"Don't! I can't miss him, no—"

But it was too late. Frank was staring into the headlights, squarely in the center of the hood, and he was getting closer and closer.

Frank Collins threw himself out of the way at the last possible sec-ond, Eve swerved wildly in the opposite direction to miss him, and some-how, they didn't kill Shane's dad.

"What the hell are you *doing*?" Eve yelled at Shane. She was shaking all over. So was Shane. "You want to run him over, do it on your own time! *God!*"

"Look behind you," Shane whispered.

There were people coming after them. A *lot* of people. They'd been hiding in the alley, Claire guessed. They had guns, and now they opened fire. The car shuddered, and the back window exploded into cracks, then fell with a crash all over Claire's neck.

"Get up here!" Shane said, and grabbed her hands to haul her into the front seat. "Keep your head down!"

Eve had sunk down on the driver's side, barely keeping her eyes above the dashboard. She was panting hoarsely, panicked, and more gunshots were rattling the back of the car. Something hit the front window, too, adding more cracks and a round, backward splash of a hole.

"Faster!" Shane yelled. Eve hit the gas hard, and whipped around a slower-moving van. The firing ceased, at least for now. "You see why I didn't want you to stop?"

"Okay, your father is officially *off my Christmas list!*" Eve yelled. "Oh my God, look at my car!"

Shane barked out a laugh. "Yeah," he agreed. "That's what's important."

"It's better than thinking about what would have happened," Eve said. "If Michael had been with us—"

Claire thought about the mobs Richard had talked about, and the dead vampires, and felt sick. "They'd have dragged him off," she said. "They'd have killed him."

Michael had been right about Shane's dad, but then, Claire had never really doubted it. Neither had Shane, from the sick certainty on his face. He wiped his eyes with his forearm, which really didn't help much; they were all dripping wet, from head to toe.

"Let's just get to the building," Shane said. "We can't do much until we find Richard."

Only it wasn't that simple, even getting in. The underground parking was crammed full of cars, parked haphazardly at every angle. As Eve inched through the shadows, looking for any place to go, she shook her head. "If we do manage to get people to leave, they won't be able to take their cars. Everybody's blocked in," she said. "This is massively screwed up." Claire, for her part, thought some of it seemed deliberate, not just panic. "Okay, I'm going to pull it against the wall and hope we can get out if we need to."

The elevator was already locked down, the doors open but the lights off and buttons unresponsive. They took the stairs at a run.

The first-floor door seemed to be locked, until Shane pushed on it harder, and then it creaked open against a flood of protests.

The vestibule was full of people.

Morganville's City Hall wasn't all that large, at least not here in the lobby area. There was a big, sweeping staircase leading up, all grand marble and polished wood, and glass display cases taking up part of one wall. The License Bureau was off to the right: six old-time bank windows, with bars, all closed. Next to each window was a brass plaque that read what the windows were supposed to deliver: RESIDENTIAL LICENSING, CAR REGISTRATION, ZONING CHANGE REQUESTS, SPECIAL PERMITS, TRAFFIC VIOLATIONS, FINE PAYMENTS, TAXES, CITY SERVICES.

But not today.

The lobby was jammed with people. Families, mostly—mothers and fathers with kids, some as young as infants. Claire didn't see a single vampire in the crowd, not even Michael. At the far end, a yellow Civil Defense sign indicated that the door led to a Safe Shelter, with a tornado graphic next to it. A policeman with a bullhorn was yelling for order, not that he was getting any; people were pushing, shoving, and shouting at one another. "The shelter is now at maximum capacity! Please be calm!"

"Not good," Shane said. There was no sign of Richard, although there were at least ten uniformed police officers trying to manage the crowd. "Upstairs?"

"Upstairs," Eve agreed, and they squeezed back into the fire stairs and ran up to the next level. The sign in the stairwell said that this floor contained the mayor's office, sheriff's office, city council chambers, and something called, vaguely, Records.

The door was locked. Shane rattled it and banged for entrance, but nobody came to the rescue.

"Guess we go up," he said.

The third floor had no signs in the stairwell at all, but there was a symbol—the Founder's glyph, like the one on Claire's bracelet. Shane turned the knob, but again, the door didn't open. "I didn't think they could do that to fire stairs," Eve said.

"Yeah, call a cop." Shane looked up the steps. "One more floor, and then it's just the roof, and I'm thinking that's not a good idea, the roof."

"Wait." Claire studied the Founder's glyph for a few seconds, then shrugged and reached out to turn the knob.

Something clicked, and it turned. The door opened.

"How did you . . . ?"

Claire held up her wrist, and the gold bracelet. "It was worth a shot. I thought, maybe with a gold bracelet—"

"Genius. Go on, get inside," Shane said, and hustled them in. The door clicked shut behind them, and locked with a snap of metal. The hallway seemed dark, after the fluorescent lights in the stairs, and that was because the lights were dimmed way down, the carpet was dark, and so was the wood paneling.

It reminded Claire eerily of the hallway where they'd rescued Myrnin, only there weren't as many doors opening off it. Shane took the lead—of course—but the doors they could open were just simple offices, nothing fancy about them at all.

And then there was a door at the end of the hall with the Founder's Symbol etched on the polished brass doorknob. Shane tried it, shook his head, and motioned for Claire.

It opened easily at her touch.

Inside were—apartments. Chambers? Claire didn't know what else to call them; there was an entire complex of rooms leading from one central area.

It was like stepping into a whole different world, and Claire could tell that it had once been beautiful: a fairy-tale room, of rich satin on the walls, Persian rugs, delicate white and gold furniture.

"Michael? Mayor Morrell? Richard?"

It was a queen's room, and somebody had completely wrecked it. Most of the furniture was overturned, some kicked to pieces. Mirrors smashed. Fabrics ripped.

Claire froze.

Lying on the remaining long, delicate sofa was François, Bishop's other loyal vampire buddy, who'd come to Morganville along with Ysandre as his entourage. The vampire looked completely at ease—legs crossed at the ankles, head propped on a plump satin pillow. A big crystal glass of something in dark red rested on his chest.

He giggled and saluted them with the blood. "Hello, little friends," he said. "We weren't expecting you, but you'll do. We're almost out of refreshments."

"Out," Shane said, and shoved Eve toward the door.

It slammed shut before she could reach it, and there stood Mr. Bishop, still dressed in his long purple cassock from the feast. It was still torn on the side, where Myrnin had slashed at him with the knife.

There was something so ancient about him, so completely uncaring, that Claire felt her mouth go dry. "Where is she?" Bishop asked. "I know you've seen my daughter. I can smell her on you."

"Ewww," Eve said, very faintly. "So much more than I needed to know."

Bishop didn't look away from Claire's face, just pointed at Eve. "Silence, or be silenced. When I want to know your opinion, I'll consult your entrails."

Eve shut up. François swung his legs over the edge of the sofa and sat up in one smooth motion. He downed the rest of his glass of blood and let the glass fall, shedding crimson drops all over the pale carpet. He'd gotten some on his fingers. He licked them, then smeared the rest all over the satin wall.

"Please," he said, and batted his long-lashed eyes at Eve. "Please, say something. I love entrails."

She shrank back against the wall. Even Shane stayed quiet, though Claire could tell he was itching to pull her to safety. *You can't protect me,* she thought fiercely. *Don't try.*

"You don't know where Amelie is?" Claire asked Bishop directly. "How's that master plan going, then?"

"Oh, it's going just fine," Bishop said. "Oliver is dead by now.

Myrnin—well, we both know that Myrnin is insane, at best, and homicidal at his even better. I'm rather hoping he'll come charging to your rescue and forget who you are once he arrives. That would be amusing, and very typical of him, I'm afraid." Bishop's eyes bored into hers, and Claire felt the net closing around her. "Where is Amelie?"

"Where you'll never find her."

"Fine. Let her lurk in the shadows with her creations, until hunger or the humans destroy them. This doesn't have to be a battle, you know. It can be a war of attrition just as easily. I have the high ground." He gestured around the ruined apartment with one lazy hand. "And of course, I have everyone here, whether they know it or not."

She didn't hear him move, but flinched as François trailed cold fingers across the back of her neck, then gripped her tightly.

"Just like that," Bishop said. "Just precisely like that." He nodded to François. "If you want her, take her. I'm no longer interested in Amelie's pets. Take these others, too, unless you wish to save them for later."

Claire heard Shane whisper, "No," and heard the complete despair in his voice just as Bishop's follower wrenched her head over to the side, baring her neck.

She felt his lips touch her skin. They burned like ice.

"Ah!" François jerked his head back. "You little peasant." He used a fold of her shirt to take hold of the silver chain around her neck, and broke it with a sharp twist.

Claire caught the cross in her hand as it fell.

"May it comfort you," Bishop said, and smiled. "My child."

And then François bit her.

"Claire?" Somewhere, a long way off, Eve was crying. "Oh my God, Claire? Can you hear me? Come on, please, *please* come back. Are you sure she's got a pulse?"

"Yes, she's got a pulse." Claire knew that voice. Richard Morrell. But why was he here? Who called the police? She remembered the accident with the truck—no, that was before.

Bishop.

Claire slowly opened her eyes. The world felt very far away, and safely muffled for the moment. She heard Eve let out a gasp and a flood of words, but Claire didn't try to identify the meaning.

I have a pulse.

That seemed important.

My neck hurts.

Because a vampire had bitten her.

Claire raised her left hand slowly to touch her neck, and found a huge wad of what felt like somebody's shirt pressed against her neck.

"No," Richard said, and forced her hand back down. "Don't touch it. It's still closing up. You shouldn't move for another hour or so. Let the wounds close."

"Bit," Claire murmured. "He bit me." That came in a blinding flash, like a red knife cutting through the fog. "Don't let me turn into one."

"You won't," Eve said. She was upside down—no, Claire's head was in her lap, and Eve was leaning over her. Claire felt the warm drip of Eve's tears on her face. "Oh, sweetie. You're going to be okay. Right?" Even upside down, Eve's look was panicked as she appealed to Richard, who sat on her right.

"You'll be all right," he said. He didn't look much better than Claire felt. "I have to see to my father. Here." He moved out of the way, and someone else sat in his place.

Shane. His warm fingers closed over hers, and she shivered when she realized how cold she felt. Eve tucked an expensive velvet blanket over and around her, fussing nervously.

Shane didn't say anything. He was so *quiet*.

"My cross," Claire said. It had been in her hand. She didn't know where it was now. "He broke the chain. I'm sorry—"

Shane opened her fingers and tipped the cross and chain into her hand. "I picked it up," he said. "Figured you might want it." There was something he wasn't saying. Claire looked at Eve to find out what it was, but she wasn't talking, for a change. "Anyway, you're going to be okay. We're lucky this time. François wasn't that hungry." He closed her fingers around the cross and held on.

His hands were shaking. "Shane?"

"I'm sorry," he whispered. "I couldn't move. I just *stood there*."

"No, he didn't," Eve said. "He knocked Franny clear across the room and he would have staked him with a chair leg, except Bishop stepped in."

That sounded like Shane. "You're not hurt?" Claire asked.

"Not much."

Eve frowned. "Well—"

"Not much," Shane repeated. "I'm okay, Claire."

She kind of had to take that at face value, at least right now. "What time—"

"Six fifteen," Richard said, from the far corner of the small room. This, Claire guessed, had been some kind of dressing area for Amelie. She saw a long closet to the side. Most of the clothes were shredded and scattered in piles on the floor. The dressing table was a ruin, and every mirror was broken.

François had had his fun in here, too.

"The storm's heading for us," Eve said. "Michael never got to Richard, but he got to Joe Hess, apparently. They evacuated the shelters. Bishop was pretty mad about that. He wanted a lot of hostages between him and Amelie."

"So all that's left is us?"

"Us. And Bishop's people, who didn't leave. And Fabulous Frank Collins and his Wild Bunch, who rolled into the lobby and now think they've won some kind of battle or something." Eve rolled her eyes, and for an instant was back to her old self. "Just us and the bad guys."

Did that make Richard—no. Claire couldn't believe that. If anyone in Morganville had honestly tried to do the right thing, it was Richard Morrell.

Eve followed Claire's look. "Oh. Yeah, his dad got hurt trying to stop Bishop from taking over downstairs. Richard's been trying to take care of him, and his mom. We were right about Sullivan, by the way. Total backstabber. Yay for premonitions. Wish I had one right now that could help get us out of this."

"No way out," Claire said.

"Not even a window," Eve said. "We're locked in here. No idea where Bishop and his little sock monkey got off to. Looking for Amelie, I guess. I wish they'd just kill each other already."

Eve didn't mean it, not really, but Claire understood how she felt. Distantly. In a detached, shocked kind of way.

"What's happening outside?"

"Not a clue. No radios in here. They took our cell phones. We're"— the lights blinked and failed, putting the room into pitch darkness— "screwed," Eve finished. "Oh man, I should not have said that, should I?"

"Power's gone out to the building, I think," Richard said. "It's probably the storm."

Or the vampires screwing with them, just because they could. Claire didn't say it out loud, but she thought it pretty hard.

Shane's hand kept holding hers. "Shane?"

"Right here," he said. "Stay still."

"I'm sorry. I'm really, really sorry."

"What for?"

"I shouldn't have gotten angry with you, before, about your dad. . . ."

"Not important," he said very softly. "It's okay, Claire. Just rest."

Rest? She couldn't rest. Reality was pushing back in, reminding her of pain, of fear, and most important, of time.

There was an eerie, ghostly sound now, wailing, and getting louder.

"What is that?" Eve asked, and then, before anybody could answer, did so herself. "Tornado sirens. There's one on the roof."

The rising, falling wail got louder, but with it came something else—a sound like water rushing, or—

"We need to get to cover," Richard said. A flashlight snapped on, and played over Eve's pallid face, then Shane's and Claire's. "You guys, get her over here. This is the strongest interior corner. That side faces out toward the street."

Claire tried to get up, but Shane scooped her in his arms and carried her. He set her down with her back against a wall, then got under the blanket next to her with Eve on his other side. The flashlight turned away from them, and in its sweep, Claire caught sight of Mayor Morrell. He was a fat man, with a politician's smooth face and smile, but he didn't look anything like she remembered now. He seemed older, shrunken inside his suit, and very ill.

"What's wrong with him?" Claire whispered.

Shane's answer stirred the damp hair around her face. "Heart attack," he said. "At least, that's Richard's best guess. Looks bad."

It really did. The mayor was propped against the wall a few feet from them, and he was gasping for breath as his wife (Claire had never seen her before, except in pictures) patted his arm and murmured in his ear. His face was ash gray, his lips turning blue, and there was real panic in his eyes.

Richard returned, dragging another thick blanket and some pillows. "Everybody cover up," he said. "Keep your heads down." He covered his mother and father and crouched next to them as he wrapped himself in another blanket.

The wind outside was building to a howl. Claire could hear things hitting the walls—dull thudding sounds, like baseballs. It got louder. "Debris," Richard said. He focused the light on the carpet between their small group. "Maybe hail. Could be anything."

The siren cut off abruptly, but that didn't mean the noise subsided; if anything, it got louder, ratcheting up from a howl to a scream—and then it took on a deeper tone.

"Sounds like a train," Eve said shakily. "Damn, I was really hoping that wasn't true, the train thing—"

"Heads down!" Richard yelled, as the whole building started to shake. Claire could feel the boards vibrating underneath her. She could see the walls bending, and cracks forming in the bricks.

And then the noise rose to a constant, deafening scream, and the whole outside wall sagged, dissolved into bricks and broken wood, and disappeared. The ripped, torn fabric around the room took flight like startled birds, whipping wildly through the air and getting shredded into ever-smaller sections by the wind and debris.

The storm was screaming as if it had gone insane. Broken furniture and shards of mirrors flew around, smashing into the walls, hitting the blankets.

Claire heard a heavy groan even over the shrieking wind, and looked up to see the roof sagging overhead. Dust and plaster cascaded down, and she grabbed Shane hard.

The roof came down on top of them.

Claire didn't know how long it lasted. It seemed like forever, really—the screaming, the shaking, the pressure of things on top of her.

And then, very gradually, it stopped, and the rain began to hammer down again, drenching the pile of dust and wood. Some of it trickled down to drip on her cheek, which was how she knew.

Shane's hand moved on her shoulder, more of a twitch than a conscious motion, and then he let go of Claire to heave up with both hands. Debris slid and rattled. They'd been lucky, Claire realized—a heavy wooden beam had collapsed in over their heads at a slant, and it had held the worst of the stuff off them.

"Eve?" Claire reached across Shane and grabbed her friend's hands. Eve's eyes were closed, and there was blood trickling down one side of her face. Her face was even whiter than usual—plaster dust, Claire realized.

Eve coughed, and her eyelids fluttered up. "Mom?" The uncertainty in her voice made Claire want to cry. "Oh God, what happened? Claire?"

"We're alive," Shane said. He sounded kind of surprised. He brushed fallen chunks of wood and plaster off Claire's head, and she coughed, too. The rain pounded in at an angle, soaking the blanket that covered them. "Richard?"

"Over here," Richard said. "Dad? Dad—"

The flashlight was gone, rolled off or buried or just plain taken away by the wind. Lightning flashed, bright as day, and Claire saw the tornado that had hit them still moving through Morganville, crashing through buildings, spraying debris a hundred feet into the air.

It didn't even look *real.*

Shane helped move a beam off Eve's legs—thankfully, they were just bruised, not broken—and crawled across the slipping wreckage toward Richard, who was lifting things off his mother. She looked okay, but she was crying and dazed.

His father, though . . .

"No," Richard said, and dragged his father flat. He started administering CPR. There were bloody cuts on his face, but he didn't seem to care about his own problems at all. "Shane! Breathe for him!"

After a hesitation, Shane tilted the mayor's head back. "Like this?"

"Let me," Eve said. "I've had CPR training." She crawled over and took in a deep breath, bent, and blew it into the mayor's mouth, watching for his chest to rise. It seemed to take a lot of effort. So did what Richard was doing, pumping on his dad's chest, over and over. Eve counted slowly, then breathed again—and again.

"I'll get help," Claire said. She wasn't sure there *was* any help, really, but she had to do something. When she stood up, though, she felt dizzy and weak, and remembered what Richard had said—she had holes in her neck, and she'd lost a lot of blood. "I'll go slow."

"I'll go with you," Shane said, but Richard grabbed him and pulled him down.

"No! I need you to take over here." He showed Shane how to place his hands, and got him started. He pulled the walkie-talkie from his belt and tossed it to Claire. "Go. We need paramedics."

And then Richard collapsed, and Claire realized that he had a huge piece of metal in his side. She stood there, frozen in horror, and then punched in the code for the walkie-talkie. "Hello? Hello, is anybody there?"

Static. If there was anybody, she couldn't hear it over the interference and the roaring rain.

"I have to go!" she shouted at Shane. He looked up.

"No!" But he couldn't stop her, not without letting the mayor die, and after one helpless, furious look at her, he went back to work.

Claire slid over the pile of debris and scrambled out the broken door, into the main apartment.

There was no sign of François or Bishop. If the place had been wrecked before, it was unrecognizable now. Most of this part of the building was gone, just—gone. She felt the floor groan underneath her, and moved fast, heading for the apartment's front door. It was still on its hinges, but as she pulled on it, part of the frame came out of the wall.

Outside, the hallway seemed eerily unmarked, except that the roof overhead—and, Claire presumed, all of the next floor above—was missing. It was a hallway open to the storm. She hurried along it, glad now for the flashes of lightning that lit her way.

The fire stairs at the end seemed intact. She passed some people huddled there, clearly terrified. "We need help!" she said. "There are people hurt upstairs—somebody?"

And then the screaming started, somewhere about a floor down, lots of people screaming at the same time. Those who were sitting on the stairs jumped to their feet and ran up, toward Claire. "No!" she yelled. "No, you can't!"

But she was shoved out of the way, and about fifty people trampled past her, heading up. She had no idea where they'd go.

Worse, she was afraid their combined weight would collapse that part of the building, including the place where Eve, Shane, and the Morrells were.

"Claire?" Michael. He came out of the first-floor door, and leaped two flights of stairs in about two jumps to reach her. Before she could protest, he'd grabbed her in his arms like an invalid. "Come on. I have to get you out of here."

"No! No, go up. Shane, they need help. Go up; leave me here!"

"I can't." He looked down, and so did she.

Vampires poured into the stairwell below. Some of them were fighting, ripping at one another. Any human who got between them went down screaming.

"Right. Up it is," he said, and she felt them leave the ground in one powerful leap, hitting the third-floor landing with catlike grace.

"What's happening?" Claire twisted to try to look down, but it didn't make any sense to her. It was just a mob, fighting one another. No telling who was on which side, or even why they were fighting so furiously.

"Amelie's down there," Michael said. "Bishop's trying to get to her, but he's losing followers fast. She took him by surprise, during the storm."

"What about the people—I mean, the humans? Shane's dad, and the ones who wanted to take over?"

Michael kicked open the door to the third-floor roofless hallway. The people who'd run past Claire were milling around in it, frightened and babbling. Michael brought down his fangs and snarled at them, and they scattered into whatever shelter they could reach—interior offices, mostly, that had sustained little damage except for rain.

He shoved past those who had nowhere to go, and down to the end of the hall. "In here?" He let Claire slide down to her feet, and his gaze focused on her neck. "Someone bit you."

"It's not so bad." Claire put her hand over the wound, trying to cover it up. The wound's edges felt ragged, and they were still leaking blood, she thought, although that could have just been the rain. "I'm okay."

"No, you're not."

A gust of wind blew his collar back, and she saw the white outlines of marks on his own neck. "Michael! Did you get bitten, too?"

"Like you said, it's nothing. Look, we can talk about that later. Let's get to our friends. First aid later."

Claire opened the door and stepped through . . . and the floor collapsed underneath her.

She must have screamed, but all she heard was the tremendous cracking sound of more of the building falling apart underneath and around her. She turned toward Michael, who was frozen in the doorway, illuminated in stark white by a nearby lightning strike.

He reached out and grabbed her arm as she flung it toward him, and then she was suspended in midair, wind and dust rushing up around her, as the floor underneath fell away. Michael pulled, and she almost flew, weightless, into his arms.

"Oh," she whispered faintly. "Thanks."

He held on to her for a minute without speaking, then said, "Is there another way in?"

"I don't know."

They backed up and found the next office to the left, which had suspicious-looking cracks in its walls. Claire thought the floor felt a little unsteady. Michael pushed her back behind him and said, "Cover your eyes."

Then he began ripping away the wall between the office and Amelie's apartments. When he hit solid red brick, he punched it, breaking it into dust.

"This isn't helping keep things together!" Claire yelled.

"I know, but we need to get them out!"

He ripped a hole in the wall big enough to step through, and braced himself in it as the whole building seemed to shudder, as if shifting its weight. "The floor's all right here," he said. "You stay. I'll go."

"Through that door, to the left!" Claire called. Michael disappeared, moving fast and gracefully.

She wondered, all of a sudden, why he wasn't downstairs. Why he wasn't fighting, like all the others of Amelie's blood.

A couple of tense minutes passed, as she stared through the hole; nothing seemed to be happening. She couldn't hear Michael, or Shane, or anything else.

And then she heard screaming behind her, in the hall. *Vampires*, she thought, and quickly opened the door to look.

Someone fell against the wood, knocking her backward. It was François. Claire tried to shut the door, but a bloodstained white hand wormed through the opening and grabbed the edge, shoving it wider.

François didn't look even remotely human anymore, but he did look absolutely desperate, willing to do anything to survive, and very, very angry.

Claire backed up, slowly, until she was standing with her back against the far wall. There wasn't much in here to help her—a desk, some pens and pencils in a cup.

François laughed, and then he growled. "You think you're winning," he said. "You're not."

"I think you're the one who has to worry," Michael said from the hole in the wall. He stepped through, carrying Mayor Morrell in his arms. Shane and Eve were with him, supporting Richard's sagging body between them. Mrs. Morrell brought up the rear. "Back off. I won't come after you if you run."

François' eyes turned ruby, and he threw himself at Michael, who was burdened with the mayor.

Claire grabbed a pencil from the cup and plunged it into François' back.

He whirled, looking stunned . . . and then he slowly collapsed to the carpet.

"That won't kill him," Michael said.

"I don't care," Eve said. "Because that was *fierce.*"

Claire grabbed the vampire's arms and dragged him out of the way, careful not to dislodge the pencil; she wasn't really sure how deep it had gone, and if it slipped out of his heart, they were all in big trouble. Michael edged around him and opened the door to check the corridor. "Clear," he said. "For the moment. Come on."

Their little refugee group hurried into the rainy hall, squishing through soggy carpet. There were people hiding in the offices, or just pressed against the walls and hoping not to be noticed. "Come on," Eve said to them. "Get up. We're getting out of here before this whole thing comes down!"

The fighting in the stairwell was still going on—snarling, screams, bangs, and thuds. Claire didn't dare look over the railing. Michael led them down to the locked second-floor entrance. He pulled hard on it, and the knob popped off—but the door stayed locked.

"Hey, Mike?" Shane had edged to the end of the landing to look over the railing. "Can't go that way."

"I know!"

"Also, time is—"

"I know, Shane!" Michael started kicking the door, but it was reinforced, stronger than the other doors Claire had seen. It bent, but didn't open.

And then it did open . . . from the inside.

There, in his fancy but battered black velvet, stood Myrnin.

"In," he said. "This way. Hurry."

The falling sensation warned Claire that the door was a portal, but she didn't have time to tell anybody else, so when they stepped through into Myrnin's lab, it was probably kind of a shock. Michael didn't pause; he pushed a bunch of broken glassware from a lab table and put Mr. Morrell down on it, then touched pale fingers to the man's throat. When he found nothing, he started CPR again. Eve hurried over to breathe for him.

Myrnin didn't move as the refugees streamed in past him. He was standing with his arms folded, a frown grooved between his brows. "Who are all these people?" he asked. "I am not an innkeeper, you know."

"Shut up," Claire said. She didn't have any patience with Myrnin right now. "Is he okay?" She was talking to Shane, who was easing Richard onto a threadbare rug near the far wall.

"You mean, except for the big piece of metal in him? Look, I don't know. He's breathing, at least."

The rest of the refugees clustered together, filtering slowly through the portal. Most of them had no idea what had just happened, which was good. If they'd been part of Frank's group, intending to take over Morganville, that ambition was long gone. Now they were just people, and they were just scared.

"Up the stairs," Claire told them. "You can get out that way."

Most of them rushed for the exit. She hoped they'd make it home, or at least to some kind of safe place.

She hoped they had homes to go back to.

Myrnin glared at her. "You do realize that this was a *secret* laboratory, don't you? And now half of Morganville knows where it is?"

"Hey, I didn't open the door; you did." She reached over and put her hand on his arm, looking up into his face. "Thank you. You saved our lives."

He blinked slowly. "Did I?"

"I know why you weren't fighting," Claire said. "The drugs kept you from having to. But . . . Michael?"

Myrnin followed her gaze to where Eve and Michael remained bent over the mayor's still form. "Amelie let him go," he said. "For now. She could claim him again at any time, but I think she knew you needed help." He uncrossed his arms and walked over to Michael to touch his shoulder. "It's no use," he said. "I can smell death on him. So can you, if you try. You won't bring him back."

"No!" Mrs. Morrell screamed, and threw herself over her husband's body. "No, you have to try!"

"They did," Myrnin said, and retreated to lean against a convenient wall. "Which is more than I would have." He nodded toward Richard. "He might live, but to remove that metal will require a chirurgeon."

"You mean, a doctor?" Claire asked.

"Yes, of course, a doctor," Myrnin snapped, and his eyes flared red. "I know you want me to feel some sympathy for them, but that is not who I am. I care only about those I know, and even then, not all that deeply. Strangers get nothing from me." He was slipping, and the anger was coming back. Next it would be confusion. Claire silently dug in her pockets. She'd put a single glass vial in, and miraculously, it was still unbroken.

He slapped it out of her hand impatiently. "I don't need it!"

Claire watched it clatter to the floor, heart in her mouth, and said, "You do. You know you do. Please, Myrnin. I don't need your crap right now. Just *take your medicine.*"

She didn't think he would, not at first, but then he snorted, bent down, and picked up the vial. He broke the cap off and dumped the liquid into his mouth. "There," he said. "Satisfied?" He shattered the glass in his fingers, and the red glow in his eyes intensified. "Are you, little Claire? Do you enjoy giving me orders?"

"Myrnin."

His hand went around her throat, choking off whatever she was going to say.

She didn't move.

His hand didn't tighten.

The red glow slowly faded away, replaced by a look of shame. He let go of her and backed away a full step, head down.

"I don't know where to get a doctor," Claire said, as if nothing had happened. "The hospital, maybe, or—"

"No," Myrnin murmured. "I will bring help. Don't let anyone go through my things. And watch Michael, in case."

She nodded. Myrnin opened the portal doorway in the wall and stepped through it, heading—where? She had no idea. Amelie had, Claire thought, shut down all the nodes. But if that was true, how had they gotten here?

Myrnin could open and close them at will. But he was probably the only one who could.

Michael and Eve moved away from Mayor Morrell's body, as his wife stood over him and cried.

"What can we do?" Shane asked. He sounded miserable. In all the confusion, he'd missed her confrontation with Myrnin. She was dimly glad about that.

"Nothing," Michael said. "Nothing but wait."

When the portal opened again, Myrnin stepped through, then helped someone else over the step.

It was Theo Goldman, carrying an antique doctor's bag. He looked around the lab, nodding to Claire in particular, and then moved to where Richard was lying on the carpet, with his head in his mother's lap. "Move back, please," he told her, and knelt down to open his bag. "Myrnin. Take her in the other room. A mother shouldn't see this."

He was setting out instruments, unrolling them in a clean white towel. As Claire watched, Myrnin led Mrs. Morrell away and seated her in a chair in the corner, where he normally sat to read. She seemed dazed now, probably in shock. The chair was intact. It was just about the only thing in the lab that was—the scientific instruments were smashed, lab tables overturned, candles and lamps broken.

Books were piled in the corners and burned, reduced to scraps of leather and curling black ash. The whole place smelled sharply of chemicals and fire.

"What can we do?" Michael asked, crouching down on Richard's other side. Theo took out several pairs of latex gloves and passed one set to Michael. He donned one himself.

"You can act as my nurse, my friend," he said. "I would have brought my wife—she has many years of training in this—but I don't want to leave my children on their own. They're already very frightened."

"But they're safe?" Eve asked. "Nobody's bothered you?"

"No one has so much as knocked on the door," he said. "It's a very good hiding place. Thank you."

"I think you're paying us back," Eve said. "Please. Can you save him?"

"It's in God's hands, not mine." Still, Theo's eyes were bright as he looked at the twisted metal plate embedded in Richard's side. "It's good that he's unconscious, but he might wake during the procedure. There is chloroform in the bag. It's Michael, yes? Michael, please put some on a cloth and be ready when I tell you to cover his mouth and nose."

Claire's nerve failed around the time that Theo took hold of the piece of steel, and she turned away. Eve already had, to take a blanket to Mrs. Morrell and put it around her shoulders.

"Where's my daughter?" the mayor's wife asked. "Monica should be here. I don't want her out there alone."

Eve raised her eyebrows at Claire, clearly wondering where Monica was.

"The last time I saw her, she was at school," Claire said. "But that was before I got the call to come home, so I don't know. Maybe she's in shelter in the dorm?" She checked her cell phone. No bars. Reception was usually spotty down here in the lab, but she could usually see something, even if it was only a flicker. "I think the cell towers are down."

"Yeah, likely," Eve agreed. She reached over to tuck the blanket around Mrs. Morrell, who leaned her head back and closed her eyes, as if the strength was just leaking right out of her. "You think this is the right thing to do? I mean, do we even know this guy or anything?"

Claire didn't, really, but she still wanted to like Theo, in much the same way as she liked Myrnin—against her better sense. "I think he's okay. And it's not like anybody's making house calls right now."

The operation—and it was an operation, with suturing and everything—took a couple of hours before Theo sat back, stripped off the gloves, and sighed in quiet satisfaction. "There," he said. Claire and Eve got up to walk over as Michael rose to his feet. Shane had been hanging on the edges, watching in what Claire thought looked like queasy fascination. "His pulse is steady. He's lost some blood, but I believe he will be all right, provided no infection sets in. Still, this century has those wonderful antibiotics, yes? So that is not so bad." Theo was almost beaming. "I must say, I haven't used my surgical skills in years. It's very exciting. Although it makes me hungry."

Claire was pretty sure Richard wouldn't want to know that. She knew she wouldn't have, in his place.

"Thank you," Mrs. Morrell said. She got up from the chair, folded the blanket and put it aside, then walked over to shake Theo's hand with simple, dignified gratitude. "I'll see that my husband compensates you for your kindness."

They all exchanged looks. Michael started to speak, but Theo shook his head. "That's quite all right, dear lady. I am delighted to help. I recently lost a son myself. I know the weight of grief."

"Oh," Mrs. Morrell said, "I'm so sorry for your loss, sir." She said it as if she didn't know her husband was lying across the room, dead.

Tears sparkled in his eyes, Claire saw, but then he blinked them away and smiled. He patted her hand gently. "You are very generous to an old man," he said. "We have always liked living in Morganville, you know. The people are so kind."

Shane said, "Some of those same people killed your son."

Theo looked at him with calm, unflinching eyes. "And without forgiveness, there is never any peace. I tell you this from the distance of many centuries. My son gave his life. I won't reply to his gift with anger, not even for those who took him from me. Those same poor, sad people will wake up tomorrow grieving their own losses, I think, if they survive at all. How can hating them heal me?"

Myrnin, who hadn't spoken at all, murmured, "You shame me, Theo."

"I don't mean to do so," he said, and shrugged. "Well. I should get back to my family now. I wish you all well."

Myrnin got up from his chair and walked with Theo to the portal. They all watched him go. Mrs. Morrell was staring after him with a bright, odd look in her eyes.

"How very strange," she said. "I wish Mr. Morrell had been available to meet him."

She spoke as if he were in a meeting downtown instead of under a sheet on the other side of the room. Claire shuddered.

"Come on, let's go see Richard," Eve said, and led her away.

Shane let out his breath in a slow hiss. "I wish it were as simple as Theo thinks it is, to stop hating." He swallowed, watching Mrs. Morrell. "I wish I could, I really do."

"At least you want to," Michael said. "It's a start."

They stayed the night in the lab, mainly because the storm continued outside until the wee hours of the morning—rain, mostly, with some hail. There didn't seem to be much point running out in it. Claire kept checking her phone, Eve found a portable radio buried in piles of junk at the back of the room, and they checked for news at regular intervals.

Around three a.m. they got some. It was on the radio's emergency alert frequency.

All Morganville residents and surrounding areas: we remain under severe thunderstorm warnings, with high winds and possible flooding, until seven a.m. today. Rescue efforts are under way at City Hall, which was partially destroyed by a tornado that also leveled several warehouses and abandoned buildings, as well as one building in Founder's Square. There are numerous reports of injuries coming in. Please remain calm. Emergency teams are working their way through town now, looking for anyone who may be in need of assistance. Stay where you are. Please do not attempt to go out into the streets at this time.

It started to repeat. Eve frowned and looked up at Myrnin, who had listened as well. "What aren't they saying?" she asked.

"If I had to guess, their urgent desire that people stay within shelter would tell me there are other things to worry about." His dark eyes grew distant for a moment, then snapped back into focus. "Ibid nothing."

"What?" Eve seemed to think she'd misheard.

"Ibid nothing carlo. I don't justice."

Myrnin was making word salad again—a precursor to the drugs wearing off—more quickly than Claire had expected, actually, and that was worrying.

Eve sent Claire a look of alarm. "Okay, I didn't really understand that at all—"

Claire put a hand on her arm to silence her. "Why don't you go see Mrs. Morrell? You too, Shane."

He didn't like it, but he went. As he did, he jerked his head at Michael, who rose from where he was sitting with Richard and strolled over.

Casually.

"Myrnin," Claire said. "You need to listen to me, okay? I think your drugs are wearing off again."

"I'm fine." His excitement level was rising; she could see it—a very light flush in his face, his eyes starting to glitter. "You worry over notebook."

There was no point in trying to explain the signs; he never could identify them. "We should check on the prison," she said. "See if everything's still okay there."

Myrnin smiled. "You're trying to trick me." His eyes were getting darker, endlessly dark, and that smile had edges to it. "Oh, little girl, you don't know. You don't know what it's like, having all these guests here, and all this"—he breathed in deeply—"all this blood." His eyes focused on her throat, with its ragged bite mark hidden under a bandage Theo had given her. "I know it's there. Your mark. Tell me, did François—"

"Stop. Stop it." Claire dug her fingers into her palms. Myrnin took a step toward her, and she forced herself not to flinch. She knew him, knew what he was trying to do. "You won't hurt me. You need me."

"Do I?" He breathed deeply again. "Yes, I do. Bright, so bright. I can feel your energy. I know how it will feel when I . . ." He blinked, and horror sheeted across his face, fast as lightning. "What was I saying? Claire? What did I just say?"

She couldn't repeat it. "Nothing. Don't worry. But I think we'd better get you to the cell, okay? Please?"

He looked devastated. This was the worst part of it, she thought, the mood swings. He'd tried so hard, and he'd helped, he really had—but he wasn't going to be able to hold together much longer. She was seeing him fall apart in slow motion.

Again.

Michael steered him toward the portal. "Let's go," he said. "Claire, can you do this?"

"If he doesn't fight me," she said nervously. She remembered one afternoon when his paranoia had taken over, and every time she'd tried to establish the portal, he'd snapped the connection, sure something was waiting on the other side to destroy him. "I wish we had a tranquilizer."

"Well, you don't," Myrnin said. "And I don't like being stuck with your needles, you know that. I'll behave myself." He laughed softly. "Mostly."

Claire opened the door, but instead of the connection snapping clear to the prison, she felt it shift, pulled out of focus. "Myrnin, stop it!"

He spread his hands theatrically. "I didn't do anything."

She tried again. The connection bent, and before she could bring it back where she wanted it, an alternate destination came into focus.

Theo Goldman fell out of the door.

"Theo!" Myrnin caught him, surprised out of his petulance, at least for the moment. He eased the other vampire down to a sitting position against the wall. "Are you injured?"

"No, no, no—" Theo was gasping, though Claire knew he didn't need air, not the way humans did. This was emotion, not exertion. "Please, you have to help, I beg you. Help us, help my family, please—"

Myrnin crouched down to put their eyes on a level. "What's happened?"

Theo's eyes filled with tears that flowed over his lined, kind face. "Bishop," he said. "Bishop has my family. He says he wants Amelie and the book, or he will kill them all."

FOURTEEN

Theo hadn't come straight from Common Grounds, of course; he'd been taken to one of the open portals—he didn't know where—and forced through by Bishop. "No," he said, and stopped Michael as he tried to come closer. "No, not you. He only wants Amelie, and the book, and I want no more innocent blood shed, not yours or mine. Please. Myrnin, I know you can find her. You have the blood tie and I don't. Please find her and bring her. This is not our fight. It's family; it's father and daughter. They should end this, face-to-face."

Myrnin stared at him for a long, long moment, and then cocked his head to one side. "You want me to betray her," he said. "Deliver her to her father."

"No, no, I wouldn't ask for that. Only to—to let her know what price there will be. Amelie will come. I know she will."

"She won't," Myrnin said. "I won't let her."

Theo cried out in misery, and Claire bit her lip. "Can't you help him?" she said. "There's got to be a way!"

"Oh, there is," Myrnin said. "There is. But you won't like it, my little Claire. It isn't neat, and it isn't easy. And it will require considerable courage from you, yet again."

"I'll do it!"

"No, you won't," Shane and Michael said, at virtually the same time. Shane continued. "You're barely on your feet, Claire. You don't go anywhere, not without me."

"And me," Michael said.

"Hell," Eve sighed. "I guess that means I have to go, too. Which I may not ever forgive you for, even if I don't die horribly."

Myrnin stared at each of them in turn. "You'd go. All of you." His lips stretched into a crazy, rubber-doll smile. "You are the best toys, you know. I can't imagine how much *fun* it will be to play with you."

Silence, and then Eve said, "Okay, that was extra creepy, with whipped creepy topping. And this is me, changing my mind."

The glee faded from Myrnin's eyes, replaced with a kind of lost desperation that Claire recognized all too well. "It's coming. Claire, it's coming, I'm afraid. I don't know what to do. I can feel it."

She reached out and took his hand. "I know. Please, try. We need you right now. Can you hold on?"

He nodded, but it was more a convulsive response than confirmation. "In the drawer by the skulls," he said. "One last dose. I hid it. I forgot."

He did that; he hid things and remembered them at odd moments—or never. Claire dashed off to the far end of the room, near where Richard slept, and opened drawer after drawer under the row of skulls he'd nailed to the wall. He'd promised that they were all clinical specimens, not one of them victims of violence. She still didn't altogether believe him.

In the last drawer, shoved behind ancient rolls of parchment and the mounted skeleton of a bat, were two vials, both in brown glass. One, when she pried up the stopper, proved to be red crystals.

The other was silver powder.

She put the vial with silver powder in her pants pocket—careful to use the pocket without a hole in it—and brought the red crystals back to Myrnin. He nodded and slipped the vial into his vest pocket, inside the coat.

"Aren't you going to take them?"

"Not quite yet," he said, which scared the hell out of her, frankly. "I can stay focused a bit longer. I promise."

"So," Michael said, "what's the plan?"

"This."

Claire felt the portal snap into place behind her, clear as a lightning strike, and Myrnin grabbed the front of her shirt, swung her around, and threw her violently through the doorway.

She seemed to fall a really, really long time, but she hit the ground and rolled.

She opened her eyes on pitch darkness, smelling rot and old wine.

No.

She knew this place.

She was trying to get up when something else hit her from behind—Shane, from the sound of his angry cursing. She writhed around and slapped a hand over his mouth, which made him stop in midcurse. "Shhhh," she hissed, as softly as she could. Not that their rolling around on the floor hadn't rung the dinner bell loud and clear, of course.

Damn you, Myrnin.

A cold hand encircled her wrist and pulled her away from Shane, and when she hit out at it, she felt a velvet sleeve.

Myrnin. Shane was scrambling to his feet, too.

"Michael, can you see?" Myrnin's voice sounded completely calm.

"Yes." Michael's didn't. At *all.*

"Then *run*, damn you! I've got them!"

Myrnin followed his own advice, and Claire's arm was almost yanked from its socket as he dragged her with him. She heard Shane panting on his other side. Her foot came down on something springy, like a body, and she yelped. The sound echoed, and from the darkness on all sides, she heard what sounded like fingers tapping, sliding, coming closer.

Something grabbed her ankle, and this time Claire screamed. It felt like a wire loop, but when she tried to bat at it, she felt fingers, a thin, bony forearm, and nails like talons.

Myrnin skidded to a halt, turned, and stomped. Her ankle came free, and something in the darkness screamed in rage.

"Go!" He roared—not to them, but to Michael, Claire guessed. She saw a flash of something up ahead that wasn't quite light—the portal? That looked like the kind of shimmer it made when it was being activated.

Myrnin let go of her wrist, and shoved her forward.

Once again, she fell. This time, she landed on top of Michael.

Shane fell on top of her, and she gasped for air as all the breath was driven out of her. They squirmed around and separated. Michael pulled Eve to her feet.

"I know this place," Claire said. "This is where Myrnin—"

Myrnin stepped through the portal and slammed it shut, just as Amelie had done not so long ago. "We won't come back here," he said. "Out. Hurry. We don't have much time."

He led the way, long black coat flapping, and Claire had to dig deep to keep up, even with Shane helping her. When he slowed down and started to pick her up, she swatted at him breathlessly. "No, I'll make it!"

He didn't look so sure.

At the end of the stone hallway, they took a left, heading down the dark, paneled hall that Claire remembered, but they passed up the door she remembered as Myrnin's cell, where he'd been chained.

He didn't even slow down.

"Where are we going?" Eve gasped. "Man, I wish I'd worn different shoes—"

She cut herself off as Myrnin stopped at the end of the hallway. There was a massive wooden door there, medieval style with thick, hand-hammered iron bands, and the Founder's Symbol etched into the old wood.

He hadn't even broken a sweat. Of course. Claire windmilled her arms as she stumbled to a halt, and braced herself against the wall, chest heaving.

"Shouldn't we be armed?" Eve asked. "I mean, for a rescue mission, generally people go armed. I'm just pointing that out."

"I don't like this," Shane said.

Myrnin didn't move his gaze away from Claire. He reached out and took her hand in his. "Do you trust me?" he asked.

"I will if you take your meds," she said.

He shook his head. "I can't. I have my reasons, little one. Please. I must have your word."

Shane was shaking his head. Michael wasn't seeming any too confident about this, either, and Eve—Eve looked like she would gladly have run back the other way, if she'd known there was any other choice than going back into that darkness.

"Yes," Claire said.

Myrnin smiled. It was a tired, thin sort of smile, and it had a hint of sadness in it. "Then I should apologize now," he said. "Because I'm about to break that trust most grievously."

He dropped Claire's hand, grabbed Shane by the shirt, and kicked open the door.

He dragged Shane through with him, and the door slammed behind him before any of them could react—even Michael, who hit the wood just an instant later, battering at it. It was built to hold out vampires, Claire realized. And it would hold out Michael for a long, long time.

"Shane!" She screamed his name and threw herself against the wood, slamming her hand over and over into the Founder's Symbol. "Shane, no! Myrnin, bring him back. Please, don't do this. Bring him *back*. . . ."

Michael whirled around, facing the other direction. "Stay behind me," he said to Eve and Claire. Claire looked over her shoulder to see doors opening, up and down the hall, as if somebody had pressed a button.

Vampires and humans alike came out, filling the hallway between the three of them, and any possible way out.

Every single one of them had fang marks in their necks, just like the ones in Claire's neck.

Just like the ones in *Michael's* neck.

There was something about the way he was standing there, so still, so quiet. . . .

And then he walked away, heading for the other vampires.

"Michael!" Eve started to lunge after him, but Claire stopped her.

When Michael reached the first vampire, Claire expected to see some kind of a fight—*something*—but instead, they just looked at each other, and then the man nodded.

"Welcome," he said, "Brother Michael."

"Welcome," another vampire murmured, and then a human.

When Michael turned around, his eyes had shifted colors, going from sky blue to dark crimson.

"Oh *hell*," Eve whispered. "This isn't happening. It can't be."

The door opened behind them. On the other side was a big stone hall, something straight out of a castle, and the wooden throne that Claire remembered from the welcome feast was here, sitting up on a stage. It was draped in red velvet.

Sitting on the throne was Mr. Bishop.

"Join us," Bishop said. Claire and Eve looked at each other. Shane was lying on the stone floor, with Myrnin's hand holding him facedown. "Come in, children. There's no point anymore. I've won the night."

Claire felt like she'd stepped off the edge of the world, and everything was just . . . gone. Myrnin wouldn't look at her. He had his head bowed to Bishop.

Eve, after that first look, returned her attention to Michael, who was walking toward them.

It was not the Michael they knew—not at all.

"Let Shane go," Claire said. Her voice trembled, but it came out clearly enough. Bishop raised one finger, and Michael lunged forward, grabbed Eve by the throat, and pulled her close to him with his fangs bared. "No!"

"Don't give me orders, child," Bishop said. "You should be dead by now. I'm almost impressed. Now, rephrase your request. Something with a *please*."

Claire licked her lips and tasted sweat. "Please," she said. "Please let Shane go. Please don't hurt Eve."

Bishop considered, then nodded. "I don't need the girl," he said. He nodded to Michael, who let Eve go. She backed away, staring at him in disbelief, hands over her throat. "I have what I want. Don't I, Myrnin?"

Myrnin pulled up Shane's shirt. There, stuffed in his waistband at the back, was the book.

No.

Myrnin pulled it free, let Shane up, and walked to Bishop. *I'm about to break that trust most grievously,* he'd said to Claire. She hadn't believed him until this moment.

"Wait," Myrnin said, as Bishop reached for it. "The bargain was for Theo Goldman's family."

"Who? Oh, yes." He smiled. "They'll be quite safe."

"And unharmed," Myrnin said.

"Are you putting conditions on our little agreement?" Bishop asked. "Very well. They go free, and unharmed. Let all witness that Theo Goldman and his family will take no harm from me or mine, but they are not welcome in Morganville. I will not have them here."

Myrnin inclined his head. He lowered himself to one knee in front of the throne, and lifted the book in both hands over his head, offering it up.

Bishop's fingers closed on it, and he let out a long, rattling sigh. "At last," he said. "At last."

Myrnin rested his forearms across his knee, but didn't try to rise. "You said you also required Amelie. May I suggest an alternative?"

"You may, as I'm in good humor with you at the moment."

"The girl wears Amelie's sigil," he said. "She's the only one in town who wears it in the old way, by the old laws. That makes her no less than a part of Amelie herself, blood for blood."

Claire stopped breathing. It seemed as if every head turned toward her, every pair of eyes stared. Shane started to come toward her.

He never made it.

Michael darted forward and slammed his friend down on the stones, snarling. He held him there. Myrnin rose and came to Claire, offering her his hand in an antique, courtly gesture.

His eyes were still dark, still mostly sane.

And that was why she knew she could never really forgive him, ever again. This wasn't the disease talking.

It was just Myrnin.

"Come," he said. "Trust me, Claire. Please."

She avoided him and walked on her own to the foot of Bishop's throne, staring up at him.

"Well?" she asked. "What are you waiting for? Kill me."

"Kill you?" he repeated, mystified. "Why on earth would I do such a foolish thing? Myrnin is quite right. There's no point in killing you, none at all. I need you to run the machines of Morganville for me. I have already declared that Richard Morrell will oversee the humans. I will allow Myrnin the honor of ruling those vampires who choose to stay in my kingdom and swear fealty to me."

Myrnin bowed slightly, from the waist. "I am, of course, deeply grateful for your favor, my lord."

"One thing," Bishop said. "I'll need Oliver's head."

This time, Myrnin smiled. "I know just where to find it, my lord."

"Then be about your work."

Myrnin gave a bow, flourished with elaborate arm movements, and to Claire's eyes, it was almost mocking.

Almost.

While he was bowing, she heard him whisper, "Do as he says."

And then he was gone, walking away, as if none of it meant anything to him at all.

Eve tried to kick him, but he laughed and avoided her, wagging a finger at her as he did.

They watched him skip away down the hall.

Shane said, "Let me up, Michael, or fang me. One or the other."

"No," Bishop said, and snapped his fingers to call Michael off when he snarled. "I may need the boy to control his father. Put them in a cage together."

Shane was hauled up and marched off, but not before he said, "Claire, I'll find you."

"I'll find you first," she said.

Bishop broke the lock on the book that Myrnin had given him, and opened it to flip the pages, as if looking for something in particular. He ripped out a page and pressed the two ends together to make a circle of paper, thickly filled with minute, dark writing. "Put this on your arm," he said, and tossed it to Claire. She hesitated, and he sighed. "Put it on, or one of the many hostages to your good behavior will suffer. Do you understand? Mother, father, friends, acquaintances, complete strangers. You are not Myrnin. Don't try to play his games."

Claire slipped the paper sleeve over her arm, feeling stupid, but she didn't see any alternatives.

The paper felt odd against her skin, and then it sucked in and clung to her like something alive. She panicked and tried to pull it off, but she couldn't get a grip on it, so closely was it sticking to her arm.

After a moment of searing pain, it loosened and slipped off on its own.

As it fluttered to the floor, she saw that the page was blank. Nothing on it at all. The dense writing that had been on it stayed on her arm—no, *under the skin*, as if she'd been tattooed with it.

And the symbols were *moving*. It made her ill to watch. She had no idea what it meant, but she could feel something happening inside, something . . .

Her fear faded away. So did her anger.

"Swear loyalty to me," Bishop said. "In the old tongue."

Claire got on her knees and swore, in a language she didn't even know, and not for one moment did she doubt it was the right thing to do. In fact, it made her happy. Glowingly happy. Some part of her was screaming, *He's making you do this!* but the other parts really didn't care.

"What shall I do with your friends?" he asked her.

"I don't care." She didn't even care that Eve was crying.

"You will, someday. I'll grant you this much: your friend Eve may go. I have absolutely no use for her. I will show I am merciful."

Claire shrugged. "I don't care."

She did, she knew she did, but she couldn't make herself feel it.

"Go," Bishop said, and smiled chillingly at Eve. "Run away. Find Amelie and tell her this: I have taken her town away, and all that she values. Tell her I have the book. If she wants it back, she'll have to come for it herself."

Eve angrily wiped tears from her face, glaring at him. "She'll come. And I'll come with her. You don't own jack. This is *our* town, and we're going to kick you out if it's the last thing we do."

The assembled vampires all laughed. Bishop said, "Then come. We'll be waiting. Won't we, Claire?"

"Yes," she said, and went to sit down on the steps by his feet. "We'll be waiting."

He snapped his fingers. "Then let's begin our celebration, and in the morning, we'll talk about how Morganville will be run from now on. According to *my* wishes."

TRACK LIST

I had an especially great track list to help me through this book, and I thought you might enjoy listening along. Don't forget: musicians need love and money, too, so buy the CDs or pay for tracks.

"On and On"	Nikka Costa
"Everybody Got Their Something"	Nikka Costa
"Above the Clouds"	Delirium & Shelly Harland
"2 Wicky"	Hooverphonic
"Is You Is or Is You Ain't My Baby"	Rae & Christian Remix, Dinah Washington
"Enjoy the Ride"	Morcheeba
"Hate to Say I Told You So"	The Hives
"See You Again"	Miley Cyrus
"Fever"	Sarah Vaughn, Verve Remix
"Peter Gunn"	Max Sedgley Remix, Sarah Vaughn
"Blade"	Spacekid & Maxim Yul Remix, Warp Brothers
"Aly, Walk with Me"	The Raveonettes
"Hunting for Witches"	Bloc Party
"Cuts You Up"	Peter Murphy
"Hurt"	Christina Aguilera
"Run"	Gnarls Barkley
"Electrofog"	Le Charme
"Where I Stood"	Missy Higgins
"Children (Dream Version)"	Robert Miles
"Grace"	Miss Kittin

"Walkie Talkie Man"	Steriogram
"Living Dead Girl"	Rob Zombie
"Saw Something"	Dave Gahan
"Boy with a Coin"	Iron & Wine
"Fever"	Stereo MC's
"Kaybettik"	Candan Ercetin
"Playing with Uranium"	Duran Duran
"Staring at the Sun"	TV on the Radio
"The Moment I Said It"	Imogen Heap
"This Is the Sound"	The Last Goodnight
"Juicy"	Better Than Ezra
"One Week of Danger"	The Virgins
"Wolf Like Me"	TV on the Radio
"Poison Kiss"	The Last Goodnight
"Beat It"	Fall Out Boy
"Old Enough"	The Raconteurs
"I Will Possess Your Heart"	Death Cab for Cutie

CARPE CORPUS

For absent friends Tim and Ter. I miss you.

For my dear and constant Cat.

And for present friends Pat, Jackie, Jo, Sharon, Heidi, Bill, and all of ORAC!

ACKNOWLEDGMENTS

There were many people who helped me out with technical review, including:

Amie
Jenn Clack
Stephanie Hill
Alan Balthrop
Loa Ledbetter
CJ
Minde Briscoe
Trisha
Joann Casper
Lisa Lapkovitch
Bethany
Virginia
Sharon Sams

Also, a special note for someone I left out of the dedication for *Feast of Fools* even though I promised to put her in:

Sarah Magilnick

Sarah, I'm very sorry for leaving you out. It was completely my fault.

ONE

"Happy birthday, honey!"

In the glow of the seventeen candles on Claire's birthday cake, her mother looked feverishly happy, wearing the kind of forced smile that was way too common around the Danvers house these days.

It was way too common all over Morganville, Texas. People smiled because they had to, or else.

Now it was Claire's turn to suck it up and fake it.

"Thanks, Mom," she said, and stretched her lips into something that didn't really feel like a smile at all. She rose from her chair at the kitchen table to blow out the candles. All seventeen of the flames guttered and went out at her first puff. *I wish . . .*

She didn't dare wish for *anything*, and that, more than anything else, made frustration and anger and grief roll over her in a hot, sticky wave. This wasn't the birthday she'd been planning for the past six months, since she'd arrived in Morganville. She'd been counting on a party at her home, with her friends. Michael would have played his guitar, and she could almost see that lost, wonderful smile he had when he was deep in the music. Eve, cheerfully and defiantly Goth, would have baked some outrageous and probably inedible cake in the shape of a bat, with licorice icing and black candles. And Shane . . .

Shane would have . . .

Claire couldn't think about Shane, because it made her breath lock up in her throat, made her eyes burn with tears. She missed him. No, that was wrong . . . *missed him* was too mild. She *needed* him. But Shane was locked up in a cage in the center of town, along with his father, the idiot vampire hunter.

She still couldn't quite get her head around the fact that Morganville—a normal, dusty Texas town in the middle of nowhere—was run by vampires. But she could believe *that* more easily than the idea that Frank Collins was somehow going to make it all better.

After all, she'd met the man.

Bishop—the new master vampire of Morganville—was planning something splashy in the way of executions for Frank and Shane, which apparently was the old-school standard for getting rid of humans with ideas of grandeur. Nobody had bothered to fill her in on the details, and she guessed she should be grateful for that. It would certainly be medievally awful.

The worst thing about that, for Claire, was that there seemed to be nothing she could do to stop it. *Nothing.* What was the use of being a main evil minion if you couldn't even enjoy it—or save your own friends?

Evil minion. Claire didn't like to think of herself that way, but Eve had flung it at her the last time they'd spoken.

And of course, as always, Eve was right.

A slice of birthday cake—vanilla, with vanilla frosting and little pastel sprinkles (and the exact opposite of what Eve would have baked)— landed in front of her, on her mom's second-best china. Mom had made the cake from scratch, even the frosting; she didn't believe in ready-made anything. It'd be delicious, but Claire already knew that she wouldn't care. Eve's fantasy cake would have tasted awful, left her teeth and tongue black, and Claire would have loved every bite.

Claire picked up her fork, blinked back her tears, and dug into her birthday treat. She mumbled, "Wonderful, Mom!" around a mouthful of cake that tasted like air and sadness.

Her dad seated himself at the table and accepted a slice, too. "Happy birthday, Claire. Got any plans for the rest of the day?"

She'd had plans. All kinds of plans. She'd imagined this party a million times, and in every single version, it had ended with her and Shane alone.

Well, she was alone. So was he.

They just weren't alone *together*.

Claire swallowed and kept her gaze down on the plate. She was about to say the honest truth: *no.* She didn't have any plans. But the thought of being stuck here all day with her parents, with their frightened eyes and joyless smiles, was too much for her. "Yeah," she said. "I'm . . . supposed to go to the lab. Myrnin wants me."

Myrnin was her boss—her *vampire* boss—and she hated him. She hadn't always hated him, but he'd betrayed her one time too many, and the last time had been a doozy: he'd turned her and Michael and Shane over to their worst enemy, just because it was easier for him than being loyal to them when things got tough.

She could practically hear Shane's voice, heavy on the irony: *Well, he's a vampire. What did you expect?*

Something better, she guessed. And maybe that made her an idiot, because, hey, vampire, and Myrnin had never been big on sanity anyway. She would have refused to work for him after that . . . only she couldn't refuse anything Bishop ordered her to do directly. Magic. Claire didn't believe in magic—that was, as far as she was concerned, just science that hadn't been fully investigated yet—but this felt uncomfortably close to meeting the standard definition.

She didn't like to think of that moment when she became—as Eve had so clearly put it—the pawn of evil, because she was afraid, down in the sickest depths of her nightmares, that she'd made the wrong choice. As she reached for her glass of Coke, her long-sleeved shirt slipped back on her forearm to reveal what Bishop had done to her—blue ink, like some tribal biker tattoo, only this ink *moved*. Watching it slowly revolve and writhe under her skin made her sick.

No such thing as magic. No such thing.

Claire tugged her sleeve back down to hide it—not from her parents; they couldn't see anything wrong with her arm at all. It was something only she could see, and the vampires. She thought that it had gotten a little lighter since the day that Bishop had forced it on her, but maybe that was just wishful thinking. *If it fades out enough, maybe it'll stop working.* Stop forcing her to obey him when he gave her orders.

She had no way of knowing whether it was getting weaker, one way or the other, unless she was willing to risk openly defying Bishop. That was slightly less healthy than swimming in a shark tank, smeared with fish oil and wearing a big Eat Me sign.

She'd ransacked Myrnin's library, looking for any hint of what Bishop had done to her, and how to get rid of it, but if the information was there, he'd hidden it away too well for her to find. *For your own good,* he'd probably have said, but she wouldn't believe him. Not anymore. Myrnin did only what was good for him, and no one else.

At least she could define what the tattoo had done to her—it had taken away her will to say no to Mr. Bishop. *It's not magic,* she told herself for the thousandth time today. *It's not magic because there's no such thing as magic. Everything has an explanation. We just may not understand it yet, but this tattoo thing has rules and laws, and there's got to be a way to make it go away.*

Claire again tugged down the sleeve over the tattoo, and her fingers skimmed over the gold bracelet she still wore. Amelie's bracelet, with the symbol on it of the former vampire ruler of Morganville. Before Mr. Bishop had arrived, it had been a mark of Protection . . . it meant she owed Amelie taxes, usually in the form of money, services, and donated blood, and in return Amelie—and the other vampires—would play nice. It was sort of like the Mafia, with fangs. And it hadn't always worked, but it had been a lot better than walking around Morganville as a free lunch.

Now, though, the bracelet wasn't such an asset. She hadn't seen or heard from Amelie in weeks, and all of Amelie's allies seemed to be MIA. The most prominent vampires in Morganville were in hiding, or maybe even dead . . . or else they were under Bishop's control, and they had no real will of their own. Seemed like that was happening more and more as time went along. Bishop had decided it was more trouble to kill the opposition than to convert them.

Just like he'd converted her, although she was pretty much the only human he'd bothered to put directly under his thumb. He didn't have a very high opinion of people, generally.

Claire finished her cake, and then dutifully opened the birthday presents her parents brought to the table. Dad's package—wrapped by Mom, from the neat hospital corners on it—contained a nice silver necklace with a delicate little heart on it. Mom's package revealed a dress—Claire never wore dresses—in a color and cut that Claire was sure would be drastically unflattering on her smallish frame.

But she kissed them both and thanked them, promised to try the dress on later, and modeled the necklace for her dad when her mom buzzed off to the kitchen to put away the rest of the cake. She put it on over the cross necklace Shane had given her.

"Here," Dad said, trying to be helpful. "I'll get that other one off."

"No!" She slapped a hand over Shane's necklace and backed away, eyes wide, and Dad looked hurt and baffled. "Sorry. I . . . I never take this one off. It . . . was a gift."

He understood then. "Oh. From that boy?"

She nodded, and tears prickled at her eyes again, burning hot. Dad opened his arms and held her tight for a moment, then whispered, "It'll be okay, honey. Don't cry."

"No, it won't," she said miserably. "Not if we don't *make* it okay, Dad. Don't you understand that? We have to *do* something!"

He pushed her back to arm's length and studied her with tired, faded eyes. He hadn't been in good health for a while, and every time she saw him, Claire worried a little more. *Why couldn't they leave my parents out of this? Why did they drag them here, into the middle of this?*

Things had been fine before—well, maybe not fine, but stable. When she'd come to attend college at Texas Prairie University, she'd had to leave the crazy-dangerous dorm to find some kind of safety, and she'd ended up rooming at the Glass House, with Eve and Shane and Michael. Mom and Dad had remained safely far away, out of town.

Or they had, until Amelie had decided that luring them here would help control Claire better. Now they were Morganville residents. Trapped.

Just like Claire herself.

"We tried to leave, honey. I packed your mom up the other night and headed out, but our car died at the city limits." His smile looked frail and broken around the edges. "I don't think Mr. Bishop wanted us to leave."

Claire was a little bit relieved that at least they'd tried, but only for a second—then she decided that she was a lot more horrified. "*Dad!* Please don't try that again. If the vampires catch you outside the city limits—" Nobody left Morganville without permission; there were all kinds of safeguards to prevent it, but the fact that the vampires were ruthless about tracking people down was enough to deter most.

"I know." He put his warm hands on either side of her face, and looked at her with so much love that it broke her heart. "Claire, you think you're ready to take on the world, but you're not. I don't want you in the middle of all this. You're just too *young*."

She gave him a sad smile. "It's too late for that. Besides, Dad, I'm not a kid anymore—I'm seventeen. Got the candles on the cake to prove it and everything."

He kissed her forehead. "I know. But you'll always be five years old to me, crying about a skinned knee."

"That's embarrassing."

"I felt the same way when my parents said it to me." He watched as she fiddled with Shane's cross necklace. "You're going to the lab?"

"What? Oh, yeah."

He knew she was lying, she could tell, and for a moment, she was sure he'd call her on it. But instead he said, "Please just tell me you're not going out today to try to save your boyfriend. Again."

She put her hands over his. "Dad. Don't try to tell me I'm too young. I know what I feel about Shane."

"I'm not trying to do that at all," her father said. "I'm trying to tell you that right now, being in love with *any* boy in this town is dangerous.

Being in love with *that* boy is suicidal. I wouldn't be thrilled under normal circumstances, and this is isn't even close to normal."

No kidding. "I won't do anything stupid," she promised. She wasn't sure she could actually keep that particular vow, though. She'd happily do something stupid if it gave her a single moment with Shane. "Dad, I need to go. Thanks for the necklace."

He stared at her so hard that she thought for a second he'd lock her in her room or something. Not that she couldn't find a way out, of course, but she didn't want to make him feel any worse than she had to.

He finally sighed and shook his head. "You're welcome, honey. Happy birthday. Be careful."

She stood for a moment, watching him play with his piece of birthday cake. He didn't seem hungry. He was losing weight, and he looked older than he had just a year ago. He caught her look. "Claire. I'm *fine.* Don't make that face."

"What face?"

Innocence wasn't going to work on him. "The my-dad's-sick-and-I-feel-guilty-for-leaving face."

"Oh, that one." She tried for a smile. "Sorry."

In the kitchen, her mom was buzzing around like a bee on espresso. As Claire put the plates in the sink, her mother chattered a mile a minute—about the dress, and how she just knew Claire would look perfect in it, and they really should make plans to go out to a nice restaurant this week and celebrate in style. Then she went on about her new friends at the Card Club, where they played bridge and some kind of gin rummy and sometimes, daringly, Texas Hold 'Em. She talked about everything but what was all around them.

Morganville looked like a normal town, but it wasn't. Casual travelers came and went, and never knew a thing; even most of the college students stayed strictly on campus and put in their time without learning a thing about what was *really* going on—Texas Prairie University made sure it was a world unto itself. For people who lived here, the real residents, Morganville was a prison camp, and they were all inmates, and they were all too afraid to talk about it out in the open. Claire listened with her patience stretching thin as plastic wrap, ready to rip, and finally interrupted long enough to get in a hasty, "Thanks," and, "Be back soon; love you, Mom."

Her mother stopped and squeezed her eyes shut. "Claire," she said in an entirely different tone—a genuine one. "I don't want you to go out today. I'd like you to stay home, please."

Claire paused in the doorway. "I can't, Mom," she said. "I'm not going to be a bystander in all this. If you want to be, I understand, but that's not how you raised me."

Claire's mom broke a plate. Just smashed it against the side of the sink into a dozen sharp-edged pieces that skittered all over the counter and floor.

And then she just stood there, shoulders shaking.

"It's okay," Claire said, and quickly picked up the broken pieces from the floor, then swept the rest off the counter. "Mom—*it's okay*. I'm not afraid."

Her mom laughed. It was a brittle, hysterical little laugh, and it scared Claire down to her shoes. "You're not? Well, I am, Claire. I'm as afraid as I've ever been in my life. *Don't go.* Not today. Please stay home."

Claire stood there for a few seconds, took a deep breath, and dumped the broken china in the trash.

"I'm sorry, but I really need to do this," she said. "Mom—"

"Then go." Her mother turned back to the sink and picked up another plate, which she dipped into soapy water and began to scrub with special viciousness, as if she intended to wash the pink roses right off the china.

Claire escaped back to her room, put the dress in her closet, and grabbed up her battered backpack from the corner. As she was leaving, she caught sight of a photograph taped to her mirror. Their Glass House formal picture—Shane, Eve, herself, and Michael, caught midlaugh. It was the only photo she had of all of them together. She was glad it was such a happy one, even if it was overexposed and a little out of focus. Stupid cell phone cameras.

On impulse, she grabbed the photo and stuck it in her backpack.

The rest of her room was like a time warp—Mom had kept all her

things from high school and junior high, all her stuffed animals and posters and candy-colored diaries. Her Pokémon cards and her science kits.
Her glow-in-the-dark stick-on stars and planets on the ceiling. All her
certificates and medals and awards.

It felt so far away now, like it belonged to someone else. Someone who
wasn't facing a shiny future as an evil minion, and trapped in Morganville
forever.

Except for her parents, the photograph was really the only thing in
this whole house that she'd miss if she never came back.

And that was, unexpectedly, kind of sad.

Claire stood in the doorway for a long moment, looking at her past,
and then she closed the door and walked away to whatever the future
held.

TWO

Morganville didn't look all that different now from when Claire had first come to town, and she found that really, really odd. After all, when the evil overlords took over, you'd think it would have made some kind of visible difference, at least.

But instead, life still went on—people went to work, to school, rented videos, and drank in bars. The only real difference was that nobody roamed around alone after dark. Not even the vampires, as far as she knew. The dark was Mr. Bishop's hunting time.

Even that wasn't as much of a change as you'd think, though. Sensible people in Morganville had *never* gone out after dark if they could help it. Instincts, if nothing else.

Claire checked her watch. Eleven a.m.—and she really didn't have to go to the lab. In fact, the lab was the last place she wanted to be today. She didn't want to see her supposed boss Myrnin, or hear his rambling crazy talk, or have to endure his questions about why she was so angry with him. He knew why she was angry. He wasn't *that* crazy.

Her dad had been right on the money. She intended to spend the day trying to help Shane.

First step: see the mayor of Morganville—Richard Morrell.

Claire didn't have a car, but Morganville wasn't all that big, really, and she liked walking. The weather was still good—a little cool even during the day now, but crisp instead of chilly. It was what passed for winter in west Texas, at least until the snowstorms. They'd had a few days of fall, which meant the leaves were a sickly yellow around the edges instead of dark green. She'd heard that fall was a beautiful season in other parts of the country and the world, but around here, it was more or less a half hour between blazing summer and freezing winter.

As she walked, people noticed her. She didn't like that, and she wasn't used to it; Claire had always been one of the Great Anonymous Geek Army, except when it came to a science fair or winning some kind of academic award. She'd never stood out physically—too short, too thin, too small—and it felt weird to have people focus on her and nod, or just plain stare.

Word had gotten around that she was Bishop's errand girl. He'd never made her *do* anything, really, but he made her carry his orders.

And bad things happened. Making her do it, while she was still wearing Amelie's bracelet, was Bishop's idea of a joke.

All the staring made the walk feel longer than it really was.

As she jogged up the steps to Richard's replacement office—the old one having been mostly trashed by a tornado at City Hall—she wondered if the town had appointed Richard as mayor just so they didn't have to change any of the signs. His father—the original Mayor Morrell, one of those Texas good ol' boys with a wide smile and small, hard eyes—had died during the storm, and now his son occupied a battered old storefront with a paper sign in the window that read, MAYOR RICHARD MORRELL, TEMPORARY OFFICES.

She would be willing to bet that he wasn't very happy in his new job. There was a lot of that going around.

A bell tinkled when Claire opened the door, and her eyes adjusted slowly to the dimness inside. She supposed he kept the lights low out of courtesy to vampire visitors—same reason he'd had the big glass windows in front blacked out. But it made the small, dingy room feel like a cave to her—a cave with bad wallpaper and cheap, thin carpeting.

Richard's assistant looked up and smiled as Claire shut the door.

"Hey, Claire," she said. Nora Harris was a handsome lady of about fifty, neatly dressed in dark suits most of the time, and had a voice like warm chocolate butter sauce. "You here to see the mayor, honey?"

Claire nodded and looked around the room. She wasn't the only person who'd come by today; there were three older men seated in the waiting area, and one geeky-looking kid still working off his baby fat, wearing a T-shirt from Morganville High with their mascot on it—a snake, fangs exposed. He looked up at her, eyes wide, and pretty obviously scared, and she smiled slightly to calm him down. It felt weird, being the person other people were scared to see coming.

None of the adults looked at her directly, but she could feel them studying her out of the corners of their eyes.

"He's got a full house today, Claire," Nora continued, and nodded toward the waiting area. "I'll let him know you're here. We'll try to work you in."

"She can go ahead of me," one of the men said. The others looked at him, and he shrugged. "Don't hurt none to be nice."

But it wasn't being nice; Claire knew that. It was simple self-interest, sucking up to the girl who acted as Bishop's go-between to the human community. She was *important* now. She hated every minute of that.

"I won't be long," she said. He didn't meet her gaze at all.

Nora gestured her toward the closed door at the back. "I'll let him know you're coming. Mr. Golder, you'll be next as soon as she's done."

Mr. Golder, who'd given up his place for Claire, nodded back. He was a sun-weathered man, skin like old boots, with eyes the color of dirty ice. Claire didn't know him, but he smiled at her as she passed. It looked forced.

She didn't smile back. She didn't have the heart to pretend.

Claire knocked hesitantly on the closed door as she eased it open, peeking around the edge like she was afraid to catch Richard doing something . . . well, nonmayorly. But he was just sitting behind his desk, reading a file folder full of papers.

"Claire." He closed the file and sat back in his old leather chair, which creaked and groaned. "How are you holding up?" He stood up to offer her his hand, which she shook, and then they both sat down. She'd gotten so used to seeing Richard in a neatly pressed police uniform that it still felt odd to see him in a suit—a nice pin-striped one today, in gray, with a blue tie. He wasn't that old—not even thirty, she'd guess—but he carried himself like somebody twice his age.

They had that in common, she guessed. She didn't feel seventeen these days, either.

"I'm okay," she said, which was a lie. "Hanging in there. I came to—"

"I know what you're going to ask," Richard said. "The answer's still no, Claire." He sounded sorry about it, but firm.

Claire swallowed hard. She hadn't expected to get a no right off the bat. Richard usually heard her out. "Five minutes," she said. "Please. Haven't I earned it?"

"Definitely. But it's not my call. If you want permission to see Shane, you have to go to Bishop." Richard's eyes were kind, but unyielding. "I'm doing all I can to keep him alive and safe. I want you to know that."

"I know you are, and I'm grateful. Really." Her heart sank. Somehow, she'd had her hopes up, even though she'd known it wouldn't work out, today of all days. She studied her hands in her lap. "How is he doing?"

"Shane?" Richard laughed softly. "How do you expect him to be? Pissed off. Angry at the world. Hating every minute of this, especially since he's stuck in there with nobody but his father for company."

"But you've seen him?"

"I've dropped in," Richard said. "Official duties. So far, Bishop hasn't seen fit to yank my chain and make me stop touring the cells, but if I try to get you in . . ."

"I understand." She did, but Claire still felt heartsick. "Does he ask—"

"Shane asks about you every day," Richard said very quietly. "Every single day. I think that boy might really love you. And I never thought I'd be saying that about Shane Collins."

Her fingers were trembling now, a fine vibration that made her clench them into fists to make it stop. "It's my birthday." She had no idea why she said that, but it seemed to make sense at the time. It seemed *important*. Looking up, she saw she'd surprised him with that, and he was temporarily at a loss for words.

"Offering congratulations doesn't seem too appropriate," he said. "So. You're seventeen, right? That's old enough to know when you're in over your head. Claire, just go home. Spend the day with your parents, maybe see your friends. Take care of yourself."

"No. I want to see Shane," she said.

He shook his head. "I really don't think that's a very good idea."

He meant well; she knew that. He came around the desk and put his hand on her shoulder, a kind of half hug, and guided her back out the door.

I'm not giving up. She thought it, but she didn't say it, because she knew he wouldn't approve.

"Go home," he said, and nodded to the man whose appointment Claire had taken. "Mr. Golder? Come on in. This is about your taxes, right?"

"Getting too damn expensive to live in this town," Mr. Golder growled. "I ain't got that much blood to give, you know."

Claire hoisted her backpack and went out to try something else that might get her in to see Shane.

Of course, it was something a lot more dangerous.

She tried to talk herself out of it, but in the end, Claire went to the last place she wanted to go—to Founder's Square, the vampire part of town. In broad daylight, it seemed deserted; regular people didn't venture here anymore, not even when the sun was blazing overhead, although it was a public park. There were some police patrolling on foot, and sometimes she could believe there were shapes flitting through the shadows under the trees, or in the dark spaces of the large, spacious buildings that faced the parklike square.

Those weren't people, though. Not technically.

Claire trudged down the white, smooth sidewalks, head down, feeling the sun beat on her. She watched the grimy, round tips of her red lace-up sneakers. It was almost hypnotic after a while.

She came to a stop as the tips of her shoes bumped into the first of a wide expanse of marble stairs. She looked up—and up—at the largest building on the square: big columns, lots of steps, one of those imposing Greek temple styles. This was the vampire equivalent of City Hall, and inside . . .

"Just go on already," she muttered to herself, and hitched her backpack to a more comfortable position as she climbed the steps.

Claire felt two things as the edge of the roof's shadow fell over her—relief, from getting out of the sun, and claustrophobia. Her footsteps slowed, and for a second she wanted to turn around and take Richard's advice—just go home. Stay with her parents. Be safe.

Pretend everything was normal, like her mom did.

The big, shiny wooden doors ahead of her swung open, and a vampire stood there, well out of the direct glare of sunlight, watching her with the nastiest smile she'd ever seen. Ysandre, Bishop's token sex-kitten vamp, was beautiful, and she knew it. She posed like a Victoria's Secret model, as if at any moment an unexpected photo shoot might begin.

Just now, she was wearing a skintight pair of low-rise blue jeans, a tight black crop top that showed acres of alabaster skin, and a pair of black low-heeled sandals. Skank-vamp casual day wear. She smoothed waves of shiny hair back from her face and continued to beam an evil smile from lips painted with Hooker Red #5.

"Well," she said low in her throat, sweet as grits and poisoned molasses, "look what the cat dragged in. Come on, little Claire. Y'all are letting all the dark out."

Claire had hoped that Ysandre was dead, once and for all; she'd thought that was pretty much inevitable, since the last time she'd seen her Ysandre had been in Amelie's hands, and Amelie hadn't been in a forgiving kind of mood.

But here she was, without a mark on her. Something had gone really wrong for Ysandre to still be alive, but Claire had no real way of finding out what. Ysandre might tell her, but it would probably be a lie.

Claire, lacking any other real choice, came inside. She stayed as far away from the skank as she could, careful not to meet the Vampire Stare of Doom. She wasn't sure that Ysandre had the authority to hurt her, but it didn't seem smart to take chances.

"You come to talk to Mr. Bishop?" Ysandre asked. "Or just to moon around after that wretched boy of yours?"

"Bishop," Claire said. "Not that it's any of your business, unless you're just a glorified secretary with fangs."

Ysandre hissed out a laugh as she locked the doors behind them. "Well, you're growing a pair, Bite-size. Fine, you skip off and see our lord and master. Maybe I'll see him later, too, and tell him you'd be better at your job if you didn't talk so much. Or at all."

It was hard to turn her back on Ysandre, but Claire did it. She heard the vampire's hissing chuckle, and the skin on the back of her neck crawled.

There was a touch of ice there, and Claire flinched and whirled to see her trailing pale, cold fingers in the air where the back of Claire's neck had been.

"Where'd you learn to be a vampire?" Claire demanded, angry because she was scared and hating it. "The movies? Because you're one big, walking, stupid cliché, and you know what? *Not impressed.*"

They stared at each other. Ysandre's smile was wicked and awful, and Claire didn't know what to do, other than stare right back.

Ysandre finally laughed softly and melted into the shadows.

Gone.

Claire took a deep breath and went on her way—a way she knew all too well. It led down a hushed, carpeted hallway into a big, circular atrium armored in marble, with a dome overhead, and then off to the left, down another hallway.

Bishop always knew when she was coming.

He stared right at her as she entered the room. There was something really unsettling about the way he watched the door, waiting for her. As bad as his stare was, though, his smile was worse. It was full of satisfaction, and ownership.

He was holding a book open in his hand. She recognized it, and a chill went down her spine. Plain leather cover with the embossed symbol of the Founder on it. That book had nearly gotten her killed the first few weeks she'd been in Morganville, and that had been well before she'd had any idea of its power.

It was a handwritten account, written mostly in Myrnin's code, with all his alchemical methods. All the secrets of Morganville, which he'd documented for Amelie. It had details even Claire didn't know about the town. About Ada. About *everything*.

It also contained jotted-down notes for what she could think of only as magic spells, like the one that had embedded the tattoo in her arm. She had no idea what else was in it, because Myrnin himself couldn't remember, but Bishop had wanted that book very, very badly. It was the most important thing in Morganville to him—in fact, Claire suspected it was why he'd come here in the first place.

He snapped the book closed and slipped it into the inside pocket of his jacket, where a religious person might keep a copy of the Bible handy.

The room he'd taken over for his own was a big, carpeted office, with a small, fancy sofa and chairs at one end of it, and a desk at the other. Bishop never sat at the desk. He was always standing, and today was no different. Three other vampires sat in visitors' chairs—Myrnin, Michael Glass, and a vamp Claire didn't recognize . . . she wasn't even sure whether it was a man or a woman, actually. The bone structure of the pale face looked female, but the haircut wasn't, and the hands and arms looked too angular.

Claire focused on the stranger to avoid looking at Michael. Her friend—and he *was* still her friend; he couldn't help being in this situation any more than she could—wouldn't meet her eyes. He was angry and ashamed, and she wished she could help him. She wanted to tell him, *It's not your fault,* but he wouldn't believe that.

Still, it was true. Michael didn't have a magic tattoo on his arm; instead, he had Bishop's fang marks in his neck, which worked just as well for the life-challenged. She could still see the livid shadow of the scars on his pale skin.

Bishop's bite was like a brand of ownership.

"Claire," Bishop said. He didn't sound pleased. "Did I summon you for some reason I've forgotten?"

Claire's heart jumped as if he'd used a cattle prod. She willed herself not to flinch. "No, sir," she said, and kept her voice low and respectful. "I came to ask a favor."

Bishop—who was wearing a plain black suit today, with a white shirt that had seen brighter days—picked a piece of lint from his sleeve. "Then the answer is no, because I don't grant favors. Anything else?"

Claire wet her lips and tried again. "It's a small thing—I want to see Shane, sir. Just for a few—"

"I said *no*, as I have half a hundred times already," Bishop said, and she felt his anger crackle through the room. Michael and the strange vamp both looked up at her, eyes luminously threatening—Michael against his will, she was sure. Myrnin—dressed in some ratty assortment of Goodwill-reject pants and a frock coat from a costume shop, plus several layers of cheap, tacky Mardi Gras beads—just seemed bored. He yawned, showing lethally sharp fangs.

Bishop glared at her. "I am very tired of you making this request, Claire."

"Then maybe you should say yes and get it over with."

He snapped his fingers. Michael got to his feet, pulled there like a puppet on a string. His eyes were desperate, but there seemed to be nothing he could do about it. "Michael. Shane is your friend, as I recall."

"Yes."

" 'Yes, *my lord Bishop.*' "

Claire saw Michael's throat bob as he swallowed what must have been a huge chunk of anger. "Yes," he said. "My lord Bishop."

"Good. Fetch him here. Oh, and bring some kind of covering for the floor. We'll just remove this irritation once and for all."

Claire blurted out, "No!" She took a step forward, and Bishop's stare locked tight onto her, forcing her to stop. "Please! I didn't mean . . . Don't hurt him! You can't hurt him! Michael, don't! Don't do this!"

"I can't help it, Claire," he said. "You know that."

She did. Michael walked away toward the door. She could see it all happening, nightmarishly real—Michael bringing Shane back here, forcing him to his knees, and Bishop . . . Bishop . . .

"I'm sorry," Claire said, and took a deep, trembling breath. "I won't ask again. Ever. I swear."

The old man raised his thick gray eyebrows. "Exactly my point. I remove the boy, and I remove any risk that you won't keep your word to me."

"Oh, don't be so harsh, old man," Myrnin said, and rolled his eyes. "She's a teenager in love. Let the girl have her moment. It'll hurt her more, in the end. Parting is such sweet sorrow, according to the bards. I wouldn't know, myself. I never parted anyone." He mimed ripping someone in half, then got an odd expression on his face. "Well. Just the one time, really. Doesn't count."

Claire forgot to breathe. She hadn't expected Myrnin, of all of them, to speak up, even if his support had been more crazy than useful. But he'd given Bishop pause, and she kept very still, letting him think it over.

Bishop gestured, and Michael paused on his way to the door. "Wait, Michael," Bishop said. "Claire. I have a task for you to do, if you want to keep the boy alive another day."

Claire felt a trembling sickness take hold inside. This wasn't the first time, but she always assumed—had to!—that it would be the *last* time. "What kind of task?"

"Delivery." Bishop walked to the desk and flipped open a carved wooden box. Inside was a small pile of paper scrolls, all tied up with red ribbon and dribbled with wax seals. He picked one seemingly at random to give her.

"What is it?"

"You know what it is."

She did. It was a death warrant; she'd seen way too many of them. "I can't—"

"I can order you to take it. If I do, I won't feel obliged to offer you any *favors*. This is the best deal you are going to get, little Claire: Shane's life for the simple delivery of a message," Bishop said. "And if you won't do it, I will send someone else, Shane dies, and you have a most terrible day."

She swallowed. "Why give me the chance at all? It's not like you to bargain."

Bishop showed his teeth, but not his fangs—those were kept out of sight, but that didn't make him any less dangerous. "Because I want you to understand your role in Morganville, Claire. You belong to me. I could order you to do it, with a simple application of will. Instead, I am allowing you to *choose* to do it."

Claire turned the scroll in her fingers and looked down at it. There was a name on the outside of it, written in old-fashioned black calligraphy. *Detective Joe Hess.*

She looked up, startled. "You can't—"

"Think very carefully about the next thing you say," Bishop interrupted. "If it involves telling me what I can or can't do in my own town, they will be your last words, I promise you."

Claire shut her mouth. Bishop smiled.

"Better," he said. "If you choose to do so, go deliver my message. When you come back, I'll allow you to see the boy, just this once. See how well we can get along if we try?"

The scroll felt heavy in Claire's hand, even though it was just paper and wax.

She finally nodded.

"Then go," Bishop said. "Sooner started, sooner done, sooner in the arms of the one you love. There's a good girl."

Michael was looking at her. She didn't dare meet his eyes; she was afraid that she'd see anger there, and betrayal, and disappointment. It was one thing to be forced to be the devil's foot soldier.

It was another thing to choose to do it.

Claire walked quickly out of the room.

By the time she hit the marble steps and the warm sun, she was running.

THREE

*D*etective Joe Hess.

Claire turned the scroll over and over in sweaty fingers as she walked, wondering what would happen if she just tossed it down a storm drain. Well, obviously, Bishop would be *pissed*. And probably homicidal, not that he wasn't mostly that all the time. Besides, what she was carrying might not be anything bad. Right? Maybe it just *looked* like a death warrant. Maybe it was a decree that Friday was ice cream day or something.

A car cruised past her, and she sensed the driver staring at her, then speeding up. *Nothing to see here but a sad, stupid evil pawn*, she thought bitterly. *Move along.*

The police station was in City Hall as well, and the entire building was being renovated, with work crews ripping out twisted metal and breaking down stone to put in new braces and bricks. The side that held the jail and the police headquarters area hadn't been much damaged, and Claire headed for the big, high counter that was manned by the desk sergeant.

"Detective Joe Hess," she said. "Please."

The policeman barely glanced up at her. "Sign in; state your name and business."

She reached for the clipboard and pen and carefully wrote her name. "Claire Danvers. I have a delivery from Mr. Bishop."

There were other things going on in the main reception area—a couple of drunks handcuffed to a huge wooden bench, some lawyers getting a cup of coffee from a big silver pot near the back.

Everything stopped. Even the drunks.

The desk sergeant looked up, and she saw a weary anger in his eyes before he put on a blank, hard expression. "Have a seat," he said. "I'll see if he's here."

He turned away and picked up a phone. Claire didn't watch him make the call. She was too lost in her own misery. She stared down at the writing on the scroll and wished she knew what was inside—but then, it might make it worse if she did know. *I'm only a messenger.*

Yeah, that was going to make her sleep nights.

The desk sergeant spoke quietly and hung up, but he didn't come back to the counter. Avoiding her, she assumed; she was getting used to that. The good people avoided her, the bad people sucked up to her. It was depressing.

Her tattoo itched. She rubbed the cloth of her shirt over it, and watched the reinforced door that led into the rest of the police station.

Detective Hess came out just about a minute later. He was smiling when he saw her, and that hurt. Badly. He'd been one of the first adults to really be helpful to her in Morganville—he and his partner, Detective Lowe, had gone out of their way for her not just once, but several times. And now she was doing *this* to him.

She felt sick as she rose to her feet.

"Claire. Always a pleasure," he said, and it sounded like he actually meant it. "This way."

The desk sergeant held out a badge as she passed. She clipped it on her shirt and followed Joe Hess into a big, plain open area. His desk was near the back of the room, next to a matching one that had his partner's nameplate on the edge. Nothing fancy. Nobody had a lot of personal stuff on their desks. She supposed that maybe it wasn't a good idea to have breakables, if you interviewed angry people all day.

She settled into a chair next to his desk, and he took a seat, leaned forward, and rested his elbows on his knees. He had a kind face, and he wasn't trying to intimidate her. In fact, she had the impression he was trying to make it easy on her.

"How are you holding up?" he asked her, which was the same thing Richard Morrell had said. She wondered if she looked that damaged. Probably.

Claire swallowed and looked down at her hands, and the scroll held in her right one. She slowly stretched it out toward him. "I'm sorry," she said. "Sir, I'm . . . so sorry." She wanted to explain to him, but there really didn't seem to be much to excuse it at the moment. She was here. She was doing what Bishop wanted her to do.

This time, she'd chosen to do it.

No excuse for that.

"Don't blame yourself," Detective Hess said, and plucked the scroll from her fingers. "Claire, none of this is your fault. You understand that, right? You're not to blame for Bishop, or anything else that's screwed up around here. You did your best."

"Wasn't good enough, was it?"

He watched her for another long second, then shook his head and snapped the seals on the scroll. "If anybody failed, it was Amelie," he said. "We just have to figure out how to survive now. We're in uncharted territory."

He unrolled the scroll. His hands were steady and his expression carefully still. He didn't want to scare her, she realized. He didn't want her to feel guilty.

Detective Hess read the contents of the paper, then let it roll up again into a loose curl. He set it on his desk, on top of a leaning tower of file folders.

She had to ask. "What is it?"

"Nothing you need to worry about," he said, which couldn't have been true. "You did your job, Claire. Go on, now. And promise me . . ." He hesitated, then sat back in his chair and opened a file folder so he could look busy. "Promise me you won't do anything stupid."

She couldn't promise that. She had the feeling she'd already been stupid three or four times since breakfast.

But she nodded, because it was really all she could do for him.

He gave her a distracted smile. "Sorry. Busy around here," he said. That was a lie; there was almost nobody in the room. He tapped a pencil on the open file. "I've got court this morning. You go on now. I'll see you soon."

"Joe—"

"Go, Claire. Thank you."

He was going to protect her; she could see that. Protect her from the consequences of what she'd done.

She couldn't think how she would ever really pay him back for that.

As she walked out, she felt him watching her, but when she glanced back, he was concentrating on his folder again.

"Hey, Claire? Happy birthday."

She *would not* cry.

"Thanks," she whispered, and choked on the word as she opened the door and escaped from whatever awful thing she'd just brought to his desk.

It was nearly one o'clock when she made it back to Bishop's office—not so much because it was a long trip as because she had to stop, sit, and cry out her distress in private, then make sure she'd scrubbed away any traces before she headed back. Ysandre would be all over it if she didn't.

And Bishop.

Claire thought she did a good job of looking calm as Ysandre waved her back to the office. Bishop was just where he'd been, although the third vampire, the stranger, was gone.

Michael was still there.

Myrnin was trying to build an elaborate abstract structure out of paper clips and binder clips, which was one of his less crazy ways to pass the time.

"The prodigal child returns," Bishop said. "And how did Detective Hess take the news?"

"Fine." Claire wasn't going to give him anything, but even that seemed to amuse him. He leaned on the corner of his desk and crossed his arms, staring at her with a faint, weird smile.

"He didn't tell you, did he?"

"I didn't ask."

"What a civilized place Morganville is." Bishop made that into an insult. "Very well, you've done your duty. I suppose I'll have to keep my half of the bargain." He glanced at Myrnin. "She's your pet. Clean up after her."

Myrnin gave Bishop a lazy salute. "As my master commands." He stood with that unconscious vampire grace that made Claire feel heavy, stupid, and slow, and his bright black eyes locked with hers for a long moment. If he was trying to tell her something, she had no idea what it was. "Out, girl. Master Bishop has important work to do here."

What? she wondered. *Working on his evil laugh? Interviewing backup minions?*

Myrnin crossed the room and closed ice-cold fingers around her arm. She pulled in a breath for a gasp, but he didn't give her time to react; she was yanked along with him down the hall, moving at a stumbling run.

She looked back at Michael mutely, but he couldn't help her. He was just as trapped as she was.

Myrnin stopped only when there were two closed doors, and about a mile of hallway, between them and Mr. Bishop.

"Let go of me!" Claire spat, and tried to yank free. Myrnin looked down at her arm, where his pale fingers were still wrapped around it, and raised his eyebrows as if he couldn't quite figure out what his hand was doing. Claire yanked again. "Myrnin, *let go!*"

He did, and stepped back. She thought he looked disappointed for a flicker of a second, and then his loony smile was firmly in place. "Will you be a good little girl, then?" She glared at him. "Ah. Probably not. All right, then, on your head be it, Claire, and let's do our best to keep your head attached to the rest of you. Come. I'll take you to your boy, since evidently our mutual benefactor is in a giving sort of mood."

He turned, and the skirts of his frock coat flared. He was wearing flip-flops again, and his feet were dirty, though he didn't smell too bad in general. The layers of cheap metallic beads clicked and rattled as he walked, and the slap of his shoes made him just about the noisiest vampire Claire had ever heard.

"Are you taking your medicine?" she asked. Myrnin sent her a glance over his shoulder, and once again, she didn't know what that look meant at all. "Is that a no?"

"I thought you hated me," he said. "If you do, you shouldn't really care, should you?"

He had a point. Claire shut up and hurried along as he walked down a long, curved hallway to a big wooden door. There was a vampire guard on the door, a man who'd probably been Asian in his regular life, but was now the color of old ivory. He wore his hair long, braided in the back, and he wasn't much taller than Claire.

Myrnin exchanged some Chinese-sounding words with the other vampire—who, like Michael, sported Bishop's fang marks in his neck—and the vampire unlocked the door and swung it open.

This was as far as Claire had ever been able to get before. She felt a wave of heat race through her, and then she shivered. Now that she was here, actually walking through the door, she felt faintly sick with anticipation. *If they've hurt him . . .* And it had been so long. What if he didn't even want to see her at all?

Another locked door, another guard, and then they were inside a plain stone hallway with barred cells on the left side. No windows. No light except for blazing fluorescent fixtures far overhead. The first cell was empty. The second held two humans, but neither one was Shane. Claire tried not to look too closely. She was afraid she might know them.

The third cell had two small cots, one on each side of the tiny room, and a toilet and sink in the middle. Nothing else. It was almost painfully neat. There was an old man with straggly gray hair asleep on one of the beds, and it took Claire a few seconds to realize that he was Frank Collins, Shane's dad. She was used to seeing him awake, and it surprised her to see him so . . . fragile. So helpless and old.

Shane was sitting cross-legged on the other bed. He looked up from the book he was reading, and jerked his head to get the hair out of his eyes. The guarded, closed look on his face reminded Claire of his father, but it shattered when Shane saw her.

He dropped the book, surged to his feet, and was at the bars in about one second flat. His hands curled around the iron, and his eyes glittered wildly until he squeezed them shut.

When he opened them again, he'd gotten himself under control. Mostly.

"Hey," Shane said, as calmly as if they'd just run into each other in the hallway at the Glass House, their strange little minifraternity. As if whole months hadn't gone by since they'd been parted. "Imagine seeing you around here. Happy birthday to you, and all."

Claire felt tears burn in her eyes, but she blinked them back and put on a brave smile. "Thanks," she said. "What'd you get me?"

"Um . . . a shiny diamond." Shane looked around and shrugged. "Must have left it somewhere. You know how it is, out all night partying, you get baked and forget where you left your stuff. . . ."

She stepped forward and wrapped her hands around his. She felt tremors race through him, and Shane sighed, closed his eyes, and rested his forehead against the bars. "Yeah," he whispered. "Shutting up now. Good idea."

She pressed her forehead against his, and then her lips, and it was hot and sweet and desperate, and the feelings that exploded inside her made her shake in reaction. Shane let go of the bars and reached through to run his fingers through her soft, short hair, and the kiss deepened, darkened, took on a touch of yearning that made Claire's heart pound.

When their lips finally parted, they didn't pull away from each other. Claire threaded her arms through the bars and around his neck, and his hands moved down to her waist.

"I hate kissing you through prison bars," Shane said. "I'm all for re-straint, but self-restraint is so much more fun."

Claire had almost forgotten that Myrnin was still there, so his soft chuckle made her flinch. "There speaks a young man with little practical experience," he said, yawned, and draped himself over a bench on the far side of the wall. He propped his chin up on the heel of one hand. "Enjoy that innocence while you can."

Shane held on to her, and his dark eyes stared into hers. *Ignore him*, they seemed to say. *Stay with me.*

She did.

"I'm trying to get you out," she whispered. "I really am."

"Yeah, well . . . it's no big deal, Claire. Don't get yourself in trouble. Wait, I forgot who I'm talking to. What kind of trouble are you in today, anyway?"

"I'm not. Don't worry."

"I've got nothing to do but worry, mostly about you." Shane was looking very serious now, and he tilted her head up to force her to meet his eyes again. "Claire. What's he got you doing?"

"You're worried about *me*?" She laughed, just a little, and it sounded panicked. "You're the one in a cage."

"Kind of used to that, you know. Claire, tell me. Please."

"I . . . I can't." That wasn't true. She *could*. She just desperately didn't want to. She didn't want Shane to know any of it. "How's your father holding up?"

Shane's eyebrows rose just a little. "Dad? Yeah, well. He's okay. He's just . . . you know."

And that, Claire realized, was what she was afraid of—that Shane had forgiven his father for all his crazy stunts. That the Collins boys were together again, united in their hatred of Morganville in general.

That Shane was back in the vampire-slayer fold. If that happened Bishop would *never* let him out of his cell.

Shane read it in her face. "Not like that," he said, and shook his head. "It's pretty close quarters in here. We have to get along, or we'd kill each other. We decided to get along, that's all."

"Yeah," said a deep, scratchy voice from the other bunk. "It's been one big, sloppy bucket of joy, getting to know my son. I'm all teary-eyed and sentimental."

Shane rolled his eyes. "Shut up, Frank."

"That any way to talk to your old man?" Frank rolled over, and Claire saw the hard gleam of his eyes. "What's your collaborator girl doing here? Still running errands for the vampires?"

"Dad, Christ, will you *shut up?*"

"This is the two of you getting along?" Claire whispered.

"You see any broken bones?"

"Good point." This was not how she'd imagined this moment going, except for the kissing. Then again, the kissing was better than she'd dared believe was possible. "Shane—"

"Shhhh," he whispered, and pressed his lips to her forehead. "How's Michael?" She didn't want to talk about Michael, so she just shook her head. Shane swallowed hard. "He's not . . . dead?"

"Define *dead* around here," Claire said. "No, he's okay. He's just . . . you know. Not himself."

"Bishop's?" She nodded. He closed his eyes in pain. "What about Eve?"

"She's working. I haven't seen her in a couple of weeks." Eve, like everyone else in Morganville, treated Claire like a traitor these days, and Claire honestly couldn't blame her. "She's really busted up about Michael. And you, of course."

"No doubt," Shane said softly. He seemed to hesitate for a heartbeat. "Have you heard anything about me and my dad? What Bishop has planned for us?"

Claire shook her head. Even if she knew—and she didn't, in detail—she wouldn't have told him. "Let's not talk about it. Shane—I've missed you so much—"

He kissed her again, and the world melted into a wonderful spinning blend of heat and bells, and it was only when she finally, regretfully pulled back that she heard Myrnin's mocking, steady clapping.

"Love conquers all," he said. "How quaint."

Claire turned on him, feeling fury erupt like a volcano in her guts. *"Shut up!"*

He didn't even bother to glance at her, just leaned back against the wall and smiled. "You want to know what he's got planned for you, Shane? Do you really?"

"Myrnin, don't!"

Shane reached through the bars and grabbed Claire's shoulders, turning her back to face him. "It doesn't matter," he said. "*This* matters, right now. Claire, we're going to get out of this. We're going to live through it. Both of us. Say it with me."

"Both of us," she repeated. "We're going to live."

Myrnin's cold hand closed around her wrist, and he dragged her away from the bars. The last thing she let go of was Shane's hand.

"Hey!" Shane yelled as Claire fought, lost, and was pulled through the door. "Claire! We've going to live! Say it! *We're going to live!*"

Myrnin slammed the door. "Theatrical, isn't he? Come on, girl. We have work to do."

She tried to shake him off. "I'm not going anywhere with you, you traitor!"

Myrnin didn't give her a choice; he half dragged, half marched her away from the first vampire guard, then the second, and then pulled her into an empty, quiet room off the long hallway. He shut the door with a wicked boom and whirled to face her.

Claire grabbed the first thing that came to hand—it happened to be a heavy candlestick—and swung it at his head. He ducked, rushed in, and effortlessly took it away from her. "Girl. *Claire!*" He shook her into stillness. His eyes were wide and very dark. Not at all crazy. "If you want the boy to live, you'll stop fighting me. It's not productive."

"What, I should just stand here and let you bite me? Not happening!" She tried to pull away, but he was as solid as a granite statue. Her bones would break before his grip did.

"Why on earth would I bite you?" Myrnin asked, very reasonably. "I don't work for Bishop, Claire. I never have. I thought you certainly had enough brains to understand that."

Claire blinked again. "Are you trying to tell me that *you're still on our side?*"

"Define *our*, my dear."

"The side of . . ." Well, he was right. It was a little tough to define. "You know. Us!"

Myrnin actually laughed, let go, and stuffed his hands casually into the pockets of his frock coat. "Us, indeed. I understand you might be skeptical. You have reason. Perhaps I should allow someone else to convince you— Ah. Right on time."

She wouldn't have believed him, not for a second, except that a section of the wall opened, there was a flash of white-hot light, and a woman stepped through, followed by a long line of people.

The woman was Amelie, vampire queen of Morganville—though she didn't look anything like the perfect pale princess that Claire had always seen. Amelie had on black pants, a black zip-up hoodie, and *running shoes*.

So wrong.

And behind her was the frickin' vampire *army*, led by Oliver, all in black, looking scarier than Claire could remember ever seeing him—he usually at least tried to look nondangerous, but today, he obviously didn't care. He wore his graying hair tied back in a ponytail, and it pulled his face into an unsmiling mask.

He crossed his arms and looked at Myrnin and Claire like they were something slimy he'd found on his coffee shop floor.

"Myrnin," Amelie said, and nodded graciously. He nodded back, like they were passing on the street. Like it was just a normal day. "Why did you involve the girl?"

"Oh, I had to. She's been quite difficult," he said. "Which helped convince Bishop that I am, indeed, his creature. But I think it's best if you leave her behind for now, and me as well. We have more work to do here, work that can't be done in hiding."

Claire opened her mouth, then closed it without thinking of a single coherent question to ask. Oliver dismissed both of them with a shake of his head and signaled his vampire shock troops to fan out around the room on either side of the door to the hallway.

Amelie lingered, a trace of a frown on her face. "Will you protect her, Myrnin? I was loath to let you lead her this far into the maze; I should

RACHEL CAINE

258

hate to think you'd abandon her on a whim. I do owe her Protection." Her pale gray eyes bored into his, colder than steel in winter. "Be careful what you say. I will hold you to your answer."

"I'll defend the girl with my last breath," he promised, and clasped his hand dramatically to the chest of his ragged frock coat. "Oh, wait. That doesn't mean much, does it, since I gasped that last breath before the Magna Carta was dry on the page? I mean, of course I'll look after her, with whatever is left of my life."

"I'm not joking, jester."

He suddenly looked completely sober. "And I'm not laughing, my lady. I'll protect her. You have my word on it."

Claire's head was spinning. She looked from Myrnin to Amelie to Oliver, and finally thought of a decent question to ask. "Why are you *here*?"

"They're here to rescue your boyfriend," Myrnin said. "Happy birthday, my dear."

Amelie sent him a sharp, imperious look. "Don't lie to the girl, Myrnin. It's not seemly."

Myrnin bowed his head very slightly. Claire could still see a manic smile trembling on his lips.

Amelie transferred her steady gray gaze to Claire. "Myrnin has been helping us gain entry to the building. There are things we are doing to retake Morganville, but it is a process that will take some time. Do you understand?"

It hit Claire a little late. "You're . . . you're *not* here to rescue Shane?"

"Of course not," Oliver said scornfully. "Don't be stupid. What possible strategic value does your boyfriend hold for us?"

Claire bit her lip on an instinctive argument and forced herself to *think*. It wasn't easy; all she wanted to do was scream at him. "All right," she finally said. "I'm going to *make* him strategically valuable to you. How's that?"

Myrnin slowly raised his head. He had a warning look on his face, which she ignored completely.

"If you don't rescue Shane *and his father*, I'm not going to help keep Myrnin on track, and I'll destroy the maintenance drugs and the serum we were working on. I'm guessing you still want to avoid getting on the crazy train, right?" Because that was where all the vampires were headed, even Oliver and Amelie.

When she'd first come to Morganville, she'd thought they were immortal and perfect, but in many ways, that was all just a front. The reason there were no other vampires out there in the world—or very few, anyway—was that over the years, their numbers had gradually declined, and their ability to make other vampires had slipped away. It was a kind of disease, something nasty and progressive, although they'd been in denial about it for a very long time.

Amelie had created Morganville to be their last, best hope of survival. But the disease hadn't gotten better; it had gotten worse, and seemed to be affecting them faster and faster these days. Claire had learned to pick up the subtle signs by now, and they were already visible—tremors in the pale hands, sometimes up the arms. Soon, it'd be worse. They were all terrified of it. They had good reason to be.

Myrnin had developed a maintenance drug, but they needed a cure. Badly. And with Myrnin slipping fast, Claire was the key to getting that done.

There was a profound silence in the room, and for a second, Claire's angry resolve faltered. Then she saw the look in Oliver's eyes. *Oh no you don't*, she thought. *Don't you look smug.*

"We do this my way," Claire said, "or I'll destroy all the work and let you all die."

"Claire," Myrnin murmured. He sounded horrified. Good. She was glad. "You can't mean that."

"I *do* mean it. All your work, all your research. If you let Bishop kill Shane, none of it matters to me anyway." She was scared to say this, but in a way, it was a relief. "It's not all about you and your stupid ancient feuds. There are living people in this town. We have *lives*. We *matter!*" She'd let the lid off her simmering, terrified anger, and now it was boiling all over the place. She whirled on Myrnin. "*You!* You *gave* us to him! You turned on us when we *needed you!* And *you*"—Amelie, this time—"*you didn't even care.*

Where have you *been*? I thought you were different; I thought you wanted to help—but you're just like the rest of them; you're just—"

"Claire." Just the one word, but from Amelie that was all it took to stop Claire in her tracks. "What else could I do? Bishop turned enough of my followers that any action I would take would have been against my own people. It would have been a fight to the death, and that fight would have destroyed everyone you or I love. I had to withdraw and allow him to think he had triumphed. Myrnin did what he could to protect you and all your friends, while we found another way."

Claire snorted out a bitter little laugh. "Sure he did."

"You're all alive, I believe, unlike most who've crossed Bishop throughout his life. You might think on how unlikely that is, so long after he should have lost interest and torn you and my town apart." Amelie's face was as hard as carved marble. "My father has no interest in *administering*. Only in destroying. Myrnin has been persuading him to at least try to keep Morganville alive, and putting himself at constant risk to do so."

Claire didn't want to believe it, but when she actually thought about it, she remembered how often Bishop had ordered people killed, and how often Myrnin—or Myrnin and Michael!—had managed to distract him from carrying it out. "Michael," Claire said slowly. "You turned Michael back, didn't you? He's not really Bishop's anymore."

Amelie and Oliver exchanged looks, and Oliver shrugged very slightly. "She is a quick study," he said. "I never said otherwise. Unless the boy's a bad actor."

"If he were a bad actor, he'd be long dead by now," Amelie said. "Claire—you must not treat Michael any differently. For his life's sake, you must not. Now, I need you to go with Myrnin. The serum you've cultured from Bishop's blood is of vital importance to us now; we need to treat all those we can reach, and we must have enough of a supply to do the job. I rely upon you for that, Claire."

"Why should I help you at all?" Claire asked, and felt a tremor of pure chill along the back of her neck when Amelie's gray eyes sharpened their focus on her. "You haven't promised me anything. I want you to swear you'll get Shane and his father out of there alive."

Oliver growled, and from her peripheral vision she saw the ivory flash of his fangs. "You're going to permit this puppy to bark at you?"

"What I do is my affair, Oliver." Amelie let a long, long moment pass before she said, "Very well, Claire, you have my word that we will retrieve Shane and his father before they are executed. What else?"

Claire hadn't really been prepared to win that argument. She blinked, searched for another demand, and came up with nothing in particular.

Then she did. "I . . . want you to promise me that when this is over, you're going to change things in Morganville."

Amelie looked, for a moment, perplexed. "Change things? What sort of things?"

"No more hunting humans," she said. "No more owning people. You'll make everybody equal around here."

"You're speaking of things you don't understand. These things are required for us to survive in relative security. I won't put my people at further risk, nor leave them at the whims and mercies of yours. I've seen too many centuries of death and destruction." Amelie shook her head. "No, if that is your price, then it's too high for me to pay, Claire. Do as you will, but I won't betray all we've built here to accommodate your sentimental idea of modern life."

Claire had been raised to be kind, to agree, to *help*, and for just a second, locked in a stare with the Founder of Morganville, she wanted to give up.

The only thing that stopped her was imagining what Shane would have said, if he'd been standing in her place.

"No," she said, and felt her heart flutter madly in panic. Her whole body was shaking, pleading for her to run, avoid the confrontation. "You hear what you're saying, right? You want to save your people at the cost of human lives. I won't agree to that; I *can't*. Deal's off. I'm not helping you anymore. And the first chance I get, I tell Bishop about Myrnin, too."

Amelie turned on her hard and fast, and before she knew what was happening Claire felt a cold hand around her throat, and she was smashed up against the wall. Claire screamed and slammed her eyes shut, but not fast enough to block out the rage on Amelie's face, or the wicked-sharp white fangs and staring eyes.

She felt Amelie's cool breath on her throat, and heard Myrnin murmur something under his breath, something in a language she couldn't understand. He sounded horrified.

Amelie's hard, cold hands let go of her throat. Instead, they fastened around Claire's shoulders and shook her. Claire's skull bounced off of brick, and she winced and saw stars. "*Open your eyes!*" Amelie barked. Claire did, blinking away confusion. "I have *never* met such a vexing, foolish human being in my entire life. There are *eight hundred vampires* in the world, Claire. In the *world*. Fewer each day. We are hunted, we are sick, we are *dying*. There are billions of you! I *will not* put you *first!*" That last was a raw, furious hiss, and it sparked something terrible in Amelie's eyes, something out of control and hungry. "I *will* save my people!"

Behind her, another vampire stepped out of the shadows and said, very quietly, "Amelie. None of this is Claire's fault. You know that. And she's right. It's the same thing I told you fifty years ago. You got mad then, too, as I recall."

The vampire taking Claire's side was Sam Glass, Michael's grandfather; he still looked college-age, even after all these years. He was probably the only one of the nonbreathing who could have stepped in on Claire's behalf—or would have.

He touched Amelie's shoulder.

She turned on him, but he wrapped her in his arms, and for a second, one second, Amelie let herself be held before she pushed him away and stalked to the far corner of the room, agitation in every movement. "Oh, just get her out," she said. "Myrnin, get her *out*. Now! Before I do something I regret. Or possibly, which I don't."

Claire could hardly breathe, much less protest. Myrnin took her hand in his and yanked, hard. She brushed by Oliver, whose eyes were flaring in hunting-vampire colors, and felt a low-decibel growl fill the room.

Myrnin shoved her toward what looked like a blank wall, and for an instant of panic Claire thought she was going to hit it face-first . . . and then she felt the telltale tingle of one of Myrnin's stable wormhole portals, his alchemical travel network that led to some of the most dangerous places in Morganville. The wall dissolved in a swirl of mist, and Claire had the feeling of helplessly falling into the dark, with no idea of where she'd land. It seemed to last forever, but then she was stumbling out . . . into her *home.*

FOUR

The Glass House was pretty much as she'd last left it, when she'd packed her pitifully few belongings and moved in with her parents after they'd been brought to Morganville. The house seemed quiet, lonely, somehow sad and colorless. That was just its mood. Shane's things were still strewn around—a new game console that he'd only just gotten hooked up, games piled in the corners along with his Wii controllers, his ratty old black sweatshirt crumpled on the corner of the couch. Claire walked to it, sat down, and pulled it into her lap like a pet, then held it up to her face and breathed.

I'm home. It felt wonderful and sad and horrible, all at the same time.

Holding Shane's shirt was like having him holding her, just for a moment.

When she looked up, Myrnin was watching her. "What?" she demanded. He shrugged and turned away. "Why did you bring me here?"

"I had to bring you somewhere," Myrnin said. "I thought perhaps you would enjoy this more than, say, the sewage treatment plant."

Michael's guitar lay in its case on the floor near the bookcases. Some of Eve's magazines still littered the coffee table, edges curling up from neglect more than use.

It still smelled so *familiar*, and Claire felt the loss of Shane, of her friends, hit her hard once again.

"Is Eve here?" she asked him, but Myrnin didn't answer.

Eve did, from the kitchen doorway. "Where else would I be?" she asked. She leaned against the doorjamb and crossed her arms, staring at them. "What are you doing in my house, freaks?"

"Hey, it's my house, too!" Claire knew she sounded defensive, but she couldn't help it. From the very first time they'd met, Eve had been on her side—always in her corner, always believing her. Believing *in* her, which was even more important.

It hurt that all that had changed now.

Eve's face was a rice-powder mask, aggressively marked up with black lipstick and way too much eyeliner. Her black hair was pulled back into a severe ponytail, and she was wearing a skintight black knit shirt with a red skull on the front, and oversize cargo pants with loads of pockets and chains. Heavy combat-style boots.

Eve was ready to kick ass, and she wouldn't bother to take names while she was at it.

"I'm serious," Eve said. "I'm giving you about five seconds to get out of my house. And take your pet leech with you before I play a game of Pin the Stake in the Vamp."

Claire held Shane's sweatshirt in her arms for comfort. "Aren't you going to at least ask how they are?"

Eve stared at her with eyes like burned black holes. "I've got sources," she said. "My boyfriend's still evil. Your boyfriend's still in jail. You're still sucking up to the Dark Lord of Mordor. By the way, I'm going to start calling you Gollum, you little creep."

"Eve, wait. It's not like that—"

"Actually, it is exactly like that," Myrnin said. "We should go, Claire. Now."

He tried to take her hand; she shook him off and moved closer to Eve, who straightened from her slouch and slipped one hand into a pocket on her cargo pants. "I'm not screwing around, Claire. *Get out of my house!*"

"I *live here!*"

"No, you *used to* live here!" That came out of Eve's blackened lips in a raw, vicious snarl. "This is still Michael's house, and no matter what's happened to him, I'm going to defend it, do you understand? I'm not letting you—"

"Michael's not evil," Claire blurted out desperately. "He's working for Amelie."

Eve stopped, lips parted, eyes wide.

"Claire," Myrnin warned softly from behind her. "Secrets are best kept cold."

"Not from her." Claire tried again, desperate to see some of that anger leave her friend. "Michael's working for Amelie. He's not on Bishop's side. He'd want me to tell you that. He never left us, Eve. He never left *you.*"

Silence. Dead, cold silence, and in it, Claire could hear Eve's breathing. Nothing else.

Eve took her hand out of her pocket. She was holding a knife.

"So this is Bishop's latest game? Taunt the loser? See how crazy you can make me? Because honestly, that's not much of a challenge—I'm pretty crazy already." Her dark eyes sparkled with tears. "Runs in my family, I guess."

"Claire isn't lying to you," Myrnin said, and stepped around Claire to block any threatening moves Eve might make. "Do you have to be so full of—"

Eve lunged at him. Myrnin didn't seem to move at all, but suddenly he had her from behind, arms pinned, and the knife was spinning on the floor and skidding to bump into Claire's feet. Eve didn't even have time to scream. Once he had her, she wasn't able to, because his hand was across her mouth, muffling any sounds.

Myrnin's eyes sparked an unholy color of red, and he brushed his lips against Eve's pale neck. "—so full of useless bravado?" he finished, in exactly the same tone as before. "She didn't lie to you. She's an awful liar, when it comes down to it. That's what makes her so terrifyingly useful to us—we always know where we stand with little

Claire. Now play *nicely*, make-believe dead girl. Or I will fulfill your darkest wishes."

He shoved Eve away, toward Claire, who kicked the knife far out of anybody's reach. Eve whirled, evidently (and understandably) finding Myrnin more of a threat. Under the rice-powder makeup, her face was flushed, her eyes shining with fear.

Myrnin circled like a hyena. He grinned like one, too.

"Call him off," Eve said. "Claire, *call him off!*"

"Myrnin, leave Eve alone. Please?" Which was about the closest Claire dared come to telling Myrnin to do anything, especially when he had that particular glow in his eyes. He was enjoying this. "I need to talk to her, and I can't do that if you're scaring the crap out of her. Please."

He paced a few more steps, and she saw him get control of himself with a real physical effort. He sat down in a chair at the dining table and put his dirty feet up. "Fine," he said, and crossed his arms. "Talk. I'll just wait, shall I? Because *my* mission to save this town is of no importance whatsoever next to your *girl talk.*"

Claire rolled her eyes. "Oh, shut *up*, you medieval drama queen." Now that he was sitting down and the glow was gone from his eyes, she could say it, and he could acknowledge it with a snort and a roll of his shoulders. "Eve, I tried to call. I tried to come by and see you." She was talking to her friend now, and Eve was staring right at her, not at Myrnin, as if Claire were the actual threat in the room. "Eve?"

"I heard you."

"And?"

"And I'm thinking," she said. "Because you've been awfully chummy with Fang-Daddy Bishop. You're his little pet, scurrying around all over town, delivering his little love notes. Right?"

Claire couldn't really dispute that. "Not like I had a choice," she said. "Believe me, I'd rather not be in the middle of this, but he knew I belonged to Amelie. I was just another thing to take away from her, that's all. He likes making her squirm by using me."

Eve thawed just a tiny bit. "Sucks to be the object lesson."

"You have no idea."

"He hasn't, you know . . . ?" Eve mimed the fang thing, just in case Claire thought she meant something else. Then she looked worried about that, too.

"He's not interested in me at all," Claire assured her. "I'm just some pawn for him to move around on the chessboard. And besides, Myrnin looks after me." Myrnin waved his hand in the air, halfway between a dismissal and a prince's lazy wave of acknowledgment. "He won't let Bishop hurt me." Well . . . not much. If he was paying attention. "How about you?"

"It's been quiet," Eve said, and looked away for a moment. "My brother's been coming around to check on me."

Jason? Wow, that was not the most comforting thing Claire could think of. "Tell me you're kidding."

"No, he's . . . I think he finally has his head on straight. He seems . . . different. Besides, I need somebody on my side, and he's the only one still around."

"Jason is the one who *sold us out* at the feast; do you remember that? He kicked this whole thing off! Talk about me being Bishop's favorite—at least I didn't choose it!" Not until today, anyway.

Eve sent her a fierce glare. "Jason's still my brother. Hey, I wish he wasn't, but it's not like I got to pick my family!"

"You sound like Shane talking about his dad."

"Did you just come here to insult me, or do you have a *point*? Because if you don't, I need to get to work." Eve pushed away from the doorway and snatched up a patent-leather backpack and a set of keys, which she rattled impatiently. "That's Latin for *get the hell out*, by the way. I'd think a college girl like you would know that."

Myrnin slowly sat up, eyes going wider. "I'm sorry, little pale creature—did you just give us an order?"

"Not so much you as her, but yeah, if you want to take it that way. Sure, you knockoff Lestat. Get the hell out of my house." Eve waited expectantly, but nothing happened. "Damn, that really doesn't work anymore, does it?"

"Not since the owner of the house turned vampire," Myrnin said, and stood up in that eerie way he had, as if gravity had just been canceled in his neighborhood. "Please feel free to try to make me leave. I'd quite enjoy it."

"Myrnin." Claire sighed. "Eve. We're not enemies, okay? Stop poking at each other."

That got her stares from both of them. Not nice ones.

"We're just . . . passing through," Claire said, and felt a surge of real regret. "On our way to . . . Where are we going?"

"Somewhere remote," Myrnin said. "And I don't intend to tell your angry little friend about it in any case. Finish your babble. It's time to go."

As if it was his idea, and they weren't getting tossed out. Claire couldn't resist rolling her eyes.

She caught Eve doing the same thing, and they shared sudden, sheepish grins.

"Sorry," Claire murmured. "Honest, Eve. I miss you."

"Yeah," Eve said. "Miss you, too, freak. Wish I didn't, sometimes, but there you go."

Claire wasn't sure which of them moved first, but it really didn't matter; they both put their arms out, and the hug felt warm and good and real. Eve kissed her quickly on the cheek, then let go and hurried out, hiding her tears. "I'm leaving!" she shouted back, and disappeared into the hallway. "That means you should, too!" The front door slammed.

As Myrnin opened the portal in the wall, Claire grabbed up Shane's sweatshirt and pulled it on over her clothes. It was huge on her. She rolled up the sleeves, and couldn't resist lifting the neck to smell it one more time.

Myrnin smirked. "There is no drama so great as that of a teenage girl," he said.

"Except yours."

"Did no one ever teach you to respect your elders?" He grabbed her by the shoulder and pushed her through the portal. "Mind the gap. Oh, and you have black lipstick on your cheek."

They came out in a dim, damp basement—a generic sort of place, full of molding boxes. "You take me to the nicest places," Claire said, and sneezed. Myrnin shoved boxes out of his way without bothering to answer, uncovering a set of iron steps that looked to be more rust than actual iron. Claire followed him up, testing every tread carefully along the way. The whole thing seemed ready to collapse, but they made it to the top, which featured . . . a locked door.

Myrnin patted his pockets, sighed, and punched the lock with his fist. It shattered. The door sagged open, and he bowed to her like an old-school gentleman. Which he was, she supposed, on his good days.

"Where are we?"

"Morganville High School."

Claire hadn't ever set foot in the place. She'd started her senior year at the age of fifteen, courtesy of her mutant freak-smart brain, but as they stepped out into the hallway, she felt like she'd traveled back in time. Only a year, actually, which made it especially weird.

Scarred, polished linoleum floors. Industrial green walls. Battered rows of lockers stretching the length of the hallway, most secured with dial locks. Butcher-paper posters and banners advertising the Drama Club's production of *Annie Get Your Gun* and the band bake sale. The place smelled like industrial cleaners, sweat, and stress.

Claire paused to stare at the oversize painted mascot on the cinder-block wall at the end of the hallway.

"What?" Myrnin asked impatiently.

"Seriously. You guys have no sense of subtlety, do you?" It was the same image the boy at Richard Morrell's office had worn on his T-shirt: a menacing viper lunging, with fangs displayed. *Cute.*

"I have no idea what you mean. Come on. We have very little time before classes let out—"

A loud bell clattered, and all up and down the hallway, doors banged open, releasing floods of young people Claire's own age, or close to it. Myrnin grabbed Claire's arm and yanked her onward, fast.

School. It was surreal how normal it all seemed—like nobody could handle the truth, so they just kept on with all the surface lies, and in that sense, Morganville High was just like the rest of the town. All the chatter seemed falsely bright, and kids walked in thick groups, seeking comfort and protection.

They all avoided Myrnin and Claire, although *everybody* looked at them. She heard people talking. *Great. I'm famous in high school, finally.*

Another quick left turn led through a set of double doors, and the noise of feet, talk, and locker doors slamming faded behind them into velvety silence. Myrnin prodded her onward. More classrooms, but these were dark and empty.

"They don't use this part of the building?" Claire asked.

"No need for it," Myrnin said. "It was built with a plan that the human population of Morganville would grow. It hasn't."

"Can't imagine why," Claire muttered. "Such a great place to live and all. You'd think there'd be people just dying to get in. Operative word, dying."

He didn't bother to debate it. There was another door at the end of the hall, and this one had a shiny silver dead-bolt lock on it.

Myrnin knocked.

After a long moment of silence, the dead bolt was pulled back with a metallic *clank*, and the door swung open.

"Dr. Mills?" Claire was surprised. She hadn't heard much about Dr. Mills, ER doctor and their sometime lab assistant, for weeks. He'd dropped out of sight, along with his family. She'd tried to find out what had happened to him, but she'd been afraid it would be bad news. Sometimes, it was just better not to know.

"Claire," he said, and stepped back to let her and Myrnin inside the room. He closed and locked the door before turning a tired smile in her direction. "How are you, kid?"

"Um, fine, I guess. I was worried—"

"I know." Dr. Mills was middle-aged and kind of average in every way, except his mind, which was—even by Claire's standards—pretty sharp. "Mr. Bishop got word that I was doing research on vampire blood. He wanted it stopped—it's not in his best interest for anyone to get better right now, if you know what I mean. We had to move quickly. Myrnin relocated us." He nodded warily to Myrnin, who gave him a courtly sort of wave of acknowledgment.

"Your family, too?"

"My wife and kids are in the next room," he said. "It's not what you might call comfortable, but it's safe enough. We can use the gym showers at night. There's food in the cafeteria, books in the library. It's about the best safe haven we could have." Dr. Mills looked at Claire closely, and frowned. "You look tired."

"Probably," she said. "So . . . this is the new lab?"

"Seems like we always have a new one, don't we? At least this one has most of what we need." He gestured around vaguely. The room had clearly been intended to be a science classroom; it had the big granite-topped tables, equipped with sinks and built-in gas taps. At the back of the room were rows and rows of neat shelves filled with glass-ware and all kinds of bottled and labeled ingredients. One thing about Morganville—the town really did invest in education. "I've made some unexpected progress."

"Meaning?" Myrnin turned to look at him, suddenly not at all fey and weird.

"You know I've been trying to trace the origins of the disease?"

"The origins are not as important as developing an effective and con-sistent palliative treatment, not to mention mass producing the cure," Myrnin said. "As I've told you before. Loudly."

Dr. Mills looked at Claire for support, and she cleared her throat. "I think we can do both," she said. "I mean, it's important to know where something came from, too."

"That's the thing," Dr. Mills said. "It didn't seem to come from *anywhere*. There weren't any other vampire diseases; everything I tested within the medium of their blood went down without a fight, from colds and flu to cancer. Granted, I can't get my hands on some of the top-level contagious viruses, but I don't see anything in common be-tween this disease and any other, except one."

Myrnin forgot his objections and came closer. "Which one?"

"Alzheimer's disease. It's a progressive degenerative disease of—"

Myrnin gestured sharply. "I know what it is. You said it had things in common."

"The progress of the disease is similar, yes, but here's the thing: Bishop's blood contains antibodies. It's the *only* blood that contains antibodies. That means that there is a cure, and Bishop took it, because he contracted the disease and recovered."

Myrnin turned slowly and raised his eyebrows at Claire. It was a mild expression, but the look in his eyes was fierce. "Interpret, please."

"Bishop might have done this on purpose," she said. "Right, Dr. Mills? He might have developed this disease and deliberately spread it—used the cure only for himself. But why would he do that?"

"I have no idea."

Myrnin stalked away, moving in jerky, agitated strides; when a lab stool got in his way, he picked it up and smashed it into junk against the wall without so much as pausing. "Because he wants control," he said. "And revenge. It's perfect. He can once again decide who lives, who dies—he had that power once, until we took it from him. We thought he was destroyed. We were *sure.*"

"You and Amelie," Claire said. There was a long, ugly history behind all this—she didn't understand it and didn't really want to, but she knew that at some point, maybe hundreds of years ago, Amelie had tried to kill Mr. Bishop once and for all. "But you failed. And this is his way of hitting you back. Hitting you all back at once."

Myrnin stopped, facing a blank corner for a moment without replying. Then he slowly walked back toward them and took a seat on one of the lab stools that hadn't been destroyed, flipping back the tails of his frock coat as he sat. "So it is deliberate, this bane."

"Apparently," Claire said. "And now he's got you where he wants you."

Myrnin smiled. "Not quite." He gestured around the lab. "We do have weapons."

Most of the granite-topped tables had metal pans spread with drying reddish crystals. Claire nodded toward them with a frown. "I thought we were going with the liquid version of that stuff?" *That stuff* being the maintenance drug that she and Myrnin had developed—or at least refined to the point of being useful—that acted to keep the vampire disease's worst effects at bay. It wasn't a cure; it helped, but it had diminishing returns, at best.

"We were," Dr. Mills said. "But it takes longer to distill the liquid form than it does to manufacture the crystals, and we need to medicate more and more of the vampires—so here we are. Two prongs of attack."

"What about the cure?" He didn't look happy, and Claire's heart shrank down to a small, tight knot in her chest. "What's wrong?"

"Unfortunately, the sample of Bishop's blood we had degraded quickly," he said. "I was able to culture a small amount of serum out of it, but I'm going to need more of the base to really develop enough to matter."

"How much more of his blood do you need?"

"Pints," he said apologetically. "I know. Believe me, I know what you're thinking."

Claire was thinking of exactly how stupidly suicidal it would be to try to get *drops* of Bishop's blood, never mind pints. Myrnin had managed it once, but she doubted even he could pull it off twice without being staked and sunbathed to death. But she wasn't willing to give up, either. "We'd have to drug him," she said.

Myrnin looked up from fiddling with glassware on the table. "How? He's not one of those partial to human food and drink. And I doubt any of us could get close enough to give him a shot large enough to matter."

Claire pulled in a deep breath as it occurred to her in a cold and blinding flash. "We have to drug him through what it is he *does* drink."

"From everything I've heard about Bishop, he doesn't drink from blood bags," Dr. Mills said. "He only feeds from live victims."

Claire nodded. "I know." She felt sick saying it, so sick she almost couldn't speak at all. "But it's the only way to get to him—if you really want to end this."

The two men looked at her—one older than her, the other infinitely older—and for just a moment, they had the same expression on their faces: as if they'd never seen her before.

Myrnin said thoughtfully, "It's an idea. I'll have to give it some thought. The problem is that loading blood with sufficient poison to affect Bishop will certainly kill a human subject."

Poison. She'd been thinking of some kind of knockout drug—but that wouldn't work, she realized. Doses big enough to affect a vampire would be poison to humans in their bloodstream. "Does he always drink from humans?"

Myrnin flinched. She knew why; she knew Myrnin had drained a couple of vampire assistants he'd had, which was strictly against the rules. He'd done it accidentally, kind of, when he was crazy. "Not . . . always," he said, very quietly. "There are times—but he'd have to be greatly angered."

"Yeah, like that's a trick," Claire said. "Would it kill a vampire to put that amount of poison in his bloodstream?"

"The drugs would not necessarily kill a vampire," Myrnin said. "Bishop draining him certainly would."

The silence stretched. Myrnin looked down at his dirty feet in those ridiculous flip-flops. In the other room, Claire heard a child singing her ABCs, and then a woman's quiet voice hushing her.

"Myrnin," Claire said. "It doesn't have to be you."

Myrnin raised his head and fixed his gaze on hers.

"Of course it doesn't," he said. "But it will have to be someone you know. Someone you might perhaps like. Of all the people in Morganville, Claire, I never expected you to turn so cold to that possibility."

She shivered deep inside from the disappointment in his voice, and fisted her hands in the folds of Shane's oversize sweatshirt. "I'm not cold," she said. "I'm desperate. And so are you."

"Yes," Myrnin said. "That's unfortunately quite true."

He turned away, clasped his hands behind his back, and began to pace the far end of the room, turn after turn, head down.

Dr. Mills cleared his throat. "If you have some time, I need help bottling the serum I do have. There's enough for maybe twenty vampires—thirty if I stretch it. No more."

"Okay," Claire said, and followed him to the other side of the room, where a beaker and tiny bottles waited. She poured and handed him bottles to place the needle-permeable caps on with a metal crimper. The serum was milky and slightly pink. "How long does it take to work?"

"About forty-eight hours, according to my tests," he said. "I need to give it to Myrnin; he's the worst case we have who isn't already confined in a cell."

"He won't let you," Claire said. "He thinks he needs to be crazy so that Bishop can't sense that he's still working for Amelie."

Dr. Mills frowned at her. "Is that true?"

"I think he needs to be crazy," she said. "Just probably not for the reason he says."

Myrnin refused the shot. Of course. But he took pocketfuls of the medicine and disposable syringes, and escorted Claire back out of the lab. She heard the lock snap shut behind them.

"Are Dr. Mills and his family safe in there?" she asked. Myrnin didn't answer. "Are they?"

"As safe as anyone is in Morganville," he said, which really wasn't an answer. He stopped and leaned against a wall and closed his eyes. "Claire. I'm afraid. . . ."

"What?"

He shook his head. "I'm just afraid. And that's rare. That's so very rare."

He sounded lost and uncertain, the way he sometimes did when the disease began to take hold—but this was different. This was the real Myrnin, not the confused one. And it made Claire afraid, too.

She reached out and took his hand. It felt like a real person's hand, just cold. His fingers tightened on hers, briefly, and then released.

"I believe that it's time for you to learn some things," he said. "Come."

He pushed off from the wall, and led her at a brisk walk toward the portal, flip-flops snapping with urgency.

FIVE

Myrnin's actual lab was a deserted wreck.

Whether it was Bishop's goons, vandals, or just Myrnin being crazy, there was even more destruction now than the last time Claire had seen the place. Virtually all the glass had been shattered; it covered the floor in a deadly glitter. Tables had been overturned and splintered. Books had been ripped to shreds, with the leather and cloth covers gutted and empty, tossed on piles of trash.

The whole place smelled foul with spilled chemicals and molding paper.

Myrnin said nothing as they descended the steps into the mess, but on the last step, he paused and sat down—more like *fell* down, actually. Claire wasn't sure what to do, so she waited.

"You okay?" she finally asked. He slowly shook his head.

"I've lived here a long time," Myrnin said. "Mostly by choice, as it happens; I've always preferred a lab to a palace, which Amelie never really understood, although she humored me. I know it's only a place, only things. I didn't expect to feel so much . . . loss." He was silent again for a moment, and then sighed. "I shall have to rebuild again. But it will be a bother."

"But . . . not right now, right?" Because the last thing Claire wanted to do was get a broom and a dump truck to pick up all that broken glass when the fate of Morganville was riding on their staying focused.

"Of course not." He leaped up and—to her shock—walked across the broken glass. *In flip-flops.* Not even pausing when the glass got ankle-deep. Claire looked down at her own shoes—high-top sneakers—and sighed. Then she very carefully followed him, shoving a path through the glass as she went while Myrnin heedlessly crunched his way through.

"You're hurting yourself!" she called.

"Good," he shot back. "Life is pain, child. Ah! Excellent." He crouched down, brushed a clear spot on the floor, and picked up something that looked like a mouse skeleton. He examined it curiously for a few seconds, then tossed it over his shoulder. Claire ducked as it sailed past. "They didn't find it."

"Find what?"

"The entrance," he said. "To the machine."

"What machine?"

Myrnin smiled his best, looniest smile at her, and punched his fist down into the bare floor, which buckled and groaned. He punched again, and again—and an entire six-foot section of the floor just *collapsed* into a big black hole. "I covered it over," he said. "Clever, yes? It used to be a trapdoor, but that seemed just a bit too easy."

Claire realized her mouth was gaping open. "We could have fallen right through that," she said.

"Don't be overly dramatic. I calculated your weight. You were perfectly safe, so long as you weren't carrying anything too heavy." Myrnin waved at her to join him, but before she got halfway there, he jumped down into the hole and disappeared.

"Perfect." She sighed. When she finally reached the edge, she peered down, but it was pitch-black . . . and then there was the sound of a scratch, and a flame came to life, glowing on Myrnin's face a dozen feet down. He lit an oil lamp and set it aside. "Where are the stairs?"

"There aren't any," he said. "Jump."

"I can't!"

"I'll catch you. Jump."

That was a level of trust she really never wanted to have with Myrnin, but . . . there was no sign of mania in him, and he watched her with steady concentration.

"If you don't catch me, I'm totally killing you. You know that, right?"

He raised a skeptical eyebrow, but didn't dispute that. "Jump!"

She did, squealing as she fell—and then she landed in his strong, cold arms, and at close range, his eyes were wide and dark and almost—*almost*—human.

"See?" he murmured. "Not so bad as all that, was it?"

"Yeah, it was great. You can put me down now."

"What? Oh. Yes." He let her slide to the ground, and picked up the oil lamp. "This way."

"Where are we?" Because it looked like wide, industrial tunnels, obviously pretty old. Original construction, probably.

"Catacombs," he said. "Or drainage tunnels? I forget how we originally planned it. Doesn't matter; it's all been sealed off for ages. Mind the dead man, my dear."

She looked down and saw that she was standing not on some random sticks, but on *bones*. Bones in a tattered, ancient shirt and trousers. And there was a white skull staring at her from nearby, too. Claire screamed and jumped aside. "What the *hell*, Myrnin?"

"Unwanted visitor," he said. "It happens. Oh, don't worry; I didn't kill him. I didn't have to—there are plenty of safeguards in place. Now come on, stop acting like you've never seen a dead man before. I told you, this is important."

"Who was he?"

"What does it matter? He's dust, child. And we are not, as yet, although at this rate we certainly may be before we get where we're going. Come on!"

She didn't want to, but she wanted to stay inside the circle of the lamplight. Dark places in Morganville really were full of things that could eat you. She joined Myrnin, breathless, as he marched down an endlessly long tunnel that seemed to appear ten feet ahead and disappear ten feet behind them.

And suddenly, the roof disappeared, and there was a cave. A big one.

"Hold this," Myrnin said, and passed her the lamp. She juggled it, careful to avoid hot glass and metal, and Myrnin opened a rusty cabinet on the wall of the tunnel and pulled down an enormous lever.

The lamp became completely redundant as bright lights began to shine, snapping on one by one in a circle around the huge cavern. The beams glittered off a tangled mass of glass and metal, and as Claire blinked, things came into focus.

"What is that?"

"My difference engine," Myrnin said. "The latest version, at least. I built the core of it three hundred years ago, but I've added to and embroidered on it over the years. Oh, I know what you're thinking—this isn't Babbage's design, that limited and stupid thing. No, this is half art, half artifice. With a good dash of genius, if I might say so."

It looked like a huge pipe organ, with rows and rows of thin metal plates all moving and clacking together in vertical columns. The whole thing hissed with steam. In and around that were spaghetti tangles of cables, tubes, and—in some cases—colorful duct tape. There were three huge glass squares, too thick to be monitors, and in the middle was a giant keyboard with every key the size of Claire's entire hand. Only instead of letters on it, there were symbols. Some of them—many of them— she knew from her studies with Myrnin about alchemy. Some of them were vampire symbols. A few were just . . . blank, like maybe there'd been something on them once, but it had worn completely off.

Myrnin patted the dirty metal flank of the beast affectionately. It let out a hiss from several holes in the tubing. "This is Ada. She's what drives Morganville," Myrnin said. "And I want you to learn how to use her."

Claire stared at it, then at him, then at the machine once again. "You're kidding."

And the machine said, "No. He's not. Unfortunately."

Claire had seen a lot of weird stuff since moving to Morganville, but a living, steam-operated Frankenstein of a computer, built out of wood and scraps?

That was just too much.

She sat down suddenly on the hard rocks, gasping for breath, and rested her head on her trembling palms. Distantly, she heard the computer—that was what it was, right?—ask, "Did you break another one, Myrnin?" and Myrnin answered, "You are not to speak until spoken to, Ada. How many times do I have to tell you?"

Claire honestly didn't even know how to start to deal with this. She just sat, struggling to keep herself from freaking out totally, and Myrnin finally flopped down next to her. He reclined, with his arms folded behind his head, staring straight up.

"What do you want to know?" he asked.

"I don't," she said, and wiped trickles of tears from her face. "I don't want to know *anything* anymore. I think I'm going crazy."

"Well, it's always a possibility." He shrugged. "Ada is a living mind inside an artificial form. A brilliant woman—a former assistant of mine, actually. This preserved the best parts of her. I have never regretted taking the steps to integrate technology and humanity."

"Well, of course you wouldn't. I have," Ada said, from nowhere in particular. Claire shuddered. There was something not quite right about that voice, as if it was coming out of some old, cheap AM radio speakers that had been blown out a few times. "Tell your new friend the truth, Myrnin. It's the least you can do."

He closed his eyes. "Ada was dying because I had a lapse."

"In other words," the computer said acidly, "he killed me. And then he trapped me inside this box. Forever. The fact that he doesn't regret it only proves how far from human he is."

"You are *not* trapped in the box forever," Myrnin said, "as you well know. But I still need you, so you will simply have to stop your endless wailing and get on with things. If you want an escape, research your way out."

"Or you'll what?"

Myrnin's eyes snapped open, and he bared his fangs—not that he could bite the *computer*. It was just a reaction of frustration, Claire thought. "Or I'll disconnect your puzzle sets," he said, "and you can read the works of Bulwer-Lytton for entertainment for the next twenty years before I take pity on you."

Ada was notably silent in response to that, and Myrnin folded up his fangs and smiled. "Now," he said to Claire, "let me explain Ada. She is the life force that powers the town, of course; without her, we could not operate the portals, and we could not maintain the invisible fields that ensure Morganville residents stay put, and suffer memory loss if they manage to make their way out of town. The drawback is that Ada is a living being, and living beings have . . . moods. Feelings. She has been known to grow fond of people, and to sometimes interfere. Such as with your friend Michael."

"Michael?" Claire blinked, intrigued despite everything. She didn't *want* to know more. . . . Oh, hell, yes she did. She really did. "What do you mean?"

"I mean that Ada interceded to keep Michael alive, because she could. Ada's presence is most felt in the Founder Houses, which are closely linked to her; she can, with enough of an effort, manifest in them, or anywhere there is a portal, for short periods of time. In Michael's case, she chose to save his life by storing him in the matrix of the Glass House rather than allowing him to die when Oliver attempted, and failed, to turn him into a vampire."

"She didn't just save him, she *saved* him," Claire said. "Like a computer saving a crashed file."

"I suppose, if you want to put it in mundane terms." Myrnin yawned. "I told her to let him go. She ignored me. She does that."

"Frequently," Ada's disembodied voice said. "And with great satisfaction. So. You are the girl from the Glass House. Myrnin's new pet."

"I . . ." Claire wasn't sure how to respond to that, so she settled for a quick shrug. "I guess."

"You've done well," Ada said. "You work the portals without much understanding of how they function or how to create them, but I suppose that most modern children couldn't begin to construct the toys with which they play."

Claire's cell phone suddenly rang, its cheerful electronic tone startling in the silence. She jumped, flailed, and fished it out of her pocket, only to have it immediately go dark.

"Did you do that?" she asked.

"Do what?" Ada asked, but there was a dark, amused edge to the words. "Oh, do forgive. I've got little enough to occupy me down here in the *dungeon*. In my *box*."

"Ada." Myrnin sighed. "I brought her here so you could explain to her how to maintain your functions, not to have her listen to your endlessly inventive complaints."

Ada said nothing. Nothing at all. In the silence, Claire heard the steady whir and click of gears turning, and the hiss of steam—but Ada stayed quiet.

"She's pouting," Myrnin said, and heaved himself up to a sitting position. "Don't worry, my dear. You can trust Claire. Here, let me introduce you properly."

Myrnin's idea of a proper introduction was to grab Claire by the arm and haul her over in front of the machine. Before she could yell at him to let go, he slipped back a metal cover and pushed her hand down on a metal plate . . . and something pierced her palm, lightning fast, like a snakebite. Claire tried to snatch her hand back, but something—some *force*—held it in place.

She could feel blood trickling out of the hot, aching wound. "Let go!" she yelled, and kicked the machine in fury. "Hey! *Hey!*"

Ada giggled. It was a weirdly metallic sound; up close, she really didn't sound human at all, more like parts grinding together inside.

The force holding Claire's hand in place suddenly let go, and she stumbled back, clutching her burning hand to her chest and trying—without much success—to stop herself from gasping for breath. She was afraid to look, but she forced herself to open her left hand.

There was a small puncture wound in the middle of her palm, a red circle about the size of a pencil point; there was a whiter circle all around it, like a target. As Claire watched, the white faded.

Blood trickled out of the hole in her skin in fat red drops. Claire looked at Myrnin, who was standing a few feet away; he was gazing at her hand with fascination.

Ewwwwww.

Claire made a fist, willing the bleeding to stop. "What the hell was *that?*"

"That?" Myrnin didn't seem to be able to take his gaze off of her fist. "Oh, it's simple enough. Ada needed to know who you were. She'll know you now, and she'll follow your orders."

Ada made a sound suspiciously like a strangled cough.

"That doesn't explain why she *bit me!*" Claire said.

Myrnin blinked. "Blood is the fuel that drives the engine, my dear. As with us all. Ada requires regular infusions of blood to operate."

"You never heard of *plugging her in?* My God, Myrnin, you made a vampire computer?"

"I . . ." He seemed honestly unsure how to answer that, and finally gave up. "She requires about a pint of blood each month—not refrigerated blood; it should be warmed to at least room temperature, preferably to body temperature, of course. I generally feed her close to the beginning of the month, though she can, in a pinch, go weeks without nourishment. Oh, and do feed her at night. Blood is less effective when offered under the influence of the sun. We do work according to hermetic rules here, you know."

"You're insane," Claire said. She backed up against a wall and stood there staring at him. "Seriously. *Insane.*"

He didn't pay any attention to her at all. "You also need to recalibrate her once on each solstice day, winter and summer, to accommodate the shifting influences of sun and moon. You do remember the hermetic symbology I taught you, don't you? Well, the formula is quite simple. I've noted it down for you, here." Myrnin patted his jacket pockets, and finally came up with a much-scratched-out, torn scrap of grimy paper, which he offered to Claire.

She didn't take it. "This is crazy," she said again, as if it was really important that he understand it. Myrnin slowly raised his eyebrows. "You built a vampire computer. Out of *wood*. And *glass*. You're not . . . This isn't . . ."

He patted her gently on the shoulder. "This is Morganville, dear Claire. You should know by now that it would not be what you expect." With a sudden burst of energy, Myrnin took Claire's unwilling hand, slapped the paper into it, and bounced to his feet. "Ada!"

"What?" The computer sounded surly. Hurt. *She's not even real,* Claire told herself. *Yeah. She's not real, and she drinks blood. She just drank* mine.

"You will accept all commands from Claire Danvers as my own. Do you understand me?"

"All too clearly." Ada sighed. "Very well. I shall record her essence for future reference."

Myrnin turned back to Claire and folded her hand over the scrap of paper. His fingernails were filthy and sharp, and she shuddered at how cold his touch was. "Please," he said. "You must keep this safe. It's the only record of the sequence. I made it to remind myself, in case . . . when I forgot. If you get the sequence wrong, you could risk killing her. Or worse."

Claire shuddered. "What could be worse than her being here at all?"

"Turning her against us," Myrnin said. "And believe me, dear, you wouldn't want that to happen."

SIX

By the time they made their way out of Ada's cavern, it was night—full, dark night.

Which was a problem.

"We can't walk," she told Myrnin, for about the eleven hundredth time. "It's not safe out there. You really don't get it!"

"Of course I get it," he said. "There are vampires a-roaming the dark. Very frightening. I'm quaking in my beach sandals. Come on; buck up, girl. I'll protect you." And then he leered like a total freak show, which made Claire feel not so much reassured. She didn't trust him. He was starting to get that jittery, manic edge she dreaded, and he kept insisting that he couldn't take the serum yet—or even the maintenance drug, the red crystals that Claire kept in a bottle in her backpack.

Past a certain point, Myrnin was crazy enough that he thought he was normal. That was when things got really, really dangerous around him.

"We could take the portal," Claire said. Myrnin, halfway up the stairs, didn't so much as pause.

"No, we can't," he said. "Not from this node. I've shut it down. I don't want anyone else coming here anymore. They'll ruin my work."

Claire took a look around at the wreckage—the smashed glass, the shredded books, the broken furniture. In her view, there wasn't anything *left* for vandals to destroy, and even if there was, sealing up the portal wouldn't stop them; it would only inconvenience her (and Myrnin) from getting here.

Only . . . maybe that was what he intended. "What about the entrance to the cave?" she asked. He snapped his fingers as if he'd forgotten all about it.

"Excellent point."

Myrnin dragged the largest, heaviest table over, top down, and covered up with it the hole he'd made in the floor. Then he took handfuls of broken glass and mounded it up on all sides.

"What if they move the table?" she asked.

"Then they'll find Ada, and my countermeasures will likely eat them," he said happily. "Speaking of that, I really must find some lunch. Not you, dear."

Claire would have been happier if he'd had some magical way to repair it, but she supposed that would have to do. It looked like the bad guys had been through this place a dozen times already, anyway; they probably wouldn't be back and in the mood to redecorate.

Claire unzipped her backpack. At the bottom, rattling around loose, were two sharpened wooden stakes. She took one out and slipped it into her pocket. It wouldn't kill a vampire by itself, but it would paralyze one until it was removed . . . and it would weaken one enough to die by other means.

If trouble came—even if it was Myrnin himself—she'd settle for slowing it down long enough for her to run for her life.

Myrnin artistically sprinkled some more broken glass. "There," Myrnin said, and backed off to the stairs again. "What do you think?"

"Fabulous." She sighed. "Brilliant job of camouflage."

"Normally, I'd add a corpse," he said, "just to keep people at bay. But that might be good enough."

"Yeah, that's . . . good enough," she said. "Can we go now?" Before he decided to go with the corpse idea.

As she followed Myrnin out of the wreck of a shack that covered the entrance to his lair, he took the time to carefully close and padlock the door. Which was really ridiculous, because Claire could have kicked right through the rotten old boards, and she wasn't exactly She-Hulk.

Claire pulled her phone out and flipped it open, scrolling for Eve's number.

Myrnin batted it right out of her hand, straight up into the air like a jump ball, and caught it with ease. He grinned smugly, all sharp teeth at crazy angles, and put the phone in his jacket pocket. "Now, now," he chided her. "Where's your sense of adventure?"

"Off on a beach somewhere with your sanity? We can't do this. You know what happens out on the streets at night."

"I can't help that. I need some air, and besides, walking is very healthy for humans, you know." With that, Myrnin dismissed her and started walking down the narrow alley into the dark. Claire gaped for a second, then hurried after him, because the being-left-behind option didn't seem all that fantastic a choice. On her right, over the high wooden fence, she saw the looming dark bulk of the Day House. It was deserted these days. Gramma Day had moved out, temporarily, and her daughter had gone into hiding—probably for good, considering that she'd thrown in her lot with the antivampire forces in town, and that had not gone well for anybody.

Claire slowed for a second, staring at the unlit windows of the house. She could have sworn that in the cold starlight she'd seen one of those white lace curtains move. "Myrnin," she said. "Is there somebody in there?"

"Very likely." He didn't slow down. "People are hiding out in dozens of places all over Morganville, waiting."

"Waiting for what?"

"God to descend from on high and save them? Who knows?"

From the other side of the fence, Claire heard a faint, breathless giggle. She came to a stop, staring at Myrnin, who paused and looked at the fence, shook his head, and shrugged. He moved on.

But Claire was convinced that whatever was on the Day side of the fence was pacing them now, and when they got to the end of the row . . .

Bad. That will be bad.

"Myrnin, maybe we should call somebody. You know, get a cab. Or Eve, we could call Eve—"

Myrnin turned on her.

It happened fast, so *fast*, and she barely had time to gasp and duck as he came at her, a white blur in the starlight. There was a sense of hard impact, of falling, and then everything went a little soft around the edges.

Myrnin was stretched out on top of her, and as the world stopped wobbling, she realized she was flat on her back on the ground. "Get off!" she yelped, and battered at his chest with both fists. "Off!"

He put his cold hand over her mouth and lifted a single finger of his other hand to his lips. She couldn't see his face in the shadows, but she saw the gesture, and it made the panic in her shift directions from *oh my God, Myrnin's going to bite me* to *oh my God, Myrnin's trying to save me.*

Myrnin dipped his head low, so low he was well within critical vein range, and she heard him whisper, "Don't move. Stay here."

Then he was gone, just like that. As noisy as he could be at times, he could also be as silent as a shadow when he wanted.

Claire raised her head just a little to look around, but she saw nothing. Just the alley, the fence, the sky overhead with wispy clouds moving across the stars.

And Myrnin's flip-flops, which he'd left behind, lying sad and abandoned on the ground.

There was a sudden, enraged shriek from the other side of the fence, and something crashed against the wood with enough force to splinter heavy boards. Claire rolled to her feet, heart pounding, and gripped the stake in her hand hard. *Funny, I didn't think to use it on Myrnin. . . .* Maybe she'd known, deep down, that he was acting to protect her.

She hoped so. She hoped it wasn't that she couldn't see the threat in him anymore, because that would eventually get her killed.

Whatever was happening on the other side of the fence, it was bad. It sounded like tigers fighting, and as she backed up from the snarls and howls and sounds of bodies slamming around, the boards of the fence broke again, and a white hand—not Myrnin's, this was a woman's— clawed the air.

Reaching for Claire.

"I've changed my mind," Myrnin called. He sounded eerily normal. "Do go on and run, Claire. I'll catch up. This may take a few moments."

She didn't wait. She grabbed up her fallen backpack and ran for the exit of the alley, where it dumped out into the cul-de-sac next to the Day House.

A vampire car was parked there, door open, engine idling. Nobody around.

Claire hesitated, then looked inside. In the glow of the instrument panel, she couldn't see much: dark upholstery, mainly. She didn't think there was anybody inside, although it was tough to see into the back. She ducked into the cabin and flipped on the overhead light, then bounced back on her heels with the stake held in her most threatening way possible. (Which, she had to admit, probably wasn't very intimidating at all.)

Luckily, nothing lunged at her from the backseat.

Claire threw herself behind the wheel, dumped her backpack on the floorboard of the passenger side, and slammed the door. She leaned on the horn, a long blast, and yelled, "Myrnin! Come on!"

It was a risk. There was every possibility that whoever won that fight back there, it wouldn't be Myrnin opening the car door, but she had to try. He'd taken on another vampire—more than one, she thought—to save her life. The least she could do was give him fair warning that she was about to speed away and leave him behind.

It was impossible to see through the dark tinting on the windshield and windows. Claire counted to ten, slowly and deliberately, and got to a whispered *seven* before there was a casual knock on the passenger window. She yelped, fumbled, and found the switch that rolled down the glass.

Myrnin leaned in and smiled at her. "Fair lady, may I ride with you in your carriage?"

"God—get in!" He looked . . . messy. Messier than usual, anyway; his coat was shredded in places, he had bloodless scratches on his face, and his eyes were still glowing a dull, muddy red. As he slid into the passenger seat, she caught a sharp scent from him—fresh vampire blood. In the dashboard glow, she saw traces of it around his mouth and smeared on his hands. "Who was it?"

"No idea," Myrnin said, and yawned. His fangs flashed lazily. "Someone Bishop set to spy on me, no doubt. She won't be reporting back. Sadly, her companion was too fast for me. And too frightened."

He was so casual about it. Claire, freaked, made sure all the doors were locked and the windows rolled up, and then realized that they were sitting in an idling car, and she couldn't see a thing ahead of her. Of course. It was a standard-issue vampire-edition sedan. Not meant for humans at all.

Myrnin sighed. "Please, allow me."

"Do you have the faintest idea of how to drive a car?"

"I am a very fast learner."

In fact, he wasn't.

Myrnin dropped Claire off at her parents' house well before dawn, tossed her cell phone out of the car to her, and drove off still bumping into curbs and running over mailboxes with cheerful abandon. He seemed to enjoy driving. That terrified her, but he was officially the Morganville police's problem, not hers.

The weight of the day crashed in on her as she unlocked the front door, and all she wanted to do was crawl onto the sofa in the living room and go to sleep, but she smelled like dirt, old bones, and other things she didn't really want to think about. *Shower.* Mom and Dad were in bed, she guessed; their door was shut at the top of the stairs. She tiptoed past it to the far end of the hall, dumped her backpack on the bed, and pulled an old thin cotton nightgown from a drawer before heading to the bathroom.

Déjà vu struck her as she locked the door and turned on the water. Mom and Dad's Founder House was the same layout as the Glass House—which still felt more like home, even though she'd been in both houses for about the same amount of time. Even the countertops and flooring were the same. Only the Mom-approved shower curtain and bath towels were different. *I want to go back.* Claire sat down on the toilet seat and let the sadness well up inside. *I want to go back to my friends. I want to see Shane. I want all this to stop.*

Not that any genie was going to pop in and grant her wishes, unfortunately. And crying didn't make anything easier, in the end.

After the long, hot shower, she felt a little better—cleaner, anyway, and pleasantly tired. Claire used the dryer on her hair until it was a tousled mop—it was getting longer now, and brushed her shoulders when she combed it out. Her eyes looked a little haunted. She needed sleep, and about a month with nobody trying to kill her. After that, she could deal with all the chaos again. Probably.

She touched the delicate cross Shane had given her, and thought about him trapped in a cage halfway across town. Amelie had made her a promise, but it had been significantly light on specifics and timing; she also hadn't really promised to set Shane free, only to keep him from being executed.

Claire was still thinking about that when she turned on the lights in her bedroom and found Michael sitting on the bed.

"Hey!" she blurted, and grabbed a fluffy pink robe from the back of her door to cover herself up, suddenly aware of just how thin her nightgown really was. "What are you *doing?*" After the first surge of embarrassment, though, she felt an equally strong wave of delight. She hadn't seen Michael—not on his own, away from Bishop—since that horrible day when everything had gone so wrong for all of them.

As she struggled into her robe, he stood up, holding out both hands in a very Michael-ish sort of attempt at calming her down. "Wait! I'm not who you think I am. I'm not here to hurt you, Claire. Please believe me—"

Oh. He thought she still believed he was Bishop's little pet. "Yeah, you're working for Amelie, not evil anymore, I get it. That doesn't mean you can show up without warning when I'm in my nightgown!"

Michael gave her a smile of utter relief and lowered his hands. He looked a million miles tall to her just then, and when he opened his arms, she just about flew into his embrace. She came nearly up to his chin. He was a vampire, so there was no sense of warmth from his body, but there was comfort, real and strong. Michael was his own person. Always.

There was genuine love in him. She could feel it.

"Hey, kid," he said, and hugged her with care, well aware of his strength. "You doing okay?"

"I'm okay, and man, I wish everybody would stop asking me," she said, and pulled back to look at him. "What are you doing here?"

Michael's face took on hard lines, and he sat down on the bed again. Claire climbed up next to him, feeling her happiness bleed away. She picked up a pillow and hugged it absently. She needed something to hold.

"Bishop sent me out to run one of his errands," he said. "He still thinks I'm one of his good little soldiers. At least, I hope he does. This is probably his idea of a test."

"Sent you out to do what?"

"You don't want to know." Clearly, something that Michael hated. His blue eyes were shadowed, and he didn't seem to want to look at her directly. "Things are getting too dangerous for you to be in the middle of this. Promise me you won't come back to Bishop. Not even if he uses that tattoo to call for you. Just stay away from him. Handcuff yourself to a railing if you have to, but don't go back."

"But—"

"Claire." He took her hand and squeezed it. "Trust me. Please. You have to stay here. Stay safe."

She nodded mutely, suddenly more afraid than she'd been all night. "You know something. You heard something."

"It's not that simple," Michael said. "It's more of a feeling. Bishop's getting bored, and when he gets bored with something . . . he breaks it."

"You mean me?"

"I mean Morganville," he said. "I mean everything. Everybody. You're just an easy, obvious target."

Claire swallowed hard. "But you . . . you're okay, right?"

"Yeah." He sighed and ran a hand through his curling blond hair. "I'd better be. Not much of a choice anymore. Don't worry about me—if I need to get out, I will. I'm just trying to stay with it as long as I can."

Claire hated the sadness in him, and the anger, and she wished she could say something to make him feel better. Anything.

Wait—there was something. "I saw Eve."

That got an immediate response from him—his head jerked up, and his blue eyes widened. "How is she?" There was so much emotion behind the question it made Claire shiver.

"She's good," Claire said, which wasn't exactly true. "She's, uh, kind of pissed, actually. I had to tell her. About you being not really evil."

Michael sighed and closed his eyes for a moment. "I'm not sure that was a good idea."

"It will be if you go see her tonight and tell her . . . well, whatever. Oh, but watch out. She's gone all Buffy with the stakes and things."

"Sounds like what she'd do, all right." Michael was smiling now, happier than she'd seen him in months. "Maybe I'll try to see her. Thank you."

"You're welcome." She wasn't sure how much more to say, but she was tired of not telling the truth. "She really loves you, you know. She always has."

He sat for a few seconds in silence, then shook his head. "I'd better let you rest," he said. "Remember what I said. Stay here. Don't go back to Bishop."

"Aye-aye, Captain." She mock-saluted him. "Hey. I missed you, Fang Boy."

"You've been hanging around Eve too much."

"Not nearly enough. Not recently, anyway." And she was sad about that.

"I know," he said, and kissed the back of her hand. "We'll fix it. Get some sleep."

"Night," she said, and watched him walk toward the door. "Hey. How'd you get in?"

He wiggled his fingers at her in a spooky oogie-boogie pantomime. "I'm a *vampire*. I have *secret powers*," he said with a full-on fake Transylvanian accent, which he dropped to say, "Actually, your mom let me in."

"Seriously? *My* mom? Let *you* in my room? In the middle of the night?"

He shrugged. "Moms like me."

He gave her a full-on Hollywood grin, and slipped out the door.

Claire got under the covers and, for the first time all night, felt like it was safe to sleep.

In the morning—not *too* early—Claire found cereal and juice waiting for her downstairs, along with a note from her mother that she'd gone shopping, and that she hoped Claire would stay home today. It was the same sort of note Mom left every day. At least, the "hope you stay home" part.

Claire intended to, this time. She intended to right up until she looked at her calendar, and realized what day it was, and that it was circled in red with multicolored exclamation points all around it.

"Oh, *crap!*" she muttered, and pawed through her backpack, hauling out textbooks, notebooks, her much-abused laptop, floods of colored markers, and assorted change. She found the purple notebook, the one she kept for important test dates.

Today was the final exam for her physics class. Fifty percent of her grade, and no makeup tests for anything less than life support.

It's only a test. Michael said—

It wasn't only a test; it was her most important final exam. And if she didn't show up for it, she'd automatically fail a class she had no business not acing. Besides, Michael had said not to hang around *Bishop*—he hadn't said anything about going to classes. That was normal life.

She needed normal right now.

After the cereal and juice, Claire packed her backpack and set out in the cool morning for Texas Prairie University. It was a short walk from pretty much anywhere in Morganville; from her parents' house, the route took her down four residential blocks, then into Morganville's so-called business district, about six square blocks of stores. Walking in daylight showed just how much Morganville had changed since Mr. Bishop had shown up: burned-out houses on every block, with few attempts to clear them away or rebuild. Abandoned houses, doors hanging open and windows broken. Once she got into the business district, half the stores were shut, either temporarily or permanently. Oliver's coffee shop, Common Grounds, was shuttered and quiet, with a Closed sign in the dark window.

Everywhere, there was a feeling that the town was holding its breath, closing its eyes, trying to wish away its problems. The few people Claire saw trying to go about their normal lives seemed either jumpy and distracted, or as if they were putting on some false smile and happy face. It was creepy, and she felt a little bit relieved when she passed the gates of the university—open, like it was a regular sort of day—and fell in with the crowds of young people moving around the campus. TPU wasn't a huge school, but it sprawled over a fairly large area, with lots of park spaces and quads. She usually would have made a stop at the University Center for a mocha, but there wasn't time. Instead, she headed for the science building, navigating the crowds piling into Chem 101 and Intro to Geology. The physics classes were held toward the end of the hallway, and they were a lot less well attended. TPU wasn't exactly MIT on the plains; most students just wanted to get their core courses and transfer out to better schools. Most of them never had a single clue about the true nature of Morganville, because they didn't get off campus all that much—TPU prided itself on its student services.

Of course, there were also local students, destined to stay in Morganville their entire lives. Until a few months ago, she could have identified those people at a glance, because they'd be wearing identification bracelets with odd symbols on them to identify the vampire they owed their allegiance to—their Protector. Only that system had mostly broken down after Bishop's arrival. The vampires were no longer Protectors; most were out-and-out predators. No more blood banks, at least for those loyal to Bishop; they were all about hunting.

Hunting people.

So far, Bishop had seen the wisdom of keeping his hunting parties out of the TPU campus; after all, the kids here helped fund the town and keep the economy running. Most of them stayed on campus, where they had everything they needed except for the occasional trip to a store or a bar, so they didn't know much—and couldn't care less—about Morganville. Morganville didn't offer much in the way of entertainment, when you came right down to it. Even the shops were boring.

If he started allowing his vampires to hunt students, it would get very,

very bad. Claire couldn't even imagine how the fragile system Morganville was built on could survive an exposure like that—the press would show up. The government. Not even Amelie could keep control under those kinds of conditions, and Bishop wouldn't even bother to try.

Looking around, all Claire could think about was how precarious it was—and how oblivious everybody was to the tipping point.

Claire slid into her usual seat in her physics class, two minutes early. There were only about ten other people attending now; they'd started out with about twenty, but plenty had dropped out, and of those who were left, she thought she was the only one with a solid A. As in most of her classes, nobody made eye contact. Unless you had friends when you came to TPU, you weren't likely to make them casually.

Claire's professor didn't put in an appearance, but his teaching assistant did, a twenty-two-year-old Morganville native named Sanaj, who handed out sealed tests but told the students not to open them yet. Claire tapped her pen impatiently on the test, waiting for time. She expected this to be over fast—after all, she'd mastered most of the basics of this class in the first two weeks. If she was fast enough, she might be able to grab a coffee, say hello to Eve, and get the scoop on whether Michael had dropped in for a visit. She was dying to hear all about it.

The door at the bottom of the lecture hall opened, and in strolled Monica Morrell.

Claire hadn't seen her archenemy much lately, but that had mostly been good luck on her part. Monica had been highly visible—first at her dad's funeral, then taking her role as Morganville's First Sister as a blanket excuse for any kind of crazy behavior she wanted to try. Most people in town looked worn, tired, and worried, including Monica's own brother, the mayor; not Monica, though. She looked like she was deeply enjoying herself these days. She'd gone through a bad patch for a while, after losing her status as Oliver's best girl, but disgrace was something that never seemed to stick, not to her.

Monica walked slowly. She was the center of attention and loving every minute of it. She'd gone off blond again; Claire thought the new color suited her better anyway, but she doubted it would last. Monica changed her hair the way she changed her makeup—according to mood and trend.

Currently, though, she'd let her hair grow out, long and lustrous, and it was a dark, bouncy brown. Her makeup was—of course—perfect, on a perfect face flawed only by the nasty arrogance that showed in her smile. Claire was wearing blue jeans and a camp shirt over a red tee; Monica was dressed in a flirty little dress, something more suited to Hollywood than Morganville, and some impressively tall shoes in magenta that Claire was sure had come mail-order—no store in town would have carried those. In short, she looked glossy, perfect, and utterly in command of herself and everything around her.

Behind her trailed her perpetual wingmen, Gina and Jennifer. They looked good, but never as good as Monica. That was how the whole thing worked: the backup singers never took center stage.

Sanaj paused at the top of the terraced classroom in handing out the last couple of tests to look down at Monica and her groupies. "Miss?" he asked. "Can I help you?"

"Doubt it." Monica sniffed. "I'm not here for you." Her eyes focused on Claire, and she smiled. She made a little come-here motion.

Claire calmly sent her back a middle finger. Monica pouted, an effect greatly enhanced by her shiny pink lip gloss. "Don't be that way, Claire," she said. "It'd be a shame if something happened to these nice people."

The TA looked honestly shocked and offended. "Excuse me; are you threatening my students?"

Monica rolled her eyes. "Look, idiot, just sit down and shut up. This doesn't concern you. If you think it does, I'll call up my new friend. Maybe you know him?" She pulled out a tiny bejeweled phone and held it at eye level, ready to dial. "Mr. Bishop?"

Sanaj handed out the last two tests in silence and looked at Claire apologetically. "Perhaps you should talk with your friend outside," he said. "So as not to disturb the other students."

"But I'm taking the test!"

Monica began to slowly dial a number. Sanaj grew pale, watching her—he was clearly one of those who knew the score. "No," he said, and grabbed Claire's test from her desk. "I'm sorry. You can take the test once you're finished with them. Please go."

"But—"

"Go now!"

The other students had their heads down, though they were shooting Claire looks that were sympathetic, scared, or angry. Nobody tried to stand up for her.

Claire put her pen down, looked Sanaj in the eyes, and said, "Save my test. I'm coming back."

He nodded and turned away.

She walked down to meet Monica on the stage.

"Well, that was easy," Monica said, and flipped her phone closed. "Hey, loser. How goes the war? Oh, yeah, you lost."

"What do you want?" Claire was determined to get it over with, fast. She wasn't interested in fighting, or sparring, or even sarcasming. Monica smiled at her and put her phone in her tiny little purse.

"Walk with me," she said. "Let's find out."

Claire resisted making an Eve-style joke about Monica's gaudy shoes, and silently followed Monica out of the classroom. Gina and Jennifer brought up the rear guard.

Outside, the hallway was mostly deserted, except for a few students hurrying late to classes. Monica led the way around the corner to a break area with well-used chairs and study tables. She took a seat, showing off her perfectly waxed legs.

She looked like a queen on a throne. Instead of standing in front of her like some criminal waiting to be judged, Claire moved to a chair off to the side and flopped down. Monica's smile curdled. "Fine," Claire said. "You've got me. What now? The beatings will continue until my attitude improves?"

"Cut the crap," Monica said. "I'm not in the mood. What did you do to my brother?"

"Your . . ." Claire sat up slowly. "Richard? What happened to Richard?"

"Like you don't know? Please. He's *missing*. He disappeared right after he talked to you—went out the door and never came back. I know it's something you said to him. Tell me what you talked about." Her eyes narrowed at Claire's silence. "Don't make me say *please.*"

Claire tried to stand up. Gina, positioned behind her, pushed down on her shoulders and held her in the chair.

Jennifer moved in from the side and took out a folding knife.

"Tell me," Monica said, "or I promise you, this is going to get ugly. And so will you."

Claire felt a nasty, cold burst of fear. Sure, she could scream the place down, but this was *Morganville*. She wasn't sure anybody would come. And besides, Monica—who'd had a brief, shining period as the town pariah—had turned back into her usual glossy, predatory self again. Bishop had interviewed her and found her amusing. Claire figured he thought lots of nasty, stinging things were amusing, too. But he'd given her his official seal of approval and sent her out with a new sense of entitlement, which Monica had promptly translated into a mandate to hurt everyone who'd kicked her when she was down.

Some of those people were no longer around at all, which put Claire among the lucky ones.

"I went to Richard to ask him for a favor," Claire said as calmly as she could. "He tried to help, but he couldn't. So I left. The end. As far as I know, he was having a normal day; I didn't see anything or anybody weird hanging around. That's all I know."

"What kind of favor did you ask him for?" Monica asked. Out of the corner of her eye, Claire saw the glitter of the knife as it turned in Jennifer's fingers. "Let me guess. Loser boyfriend rescue favor?"

Claire didn't answer. There really wasn't any good way to go with that. Monica smiled, but it wasn't a comforting kind of smile.

"So my brother turned you down when you wanted him to use his influence to spring your skanky boyfriend, and you made him disappear," she said. "Nice. I guess you figure the next mayor might be a bigger idiot and let you have what you want."

Claire took a deep breath. "Why would I think that? Since apparently running Morganville is a family business, and you'd be next in line. Oh, I see your point. You're definitely the bigger idiot."

"Ooh, she is just *begging* for it," Gina said, and pressed cruelly hard down on Claire's shoulders. "Cut her, Jen. Give her something to think about."

"I'm serious! Why would I think a new mayor would help me any more than Richard? Look, I *like* your brother. I like him a lot more than I like you. Why would I do anything to hurt him? Am I likely to get anybody *more* likely to help me?"

Monica didn't move. She didn't say anything. Jennifer took her silence for encouragement, and put the edge of the knife on Claire's cheek.

It felt hot. Claire stopped breathing.

"You're sure," Monica said. "You don't know what happened to my brother."

Now she could breathe, because Monica hadn't nodded a go-ahead on the cutting. "No. But maybe I could find out. If you don't piss me off."

The pressure of the knife went away. Claire kept watching Monica, which was where the real threat was coming from.

"Why would you help me?" Monica asked, which was a pretty reasonable question.

"Not helping you. I'm looking to help Richard. I *like* Richard."

Monica nodded. "You do that. I'm going to give you a day. If I don't hear from Richard, or he doesn't show up alive and well, then you're the next one who disappears. And I promise you, they'll never find the body."

"If I had a nickel for every time somebody said that to me around this town . . ." Claire said, and Monica's lips quirked into something that was *almost* a smile. "Come on; you know it's true. Morganville. Come for the education, stay for the terrifying drama."

"Try being born here," Monica said.

"I know. Not easy." Claire looked up at Gina, who was still holding her down; Gina exchanged looks with Monica, then shrugged and let go. Claire flexed her shoulders. She'd probably have aches later, if not bruises. "How's your mom holding up?"

"She's . . . not, exactly. It's been hard." Monica actually thawed a little. Not that they would ever like each other, Claire thought; Monica was a bully, and a bitch, and she would always feel entitled to more than anyone around her. But there were moments when Monica was just a girl only a little older than Claire—someone who'd already lost her dad, was losing her mom, and was afraid of losing her brother.

Then she surprised Claire by asking, "Your parents okay?"

"I don't know if *okay* is the right word for it, but they're safe. For now, anyway." Claire picked up her backpack. "Mind if I go finish my test now?"

Monica raised one eyebrow. "You *want* to take the test? Seriously? I was giving you an excuse, you know. They'd let you make it up. You could probably just buy the answers." She said that as if she really couldn't imagine wanting to take any test, ever.

"I like tests," Claire said. "If I didn't, why would I still be in Morganville?"

Monica smiled this time. "Wow. Good point. It is kind of pass/fail."

Test turned in (and still ahead of everyone else), Claire headed for the University Center. Specifically, she headed for the coffee bar, which was where Eve put in her slave-wage hours pulling espresso shots for the college crowd. There was more of a line than usual; with Common Grounds being "closed for renovations" (according to the sign), more students were settling for the local fare than usual. Behind the hissing machines, Eve worked with silent concentration, barely looking up as she delivered each order, but when she said, "Mocha," and slid it across, Claire touched her on the hand.

"Hey," she said.

Eve looked up, startled, and blinked for a second, as if she had trouble remembering who Claire was, and why she was standing in front of her interrupting the flow of work.

Then she yelled, "Tim! Taking five!"

"No, you're not!" Tim, who was working the register, yelled back. "Do *not* take that apron off. Eve!"

Too late. Eve's apron hit the counter, and she ducked under the barrier to join Claire on the other side. Tim sighed and motioned one of the other register clerks to cover the espresso station as they walked away.

"One of these days, he's going to fire you for that," Claire said.

"Not today. Too busy. And he'll forget by tomorrow. Tim's kind of like a goldfish. Three-second memory." Eve looked relaxed. In fact, despite the fact that she was typically Gothed up in red and black, with clown-white makeup and bloodred lipstick, Eve looked almost . . . content. "Thanks."

Claire sipped the mocha, which was actually pretty good. "For what?"

"You know what."

"Don't, actually."

Eve's smile turned wicked around the edges. "Michael came by."

"Oh?" Claire dumped her backpack on a deserted table. "Tell."

"You're too young."

"Seventeen as of yesterday."

"Oh? *Oh.* Um . . . sorry." Eve looked deeply ashamed. "I . . . Happy birthday. Man, I can't believe I forgot that. Well, in my defense, I was kinda pissed at you."

"Yeah, I noticed that. It's okay. But you owe me a cake."

"I do?" Eve flopped into the chair across from her. "Okay. It'll probably suck, though."

Claire found herself smiling. "I hope so. Anyway. What happened with Michael?"

"Oh, you know. The usual." Eve traced a black fingernail in some carving on the tabletop—apparently Martin + Mary = HOT, or at least it had once. "We talked. He played guitar for me. It felt . . . normal for a change."

"And?"

"Like I'm going to tell you."

Claire stared at her.

"Okay, I'll tell you. *God,* don't nag, okay?" Eve scooted her chair closer. "So. We kissed for a while—did I mention what an awesome kisser he is? I did, right?—and . . ."

"And?"

"And I'm not going to end up on Blood Bank Row because I told you dirty little stories about me and Michael, Miss Barely Seventeen. So just, you know, imagine." Eve winked. "You can be really vivid if you want."

"You suck." Claire sighed.

Eve opened her mouth, then closed it again without saying a single word. Before either of them could think what to say next, a shadow fell across the table.

Claire had never seen him before, but he had the typical cool-boy-on-campus look . . . a loose black T-shirt over a nice expanse of shoulders, comfortable jeans, the usual pack full of books. Dark hair, kind of an emo cut, and expressive dark eyes beneath his bangs.

"Hi," he said, and shuffled from one foot to the other. "Umm, do you mind if I . . . ?" He pointed to the remaining chair at the table. Claire looked around. All the other tables were full.

"Knock yourself out," Eve said, and pushed his chair out with her foot. "Hope you're not allergic to girl talk."

"Not likely. I have four sisters," he said. "Hey. I'm Dean. Dean Simms." When he extended his hand for Eve to shake, Claire automatically checked his wrist. Not a Morganville native; there was no bracelet, and no sign that there had ever been one. Even those who'd gladly ditched the symbols of Protection still had the tan lines.

"Eve Rosser." From the wattage of Eve's smile, she liked what she saw across the table. "This is Claire Danvers."

"Hey." He gravely shook hands with Claire, too; she thought it was a kind of forced, formal thing for him. He seemed a little nervous. "Sorry to bust in on you. I just need a place to go over my notes before my test." He dug around in his backpack and came up with a battered spiral notebook, which had an elaborate ink-pen drawing of some kind of car doodled all over the front. He saw Claire looking at it, and a faint pink blush worked up over his cheeks. "Core classes. You get bored, right?"

"Right," she said. She'd skipped core classes—tested out of them— but she understood. She'd gotten so bored that she'd read the entire

Shakespeare library of plays, and that had been her freshman year in high school. But she'd never been a doodler. "Nice drawing."

"Thanks." He flipped open the notebook, past pages of tight, neat handwriting.

"What class?" Eve asked. "Your test."

"Um, history. World History 101."

Claire had easily bypassed that one. "Seems like you've got all the notes you need."

He smiled. It was awkward and nervous, and he quickly looked down at his pages again. "Yeah, I scribble a lot when I'm in class. It's supposed to help with memory, right?"

"Does it?" Eve asked.

"I'll tell you after the test, I guess." He focused on his notes, looking even more uncomfortable. Claire looked at Eve, who gave a tiny little *whatever* shrug.

"So," she said. "Plans for today?"

"Apart from . . ." Nothing Claire could say in front of an innocent bystander. "Well, not really. Did you know that Richard Morrell's gone missing? Monica asked me to find him."

"Back up. What?"

"Monica asked me to—"

"Yeah, that's what I thought you said. Now you're doing favors for the Morrell family? Girlfriend, there's nice, and then there's utterly dumb. You don't need to do Monica any favors. What has she ever done for you?"

"That's why it's called a favor," Claire pointed out. "Not an evening of the score. It's something you do *before* they owe you one."

"You're just asking for it. Stay out of trouble, okay? Just keep your head down. I *know* that's what Michael told you. If Shane was here, that's what he'd say, too."

Dean was doing a very good imitation of studying, but the tips of his ears had been turning pink, and now he looked up and stage-whispered, "Yeah, about that. I kind of know Shane."

Which brought the conversation to a quick halt. Dean looked around and lowered his voice even more. "I also know his dad."

"Oh God, please. *Tell* me you're not one of Frank Collins's lame-ass vampire hunters." Eve sighed. "Because if you are, dude, way to go low-profile. Buy some life insurance today, and please, make me the beneficiary."

"Not exactly a vampire hunter, but . . . I do work for Frank Collins, sort of."

Eve looked at Claire. "I think we found a good choice to replace Captain Obvious." Captain Obvious had been part of the secret vampire-hating underground when Claire had first arrived in Morganville; he'd ended up being a little *too* obvious toward the end. Obviously dead.

"Because he'd be dead before he got his first sentence out when he came face-to-face with a vampire?" Claire asked, deadpan.

"I was thinking just put him in a custom T-shirt that says, 'Hello, my name is Dean and I'm here to kill you, evil bloodsucking creatures of the night.' With an arrow pointing at his neck that says, 'Bite here.'"

Dean was flipping his attention back and forth between them in obvious consternation. "Okay, let me start over. I've been trying to find out where Shane and his father are. Do you have any idea?"

"Friend," Eve said, and pointed toward her skull-graphic-covered self. "Girlfriend." The black fingernail turned toward Claire. "Housemates." The finger gestured to include them both. "So yeah, we know. How exactly do *you* know Shane?"

"I . . . I met him when he and his mom and dad were on the run. Did he tell you about that?"

Both girls nodded. Shane's sister had been killed in a house fire; the Collins family had done the forbidden in response—they'd packed up and fled Morganville . . . with some kind of vampire help, because that was the only way to get past the barriers if you were wearing a Protection mark. Out in the world, though, things hadn't gone well. Shane's parents had each gone crazy in their own special way: his dad had become a cold, hard, vampire-hunting drunk, and his mom had turned into a depressed, possibly suicidal drunk, leaving Shane to make his way as best he could.

"I was there," Dean said. "When Mrs. Collins died. I mean, I was in the motel court. I saw Shane after he found her. Man, he was totally fucked-up."

"You were there?" Claire repeated.

"My brother was running with his dad by then, so yeah. I was around. Me and Shane kind of hit it off, because we were both getting dragged around without any say in what was happening."

"Wait a minute. Shane never said anything about coming back to Morganville with a friend," Eve said.

"Yeah, he wouldn't, because he doesn't know I'm here. Mr. Collins—Shane's dad—sent me after him. I was supposed to stay to keep an eye on Shane, kind of watch his back." Dean shook his head. "Except nothing was the way he said it would be. I didn't know where to hide, so I enrolled at TPU because it gave me an excuse to hang around. Then I kind of lost track of everybody a few weeks ago." He looked at them hopefully. "So? What do I do now?"

Claire and Eve stared at him in silence for a moment, and then Eve said, very seriously, "Look. We know Frank Collins—know, hate, whatever. And you need to give up on that evil old loser. You seem like kind of a sweet kid. Pack it in and go away. Get out while you still can."

"It wasn't supposed to be like this," Dean said. "It was supposed to be easy. I mean, the good guys were supposed to *win*, you know? The vampires were supposed to die."

"And then what, you guys take over and run the town?" Claire sighed. "Not likely. And I've met Mr. Collins. Not a good idea to give him the keys to the city, either."

Dean looked at her like he thought she was crazy, and that it really was a pity. "At least he's not a *vampire*."

"They're not all bad," Claire said.

For a split second, she thought she saw an altogether different Dean watching her—same guy, same emo haircut, but his eyes were weird. Not vampire weird. Odd weird.

Then he blinked, and it was gone, and she thought it was just her imagination. If you couldn't be paranoid in Morganville, though, where could you?

"Well, that's new to me," Dean said. He smiled, and it was a real smile. A warm one, not at all nervous. "I just always thought the whole blood-sucking thing made being bad a lock."

"What you know about vampires could fit into a mosquito's ass," Eve said, irritated. "All you know is what you grew up seeing on TV. You ever actually *meet* one?"

Dean didn't answer that, but the tips of his ears grew red and his smile disappeared as he faced Eve directly. "Yeah, well, I'm not some collaborator who's willing to apologize for what these monsters do. Maybe that's the point. Anyway—it wasn't really my choice. I just came because Frank asked, and I didn't have anyplace else to go. My brother was running with Frank, and he was all I had."

Eve's eyes remained watchful. "So where's Big Scary Bro now?"

"Dead," Dean said softly. "He got killed in the fighting. I'm all alone."

Claire stared down at the table, suddenly not interested at all in her mocha, no matter how delicious. The truth was that some of those guys—the foot soldiers, the ones who'd come along to Morganville with Frank Collins as his shock troops—well, some of those guys hadn't fared well, either in the fight or in jail. She didn't know who they were, not by name. Up until this moment, they'd just been labeled in her head as Frank Collins's minions. But they all had names, friends, lives. They all had families. Claire wouldn't know Dean's brother from any of his fellow muscle-bound biker dudes, but that didn't mean Dean didn't mourn him.

That led Claire to a terrifyingly real waking nightmare—Bishop summoning her, telling her that he'd decided to let Shane go. Shane lying there, not moving . . .

"Hey, Claire?" Eve snapped her fingers under Claire's nose, and Claire jerked so hard she slopped coffee onto the table. "Damn, girl. You space so hard, you ought to look into a career at NASA. So. We agree that Mr. Dean here is a terrible excuse for a vampire hunter, is in a whole lot of trouble if he doesn't keep his head down, and he should head for the hills if he knows what's good for him?"

"Sure," Claire said, but Dean was already looking oddly stubborn.

"I'm not going anywhere," he said. "My brother would have wanted me to finish what I started. I told Frank Collins I'd look out for Shane. I'm staying until I know they're okay."

"That's sweet, but how exactly are you going to look out for him, seeing that he's in jail?" Eve said. "Unless you want to look after his girl instead." She winked at Claire.

The tips of Dean's ears turned even redder. "That's not what I meant."

Except that Claire had the funny feeling that he did.

She avoided Eve's gaze for another few seconds, then pulled out her cell phone and checked the time. She had nowhere to be, but this was turning weirdly uncomfortable all around.

"Gotta go," she said, and grabbed up her backpack. She'd had about all the Dean time she wanted.

Eve blinked. "You barely touched the mocha!"

"Sorry. You have it."

"I *work* in a coffee bar. No. Here, Dean. Knock yourself out."

The last she saw before she ducked off into the crowds, heading for nowhere in particular, was Eve handing Dean her abandoned drink, and chatting like old friends.

Claire really didn't have a lot of ideas about what to do for the rest of the day, but one thing she did *not* intend to do was go against Michael's instructions. No way was she going anywhere near Vampire Central today. Going home didn't have much appeal, either, but it seemed the safest thing to do. As she walked, she dialed Richard Morrell's cell phone number. It went to voice mail. She tried the new chief of police next.

"Hannah Moses, go," said the brisk, calm voice on the other end.

"Hey, Hannah, it's Claire. You know, Claire Danvers?"

Hannah laughed. She was one of the few people Claire had ever met in Morganville who wasn't afraid to really laugh like she meant it. "I know who you are, Claire. How are you?"

"Fine." That was stretching the truth, Claire supposed, but not according to the standards of Morganville, maybe. "How does it feel to be in charge?"

"I'd like to say good, but you know." Claire could almost hear the shrug in the older woman's voice. "Sometimes being a know-nothing spear carrier's comforting. Don't have to know about how the war's going, just the battle in front of you." Hannah was, in real-world terms, a soldier—she'd just come back from Afghanistan a few months ago, and she was as badass a fighter as Claire could even imagine, outside of ninja TV stars. She might not do the fancy high kicks and midair spins, but she could get the job done in a real fight.

Even against vampires.

Hannah finally said, "I'm guessing you didn't call just because you missed me."

"Oh. No . . . I just . . . Did you know Richard Morrell is missing?"

"All over it," Hannah said, without a change at all in her tone. "Nothing to be concerned about. Let me guess. Monica put you onto it. I already told her it's handled."

"I don't think she believes you."

On the other end of the phone, Hannah was probably grinning. "No shit? Well, she's bad; she's not stupid. But her brother's safe enough. Don't worry. Richard can take care of himself, always has."

"Is something going on? Something I should know about?" Hannah said nothing, and Claire felt a hot prickle of shame. "Right. I forgot. I'm wearing the wrong team jersey, right?"

"Not your fault," Hannah said. "You were drafted; you didn't join up. But I can't talk strategy with you, Claire. You know that."

"I know." Claire sighed. "I wish . . . you know."

"I really do. You go home, and stay there. Understand?"

"On my way," Claire promised, and hung up.

On the other side of the street, college-adjacent businesses were starting to close up shop, even though it was still early. Nobody liked to be caught outside as night approached; it was unsafe during the day, but it was a hell of a lot worse at twilight, and after.

Claire slowed as she passed Common Grounds. The security shutters were still down, the door was closed, but there was something . . . something . . .

She crossed the street, not really sure why she did, and stood there for a few seconds, staring like an idiot at the locked door.

Then she heard the distinct, metallic sound of a dead bolt snapping back, and in slow motion, the door sagged open just a bare inch. Nothing showed but darkness.

I am not going to say, "Hello, is anyone there," like some stupid, too-dumb-to-live chick in a movie, Claire thought. *Also, I am not going in there.*

I'm really not.

The door opened another inch. More darkness. "You've got to be kidding," Claire said. "How stupid do you really think I am?"

This time, the gap opened to about a foot. Standing well back from any hint of sunlight was someone she knew: Theo Goldman, vampire and doctor.

"I'm sorry," he said. "I couldn't come to you. Will you do me the honor . . . ?"

There were a lot of vampires in Morganville who scared Claire, but Theo wasn't one of them. In fact, she liked him. She didn't blame him for trying to save his family, which included both humans and vampires. He'd done what he had to do, and she knew it hadn't been for any bad motives.

Claire stepped inside. Theo shut the door and locked it securely after her. "This way," he said. "We keep all the lights off in the front, of course. Here, allow me, my dear. I know you won't be able to see your way."

His strong, cool hand closed around her upper arm in a firm but not harsh grip, and he guided her through blind darkness, zigzagging around (she assumed) tables and chairs. When he let go, she heard a door close behind them, and Theo said, "Shield your eyes. Lights coming on."

She closed her eyes, and a flare of brightness reddened the inside of her lids. When she looked, Theo was stepping away from the light switch and moving toward the group of people sitting at the far end of the room. His dark-haired wife rose from her chair, smiling; except for her generally pale skin, she didn't look much like a vampire, really. Theo's kids and grandkids—some physically older than Claire, some younger—sat in a group playing cards. In the dark, because all the ones playing were vampires. The humans weren't here at all.

"Claire," Patience Goldman said, and extended her hand. "Thank you for coming inside."

"Um . . . no problem," she said. "Is everything okay?" It hadn't been for a while. Bishop had been thinking of killing all the Goldmans, or making them leave Morganville. Something about their being Jews. Claire didn't really understand all the dynamics of it, but she knew it was an old anger, and a very old feud.

"Yes, we are fine," Theo said. "But I wanted to tell you that we will be leaving Morganville tonight."

"You . . . what? I thought Bishop said you could stay—"

"Oh, he did," Theo said, and his kindly face took on a harder look. "Promises were made. None that I believe, of course. It's no sin for a man like him to break a promise to a man like me; after all, I am hardly better than a human to him." His wife made a sound of protest, and Theo blinked. "I did not mean that to slight you, Claire. You understand what I mean."

"Yeah." Bishop had carried over some prejudices from his human days, and a big one had to do with a dislike of Jewish people, so maybe he didn't look at Jewish vampires as being any different—any better— than mere humans, who weren't real to Bishop, anyway. "But . . . why tell me? You can't trust me, you know." She rubbed her arm under the long-sleeved T-shirt, feeling ashamed all over again. "I can't help it. If he asks me, I have to tell him about you."

Theo and his wife exchanged a look. "Actually," Patience said, "you don't. I thought you knew."

"Knew what?"

"That the influence of the charm he used on you is fading." Patience stepped forward. "May I?"

Claire had no idea what she was asking for, but since Patience was holding out her cool white hands, Claire hesitantly extended hers. Mrs. Goldman pushed the shirt sleeve up to expose the tattoo, turning it this way and that, studying it.

"Well?" Theo asked. "Can you tell?"

"It's definitely significantly weakened," his wife said. "How much, it's hard to tell, but I don't think he can compel her without a large effort. Not anymore."

That was news to Claire. Good news, actually. "Does he know what I'm thinking?"

"He never did, my dear," Patience said, and patted her hand before releasing it. "Mr. Bishop's skills are hardly all-powerful. He simply uses our fear to make them seem so." She nodded to her husband. "I think I can safely mask her from him, if he should look for her."

"Wait, what?" Claire asked.

Their eldest son, Virgil, threw down a handful of cards in annoyance and crossed his arms. "Oh, just tell her," he said. "They want to take you with us."

"*What?*"

"It's for the best," Theo said quickly. "We can escort you safely out of town. If you stay, he'll kill you, or turn you vampire so he can control you better. You simply have no options here, my dear. We only want to help you, but it has to be now. Tonight. We can't risk waiting any longer."

"That's . . . kind of sweet," Claire said carefully, and measured the distance between where she stood and the door. Not that she could outrun one vampire, much less six. "But I'm okay here. Besides, I really can't leave now. Shane—"

"Ah." Theo snapped his fingers, and his smile took on a wicked sort of tilt around the edges. "Yes, of course. The boy. As it happens, I did not forget young Mr. Collins; Clarence and Minnie have gone to fetch him. Once they arrive here, we will make sure you both are safely away."

Claire's eyes widened, and suddenly she couldn't get a breath. Her heart started to pound, first from anticipation, then from outright fear. "You . . . you decided to break Shane out of jail?"

"Call it our last good act of charity," Theo said. "Or our revenge on Mr. Bishop, if you like. Either way, it's of benefit to you, I think."

"Does Amelie know what you're doing?"

Theo's expression smoothed out into a frighteningly blank mask. "Amelie finds it better to skulk in the shadows, while people die for her lack of courage. No, she does not know. If she did, she'd no doubt have a dozen reasons why this was a mistake."

It *was* a mistake. Claire couldn't say why, but she knew it, deep down. "She promised me she'd take care of him," Claire said. "She's got a plan, Theo. You shouldn't have interfered."

"Amelie's plans are subject to her own needs, and she never bothered to include me," Theo said. "I am offering you and your boy a way out of Morganville. Now. *Tonight.* And you need never return here again."

It wasn't that simple. "My parents."

"We can take them with us as well."

"But . . . Bishop can find us," Claire said. "Vampires found Shane's family when they left town before. They killed his mother."

"Shane and his father blame vampires for what was only a very natural human despair. Shane's mother took her own life. You see that, don't you? Claire?" Theo seemed to want her to agree, and she wasn't sure why. Maybe he doubted it himself. When she didn't, he looked disappointed. "Well, it's too late now, in any case. We can discuss this once we're safely away. We will help you find a place well beyond Bishop's—and Amelie's—reach before we move on ourselves."

One of the grandsons—the middle one, Claire couldn't remember his name—made a rude sound and threw down his cards. "Grandpapa, we don't *want* to leave." The other children tried to shush him, but he stood up. "We don't! None of us do! We have lives here. We stopped running. It was safe for us. Now you want us to go out there again, start over again—"

"Jacob!" Theo's wife seemed shocked. "Don't talk to your grandfather so!"

"You never ask us. You want us all to pretend that we're still children. We're not, Grandmother. I know you and Grandpapa can't accept that; I know you don't want to let us go, but we can make our own decisions."

Mrs. Goldman seemed not to know what to say. Theo looked very thoughtful, and then nodded. "All right. I'm listening. What decision have you made?"

"To stay here," Jacob said. "We're staying here." He looked down at his brothers and sisters, who all nodded—some reluctantly, though. "You can go if you want, but we're not letting Bishop drive us out. And no matter what you say, that's what you're doing. You're just saving him the trouble of exiling us."

"If exile was what I was worried about, I would agree with you. It isn't."

"You think he'll try to kill us?" Jacob shook his head. "No. It's not the old days, Grandpapa. Nobody's hunting us here."

"If I have learned anything in my long life, it is that someone is *always* hunting us," Theo's wife said. "Now sit down, Jacob. The rest of you, sit down. We'll have no more of this. You're being rude in front of our friend."

Claire wanted to apologize, somehow; Jacob shot her a borderline-angry look, but he dropped back in his place on the floor, shoulders slumped. She'd never thought about it, but she supposed for a lot of vampires Morganville was about as good as it could get—no looking over your shoulder, waiting to be discovered. No worrying about putting down roots, making friends, having some kind of a life.

"Theo," Mrs. Goldman said, and nodded toward the door where they'd come in. "I hear someone coming."

"She has better ears than I do," Theo confessed to Claire. "Stay here. I will let them in."

"But—"

"Stay here. There's nothing to fear. You'll be with your young man soon."

He left, shutting the door behind him. Mrs. Goldman drifted quietly over to speak to her children and grandchildren in a low, urgent voice—the way moms always talked to kids who were throwing tantrums in front of company—and Claire was left not quite knowing what she ought to do. If they *had* managed to bust Shane out of jail, well, that was good, wasn't it? Maybe not according to Amelie's plan, but that didn't make it a bad thing. Not automatically.

Claire took her cell phone out and speed-dialed the Glass House. No answer, at least not on the first three rings.

On the fourth ring, she thought she heard someone pick up, but it was drowned out by a warning cry from Mrs. Goldman from behind her.

The door smashed open, and Theo came flying through, crashing into Claire and sending her to the floor. The phone skittered out of her hands and underneath the shadowy bottom of an old, upholstered chair. She couldn't breathe; Theo's shoulder had hit her in the stomach, and as she struggled to get her muscles working again, she saw black spots swimming at the edge of her vision. Her whole body felt liquid and hot, and she wasn't sure what had just happened, except that it was bad. . . .

Mrs. Goldman vaulted over Claire's body and grabbed Theo, who was feebly trying to right himself. She pulled him back into the corner, with the children, and fearlessly stood in front of all of them, fangs flashing white as she faced their enemies.

"Now, don't be doing that," said a honey-dark voice from the doorway's shadows. "There's no need for violence, is there?" The light caught on the vampire's face, and Claire felt sick. Ysandre, Bishop's icky little pet slut. She was dressed for business just now, in black leather pants and a long-sleeved heavy jacket with a hood. She could have been drawn in black and white, except for the slash of red that was her mouth. "Got something for you, missus."

She reached back, grabbed two people by the hair, and propelled them both inside. It was the Goldmans' other son and daughter, Clarence and Minnie. Vampires didn't often look beaten up, but these two did, and Claire felt a little sick at the sight of the fear on Mrs. Goldman's face.

"Let them go," she said. "Children! Come here!"

"Not so fast," Ysandre said, and yanked on the hair she was holding. "Let's talk about this first. Mr. Bishop is not too pleased with your family breaking its word to him. He allowed you to stay here, alive and free, and in return you were supposed to stay out of his business. Did you stay out of his business, sugar? Because it really doesn't look like you did, since you sent these two fine children of yours to try to break his enemies out of jail."

Claire stopped moving at all. She was curled on her side, still struggling to breathe, shaking, and now it felt like the whole world was crashing in on her. *Try. Try to break his enemies out jail.*

They hadn't done it. Shane was still a prisoner.

Ysandre hadn't come alone. She shoved the Goldman boy and girl over into the arms of their mother, and behind her a solid army of vampires filled the darkness. "Didn't know about this place," Ysandre remarked. "Didn't know it had a tunnel going right up under it, anyway. That's real convenient. Didn't even have to take a sunburn to get to you." She brushed her shiny hair back, and as she did, her gaze fell on Claire. She gave her a slow, deadly smile. "Why, lookit. It's little Miss Perfect. Oh, I think Mr. Bishop is going to be *very* disappointed in you."

Claire tried to get up and almost fell. She wasn't hurting yet, but she knew she would be. Bruises, mostly, maybe a couple of strained muscles.

Theo Goldman caught her. He'd gotten to his feet when she wasn't looking, and now he helped her stand up. At close range, she saw the misery in his eyes before he put on a fake smile for Ysandre's benefit.

"I suppose we will be going with you," he said. "For another interview with our benevolent master."

"Some of you will," she agreed. "And some of you won't." She snapped her fingers and pointed at Claire. Two big, muscular vampire guys lunged from behind her and grabbed Claire by the arms to haul her off. When Theo protested, they shoved him back with his family. "I want to introduce you to an old friend of Mr. Bishop's. This is Pennywell. I believe you may already be acquainted, though."

As she was dragged out of the room, into the dark open area of Common Grounds, Claire passed the stranger she'd seen in Bishop's office on her birthday. He—she? it was hard to tell—walked past Claire as if she didn't exist, heading into the room where the Goldmans were being held.

"Wait!" Claire yelled. "What are you going to do?"

Pennywell didn't even pause. Ysandre looked back and winked at her.

"Don't you worry about any of this, now," she cooed with false sympathy. "You've got plenty of your own problems to worry about. Goodbye, Claire."

SEVEN

There was a hidden ladder down to a surprisingly large, well-lit tunnel underneath Common Grounds. It had a false brick wall that led into one of the maze of tunnels that was big enough for cars—and there was one waiting, a big idling limousine. One of Claire's vampire captors opened the back and pushed her inside before getting in with her. The other one took the front seat, and before more than a few seconds passed, they were driving on into the hidden world underneath Morganville. "Hey," Claire said. The vampire sitting next to her in the back glanced at her, then away. He was about twice her size, and she had a feeling that he could have broken her in half with a harsh word and his little finger. "What's going to happen to them?"

He shrugged, not like he didn't know—more like he just flat didn't care enough to tell her. The Goldmans didn't mean much to him. Claire meant even less.

"What's your name?" she asked, and surprised herself. But for some reason, she wanted to know. Dean's brother—he hadn't been just some nameless Bad Guy Number Four. This vampire wasn't, either. He had a name, a history, maybe even people who cared what happened to him.

"My name is none of your business," he said, and continued to stare out the window, even though there was nothing but blurry brick out there.

"Can I call you None for short?" It was an Eve joke, but Claire didn't think she delivered it very well, because the vampire didn't even blink. He just shut her out.

She concentrated on not thinking about what might have happened to Shane.

The car burst out of the tunnel at a high rate of speed, rose up a ramp, and exited from what looked like an industrial building—another of Morganville's secret roads. They turned onto a residential street near Claire's parents' house—she recognized two of the burned-out homes and the carefully clipped hedge animals in front of the yellow clapboard house on the corner. She'd always thought the squirrel looked kind of crazy.

They didn't slow down as the limousine sped through the streets. People got out of the way—bikes, cars, even one or two pedestrians hurrying home into the sunset. The vampire driver had a blacked-out windshield, but he was still wearing sunglasses, gloves, and had most of his face covered as well. *Young*, Claire thought. Older vampires wouldn't care about the sun that much. It hurt them, but it wouldn't kill them. So maybe Bishop had recruited some new guys.

Before she could think of anything else to say that wouldn't get her killed, the limousine took a turn down a shaded wide street. At the end of it, Claire saw familiar buildings, and the big green expanse of Founder's Square.

They were taking her to Bishop.

She slid over to the far side, taking her time about it, and as the car slowed for the next turn, she tried to open the door and throw herself out.

Locked. Of course. The vampire in the back didn't even bother to look at her.

Another ramp, this one leading down under the streets, and thirty seconds later they were parked underground. Claire tried to come up with a plan, but honestly, she didn't have much. She'd lost her cell phone when

Theo had crashed into her, not that she had even a vague idea of who she could call, anyway. There was a stake hidden at the bottom of her backpack that maybe, *maybe* she could use—but only if it was one-on-one, and the one was a lot less scary than the two currently escorting her around.

"Get out," the vampire in the back said as the door locks clicked open. "Don't try to run."

She didn't want to. She wanted to save her strength for something more useful.

Whatever that useful thing was, it didn't become clear as they headed for the elevator and crowded inside. Phony not-really-music was piped into the steel-and-carpet box, making it seem that much more like a nightmare.

The elevator doors opened in a big formal room, the round one where she and Myrnin had circulated in their costumes before Mr. Bishop's welcome feast, the one that had been the starting point for everything going so wrong in Morganville. The doors to the banquet hall were closed, and her vampire guards marched her up the hallway to Bishop's office instead.

Michael opened the door. He hesitated, and almost lost his cool, then nodded and stepped aside for the three of them to come inside. There was nobody else in the room.

Not even Mr. Bishop.

"What's going on?" Claire asked. "I thought . . . Where is he?"

"Sit down and shut up," her vampire backseat guardian snarled, and shoved her into a chair. Michael looked like he might have been tempted to come to her defense, but she shook her head. *Not worth it.* Not yet, anyway.

The office door opened, and Mr. Bishop came in, wearing what looked like the same black suit and white shirt he'd been wearing the day before. There was something savage in the look he threw Claire, but he didn't pause; he walked to his desk and sat down.

He never did that. She couldn't imagine it was a good sign.

"Come here," he said. Claire didn't want to, but she felt the power woven into the tattoo on her arm snap to life. It responded to Bishop's voice—only to his—and the harder she tried to resist it, the worse it was going to hurt. But Patience Goldman was right . . . it hurt a lot less than it had before. Maybe it really was fading.

Better not to fight it and tip him off, if that was the case. She took a deep breath and let it pull her closer, right in front of his desk. Bishop leaned forward, staring up at her with cold, empty eyes, elbows braced on the polished wood surface. "Did you know what Goldman was going to do?" he asked. "Did you put him up to it?"

"No," she said. She wasn't sure whether it would help Theo if she took the blame, anyway.

Bishop stared a hole into her, then sat back and let his eyes drift half closed. "It hardly matters," he said. "I knew those people could not be trusted for any length of time. I kept watch on them. And you—I know you can't be trusted, either, little girl. I tethered you, but I didn't tame you. You're harder than you look, like my daughter, Amelie. No wonder she took you under her Protection."

"What are you going to do to the Goldmans?"

Bishop slapped his palm down on the desk, hard enough to leave his imprint half an inch deep in the wood. "I am done with restraint. This town will *learn* I am not to be taunted, not to be toyed with, not to be mocked. *You will learn.*"

Claire wanted to shoot back some smart-ass remark, but she could see the vicious anger in him, and knew it was just waiting to pounce. She stood there, silent, watching him, and then he slowly relaxed. When she started to back away, he said, "Stay there. I have something for you."

He snapped his fingers, and when the door opened, Shane walked in. She hadn't noticed it in the cell, but he was thinner than he'd been a few months ago—and he was also bruised and simmering with fury. When he saw Bishop, he lunged for him.

"No!" Claire yelled. "Shane, stop!"

He didn't, but he also didn't have to. Michael flashed across the room and got in his way, wrapping Shane in a bear hug and bringing him to a sudden halt.

"Let go!" Shane's voice was ragged, splitting and tearing under the strain of his anger. "Screw you, Michael; *let go!*"

He tried to break free. Michael didn't let him. He pushed him back, all the way to the wall, and held him there. Claire couldn't see Michael's face, but she could see part of Shane's, and she saw something change in it. Shane stopped fighting, as if he'd received some message she hadn't seen.

"I am a good master," Bishop said, as if none of that had happened. "You asked me for a birthday favor, Claire. I granted you a visit. Today, I have decided that it was a poor gift. I will give you what you want. Shane will be free to go."

Claire didn't dare to breathe, blink, move. She knew this was a trick, a cruel way to crush her hopes, and Shane's, too. "Why?" she finally said. Her lips felt numb. "Why now?"

"Because I intend to teach you both what it means to defy me, once and for all, and let you carry the tale for me," Bishop said. "Michael. Hold them, but make sure the two of them see everything. I won't have my students failing their lessons."

Bishop's control let go, and Claire stumbled backward into Michael. His arm went around her waist, and she felt the pressure of his lips close to her ear. "Stay still," he whispered. "No matter what happens, just *stay still*. Please. I'll protect you."

On Michael's other side, Shane was very, very quiet. He wasn't looking at Bishop. He was looking across at Claire, and he was scared—scared that something was going to happen to her, she realized. She tried for a smile, but wasn't sure how it came out.

Shane opened his mouth to say something, but before he could, a vampire guard came in, bringing a thin, scraggly man with a mess of graying, curling hair and a nasty scar down his face.

Shane's dad. He looked older, thinner, and even more vulnerable than he had back in his cell—nothing like the big, scary monster who'd terrified her when she'd first met him.

"Are you watching, Shane?" Bishop asked. "I want you to learn, so that you don't make the same mistakes again."

"Dad," Shane said. "Dad?"

Frank Collins put his hand out to stop Shane from trying to break free. "It's all right. Nothing he can do to me now." He faced Bishop straight on. "Been there, done that, not scared of anything you can bring to this party, bloodsucker. So just kill me and get it over with."

Bishop slowly rose from his chair, staying behind the desk.

"But, Mr. Collins, you mistake me. I'm not going to kill you. I'd never do such a thing. You're far too valuable to me."

His pale hands flashed out, grabbed Shane's dad, and jerked him forward over the desk. Claire shut her eyes as the fangs came out, and Bishop's eyes flashed red. She didn't see the actual biting, but she heard Shane screaming.

It was over in about thirty seconds. Shane never stopped fighting to get free of Michael's hold.

Claire didn't fight at all. She just couldn't.

She heard a thud as Mr. Collins's body hit the floor, and when she opened her eyes she realized that she'd been wrong about everything. Very wrong.

Bishop wasn't finished.

He gnawed at his wrist, pried open Frank Collins's mouth, and poured blood into it as he spread his other hand over the top of the man's head. Claire had seen this before—Amelie had done it to Michael—but Amelie had found it difficult and exhausting to make a new vampire.

For Bishop, it seemed easy.

"No," Shane said. "No, *stop.*"

Right there, right in front of them, Frank Collins coughed, choked, and came back to life. It looked painful, and it seemed to take forever for the thrashing and screaming to stop.

When it did, he wasn't Frank Collins. Not anymore.

He opened his eyes, and they were red.

"You see?" Bishop said, and wiped excess blood from his wrist on his black jacket. "I am not cruel. You'll never lose your father, Shane. Never again."

Claire could hear Shane's breath coming fast and ragged—more sobbing than gasping—but she couldn't look at him. She knew him; she knew he wouldn't want her to see him like this. *That's Shane. Always trying to protect me.*

Michael let Claire go. After a quick glance at her, he turned to Shane. "Don't freak out on me," he said. "Don't. This isn't the time, and it isn't the place."

Shane wasn't even looking at him. He was looking at his dad.

Frank Collins, standing next to Bishop, kept staring back at his son, and Claire didn't think that look was concern.

More like hunger.

"I hope everyone learned something today," Mr. Bishop said. "First, I know everything that goes on in Morganville. Second, I don't tolerate foolish attempts at rebellion. Third . . . well. I am so kind and merciful that no one else will die for it today. No, not even the Goldmans, before you bleat the question at me. They have been confined somewhere safe, for now, until I decide on a fitting punishment." He flicked his fingers at Michael. "See your friends home, boy. It would be a dreadful irony if they should be drained along the way by some passing stranger. Or relative."

Emphasis on the *dreadful*, Claire thought. She grabbed Shane's cold, shaking hand and forced him to look at her.

"Let's go," she said. "We have to *go*, Shane. Right now."

She wasn't really sure he understood her, but Michael helped nudge him along when he slowed down.

It was a long ten seconds until they were on the other side of the closed door, being eyed by Bishop's vampire guards. Claire felt like the last sandwich on the lunch counter.

Shane broke out of his trance when they got into the elevator.

Unfortunately.

Michael was pushing the garage button on the elevator panel, and he didn't quite see it coming. Shane got in a lucky shot to his face, fast and vicious, as Michael turned. It was hard enough that Michael, even with vampire strength, felt it, and crashed back against the wall, denting it in an uneven outline of his shoulders.

When Shane tried to follow up with a second punch, Michael caught his fist in an open palm. "There was nothing I could do, Shane," he said, but there was something behind the words. Something far kinder. "Let's wait to do the cage match when Claire isn't trapped in the middle, all right?"

She wasn't exactly in the middle, but close enough. No way could she come out of it unbruised if Shane and Michael decided to really go at it in a small, enclosed space.

Shane stopped, and, as if he'd forgotten that she was there at all, he turned to look at her. For a second there was no expression on his face, and then it all flooded in—pain, fury, relief.

And then horror.

He lowered his fist, gave Michael a look that pretty clearly said, *Later*, and turned toward Claire. There were two feet of space between them, and about a mile of separation.

"I'm so sorry," she whispered. "God, Shane, I am so *sorry*."

He shuddered and stepped forward to put his arms around her. As hugs went, it was everything wrapped together in a tangled mess—tight, a little desperate, filled with need. He needed her. He really did.

He didn't say anything as the elevator slowly descended. She listened to his breathing, and finally, he made a faint, wordless sound of pain, and pulled away from her. She held on to his hand.

"Come on," she said, and Michael held the door as the two of them stepped out into the darkened garage. Claire knew there were probably threats out there in the dark, but she didn't care. She was tired, and right now, she hated all of them so much for hurting Shane that she would have staked anybody. Amelie. Sam. *Michael*. She couldn't believe he hadn't done anything to stop it from happening. She was just now realizing that he'd stood by and . . . watched.

Shane was eerily quiet. Michael moved around them and opened the back door of his Morganville-standard vampmobile; Claire climbed in with Shane, leaving Michael alone in the front seat.

If he had any objections to the seating arrangements, he kept them to himself.

Shane held her hand tightly all the way—through the dark tunnels, then as they traveled the darkened streets. She didn't pay attention to where they were going. Right now, one place was as good as the next, as long as she still had his hand in hers. As long as they stayed together. His misery was a thick black cloud, and it felt like it was smothering them both, but at least they could cling to each other in the middle of it. She couldn't imagine what it would be like all alone.

When Michael braked the car and opened the back door, though, Claire realized that he'd taken Bishop's instructions literally.

He'd brought them home.

The decaying Victorian glory of the Glass House stretched up into the night. Live oaks fluttered their stiff little leaves in the breeze, and in the distance black, shiny grackles set up a loud racket of shrieks and rattles in a neighbor's tree. Grackles loved dusk, Claire remembered. It was their noisiest time of the day. The whole neighborhood sounded like broken glass in a blender.

She got Shane out of the car and opened the front gate. As they moved up the steps, the front door opened, and there stood Eve—not in black tonight, but in purple, with red leggings and clunky black platform shoes. She had a stake in one hand and a silver knife in the other, but as she saw them coming up the steps, she dropped both to the floor and lunged to throw herself on Shane.

He caught her in midair, out of self-defense.

"You're out!" she cried, and gave him an extra-hard squeeze before jumping back to the top of the steps and doing a victory dance that was a cross between something found in an end zone and a chorus line. "I knew you'd beat the rap, Collins! I just knew it! High five . . . "

She held up her hand for him to smack, but he just looked at her. Eve's smile and upraised palm faltered, and she looked quickly at Claire, then Michael.

"Oh God," she said, and lowered her hand. "What is it? What happened?"

"Not out here. Let's get inside," Michael said. "Now."

Shane didn't make it very far. In fact, five steps down the hallway, he gave up and just . . . stopped. He put his back to the wall, slid down to a sitting position, and sat there, staring down at his hands.

Claire didn't know what she ought to do, other than stay with him. Before she could sit down next to him, though, Eve grabbed her by the elbow and shook her hard. "Hey! What *happened?* You called the house but you got cut off. I've been out looking for you ever since, calling everybody I could think of. Hannah's out looking for you, too. What is it?"

"It's Shane's dad," Claire said. Eve let go and covered her mouth with one hand, eyes wide. She already had a sense of what was coming. "Bishop . . . he . . . he turned him into a vampire. Right in front of us." Claire looked down at Shane. "Right in front of him."

Eve didn't know what to say. She just looked at them, and finally at Michael. "You couldn't do anything about it?"

He kept his head down. "No."

"Nothing? Nothing at all?"

Michael turned and slammed his fist into the wall with so much violence the whole house seemed to shake. Eve yelped and jumped back, and almost tripped over Shane in her stacked heels.

"No," Michael said, with a kind of forced calm that made Claire ache inside. "Nothing at all. If I had, Bishop would have known he didn't have me anymore, and that was what he was waiting for. This wasn't about Shane and Claire, or about Shane's dad. This was more about finding out if I was still his bitch."

Shane slowly raised his head, and the two boys stared at each other for a long, quiet moment.

Michael crouched down. "I'd have killed him if I could have," he said. "I'm not strong enough, and he knows it. That's why he likes to keep me right there, because he knows that deep down I want to rip his head off. It's fun for him."

"So my dad was just your object lesson," Shane said. "Is that it?"

Michael reached out and put his hand on Shane's knee. He'd split the skin over his knuckles, and there was plaster dust all over his skin.

It wasn't bleeding.

"We're going to get him, Shane. We will."

"Who's we?" Shane asked wearily, and let his head fall back against the wall as he shut his eyes. "Just leave me alone, man. I'm tired. I just can't . . . I'm tired."

Eve put her hand on Michael's shoulder. "Come on," she said. "Leave him alone. He needs time."

Shane laughed dryly. It was a rattle in his throat, like the sound the grackles were making outside. "Yeah. Time. That's what I need." He didn't sound like himself. Not at all.

Michael didn't want to go, but Eve insisted, tugging on his hand until he stood up and followed her out into the living room.

Leaving Shane sitting alone on the floor.

"Hey," Claire said, and sat down beside him, arms wrapped around her knees. "You going to sit here all night?"

"Maybe."

"I just thought—"

"What? I'd snap out of it and go play some video games? Eat a taco? It's not that easy, Claire. He's my—" Shane's voice broke, then got stronger. "He was my *dad*. There was one thing in the world he was afraid of, and I just watched it happen to him. I can't even think about this right now."

"I know," she said, and leaned her head on his shoulder. "I'm so sorry."

They sat there together for a long time. Eve and Michael looked in on them from time to time. After a while, they quit looking, and Claire saw them head upstairs.

The house grew quiet.

"It's cold," Shane finally said. She was getting a little drowsy, despite the discomfort; his voice shocked her back upright again.

"Yeah, kinda. Well, it's the floor." Although it wasn't really the floor's fault, Claire supposed.

He considered that in silence for a few long seconds. "I guess it's pretty stupid to sit here all night."

"Maybe not. If it makes you feel better . . ."

He stretched out his legs with a sudden thump and sighed. "I don't see how getting cold and losing feeling in my body is going to help. Also,

I need a bed that isn't a bunk, and hasn't been the previous property of some dude named Bubba with a farting problem."

That was—almost—the old Shane. Claire sat up straight and looked up at him. After a second, he met her eyes. He didn't look happy, but he looked . . . better.

He was trying to be better.

"I forgot to say hello," he said. "Back in Bishop's office, when I saw you."

"Given the circumstances, I think we can let that slide." She swallowed, because he wasn't looking away. "It's been a while. Since . . . you know. Bishop put you behind bars."

"I did notice," he said, deadpan. "Are you asking if I have any wild men-behind-bars stories to tell you?"

"What?" She felt a blush start to burn along her jawline, then spill over her cheeks. "No! Of course not! I just . . . I don't know if—"

"Stop stammering."

"You make me stammer. You always have, when you look at me like that."

"Like what?"

"Like I'm dessert."

He licked her on the nose. She squealed and pulled back, swiping at the moisture, but then he was holding her, and his lips were warm and soft and damp, pressing on hers with genuine urgency. He didn't taste like dessert, not at all; he tasted like she imagined really good wine would taste, dark and strong and going straight to her head. Her muscles warmed and purred where he touched her, and it felt like, just for a moment, there was nothing in the world.

Nothing but this.

He broke off the kiss and pressed his hot cheek against her burning one; she felt his breath fluttering the hair above her ear. She felt him draw in a breath to say something, but she got there first.

"Don't," she whispered. "Don't tell me all the reasons why this isn't a good time, or a good idea. Don't tell me we ought to be thinking about your dad or my parents or what Bishop is doing right now. I want to be here with you. Just . . . here."

Shane said, "Well, I don't want to be here."

The world went out of focus, and her heart shattered. She'd known it was coming; she'd known that he'd changed his mind, that all that time apart had given him time to think about what he wouldn't like about her. . . . Why would somebody like Shane love her, anyway? He'd dated other girls. Better girls. Prettier and smarter and hotter. It had just been a matter of time before he noticed that she was a skinny geek.

But it hurt; oh God, it hurt so badly, like she'd been stabbed with a dagger made of ice.

She couldn't help the tears that flooded her eyes, and she couldn't hold back the sob. Shane went tense, and pushed her back to arm's length. "What?" he asked. "What did I say?"

She wanted to tell him it was all right, but it wasn't, it just *wasn't*, and it never would be. She felt like half of her was dying, and he looked at her in confusion and acted like he didn't understand what he'd done to her.

Claire scrambled away from him and bolted. It was usually Shane who ran away, but this time, she couldn't stay. She couldn't stand to be here, humiliated and stupid and hurting, and try to be nice to him, even though he needed it. Maybe even deserved it.

"Claire!" Shane tried to get up, but his feet wouldn't stay under him. "Dammit, wait—my legs went to sleep; *wait!* Claire—"

She didn't wait, but somehow, he managed to follow her, lunging after her with feet that must have been like running on concrete blocks. He tripped into her and they fell onto the couch. Claire smacked at him and tried to struggle free. "Let go!" she said around her sobs. "Just let go!"

"Not until you tell me what just happened. Claire, look at me. I don't understand why you're upset!"

He really didn't know. He was all but begging her to tell him. All right, then, fine. "Fine," she said aloud, in a voice that trembled more than she wanted. "I get it. You don't want to be with me right now. Maybe not ever. I understand, it's been a long time, and . . . your dad . . . I just . . . I can't . . . Oh, just let me *go!*"

"What in the hell are you talking about?" And then he got it. She saw him run it through his head, and his eyes widened. "Oh my God. Claire, you thought I meant I didn't want— No. God, no. When I said, 'I don't want to be here,' I meant I didn't want to be *there*. You know, sitting on the cold floor with my ass turning into an iceberg. I wanted you. I just wanted you somewhere *else*." He shook his head. "I meant it as a joke. I was going to say, 'I want to be on the *couch*.' Okay, it was stupid, I know. Sorry. I never meant you to think— Wait. Why would you think I'm not into you, anyway?"

Because I'm a girl, Claire thought. She was barely able to contain the relief welling up inside her. *Because we're all stupid and insecure and think that we're never, ever good enough.* She didn't say that, though. Some things it was better for boys not to know. "I just . . . It's been a tough day." She was still crying, and she couldn't seem to stop. "I'm sorry, Shane. I'm sorry your dad—"

"Hey." He touched her cheek. "It's bad, but I can deal. I'm more worried about you."

He always was. "Why?"

He wiped away the tears that trickled down her cheeks. "Because I'm not the one doing the crying, for one thing."

She nodded, shuddered, and started to gulp back the sobs. He waited, holding her, until she was finally quiet—relaxed in a way she hadn't been before.

Weirdly happy just to be here, with him, no matter what had happened or would happen. *This moment*, she thought. *This moment is perfect.*

"Shane?" she asked. She felt drowsy now, lazy in the warmth of his body.

"Yes?"

"*Do* you have any wild men-behind-bars stories?"

"Not really. Sorry to tease you," he said, and traced his finger down her cheek and over her lips. Slowly. "You know I spent a lot of time thinking about you, don't you? About how you look, how you smell, how you taste . . ."

"Creepy stalker boy."

He kissed her. There was something new in it, something fierce and hot and wild, and she felt needs explode inside her she didn't even recognize. Her whole body lifted, like she'd become metal to his magnet. Shane groaned and rolled her over on her back, his weight on top of her, and kept on kissing her like it was the most important thing in his world.

His lips left hers gasping for air, and traveled down her neck, around the collar of her T-shirt, and his hand dragged the fabric down to expose more skin to his kisses.

Off, Claire thought incoherently, and tried to pull the hem of her shirt up.

Shane's hand stopped hers. She looked up at him.

"Not here," he said. She waited. He looked wary. "What?"

"I was just waiting for you to say, 'Not now,' too. You know, like always."

He smiled, and it was pure Shane—full of edges and yet oddly sweet. "Claire, I just got out of *jail.* Do you honestly think I'm bucking for sainthood or something?"

Her whole body burned with a sudden burst of furious energy. *He just said yes. Oh my God.* All she could think of to say was, "Tell me how much you missed me."

"Not everything needs a speech." He was right about that. She could feel the wild energy in him, trembling right under his skin—a match for hers. "But I have to know, do you want to do this? Really?"

She'd been trying not to think about the scary mechanics of the moment. She'd asked Eve once, in that conspiracy-whisper voice girls used when they were embarrassed not to already know, whether or not the first time really hurt. Eve had said, very matter-of-factly, yes, and gone on to tell her all about her horrible first-time guy. So part of Claire's body was dreading the unknown, and part of it was screaming to jump in, no matter what happened.

"Yes," she said, and her whole body went quiet, stunned into silence. "Yes, Shane. I want to do this. I want to do it with you."

He let out his breath in a shaky laugh. "Nobody else? Not even the hot nude guy from that movie? No? Okay. No pressure." He gave her another kiss, this one fast and warm. "Upstairs?"

They slid off the couch together, hand in hand, and he led her up the stairs, looking back at her in warm glances, stopping every few steps to kiss her. By the time they made it to the top, she was tingling and shaking all over.

Shane pointed questioningly at his own door, but she shook her head. Her room was bigger, and it was at the end of the hall. More private.

He pulled in a quick, shaking breath. "Five minutes," he said. "I need a shower."

She nodded, although somehow being parted from him made it feel risky. They could change their minds at any second.

She opened her bedroom door as Shane went into the bathroom.

It hadn't occurred to Claire, but she supposed that Eve could have turned her former bedroom into anything—a Goth wardrobe warehouse, for instance, filled with skull-themed outfits. Or storage for her growing collection of vampire-slaying implements. Instead, the room was just the way Claire had left it—neat, kind of sterile, no trace of her own stuff left behind. There was a layer of dust on the sparse furniture, and the air felt cold for a few seconds, then began to warm up, as if the house sensed her presence and was eager to make her welcome again.

The big, soft bed still had sheets and layers of blankets and comforters.

She closed the door and sat down on the bed. Her hands were cold and shaking, and now that Shane wasn't here, she felt sense trying to knock itself back into her head.

No, she thought stubbornly. *No, not this time.*

It was less than five minutes before he came in, hair damp around his face, beads of water on his skin and dampening his shirt.

He leaned against the door after closing it, watching her.

"So," he said. "Maybe I should just—"

"Shut up, Shane," she said, and went to kiss him for a long, warm, lingering moment.

Then she reached behind him and locked the door. Just her and Shane, no friends banging on the door, no family ready to drag them apart. Not even a single vampire hiding in the shadows to spoil things.

For once, nothing to make either of them change their minds.

"Don't you dare ask me again if I'm sure," Claire said, and raised the hem of her T-shirt and pulled it off. The cold air glided over her flushed skin and made her shiver. She knew she was blushing, and she couldn't stop trembling, but that was all right, somehow. As she dropped the shirt to the floor, she thought, *He's seen me like this before. It's okay.*

Shane sat down on the edge of the bed, watching her with absolute concentration. She toed off her shoes, stripped away her socks, unbuttoned her jeans and unzipped them, and kicked them off into the same pile.

He's seen me like this before, too.

She reached behind her for the clasp of her bra. *But not like this.*

"Wait," he said, and pulled his own shirt off. Beneath it, his skin was paler than she remembered, his muscles more defined underneath. "I just want to keep it even."

She swallowed a nervous laugh. "Then you have to get rid of the pants."

Shane grinned at her and leaned back to work the button and zipper. "Don't blame me for the underwear," he said. "It's prison-issue."

"I am so glad you didn't say that before. Oh, and don't say that to my parents, ever."

Shane's pants hit the floor, along with his shoes and socks. Claire's gaze skimmed over him, and she felt dizzy at the sight of so much exposed skin.

"Come over here," he said. "It's cold."

He folded back the covers and slid in. She followed, feeling awkward and made of angles that didn't quite seem to know how to fit together.

Lying beside him felt strange and, at the same time, completely right. They lay inches apart, turned toward each other on their sides. Yearning, and not touching.

Shane lost his smile for a second. "You can tell me to stop anytime. Always."

"I *know.*"

"I won't be angry about that."

"Shane—"

"Anyway, I just wanted to tell you something."

"What?"

He reached out and touched the back of his hand to her face. "I love you."

Somehow, she managed not to cry, although she knew he'd see the glitter of tears in her eyes. "You said it first this time."

He looked relieved. "Yeah. Finally, huh?"

"Finally," she whispered. "I love you, too."

His arms pulled her against him, and she felt small and breathless and utterly secure. It was just a hug, a hug like all the other hugs . . . but it was different, too.

"God, you're beautiful," he said, and she felt his fingers press on her back. Oh—he was working the hooks on her bra. He'd had practice, some part of her noticed; the rest was too busy screaming in utter joy.

Then she wasn't able to think about much at all.

It wasn't like in the movies. In the movies, it was all graceful, pretty people and hot camera angles; in real life, it was a weird mix of tremendously exciting and totally awkward. Shane still had condoms in the wallet that he retrieved from his jeans. That was something they never showed in the movies (at least the ones Claire watched). He was kind of embarrassed about it, too. It made it feel real to her—a lot more real than all her old fantasies.

Shane asked a lot of questions, which felt odd at first, but then she realized that he was nervous, just as nervous as she was, and that was all right. He wanted to make her happy.

He *did* make her happy.

Despite what Eve had told her, the pain still came as a shock, leaping in an electric current through her entire body. If Shane hadn't held her and helped her through it, Claire didn't know how she would have felt about it later . . . but he did, and it got better.

And then it was all right.

And then it was *amazing*. She cried a little, and she didn't even know why, except that the emotions were just too big for her. Too overwhelming.

"It's different," Claire whispered to him in the dark as they lay there wrapped up together, warm and content. "It's different from what I thought."

"Different how?" He sounded suddenly worried. Claire kissed him.

"Good different. Different like it means something. Like right now—it doesn't feel like we're naked at all, does it?" She didn't know why she said that, but it was true; she didn't feel exposed with him. Just . . . accepted. "I'm not afraid with you. You know what I mean?"

He made a lazy *uh-huh* sound that meant he might possibly not be listening. "So it was okay."

"Okay?" She rose up on one elbow to look down on him. "Is this you fishing for compliments on your hotness?"

"Why? Did I catch one?"

"Idiot." She flopped back down and cuddled up against him. His hand caressed the small of her back in tiny circles. "I won't lie to you: that was intense. And it hurt. But . . . yeah. It was . . . amazing."

"I hate that it hurt," he said. "Next time—"

"I know. It wasn't so bad, though. Don't worry." The warm cushion of his arm under her head felt like the best pillow in the world. "I feel different. Do I look different?"

Shane brushed hair back from her face. "It's pretty dark in here, but yeah, I can see it."

She felt her eyes widen. "You can?"

"Sure." He traced a finger over her forehead. "Claire is not a virgin. Says so right there."

She felt her cheeks and forehead heat up, and smacked his arm. "You are *awful.*"

"Ah, the truth comes out."

"Seriously. I just feel . . . I do feel different. I feel like I'm someone else than I was before. You know?"

"Yeah," he said somberly. "I know. But I feel like that every day I wake up in Morganville."

She kissed him, and tasted the sadness in him. His sigh seemed to come all the way from his toes. "God, I needed you," he murmured. "I can't even tell you how many times I thought about this. The funny thing is, I don't need you any less now. I think I need you *more.*"

That, Claire thought, was a pretty good definition of love: needing someone even after you got what you thought you wanted.

After a long moment, he said, "Your dad is going to kill me. And he's probably got a right to."

She hadn't thought about her parents, but now it flooded in with a vengeance. This was going to get messy. And complicated. "It'll be okay," she whispered, and spread her hand out over his chest. He put his own hand over hers. "We'll be okay."

They fell asleep in each other's arms, and woke up late in the morning to the sound of birds.

Not grackles.

Songbirds.

EIGHT

"You are so busted," Eve said as Claire, fresh from a shower, ran down the steps shouldering her book bag.

Eve was sitting at the dining table, sipping a Coke and reading a *Cosmo* article with great concentration. She was wearing pink today—or, as Eve liked to call it, Ironic Pink. Pink shirt with poison skull and bones logo. Matching pink pedal-pushers with skulls embossed at the hems. Little pink skull hair ties on her pigtails, which stood out from her head aggressively, daring someone to mock them.

"Excuse me?" Claire kept moving. Eve barely glanced up from the article.

"Don't even try," she said. "I know that look."

"What look?" Claire shoved open the kitchen door.

"The now-I-am-a-woman look. Oh God, don't tell me, please, because then I have to feel guilty that you're seventeen and I should have been more of a den mom, right?" Claire couldn't think of anything to say. Eve sighed. "He'd better have been a good, sweet boy to you, or I swear, I'll kick his ass from here to— Hey, is that Shane's shirt?"

It was. "No." Claire hurried into the kitchen.

Michael was standing at the coffeepot, pushing buttons. He looked over at her and raised his eyebrows, but he didn't say anything.

"What?" she demanded, and dumped her book bag on the table as she poured herself a glass of orange juice. "Do I owe back rent?"

"We've got some things to talk about other than the rent."

"Like what?" She kept her stare focused on her OJ. "Like how far you're going to take this whole undercover-cop thing with Bishop, and whether or not you're going to get yourself killed? Because I'm wondering, Michael."

He took in a deep breath and ran his hands through his curly golden hair as if he wanted to rip a handful out in frustration. The cut on his hand, Claire noticed, was neatly healed without any trace of a scar. "I can't tell you anything else. I already took a huge risk telling you what I did, understand?"

"And did I rat you out? No. Because according to Patience Goldman, this"—she yanked back her sleeve and showed him the tattoo, which was barely a shadow now under her skin, and hardly moving at all—"this thing is running out of juice. I don't think he's noticed yet, but he probably will soon."

"That's why I told you to stay away from him."

"Not like I came on my own! Theo . . . " It struck her hard that she hadn't even asked, and she felt all of her good vibes of the morning flee in horror. "Oh God. Theo and his family—"

"They're okay," Michael said. "They were taken to a holding cell. I checked on them, and I told Sam. He'll get word to Amelie."

"That'll do a lot of good."

Michael glanced up at her as he poured his coffee. "You seem different today."

She was struck speechless, and she felt a blush burn its crimson onto her face. Michael's eyebrows rose, slowly, but he didn't say anything.

"Okay, that's . . . not what I meant. And don't ever play poker." He gave her a half smile to show her he wasn't going to harass her about it. Yet. "You moving back in?"

"I don't know." She swallowed and tried to get her racing heartbeat under control. "I need to talk to my parents. They're really . . . I'm just scared for them, that's all. I thought that maybe if I stayed with them, it would make things better, but I think it's made it worse. I wish I could just get them out of Morganville. Somehow."

"You can," said a voice from the kitchen doorway. It was—of all people!—Hannah Moses, looking tall, lean, and extremely dangerous in her Morganville police uniform, loaded down with a gun, riot baton, pepper spray, handcuffs, and who knew what else. Hannah was one of those women who would command attention no matter what she was wearing, but when she put on the full display, it was no contest at all. "Mind if I come in?"

"I think you're already in," Michael said, and gestured to the kitchen table. "Want some coffee to go with that breaking and entering?"

"It's not breaking and entering with a badge, especially if someone lets you in."

"And that would be . . . ?"

"Eve. Actually, I'll have some orange juice, if you've got more," Hannah said. "All coffeed out. I've been patrolling all night." She did look tired as she settled in a chair and stretched her legs out, although tired for Hannah just looked slightly less focused. She was wearing her cornrowed hair back in a complicated knot at the nape of her neck; having it away from her face emphasized the scar she'd gotten in Afghanistan, a seam that ran from her left temple over to her nose. On some women it might have been disfiguring. On Hannah, it was kind of a terrifying beauty mark. "It's getting nasty out there."

For Hannah to say that, it had to be worse than nasty. Claire poured some orange juice into a Scooby-Doo cup and handed it over before sitting down herself.

Michael said, "You're talking about getting Claire's parents out of town? How is that possible, without tipping off Bishop?"

"Oh, there's no doubt he'll know," Myrnin said, from right behind Claire—close enough that his cool breath touched the back of her neck, and she squealed and spilled her drink all over the table. "What he knows no longer matters. We *want* him to know."

"How did you get in here?" Michael asked, and from the shock on his face, he clearly hadn't seen Myrnin make his appearance, either. Myrnin, when Claire turned to look at him, was smirking. He'd had a bath; his hair, face, and hands were clean, although his clothes still held on to their well-lived-in filth.

"You'd hardly understand it if I told you. But to answer your question, Chief Moses has complete cooperation from me in bypassing the safeguards around the town. We need to get specific groups of people out of Morganville, and among those people are your parents, Claire."

She wet her lips. "Any special reason we're moving so fast now?"

"Yes," he said, and Hannah sent him a sharp look that would have stopped anybody sane. Didn't work on him, of course. "We are ready. Once Bishop starts killing, he will start with the ones we love first. That includes your parents, Claire, who will have no way to defend themselves."

He knew something. She could see it, and it scared her to death. "When?"

He spread his hands. "Unknown. But I can tell you that it's coming. Michael knows this as well."

Michael didn't say anything, but he studied the table very hard. Claire resisted an urge to fling some orange juice his way. "When can we get them out of town?"

"I'll handle getting them packed and ready to go," Hannah said. "I'm filling two buses with the most likely targets, and those are getting a mandatory evac out of Morganville in the next two hours." Claire saw a movement at the door, and noticed that Eve had slipped inside the kitchen, but was standing silently against the wall. As she watched, Shane came in, too, fresh from a shower, hair sparkling with drops. His gaze locked with hers, but he didn't come to her; he took up wall space next to Eve.

Hannah noticed them, too. "You two," she said. "You're on the bus today. Grab a bag. Pack for a couple of days. If you need more, we'll get it for you."

Eve and Shane both talked at once, an out-of-tune duet of angry denials. Eve slapped Shane on the shoulder and shut him up so she could go first. "No way. I'm not going anywhere, Hannah. End of story."

Shane added, "I'm not going anywhere if Claire stays here."

"Then she goes, too," Hannah said. "I was going to do that anyway."

But both Michael and Myrnin were shaking their heads. "She can't," Michael said. "Faded or not, that tattoo links her directly to Bishop. He'd still be able to track her down—and all the others who went with her."

"Not necessarily," Myrnin said. "There are vampires who could block his perception of her, if they traveled with her. But they are not available at present."

"Patience Goldman," Claire said. "Right?"

"If Theo had only waited one more day, this could have been avoided. I had planned to use her for that very purpose. But I suppose the fault is ours; if we'd kept him closer in our plans, he would not have acted so stupidly." Myrnin shrugged.

"I still wouldn't have gone," Claire said. "I'm not leaving Michael all by himself, pretending to be Bishop's best friend."

"Oh, thanks for that. Glad I inspire such confidence."

"Well, you don't. You're not a spy, Michael. You're a *musician*."

"The two," Myrnin said dryly, "are not mutually exclusive. But Michael is right. Our little Claire cannot leave the boundaries of Morganville, as matters stand just now. Besides, I need her at my side."

"Well, if she's not going," Shane said, "count me out of the running away party."

"Ditto," from Eve.

Hannah gave them both looks that should have made suitcases magically appear in their hands, but then she gave up and shook her head. "I can't promise you I'll be able to keep you safe. Understand?"

Eve rolled her eyes. "Have we ever *asked* for that? Like, *ever*? You know us, Hannah. We all went to the same high school—well, except for Claire. We Morganville kids have dodged vamps our whole lives. Not like it's new territory."

"Not true," Myrnin said, very soberly. "You might have played games with Morganville's tamed vampires, restrained by rules and laws. You've never really faced someone like Bishop, who has no conscience and no restraint."

"Don't care," Eve shot back. "That just means it's more important that we all stick together."

"Always some crazy fool who stays with a hurricane coming. Can't save everybody." Hannah drained her orange juice down to a pale froth on the bottom of the glass. "All right. I'm moving on. We're pulling people from the Founder Houses first, then anybody who has ties to Amelie, then people who were in the old Morrell administration. And yeah, the Morrells, too."

"Isn't Richard missing?"

"No," Hannah said. "Richard's just been working with us to get people lined up for evacuation. I told his damn sister to cool it, but she's still ringing every alarm bell she can find. Wish I could find a special bus just for her. A stinky, slow one. Preferably with a backed-up toilet."

Claire smiled at that, then remembered someone else. "The Goldmans," she said. "They need help, too. Can you get them?"

"No idea where they are," Hannah said.

"I know." Myrnin looked thoughtful. "I'm not sure, but I can try," he said. "They have no blood ties to Amelie or to Bishop, so they would be safe enough if we could get them on their way. But it's a risk including vampires in your evacuation."

"Then again, it means that we have some vampires fighting on our side if things go wrong outside of town," Hannah pointed out. "Not a bad thing."

"Provided the Goldmans will alight." He seemed about to say something else, but then he shook his head and made his hands into fists. "No, that isn't what I meant. Will *fight*. No. Provided that . . . provided . . . "

He was losing it. Claire got up and opened her backpack. She took out a small box of red crystals and handed it over; for most vampires, it would have been a massive dose. For a human, it was certain, gruesome death.

For Myrnin, it was like taking a handful of candy. He choked, swallowed, and nodded as he tossed the empty box back to her. Then he turned away, face to the corner, and braced himself with outspread arms, head down. His whole body shook.

That's not supposed to happen.

Then he spasmed so badly she thought he was going to fall. "Myrnin!"

Claire touched his shoulder; she'd never seen this happen before—not this bad, anyway. "What's wrong?"

He whispered, "Get away. Get them all away from me, now."

"But—"

"Everything smells like blood. *Get them away.*"

Claire let go and backed up, gesturing for Hannah and even Michael to follow. Nobody said a word. Shane held open the kitchen door, and they all left.

All except Claire, who stayed at the exit, watching Myrnin fight for his life and sanity, one slow second at a time.

She saw his shoulders relax, and felt her tide of worry begin to recede—until he turned toward her.

His eyes weren't red. They were *white.* Just . . . white, with the faint shadow of an iris and pupil showing through. The eyes of a corpse.

"Claire," he said, and took a step toward her.

Then he fell, hit the ground, and went completely limp.

"We could take him to the hospital," Hannah said, but not as if she thought it was a good idea. Claire was kneeling next to Myrnin, with Michael hovering near her, ready to yank her out of the way if Myrnin should suddenly surge back to bloodsucking life.

He was quiet. He looked *dead.*

"I think this is a little beyond the hospital," Claire said. "It's part of the disease. It's in his notes—he charted the progress; sometimes this happens. They just . . . collapse. They revive, but usually when they do, they're not—" Her voice failed her, and she had to clear her throat. "Not the same." Myrnin's notes, what she could remember of them, seemed to indicate that when—or if—the vampire recovered from the coma, he didn't have much left of his original personality.

Myrnin had been sick a long time. He'd lost the ability to create other vampires more than a hundred years ago; he'd begun behaving weirdly about another fifty years after, and from there it had progressed rapidly. Amelie, by contrast, was just now getting to the early physical symptoms—the occasional loss of emotional control, and the shakes.

Oliver . . . well. Who knew if Oliver's problem was the disease or just a bad attitude?

The fact that Myrnin had held out longer than at least thirty other vampires confined underground in cells was either proof that the disease didn't work the same way in everyone, or that Myrnin was incredibly determined. He hadn't wanted to take the cure . . . but there wasn't a choice now. He *had* to take it.

And she had to get him to Dr. Mills.

They carried him through the portal—well, Michael and Hannah carried him; Claire concentrated on getting them to their target location, the basement of Morganville High. "Stay here," Claire said. "I'm going to get the doctor."

"We can carry him up," Michael said. He was being charitable; he could have done it on his own, no problem, but he was letting Hannah take half the weight.

"I know," Claire said. "I just don't want to lead a really obvious parade to a secret hideout."

She didn't wait for an answer, just dashed up the steps, through the broken-locked door, and out into the hallways, dodging around oblivious teens her own age who were hustling to and from class. It was early morning, but Morganville High was in full session, and Claire had to shove her way through the crowd with a little more force than usual.

Somebody grabbed her by the back of her shirt and hauled her to a sudden stop. She flailed for escape, but it was just like always—she was too small, and he was *way* too big.

Her captor was wearing a shirt and tie, and had the drill sergeant hairstyle of school officials everywhere. He glared at her as if she was some bug he'd caught scurrying across his dinner table. "What do you think you're doing?" he demanded. "No shoving in the halls!"

"I'm not a student!" she yelled. "Let go of me!"

He got a glance at the gold bracelet on her wrist, and his eyes went wide; he quickly focused back on her face. "You're that girl—Claire. Claire Danvers. The Founder's— Sorry." He let her go so suddenly she almost toppled over. "My apologies, miss. I thought you were just another of these rude punk kids."

There were a few moments in her new, weird life when it was all worth it—worth being the freak of nature with all the baggage that had been loaded on her in Morganville.

This was one of them. She braced herself, put her hands on her hips, and glared at him with the kind of icy calm that she imagined Amelie would have brought down like a guillotine blade. "I *am* a rude punk kid," she said. "But I'm a rude punk kid you don't get to order around. Now, I'd like you to leave me alone and go to your office. And shut the door. Now."

He looked at her as if he couldn't quite believe his ears. "Excuse me?"

"You heard me. I don't need you out here causing trouble right now. *Go!*"

He looked confused, but he nodded reluctantly and headed for a door marked ADMINISTRATION farther down the hall.

"Eat your heart out, Monica," Claire murmured. "Thanks for the bitch lessons." She broke into a full run, leaving him and his petty kingdom behind.

Myrnin had taken her through darkened corridors, but she remembered the turns; she also remembered a little too late that the way was dark, and wished she'd thought to grab a flashlight somewhere along the way. There was little light coming into the hall during the last leg, and desks and chairs stacked randomly in her path; she had to slow down or end up taking an epic spill.

Finally, she saw the locked doors at the end of the hallway, and lunged around a dusty teacher's desk to batter at the heavy wood panel.

"Hey!" No answer. She knocked again. "Dr. Mills! Dr. Mills, open up; it's Claire! I need your help!"

There was no answer. She tried the door handle.

"Dr. Mills?"

The door opened without the slightest resistance.

The room was empty. No sign of a struggle—no sign of anything, actually. It looked like nobody had ever been here. All of the equipment was back on the shelves, sparkling and clean; there was no sign of the production of serum and crystals that had been going on here. The only thing that gave it away was the lack of a coating of dust.

Claire dashed for the room behind—the teacher's office and locked storage, where the Mills family had been living.

Same story. Nothing there to show they'd ever been here, not so much as a scrap of paper or a lost toy. "Oh God, they were *moved*," Claire whispered, and turned to run back to where she'd left her friends. She hoped the Mills family had been moved, at least. The alternative was much, much worse, but she couldn't see Bishop—or his henchmen—taking the time and energy to clean up after themselves. They certainly hadn't in Myrnin's lab.

Claire let out an involuntary yell because a ghostly woman—black and white, shades of gray, no color to her at all—blocked the way out.

She looked like she'd stepped right out of a photograph from the Victorian ages. Big full skirts, hair done up in a bun, body slender and graceful. She stared straight at Claire, hands clasped in front of her. There was something so creepy and *aware* about her that Claire skidded to a sudden halt, not sure what she should do, but absolutely sure she didn't want to go anywhere near that image.

Claire could see the room behind right through her body. As she watched, the ghost broke up into a mist of static, then re-formed. She put a finger to her lips, gestured to Claire, and glided away.

"Ghosts," Claire said. "Great. I'm going crazy. That's all there is to it."

Only, when she checked the other room, the ghost was still there, hovering a couple of inches above the floor. So at least she was consistently crazy.

The phantom beckoned for Claire to follow, and turned—getting thinner and thinner, disappearing, then widening again to show a back view. Not at all like a real person, more like a flat cardboard cutout making a one-eighty. It was startling and eerie, and Claire thought, *I'm not hallucinating this, because I'd never imagine that on my own.*

She followed the ghost back out into the science lab, then out into the hallway. Then into another classroom, this one empty except for desks and chalkboards. The same dusty sense of disuse lay over everything. It didn't feel like anyone had been here in years.

The ghost turned to the chalkboard, and letters formed in thin white strokes.

AMELIE HAS WHAT YOU NEED, it wrote. FIND AMELIE. SAVE MYRNIN.

"Who are you?" Claire asked. The ghost gave her a very tiny smile. It seemed annoyed, and more than a little superior.

Three letters appeared on the chalkboard. ADA.

"You're the *computer*?" Claire couldn't help it; she laughed. Not only was she talking to a blood-drinking computer, but it liked to think of itself as some gothic-novel heroine. Plucky Miss Plum the governess. "How do you— Oh, never mind, I know it's not the time. How can I find Amelie?"

USE BRACELET. Ada's black-and-white image flickered again, like a signal getting too much interference. When she re-formed, she looked strained and unhappy. HURRY. NO TIME.

"I don't know how!"

Ada looked even more annoyed, and wrote something on the board— but it was faint, and faded almost before Claire could read it. B-L-O . . . "Blood?" Claire asked. Ada herself was fading, but Claire saw her mouth the word *yes*. "Of course. What else? Why can't any of you guys ever come up with something that uses *chocolate*?"

No answer from the computer/spirit world; Ada disappeared in a puff of white mist and was gone. Claire looked around and found a thumbtack pressed into the surface of a bulletin board. She hesitated, positioned the thumbtack over her finger, and muttered, "If I get tetanus, I'm blaming you, Myrnin."

Then she stabbed the sharp point in, and came up with a few fat drops of red that she dripped onto the surface of the symbol on Amelie's bracelet.

It glowed white in the dim light. The blood disappeared into the grooves, and the whole bracelet turned warm, then uncomfortably hot against her skin. Claire gritted her teeth until she felt a scream coming on, and finally, the burning sensation faded, leaving the metal oddly cold.

And that was it. Amelie didn't magically appear. Claire wasn't sure what she'd expected, but this seemed really anticlimactic.

She stuck the thumbtack back on the board and went back to tell Hannah and Michael that she'd completely failed.

Dejected, she headed back to the basement. The hallways were deserted now, since classes were back in session. As she passed the administration office door, it opened, and the man she'd sent to his room like a little kid looked out. "Miss Danvers?" he asked. "Is there something I can do for you?"

This was every high school kid's fantasy, Claire thought, and she was tempted to tell him to do something crazy, like strip naked and run around the auditorium. But instead she just shook her head and kept on walking.

He came out of the door and got in her way.

"Could you put in a good word for me?" he asked, and when she tried to go around him, he grabbed her by the arm. He lowered his voice to a fast, harsh whisper. "Tell Mr. Bishop I can help him. I can be of use. Just tell him that!"

The big double doors leading out into the sunlight at the end of the hall crashed open, and a whole troop of people came flooding in. They all wore long, dark hooded coats, and they moved fast, with a purpose.

Faster than humans.

The two in the lead threw back their hoods, and Claire was relieved to see that one of them was Amelie, perfectly composed and looking as in charge as ever, even if she wasn't queen of Morganville anymore.

The other leader of the pack was Oliver, of course. Not so comforting.

"Milton Dyer," Amelie said. "Please take your hand off of my friend Claire. *Now.*"

The man went about as pale as his white shirt, and looked down at Claire, and his hand wrapped around her arm. He let go as if she'd suddenly become electrified.

"Now go away," Amelie said to him in that same calm, emotionless voice. "I don't wish to see you again."

"I . . . " He wet his lips. "I'm still loyal to my Protector. . . ."

"Your Protector was Charles," Amelie said. "Charles is dead. Oliver, do you have any interest in picking up Mr. Dyer's contract?"

"I really don't," Oliver said. He sounded bored.

"Then that settles things. Leave my sight, Mr. Dyer. The next time you cross my path, I'll finish you." She said it without any particular sense of menace, but Claire didn't doubt for an instant that she meant it. Neither did Mr. Dyer, who quickly retreated to his office. He didn't even dare to slam the door. It closed with a soft, careful click.

Leaving Claire in the hallway with a bunch of vampires. Old ones, she thought—Amelie and Oliver were obviously old, but the others seemed to have come through their sunlight stroll without a mark, too. Ten of them in total. Most of them didn't bother to put their hoods back and reveal their faces.

"You used the bracelet in a way that I did not teach you," Amelie said. "Who showed you how to use it to summon me?"

"Why?"

"Don't play games with me, Claire. Was it Myrnin?"

"No. It was Ada."

Amelie's gray eyes flickered, just a little, but it was enough to tell Claire that she had knowledge that Amelie wished she didn't. "I see. We'll talk of that later," she said. "Why did you use the blood call? It's intended to alert me only if you are seriously injured."

"Well, someone is. Myrnin's very sick. He's downstairs. I need to get him some help. I came to find Dr. Mills, but—"

"Dr. Mills has been relocated," Amelie said. "I thought it best, after Myrnin's ill-advised visit here. I can't tell you where he is. You understand why."

Claire knew. And she felt sick and a little angry, too. "You think I might give him away. To Bishop. Well, I wouldn't. Myrnin knew that."

"Whatever Myrnin believes, I can't take the risk. We are close to the endgame, Claire. I risk only what I must."

"You're not happy that Myrnin introduced me to Ada, are you?" Claire asked.

"Myrnin's judgment has been . . . questionable of late. As you say, he is ill. Where can we find him?"

"Downstairs, by the portal," Claire said. Amelie nodded a brisk dismissal and turned to go, along with all of her followers. "Wait! What do you want me to do?"

Amelie said nothing. Oliver, lingering behind for just a moment, said, "Stay out of our way. If you value your friends, keep them out of our way, too."

Then they were gone, moving fast and silently through the basement doorway.

Claire stood in the empty hallway for a few deep breaths, hearing the sounds of lectures continuing on inside of classrooms, student voices raised in questions or answers.

Life went on.

So weird.

She started to go down to the basement, but a vampire she didn't know blocked the entrance. "No," he said flatly. "You don't go with us."

"But—"

"No."

"Hannah and Michael—"

"They will be taken care of. Leave."

There wasn't any room for negotiation. Claire finally got the hint, and turned away to walk out of the high school the old-fashioned way . . . into the sunlight, the way Amelie and her gang had come. She had no idea where they'd come from, or where they were going.

Amelie wanted it that way.

Claire sat down on the steps of the high school for a few long minutes, shivering in the cold wind, not much warmed by the bright sun in a cloudless sky. The street outside the school looked empty—a few cars making their way around Morganville, but not much else going on.

She heard the door behind her open, and Hannah Moses clumped down in her heavy boots and offered Claire a big, elegant hand. Claire took it and stood. "Amelie's taking care of him?" she asked. Hannah nodded. "Michael went with?"

"He'll see you later," Hannah said. "Important thing is to get you out of here. I need you to help me get your parents on that bus."

"Bishop's going to find out," she said. "You know that, right? He's going to find out what you're doing."

Hannah nodded. "That's why we're doing it fast, girlfriend. So let's move."

Mom and Dad were having an argument; Claire could hear it from where she and Hannah stood on the front porch of their house, ringing the doorbell. Claire felt a sinking sensation in the pit of her stomach. Her parents didn't fight very often, but when they did, it was usually over something important.

The shouty blur of voices broke off, and about ten seconds later, the door whipped open. Claire's mom stood there, color burning high in her cheeks. She looked stricken when she caught sight of Claire, very obviously a guilty-looking earwitness to the fighting, but she rallied and gave a bright smile and gestured them both inside.

"Sheriff Hannah Moses, ma'am," Hannah said without waiting for introductions. "I don't think we've met in person before. I've known your daughter for a while now. She's good people."

She offered her hand, and Claire's mother took it for a quick shake as her eyes darted anxiously from Claire to Hannah, then back. "Is there some kind of problem, Sheriff Moses?"

"Hannah, please." Hannah really was turning on the charm, and she had an awful lot of it. "May I talk with you and your husband at the same time? This concerns both of you."

With only a single, worried look over her shoulder, her mother led the way down the long hallway and into the living room area. Same floor plan as the Glass House, but so wrenchingly different, especially now. Claire got mental whiplash from expecting to see the familiar battered couch and Michael's guitar and the cheerful stacks of books against the wall; instead, her mother's ruthlessly efficient housekeeping had made this room magazine-feature-ready, everything carefully aligned and straightened.

The only thing that wasn't ready for the photo shoot was Claire's father, who sat in one of the leather armchairs, face flushed. He had a stubborn set to his jaw, and an angry fire in his eyes that Claire hadn't seen in, well, forever. Still, he got to his feet and shook hands with Hannah, politely gesturing her to the couch while Claire's mom sank down on the other end, with Claire left to take the middle seat. Normally, her mom would have been fluttering around offering coffee and cookies and sandwiches, but not this time. She just took the other armchair and looked worried.

Hannah said, "Let's put all our cards on the table. There's a town emergency. Mr. and Mrs. Danvers, you are going to need to come with us. Pack a bag for a few nights, take whatever you need that you can't live without. I can give you about fifteen minutes."

That was . . . blunt. Claire blinked. She expected a flood of questions from her parents, but she was surprised by the silence.

Claire's parents looked at each other, and then her father nodded. "Good," he said. "I've wanted to do this for a while. Claire, go with your mother and pack. I'll be up in a second."

"Um . . ." Claire cleared her throat and tried not to look as awkward as she felt. "I'm not going, Dad."

They both looked at her as if she'd spoken in Chinese. "Of course you are," her mom said. "You're not staying here alone. Not with what we know about how dangerous it is."

"I'm sorry, but you know just enough about Morganville to get yourselves in trouble," Hannah said. "This really isn't up for discussion. You have to pack, and you have to go. And Claire can't come with you, at least not yet."

One thing about Hannah: when she said something like that, she clearly meant it. In the silence that fell, Claire felt the weight of both her parents' stares directly on her, so she looked down at her clasped hands instead. "I can't," she said. "It's complicated."

"No, it's not," her dad said, with a steely undertone in his voice she couldn't remember hearing before. "It's absolutely simple. I'm your father, you're under eighteen, and you're coming with us. I'm sorry, Chief Moses, but she's too young to be here on her own."

"Dad, you *sent* me here on my own!" Claire said.

"Why do you think we were fighting, Claire?" her mom replied. "Your father was just reminding me that I was the one who thought sending you to a school close by, just to get some experience with it, would be a good idea. *He* wanted you to go straight to MIT, although how we were going to pay for that, I really don't have any—"

Dad interrupted her. "We're not going to start this up again. Claire, we were wrong to let you go off on your own here in the first place, no matter how safe we thought it would be. And we're fixing that now. You're coming with us, and things will be better once we're out of this town."

Claire's hands formed into fists as frustration boiled up inside her. "Are you *listening* to me? It's too late for all that stuff! I can't go with you!"

She should have guessed that they'd make the wrong assumptions . . . and, in a way, the right one. "It's the boy, isn't it?" Claire's mother said. "Shane?"

"What? No!" Claire blurted out a denial that, even to her own ears, sounded lame and guilty. "No, not really. It's something else. Like I said, it's complicated."

"Oh my God . . . Claire, are you *pregnant?*"

"*Mom!*" She knew she looked as mortified as she felt, especially with Hannah looking on.

"Honey, has that boy taken advantage of you?" Her father was charging full speed down the wrong path; he even stood up to make it more dramatic. "Well?"

Claire stared at him, openmouthed, unable to even try to speak. She knew she should lie, but she just couldn't find the words.

In the ringing silence, her father said, "I want him arrested."

Hannah asked, "On what charge, sir?"

"Are you kidding? He had sex with my underage daughter!" He gave

Claire a look that was partly angry, partly wounded, and all over dangerous. "Go ahead, tell me I'm wrong, Claire."

"It . . . wasn't like that!"

Her dad transferred his glare over to Hannah. "You see? I'll swear out
a complaint if I need to."

Hannah looked perfectly comfortable. "Sir, there's no complaint to
be sworn out here. Fact is, Claire is seventeen years old, which by Texas
law makes her able to give consent on her own. Shane's only a year older
than she is. There's no laws being broken here, beyond maybe the law
of good sense, which I think you'll admit is often a casualty of our teen
years. This is a family matter, not a matter for the police."

Her father looked shocked, then even angrier. "That's insane! It has
to be illegal!"

"Well, it's not, sir, and it has nothing to do with why I'm telling you
Claire needs to stay in Morganville. That has to do with the vampires."
Hannah had deftly moved the whole thing off the subject of Shane and
sex, for which Claire was spine-meltingly grateful. "I'm telling you this
for your own good, and for Claire's own good: she stays here. She won't
be unprotected; I promise you that. We're committed to keeping her safe."

"Who's *we*?" Claire's dad wasn't giving up without a fight.

"Everybody who counts," Hannah said, and raised her eyebrows.
"Time's a-wastin', Mr. Danvers. We really can't debate this. You need to go
right now. Please go pack."

In the end, they did. Claire went to help her mother, reluctantly; she
didn't want the subject to come back to her and Shane, but it did as soon
as the door was closed. At least her father wasn't in the room. God, that
had been awkward.

"Honey." Claire paused in the act of dragging a suitcase out from
under her parents' bed, took one look at the serious expression on her
mother's face, and kept on with what she was doing. "Honey, I really
don't like your getting involved with that boy—that man. And it's not
appropriate for you to be living in that house with him. I just can't allow
that."

"Mom, could we *please* focus on not getting killed today? I promise, you can give me the I'm-so-disappointed-in-you speech tomorrow, and every day after, if you will just pack!"

Her mother opened a drawer of the dresser by the window, grabbed a few handfuls of things at random, and threw them into the open suitcase. *Not* normal. Mom made those people who worked retail clothing stores look sloppy about how they folded things. She moved on to the next drawer, then the next. Claire struggled to neaten up the mess.

"Just tell me this," her mother said as she dumped an armload of clothes from the closet onto the bed. "Are you being safe?"

Oh *lord*, Claire did not want to have the birds-and-bees part two conversation with her mother. Not now. Not ever, to be honest; they'd suffered through it once, awkwardly, and once was enough. "Yes," she said, with as calm and decisive a tone as she could manage. "He insisted." She meant that to reflect well on Shane. Of course, Mom took it the wrong way.

"You mean you *didn't*? Oh, Claire. It's your body!"

"Mom, of course I——" Claire took a deep breath. "Can we just pack? Please?"

She winced as a rain of shoes descended on the bed.

Hannah was waiting when she finally dragged the suitcase downstairs. Claire's father had come in for a few minutes, just long enough to add his few things to the pile, and then he'd tried to tote the bag himself, but Claire had insisted on doing it. The thing was fifty pounds, at least.

Hannah raised her eyebrows at Claire. *What happened?*

Claire rolled her eyes. *Don't ask.*

It was a cold, silent ride to the bus.

Richard Morrell had commandeered two genuine Greyhound buses, with plush seats and tinted windows. According to the hand-lettered sign in the front window, it was a charter heading to Midland/Odessa, but Claire suspected they'd go somewhere else as a destination.

The first bus was already being loaded by the time Claire arrived with her parents; in line to board were most of the town officials and Founder House residents, including the Morrells. Eve was there, too, holding a clipboard and checking people in at a folding table.

"Oh, look, there's your friend," Claire's mom said, and pointed. "She doesn't look very happy."

She wasn't pointing at Eve, but at Monica. Monica definitely wasn't happy. She had to be forced onto the bus, arguing the entire time with her brother, who looked harassed and angry. She'd somehow managed to shoehorn her two friends into the evacuation along with her, although Gina and Jennifer looked a lot more relieved at being given a chance to leave town. Monica was probably thinking that she stood a better chance of social queen bee-ness with Bishop than if Amelie was in charge, but she was thinking short-term; if what Myrnin said was right, and Claire had no reason to think it wasn't, then the entire social order of Morganville was about to get shattered, and being the most popular wouldn't get you anything but more face time with the firing squad.

The argument with Monica came from the fact that Richard Morrell refused to get on the bus. Well, Claire had seen that coming. He wasn't the type to run. "There's a whole town here that can't get out," he snapped at his sister, who was stubbornly resisting getting pushed toward the idling bus. "People who need looking after. I'm the mayor. I have to stay. Besides, since Dad's gone, I'm on the town council. I can't just go."

"You have got such an ego, Richard! Nobody's counting on you. Most of the stupid people in this town would claw one another apart to get out, if they thought they could."

"That's why I'm staying," he said. "Because those people need order. But I need for you to go, Monica. Please. You need to look after our mom."

Monica wavered. Claire, looking up, could see Mrs. Morrell sitting on the bus, looking out the window with a distant, remote expression. Monica had said her mother wasn't dealing very well, and she did look thin and frail and not entirely in this world.

"That is such emotional blackmail!" Monica spat. Behind her, Gina and Jennifer looked at each other, took a few quiet steps back, and mounted the stairs to board the bus, leaving Monica on her own. "Seriously, Richard. I can't believe you're sending me away like this!"

"Believe it. You're getting on, and getting out of here. Now. I need you to be safe." He hugged her, but she stiff-armed him with an angry glare, and turned and boarded without another word. She slumped into the seat behind Jennifer and Gina, next to her mother, and folded her arms in silent protest.

Richard breathed a sigh of relief, then turned to Claire's parents. "Please," he said. "We need to get these buses moving."

Claire's father shook his head.

"Dad," Claire said, and tugged on his arm. "Dad, come on."

He still hesitated, staring at Hannah, then Richard, then Claire. Still shaking his head in mute refusal.

"Dad, you have to go! Now!" Claire practically shouted. She felt sick inside, worried for them and relieved to think they'd be safe, finally, somewhere outside of Morganville. Somewhere none of this could touch them. "Mom, please. Just make him go! I don't want you here; you're just in the way!"

She said it in desperation, and she saw it hurt her parents a little. She'd said worse to them over the years; she'd had her share of *I hate you* and *I wish you were dead*, but that had been when she was just a kid and thought she knew everything.

Now she knew she didn't, but in this case, she knew more than they did.

Frustrating, because they'd never see it that way.

"Don't you talk to us like that, Claire!" her mother snapped. Her dad put a hand on her shoulder and patted, and she took a deep breath.

"All right," Dad said, "I can see you're not going to come without a fight, and I can see your friends here aren't going to help us." He paused, and Claire swallowed hard at the look in his eyes as he locked stares with Hannah, then Richard. "If anything happens to our daughter—"

"Sir," Richard said. "If you don't get on the bus, something is going to happen to all of us, and it's going to be very, very bad. Please. Just go."

"You need to do it for your daughter," Hannah added. "I think you both know that, deep down. So you let me worry about taking care of Claire. You two get on the bus. I promise you, this will be over soon."

It was a sad sort of farewell, full of tears (from Mom and Claire) and the kind of too-strong hug that meant Claire's father felt just as choked up, but wasn't willing to show it. Her mother smoothed her hair, just like she'd done since Claire was a little girl, and kissed her gently on the cheek.

"You be good," she said, and looked deep into Claire's eyes. "We're going to talk about things later."

She meant about Shane, of course. Claire sighed and nodded, and hugged her one last time. She watched them walk up the stairs and onto the bus.

Her parents took a seat near the front, with her mom next to the window. Claire gave a sad little wave, and her mom waved back. Mom was still crying. Dad looked off into the distance, jaw set tight, and didn't wave back.

The bus closed its doors with a final hiss and pulled away from the de-serted warehouse that served as a dropoff point for the departures. Three police cars fell in behind it, driven by people Hannah had handpicked.

Claire shivered, even though she was standing in the sun. *They're leaving. They're really leaving.* She felt very alone.

The bus looked so vulnerable.

"Cold?" A jacket settled around her shoulders. It smelled like Shane. "What did I miss?"

She turned, and there he was, wearing an old gray T-shirt and jeans. His leather jacket felt like a hug around her body, but it wasn't enough; she dived into the warmth of his arms, and they clung together for a moment. He kissed the top of her head. "It's okay," he said. "They'll be okay."

"No, it's not okay," she said, muffled against his chest. "It's just not."

He didn't argue. After a moment, she turned her head, and together they watched the caravan stream away toward the Morganville city limits.

"Why is it," she asked in a plaintive little voice, "that I can fight vam-pires and risk death and they can accept that, but they can't accept that I'm a woman, with my own life?"

Shane thought about that for a second; she could see him trying to work it out through the framework of his own admittedly weird child-hood. "Must be a girl thing?"

"Yeah, must be."

"So I'm guessing you told them."

"Um . . . not on purpose. I didn't expect them to be so . . . angry about it."

"You're their little girl," Shane said. "You know, when I think about it, I'd feel the same way about my own daughter."

"You would?" There was something deliciously warm about the fact that he wasn't afraid to say that to her. "So," she said, with an effort at being casual that was probably all too obvious. "You want to have a daughter, then?"

He kissed the top of her head. "Hit the brakes, girl."

But he didn't sound angry about it, or nervous. Just—as was usual with Shane—focused on what was in front of them right now. A sense of calm was slowly spreading through her, sinking deeper with every breath. It felt better when she was with him. Everything felt better.

Shane asked, "What about the Goldmans? Were they on the bus, too?"

"I didn't see the Goldmans," Claire said. "Hannah?"

Hannah Moses was still standing nearby, signing papers on a clipboard that another uniformed Morganville cop had handed her. She glanced toward the two of them. "Couldn't get to them," she said. "Myrnin was going to arrange that, but we've got no way to get them out of Bishop's control right now. The clock's running, and it's only a matter of minutes before Bishop finds out what we just did, if he hasn't already."

Richard Morrell's phone rang. He unclipped it from his belt and checked the number, then flipped it open and walked away to talk for a moment. Claire watched him pace, shoulders hunched, as he had his conversation. When he folded up the phone and came back, his face was tense. "He knows," he said. "Bishop's calling a town hall meeting for tonight at Founder's Square. Everybody must attend. Nobody stays home."

"Oh, come on. You can't get everybody in town to a meeting. What if they don't get the message? What if they just don't want to do it?" Claire asked. Even in Morganville, making people stick to rules—whatever the rules were—was like herding cats.

Richard and Hannah exchanged a look. "Bishop's not one for taking excuses," she said. "If he says everybody has to be at the meeting, he'll make it open season on anybody who isn't there. That's his style."

Richard was already nodding his agreement. "We need to get word out. Knock on every door, every business. Lock off the campus and keep the students out of this. We've got six hours before sundown. Let's not waste one minute."

Shane was drafted into helping a whole crowd of people load supplies into the warehouse—food, water, clothing, radios, survival-type stuff. Claire wasn't sure why, and she didn't think she really wanted to know; the atmosphere was quiet, purposeful, but tense. Nobody asked questions. Not now.

The first of Bishop's vampires showed up about two hours later, driving slowly past the perimeter in one of the city-issued cars with tinted windows. Hannah's strike team stopped the car, and Claire was surprised to see them fling a blanket over the vampire as he was dragged out of the shelter into the sun, and hauled off to be confined under cover.

"Most of Bishop's people are really Amelie's," Hannah explained. "Amelie would like us to keep them alive, if we can. She can turn them back, once Bishop's gone. Call it temporary insanity—not a killing kind of offense, even for vampires. We just need to keep them out of commission, that's all."

Well, that sounded deceptively easy to Claire's ears; she didn't think Bishop's converts—even the unwilling ones—would be all that eager to be put on the bench. Still, Hannah seemed to know what she was doing. Hopefully. "So that's the plan: we just grab every vamp who comes looking?"

"Not quite." Hannah gave her a slight smile. "You do know I'm not telling you the plan, right?"

Right, Claire was still on the wrong side. She glared down at her much-faded tattoo, which was still moving under her skin, but weakly, like the last flutters of a failing butterfly. It itched. "I wish this thing would just *die* already."

"Has Bishop tried to reach you through it?"

"Not recently. Or if he has, I can't feel it anymore." That would be excellent, if it really was a bad connection. Maybe she was in a no-magic-signal dead zone. "So what can I do?"

"Go knock on doors," Hannah said. "We've got a list of names that we're still looking for, for the second bus. You can go with Joe Hess."

Claire's eyes widened. "He's okay?" Because she had an instant sense memory of the feeling of that death warrant in her hands, the one she'd given to him.

"Sure," Hannah said. "Why wouldn't he be?"

Claire had no idea what had happened, but she liked Detective Hess, and at least riding around with him would give her a feeling of forward motion, of doing something useful. Everyone else seemed to have a purpose. All she could think about was that her parents were on a bus heading out of town, and she didn't know what was going to happen to them. Or *could* happen to them.

She wished she'd said a better good-bye. She wished they hadn't been so upset with her about Shane. *Well, they're going to have to get used to it*, she thought defiantly, but even to herself, it felt weak and a little selfish.

But being with Shane wasn't a mistake. She knew it wasn't.

Joe Hess was driving his own car, but it had all the cool cop stuff inside—a radio, one of those magnetic flashing lights to go on the roof, and a shotgun that was locked into a rack in the back. He was a tall, quiet man who just had a way about him that put her at ease. For one thing, he never looked at her like some annoying kid; he just looked at her as a person. A young person, true, but someone to take seriously. She wasn't quite sure how she'd earned that from him, considering the death warrant delivery.

"I'm locking the doors," he told her as she climbed into the passenger seat, half a second before the *click-thump* sound echoed through the car. "Nice to see you, Claire."

"Thanks. It's good to see you, too. What about the buses?" she said. "Are they out of town yet?"

"Amelie herself escorted them through the barrier a few minutes ago," he said. "There was a little bit of trouble at the border, nothing we couldn't handle. They're on their way. Nobody was hurt."

That eased a tight knot in her chest that she hadn't even known was there. "Where are they going— No, don't tell me. I probably don't need to know, right?"

"Probably not," he agreed, and gave her a sidelong look. "You okay?"

She looked out the car window and shrugged. "My parents are on one of those buses, that's all. I'm just worried."

He kept sending her looks as he drove, and there was a frown on his face. "And tired," he said. "When you left me, did you go back to Bishop? Did he hurt you?"

There really wasn't an easy answer to that. "He didn't hurt me," she finally said. "Not . . . personally."

"I guess that's part of what I was asking," he said. "But that doesn't answer my question, really."

"You mean, am I in need of serious therapy because of all this?" Another shrug seemed kind of appropriate. "Yeah, probably. But this is Morganville. That's not exactly the worst thing that could happen." She turned her head and looked directly at him. "What was on the scroll I gave you?"

He was quiet for so long she thought he was blowing off the question, but then he said, "It was a death warrant."

She already knew that. "Not yours, though."

"No," he said. "Someone else's."

"Whose?"

"Claire—"

"It doesn't matter. We got it reversed. It's not an issue anymore."

"I delivered it. I have a right to know."

For answer, Joe dug into the pocket of his sports jacket and pulled out a folded piece of paper, still curling at the edges, with fragments of wax clinging to the outside. He held it out to her.

Claire unfolded it. The paper was stiff and crackly, old paper, with a faintly moldy smell to it. The handwriting—Bishop's—was spiky and hard to read, but the name was done larger and underlined.

Eve Rosser.

"That's not happening," Joe said. "I just wanted you to know that. If he tells you about it, I wanted you to understand that Eve is perfectly safe, all right? Nothing will happen to her. Claire, do you understand me?"

She'd carried an order to him to kill her best friend.

Claire couldn't think. Couldn't feel anything except a vast, echoing sense of shock. She tried to read the rest of the paper, but her eyes kept moving back to Eve's name, going over and over it.

She folded up the paper and held it clutched tightly in one hand. *Breathe.* She felt light-headed and a little sick.

"Why you?" she asked faintly. "Why give it to you?"

"That's Bishop's style. He picks out people least likely to do what he wants, so he can punish them when they refuse to carry out the order. Object lessons for the rest of Morganville. He knew I wouldn't kill Eve. Not a chance. This was less about his wanting to get rid of Eve than to get rid of me."

She still felt cold. Sure, Detective Hess wouldn't have done it, but what if she'd been told to take it to someone else? Monica, maybe?

Eve might be dead right now, and it would have been all her fault.

She felt the death warrant being tugged out of her fingers. When she opened her eyes, fighting back tears, Detective Hess was slipping it back into his pocket. "I just wanted you to understand what we're up against," he said. "And to understand that no matter what happens, some of us will never do what he wants."

Claire realized that she couldn't count herself in that club. She'd already done what Bishop wanted.

More than once.

God, she *really* didn't want to think about how far she'd wandered into that swamp, but she was definitely up to her butt in alligators.

"All right, back to business." Hess handed her a piece of paper. "These are the people we still need to find," he said. "I heard about what happened with Frank Collins. You and Shane were there?"

She really wasn't up to talking about that. "Dr. Mills is with Amelie," she said. "You can cross him off this list. She isn't going to send him out of town."

All around Morganville, as they drove, there were signs things were happening—people gathering in groups, whispering at fences, and pausing to stare hard at the passing car. No vampires in sight, but then Claire wouldn't expect there to be so close to noon. "What is this?" she asked. Hess shook his head.

"There's still a pretty strong antivampire movement in town," he said. "It got stronger these last few months. I've been trying to keep them calmed down, because if they start this now, they'll just get themselves killed. And most of them aren't looking at Amelie's side as anything but another target. We can't afford that until Bishop's gone."

"So what do we do about it?"

"Nothing. Nothing we can do right now. Bishop's the one pushing the agenda, not us. If he wants a fight tonight, he's going to get one. Maybe bigger than he wants."

The fourth address on the list was an apartment—there weren't many apartment buildings in Morganville, since most people lived in single-family houses, but there were a few. Like in any small town, the complexes varied from crappy to less crappy; there was no such thing as luxury multifamily housing.

The apartment complex they stopped at was on the crappy end of the short spectrum. It was stucco over brick, painted a sun-faded pink, with two stories of apartments built into an open square on a central . . . well, Claire guessed you could call it a courtyard, if you liked a view that included a dry swimming pool with dark scum at one end, some spiky, untrimmed bushes, and an overflowing trash can.

Joe Hess checked apartment numbers. If the run-down appearance of the place bothered him, he didn't show it. When they reached number twenty-two, he banged loudly on the door. "Police, open up!" he yelled, and pushed Claire out of the way when she tried to stand next to him. He gave her a silent *stay there* gesture, and listened. She couldn't hear a thing from inside.

Neither could he, apparently. He shook his head, but as they turned to go, Claire clearly heard someone inside the apartment say, "Help."

She froze, staring at Detective Hess. He'd heard it, too, and he gestured her even farther back as he pulled his gun from the holster under his jacket. "Willie Combs? You okay in there? It's Joe Hess. Answer me, Willie!"

"Help," the voice came again, weaker this time.

Hess tried the door, but it was locked. He took in a deep breath. "Claire, you stay right there. *Do not come in.* Hear me?"

She nodded. He whirled and kicked into the door, and the cheap hollow wood splintered and flew open on the second try, sending wood and metal flying.

Detective Hess disappeared inside. Claire saw curtains fluttering and blinds tenting as people looked out to see what was going on, but nobody came outside.

Not even in the middle of the day.

It seemed like a very long time until Detective Hess came out with someone held in his arms. It was a girl about Claire's age, pretty, dressed in a Morganville High T-shirt and sweatpants, like she'd just dropped in from gym class.

She wasn't moving, and he was holding a towel on her neck.

"Call an ambulance," he ordered Claire. "Tell them it's a rush, and bring the bite kit."

"Is she—"

"She's alive," he said, and stretched her out on the concrete, still holding the towel in place. Hess looked up at her with fury shining in his eyes. "Her name is Theresa. Theresa Combs. She's the oldest of the three kids."

Claire went cold, and looked at the doorway of the apartment. "They're not—"

"Let's focus on the living," he said. "Hold this on her throat, just like this." She knelt beside him and pressed her small fingers where his larger ones were. It felt like she was pressing too hard, but he nodded. "Good. Keep doing that. I'm going to make one more sweep inside, just to be sure."

As he stepped over the girl and back into the apartment, Theresa's eyes fluttered, and she looked at Claire. Big, dark eyes. Desperate. "Help," she whispered. "Help Jimmy. He's only twelve."

Claire took her hand. "Shhhh. Just rest."

Theresa's eyes filled up with tears. "I tried," she said. "I really tried. Why is this happening to us? We didn't do anything wrong. We followed all the rules."

Claire couldn't do anything to help her, except hold her hand and keep the towel over her throat, just like Detective Hess said. When he came back to the doorway, drawn by the distant howl of an approaching siren, she looked up at him in miserable hope.

He shook his head.

They didn't speak at all until the paramedics took Theresa away. Claire stayed where she was, on her knees, staring at the blood speckling her trembling fingers. Detective Hess crouched down and handed her a moist wipe, with the attitude of somebody who'd done that sort of thing a lot. He patted her gently on the shoulder. "Deep breaths," he said. "I'm sorry you had to see that. Good job taking care of Theresa. You probably saved her life."

"Who did that to them?" Once she started wiping her hands, she really couldn't stop. "Why?"

"It's been happening all over town," Hess said. "People whose Protectors went over to Bishop. People who lost their Protectors in the fight. People whose Protectors never cared enough in the first place. Half of this town is nothing but a mobile blood supply right now." The look on his face, when she glanced up, was enough to make her shiver. "Maybe the crazies are right. Maybe we should kill all the vampires."

"Yeah," Claire said, very softly. "Because people never kill people, right?"

He had Eve's death warrant in his pocket.

He didn't argue about it.

They found another five people on Hannah's list, all safe and alive—well, one of them was drunk off his butt at the Barfly, one of the scarier local watering holes, but he was still breathing and unfanged. One by one, they were put on the bus.

By four p.m., the last bus was motoring out of Morganville, heading for parts unknown (to Claire, at least), and she was left standing with those who were left. Richard Morrell. Hannah Moses. Shane and Eve, standing there together, whispering. Joe Hess, talking on the police car radio. There were other people around, but they stayed in the shadows, and Claire had the strong suspicion that they were vampires. Amelie's vampires, getting organized for something big.

Without warning, Claire felt a burning sensation on her arm.

When she pulled back her sleeve, she saw the tattoo was swirling, like a pot of stirred ink under her skin. Bishop was trying to pull her in. She could feel the impulse to walk out of the warehouse and head for Founder's Square, but she resisted.

When she was afraid she couldn't hold back anymore, she told Shane. He put his arms around her. "I'm not letting you go anywhere," he promised. "Not without me."

The impulse felt like a string tied around her guts, pulling relentlessly. It was annoying at first. Then it hurt. Finally, she pulled free of Shane's embrace and walked in circles around the open space of the warehouse they'd used for the bus staging area, making wider and wider arcs. He intercepted her when she came close to the door, and she looked at him in silent misery. "I hate this!" she blurted. "I want this thing *out!*" And she burst into tears, because it felt overwhelming to her, this feeling of despair and anguish, of not being where she was supposed to be. This time, even Shane's presence couldn't help. The misery just came in waves, crushing her underneath. She heard Shane yelling at Richard Morrell, and then Hannah was there, saying something about helping.

Claire felt a hot sting in her arm, and then calm spread like ice through her veins. It was a relief, but it didn't touch the burning on her arm, or the anxiety boiling in her stomach. Her body still wasn't her own.

"She'll sleep for a while," Hannah said, from a long way off. "Shane, I need you."

Claire couldn't open her eyes, or tell them that she wasn't really asleep at all. She seemed to be—she got that—but she was desperately awake underneath. Painfully awake.

Shane kissed her, warm and gentle, and she felt his hand smooth her hair and trace down her cheek. *Don't leave me,* she wanted to tell him, but she couldn't make herself move or speak.

Her heartbeat thudded, slow and calm, even though she felt the panic building inside her.

She felt herself carried somewhere, tucked into a warm bed and piled with blankets.

Then silence.

Her eyes opened, as if someone else was controlling them, and as she sat up, she saw someone standing in the corner of the darkened room where they'd left her.

Ada.

The ghost put a pale, flickering finger to her lips and motioned for Claire to sit up. She did, although she had no idea why.

Ada drifted closer. Once again, she wasn't three-dimensional at all, just a flat projection on the air, like a TV character without the screen. She didn't really look human; in fact, she looked more like a game character, all smoothness and manufactured detail.

Somewhere in the dark, a cell phone rang. Claire walked over to a pile of boxes labeled EMERGENCY COMMUNICATION EQUIPMENT and ripped away tape to retrieve a cell phone. Fully charged, from the battery icon on the display. She lifted it to her ear.

"Bishop is trying to pull you to him," Ada's tinny, artificial voice said. "But I need you elsewhere."

"*You* need me."

"Of course. With Myrnin deactivated, I require someone to assist me. Take the portal to reach me."

"There's a portal?" Claire felt slow and stupid, and she didn't think it was the drugs that Hannah had given her. Ada's ghostly representation gave her a scorching look of contempt.

"I have *made* a portal," she said. "That's what I do, you silly fool. Take it, now. Six steps forward, four to your right. Go!"

The connection died on Claire's borrowed phone with a lost-signal beep. She folded the clamshell and slid it back in her pocket, and realized that someone—Shane, she guessed—had taken her shoes off for her. She put them on and walked six paces forward into the dark, then four steps to the right.

Her fourth step sent her falling through freezing-cold blackness, and then her foot touched ground, and she was someplace she recognized.

She came out in the cells where Myrnin and Amelie had confined the vampires who had become too sick to function on their own. It was an old prison, dark and damp, built out of solid stone and steel. The tornado that had raged through Morganville a few months back had damaged part of the building; Claire hadn't been involved in tracking down the escaped patients, but she knew it had been done, and the place repaired. Not that Bishop had cared, of course. Amelie had done that.

But all the cells were empty now.

Claire stumbled to a halt and wrapped her arms around her stomach, where the tug from Bishop's will felt like a white-hot wire being pulled through her skin. She braced herself against the wall, breathing hard. "I'm here," she said to the empty air. "What do you want me to do, Ada?"

Ada's ghost glided down the corridor ahead of her—still two-dimensional, but this time the view was from the back. Her stiff belled skirts drifted inches above the stone floor, and she looked back over her shoulder toward Claire in unmistakable command. *Great,* Claire thought. *It's not bad enough that Bishop has his hooks in me; now it's Myrnin's nutty computer, too. I have way too many bosses.*

Eve would have told her she needed a better job, which would include sewage treatment.

"Where are we going?" she asked Ada, not that she expected an answer. She wasn't disappointed. The prison was laid out in long hallways, and the last time Claire had been here, most of the cells had been filled with plague victims. She'd delivered their food—well, blood—to them to make sure they hadn't starved. Some had been violent; most had just been lying very still, unable to do much at all.

Where were they now?

At the end of the line was the cell where Myrnin had spent his days, off and on, when he was too dangerous to be in the lab or around anybody—even other vampires. It had been furnished with his home comforts, like a thick Turkish rug and a soft pile of blankets and pillows, his ragged armchair, and stacks of books.

No sign of Myrnin, either.

Ada glided to the end of the hall, then turned to face Claire, flickering from a back view to a front view like a jump cut in a movie.

"That's really creepy," Claire said. "You know that, right?"

Her phone rang. She opened the clamshell. "You were seeking Dr. Mills," Ada said. "He is here."

"Where?"

"Follow. He requires assistance."

Claire kept the phone to her ear as Ada turned around again and misted right through the stone wall. Claire stopped, her nose two inches away from the surface of the barrier. She slowly reached out, and although the stone looked utterly real—it even smelled real, like dust and mold—there was nothing under her hand but air. Still, her brain stubbornly told her not to take another step, or she'd end up with a bruised face at the very least. In fact, her whole body resisted the order to walk on.

Claire forced her foot to rise, inch forward, and step *into* the stone. Then the other foot, shuffling forward to match it. It didn't get any easier, not for five or six torturous inches, and then suddenly the pressure was gone, and she stepped through into a large, well-lit room.

A room full of vampires.

Claire froze as dozens of pallid faces turned toward her. She'd never gotten to know the inmates—they'd mostly been anonymous in the shadows—but she recognized a few of them. What were they doing out of their cages?

The voice on the phone at her ear snapped, impatiently, "Would you *come*, then?"

Claire blinked and saw that Ada was drifting in the middle of the room, staring at her in naked fury. "They're not going to—"

"They will not hurt you," Ada said. "Don't be absurd."

It really wasn't all that absurd. Claire had seen some of these same vampires clawing gouges in stone with their fingernails, and gnawing on their own fingers. She was like a doggie treat in a room full of rabid rottweilers.

None of them lunged at her. They stared at her as if she was a curiosity, but they didn't seem especially, well, hungry.

She followed Ada's image across the room to a small stone alcove, where she saw Dr. Mills lying very still on a cot.

"Oh no," Claire whispered, and hurried over to him. "Dr. Mills?"

He groaned and opened reddened eyes, blinking to focus on her face. "Claire," he croaked, and coughed. "Damn. What time is it?"

"Uh—almost five, I think. Why?"

"I just went to sleep at four," he said, and flopped back to full length on his cot. "God. Sorry, I'm exhausted. Forty-eight hours without more than a couple of hours down. I'm not a med student anymore."

She felt a wave of utter relief. "They didn't, you know—"

"Kill me? Other than by working me half to death?" Dr. Mills groaned and sat up, rubbing his head as if he was trying to shove his brains back inside. "Amelie wanted to use the serum to treat the worst cases first. I got everyone housed here, except for Myrnin. I have two doses left. There won't be any more if we don't get blood from Bishop to culture."

She'd almost forgotten about that. "Have you seen Myrnin?"

"Not since Amelie brought me here," Dr. Mills said. "Why?"

"He's sick," Claire said. "Very sick. I was looking for you to try to help him, but I don't know where he is now. Amelie took him, too."

He was already shaking his head. "She didn't bring him here. I haven't seen them."

Claire sensed a shadow behind her and, turning, came face-to-face with a vampire. A smallish one, just a little taller than her own modest height. It was a girl barely out of her teens, with waist-length blond hair and lovely dark eyes, who smiled at the two of them with an unsettlingly knowing expression.

"I am Naomi," she said. "This is my sister Violet." Just behind her was a slightly older girl, same dark eyes, only a little stronger in the chin, and with midnight-black hair. "We wish to thank you, Doctor, for your gift. We have not felt so well in many years."

"You're welcome," Dr. Mills said. He sounded tense, and Claire could understand why; the vamps were all on their best behavior, but that could change, and she saw a shadow of it in Naomi. "I'm sure Amelie will be along to get you soon."

The two vamps nodded, bobbed an old-fashioned curtsy, and withdrew back into the main room. There was a soft buzz of conversation building out there, a kind of whisper that sounded like a calm sea on the shore. Vampires didn't have to speak loudly to be heard, at least by one another.

"*Is* Amelie coming?" Dr. Mills asked. "Because I'm starting to feel like the special of the day around here."

Oh. He thought Claire was the scout riding ahead of the vampire cavalry. She looked around for Ada, but she didn't see any sign of her now. She'd just faded out. Claire folded up the phone and put it back in her pocket, feeling a little stupid. "I don't know," she said. "I was told you needed help."

He gave a jaw-cracking yawn, murmured an apology, and nodded. "I've got sacks of crystals, and some of the liquid. We need to distribute it all over town, make sure everybody who needs it gets medicated. It won't last for long, and it isn't the cure, but until I can get Bishop's blood, it'll have to do. Can you help me measure it into individual doses?"

Claire realized, as she was scooping measuring spoons of red crystals and putting them in bottles, that the burning urgency in her guts had finally, slowly faded away.

She pulled up her sleeve.

The tattoo was barely a shadow under her skin.

As she stared at the place where it had been, Naomi the vampire leaned over her shoulder and studied it with her. Claire flinched, which was probably what the vamp had intended, and Naomi chuckled. "I see Bishop marked you," she said. "Don't fear, child. It's almost gone now. He marked my sister once." The smile left her face, and it set in hard, cold lines. "Then he marked us both forever. Sister Amelie told us he was dead, long ago, but he isn't, is he?"

Claire shook her head, unable to say anything with fangs so close to her neck. Naomi didn't seem to be threatening, but she didn't seem to be *comforting*, either.

"Then it's come to it," Naomi said. "It's time for us to fight him. Good. For my sister's sake, I'll be happy to face him again." Naomi's cool hand stroked Claire's cheek. "Pretty child. You smell warm."

Claire shuddered. "Yeah, well, I, uh, am. I guess."

"Warm as sunlight. So was I, once." Naomi's sigh brushed Claire's skin, and then the vampire was gone, moving in a blur. The vampires were all moving faster now—recovering, Claire guessed. Growing stronger.

Dr. Mills was looking at them in satisfaction, but Claire couldn't quite get there from here. Great, they were feeling better; she could get behind that.

But now they were *healthy* vampires. Which meant they could make more vampires, and that changed everything. It changed the entire dynamic of Morganville.

Didn't it?

Her phone rang. No number displayed on the caller ID. Claire flipped it open and said, "What, Ada?"

"You must take Dr. Mills and leave," Ada said. "I will dial the portal for you. Go now."

"Would you mind telling me what—"

"Do as I say or I will leave you both alone in a room full of vampires who may crave an instant hot meal."

Myrnin's computer was such a *bitch.*

Claire snapped the phone shut. "Grab what you need," she said. "It's time to go."

Dr. Mills nodded. He'd loaded the individual doses into a couple of duffel bags, and he handed one to her as he hefted the other. He opened up a padded silver box and checked the contents.

Two syringes.

"Those are the last two doses of the serum, right?" Claire asked. "Maybe I'd better . . . ?"

He handed them over. "Make sure Myrnin gets one, and Amelie gets the other," he said. "Oliver will try to hijack one for himself. Don't let him."

Like she stood a chance of saying no to Oliver on her own, but she nodded anyway. Dr. Mills seemed relieved to have the stuff out of his hands. He looked around at the vampires, who were all turning toward them. "Maybe we should be going," he said. "I'm sure they're all grateful, but—"

"Yeah," Claire said. "Let's."

Walking through the crowd was like walking through a giant pride of lions. They might be calmly observing, but there was no mistaking the predatory gleam in their eyes as they did it. Claire caught the glitter of fangs in one or two mouths, and made sure not to make eye contact.

Naomi stepped into her path. The young vampire—well, young-*looking*—blocked the way out. "May I beg a favor?" she asked. "A small one, I assure you."

Claire licked her lips. "Sure."

"Give this to my sister Amelie," she said, and lifted a silver necklace off of her alabaster neck. It was a beautiful little thing, thin as a whisper, and it had a white cameo dangling from it. "Tell her that we are with her if she requires it."

Claire put the necklace in her pocket, and nodded. "I'll tell her." Naomi didn't move. "Did you want something else?"

"Oh, yes," Naomi said faintly. "Very badly. But you see, I know my sister. I know she would not forgive me if I did anything untoward. So you and your kind doctor must go, before we forget our promises."

Still, she didn't move.

Claire went around her. Naomi turned to watch her.

Stepping through the stone illusion seemed a whole lot easier this time, maybe because she knew staying was definitely not a good idea at all.

Ada's ghost stood in the hallway, looking furiously out of sorts with the delay. She turned and glided away at top speed. Claire broke into a run to keep up, and Dr. Mills kept pace. Ada suddenly stopped and spun her image to face them like a flat cardboard cutout, and the speaker on Claire's phone shrieked with static.

Dr. Mills went down.

"Run!" Ada screamed through the speakerphone, but Claire couldn't. She couldn't leave him behind.

Claire stopped to reach down to help him up, but he wasn't moving. There was a cut on his head, and although he was breathing, he was completely unconscious.

The cut was on the *back* of his head. He hadn't fallen that way.

Someone had hit him.

Ada tried to tell her to run away, but she stayed where she was. Ada's ghostly image screamed silently in frustration and burst into a storm of misty static.

Gone.

In the darkness, Claire felt fingers brush her hair.

"Naomi?" she asked in a faint whisper.

A dry chuckle sounded next to her ear, shockingly close. "Never met the lady. You know who I am," a male voice said. "Don't you, Claire?"

She closed her eyes.

"Hello," she said, "Mr. Collins."

NINE

S hane's dad turned on an electric light overhead, and the sudden glare made Claire wince and blink. She looked down quickly at Dr. Mills to confirm that he was still breathing, and not moving. Good. She needed all her concentration right now.

Frank Collins looked the same as he had the last time she'd seen him alive, there in Bishop's office—thin, lean, with his long graying hair down around his face, only now he was paler. He looked like a man who'd lived hard and died the same way—and there was definitely a shadow in him that hadn't been there before. A crazy, scary shine in his eyes, like a silver film. He had a few things in common with Oliver, but where Oliver came across as tough, frightening, and ultimately rational, Collins missed that last one entirely.

He was *way* too close. Claire stayed very still, trying not to let her pulse pound too hard.

"I see what my son likes about you," Frank Collins said. "You're tougher than you look."

"Thanks," she said. "Now back off."

He laughed again. It echoed off of the stone, as if he'd brought three or four copies of himself to enjoy the show. "No," he said. "I don't think so. Never done it before. Never will." He paused. "I'd like to talk to my son."

"Never going to happen," Claire said. "He doesn't want to talk to you."

Mr. Collins's smile showed more than teeth. His fangs slowly unfolded, and the edges caught the dim light. "You think he'd want you sucking plasma, too, sweetheart? It would kill him if something like that happened. So you might try to be a little more polite."

She wanted to vomit at the thought of Frank Collins biting her. "He'll kill *you*," she said. "You know he would."

"Maybe he'd try." Frank shrugged. "He wouldn't hurt you, though. I know my boy well enough to know how head over heels he is for you. He'd never touch a hair on your pretty little head. You're his weakness, Claire."

That was sickeningly true. Shane would do anything to save Claire. He'd even let his father turn him into a vampire—which might be what Freaky Frank was thinking about.

She couldn't let that happen. No way.

Claire slowly let the duffel bag she was holding thump down to the floor, and took stock of what she had to work with. Not much. Frank Collins had been turned by Bishop; he wasn't sick. She had no hope of curing him, or even treating him. This was his *natural* state of crazy.

Her backpack.

Claire let it slide down her arm, hoping that he'd think she was getting ready to make a run for it. It'd be useless to do that; she'd never make it.

Plus, he'd enjoy the chase.

As her backpack caught in the crook of her elbow, she grabbed the front zipper. Gravity helped her pull it down as the weight sagged forward.

Oh, crap.

The stakes weren't in the front pocket. She'd put them in the bigger interior, with her books. There was nothing in the front pocket but some paper clips, a highlighter, and half a candy bar. She didn't think bribing him with chocolate would get it done.

"Relax," Shane's dad said. "I'll let you go."

That seemed . . . too good to be true, but Claire was willing to take it and run. "Thanks," she said, and bent to grab Dr. Mills to pull him toward the portal.

"I didn't say *he* could go," Frank said, his smile full-tilt crazy. "I deserve a little bonus for being so accommodating."

Claire could feel her heart pounding now, even through the layers of calming drugs that Hannah had dosed her with before. Everything seemed to slow down. She didn't pause to think. She threw all her strength into grabbing the pack in both hands, twirling in place like a shot-putter, and slamming the pack into Frank Collins's back.

There were a lot of books in there, and physics was something not even vampires could ignore, especially when it hit them full force. Frank went sprawling. Claire grabbed Dr. Mills by one arm and dragged him toward the spot where Ada had been standing.

Ada flickered back into existence as she approached. The speaker in Claire's phone activated and Ada shouted, "Leave the man; get the bags!"

"Bite me," Claire snapped. She heaved, got Dr. Mills up to a sitting position, and rolled him through the portal.

Then she dashed back for the duffel bags.

Frank Collins's pale hand grabbed her wrist. She looked up, right into his scarred face and silvery eyes, and screamed. There was no way she could break free, not without leaving her hand behind. He was just that strong.

Shane's dad yanked her down to her knees on the floor. He pulled the strap of her backpack off her shoulder and ripped the tough fabric open, spilling the contents all over the floor. *Advanced Particle Physics* slipped off into the dark, along with *Fundamentals of Matrix Computations*. Out spilled two sharp-pointed wooden stakes. Out of sheer desperation, she made a grab for them, but his foot came crashing down to pin them to the floor before she could get there.

He stood there, staring at the stakes, and she saw something move over his face, like a ripple of real human pain. "Christ," he murmured. "I used to carry some just like that when I was starting out hunting them. What the hell am I doing?"

She knew what that pain was, and all of a sudden she knew how to hurt him. "You're hunting," Claire said. Her heart was beating so hard, it felt as if it would break her ribs. "That's what vamps do. Hunt people."

He shook his head silently, then looked up at her. He almost looked sane again, or as sane as Shane's father ever got. "I've been fighting vampires a long time," he said. "Killed a couple; did you know that?"

She knew. He and Shane had almost been executed for killing Brandon, even though Shane hadn't had anything to do with it. He stared down again at the hand-carved stakes sticking out from under his big, scuffed boot.

"Never ended up using stakes all that much," he said, and looked her right in the eyes. "You know why?"

She was afraid to ask.

"Because if you don't kill a vampire, it just makes them angrier," he said. "You think you can kill me with something like this?"

She swallowed hard. "Sure. Not that you're going to let me try."

"Truth is, the worst thing I ever feared was this. Being this. Shane tell you that?" She slowly nodded. "I'm sorry he had to see what happened to me. I'm sorry for all the things I did to make his life hell over the years. You understand?"

She shook her head, because she really didn't.

"You tell Shane I love him," Frank said. "I always did. Didn't show it right, I know that, but that was never his fault. I'm glad he found you. He deserves something good in his life."

And then he lifted up his boot and picked up the stakes. Claire opened her mouth, but her voice caught in her throat.

He didn't hurt her.

"You go home," he said. "You tell my son his father says good-bye. Wish I'd gotten to see him one more time, but you're right. It's probably not a good idea."

He turned away toward the darkness, with the stakes in his hand.

"I guess you should know that he loves you, too. He can't help it." Her voice echoed from the stone. She didn't know why she said it, except that she knew, with sad certainty, that she wouldn't see him again.

She thought Shane's dad hesitated, but then he shuffled on, until he was out of sight.

The instant he was gone, Claire grabbed the duffel bags, and lunged to her feet, heading for the open portal.

She stumbled out on the other side, tripped over Dr. Mills's motion-less body, and fell into Oliver's arms.

He looked at her with an absolutely disgusted expression, and dropped her on her butt on the plushly carpeted floor of Amelie's study.

"It's gone," Claire said for the four hundredth time as Oliver turned her arm this way and that, holding it under a light so bright it felt like a laser cutting into her skin. "Hey! I said it's *gone!*"

Oliver held her in place with a grip so hard she knew it would leave its own kind of tattooing. In blue, purple, and black. "And I said that Bishop would very much like us to think that it's gone," he snapped. "You were told to stay where you were. As usual, you ignored that instruction, and now you've placed us all at extreme risk of——"

"Let her go, Oliver," Amelie said from the other side of the vast, pol-ished desk. She drummed her perfect fingernails on the surface, making a light, dry tapping sound like bones dropped on marble. "The girl could have betrayed us a dozen times or more by now. She hasn't. I believe we can give her the benefit of the doubt, for now."

He let Claire go and stalked away, arms folded. This, Claire thought, was Amelie's war council—Sam Glass sat next to her in a side chair, look-ing more like Michael all the time as his red hair grew out into a mess of waves and curls. Oliver paced. Richard Morrell stood nearby, looking as if he *wanted* to pace, but was too tired to make the attempt.

Michael moved up next to Claire, put his hand on her shoulder, and led her off to the side, near where Hannah Moses leaned against the wall, looking fascinated and worried. Claire knew just how she felt. Be-ing plunged into the deep end—and this was it—meant swimming for your life, with sharks. Even the supposedly friendly ones could turn and take your leg off when they felt like it.

"Where's Myrnin?" Claire whispered. Michael shook his head. "Isn't he here? Somewhere?"

"No idea," Michael whispered back. "Amelie stashed him someplace; I just don't know where. He's not——"

"Michael," Amelie said, "I said I would give her the benefit of the doubt, not the full story. Please be quiet." She stood up, and Claire saw that she'd changed clothes again, this time to a flawless pale pink suit, something that looked like it belonged on a runway in Paris. Not what Claire would have thought you'd wear to a showdown. "Claire. Thank you for bringing the supplies that I requested from Dr. Mills. Thank you also for retrieving the good doctor. I am told that he will recover from his wound." Her light-colored, cool eyes focused on Claire, and shot right through her. "May I also see your arm?"

Always polite. That was when Amelie was the most dangerous, Claire knew. She slowly extended her arm, still holding Michael's hand on the other side for comfort. Amelie's touch was cold and light. She didn't study the skin, like Oliver had; she ran her fingertips over the surface, and then lowered Claire's arm back to her side.

"Michael," she said, "please take Claire to your friends. I am sure you would both prefer to be with them now."

"But . . ." Claire licked her lips. "Don't you want me here? To help?"

"You'll help when it's needed," Amelie said. "For now, you should be elsewhere. We will be bringing in some of my people to remove them from Bishop's influence. The process can be somewhat unsettling to witness."

Oliver made a rude noise as he continued his relentless pacing. "It's far worse when it fails," he said. "I hope you're not fond of this carpet."

Amelie ignored that. "Myrnin and Dr. Mills had told me that the work could not continue on the serum without more of Bishop's blood. Is that correct?" Claire nodded. "Difficult to achieve, I'm afraid, but I will include that in our calculations."

"We talked about drugging him."

"So Myrnin said." Amelie wasn't going to tell her anything. "It's no longer your concern. I will rely on you and your friends to be in attendance this evening. You should come prepared."

"Prepared for what?" Claire asked.

Amelie's eyebrows rose. "Anything. We are no longer following a plan. We are facing the final moves on the chessboard, and who wins will very much depend on nerve, skill, and the ability to do the unexpected. You may count on my father being ready to do his worst. We must be just as ruthless."

Claire thought about that moment in the tunnels, with Frank Collins. She hadn't felt ruthless at the end. She'd felt sad.

She didn't suppose Amelie, Oliver, or any of the rest of them would have hesitated for a second. Frank Collins was a bad guy. He'd been a bad guy as a human, right? But still . . . there was just that one moment when she'd seen him as a man who loved his son.

Maybe everybody had those moments. Even the worst people.

Maybe it didn't matter, except to her.

The door opened at the far end of the room, and two of Amelie's favorite vamp bodyguards came in, dragging a beat-up human. At least, Claire thought he was human; it was hard to tell, under all the dirt and bruises.

Oh. She knew him. It was Jason Rosser, Eve's crazy-ass brother. He looked like he'd been living in a garbage dump for months—for all Claire knew, he had been. Eve had said he'd been coming by the house, maybe even acting less insane, but right now, Claire couldn't see it. He looked like a rabid sewer rat, and as he scanned the room, he was all gleaming, crazy eyes and bared teeth.

When the guards let him go, at a nod from Amelie, Jason lunged for the Founder of Morganville. She didn't raise a hand to defend herself. She didn't have to.

Oliver met him halfway, grabbed Jason by the throat, and slammed him down onto the carpet flat on his back.

"You see?" Oliver said, and gave Amelie a freakishly calm smile. "You really should have thought about the carpet; you'll never get the smell of him out of it. Really, Amelie, you do insist on bringing home strays."

"I also put them down when necessary," she said. "This one happens to be yours, Oliver, yes? So I leave him to you for proper judgment."

Nobody said a word in protest to that. Not even Claire. Jason was nobody's friend; Claire would never, ever forget the night he'd almost killed Shane, for *nothing*. She wasn't about to speak up on his behalf.

Oliver stared deep into Jason's eyes and said, "You deserve to die, you know. Not only for the fact that you reek of guilt; I'm partial to a bit of mayhem now and then. No, you deserve to die because you broke the laws of Morganville *without my permission*." Oliver's smile widened into something out of a bad-clown nightmare. "So what then am I to do with you? You broke your word to Brandon. You broke your word to me. You had the bad taste to betray Amelie, in full public view. You took the side of that ancient reptile Bishop."

Jason *laughed*. It sounded like breaking ice. "Yeah, I did," he said. "Vamps are getting a break for doing the same thing. I get to die. Perfect. Nothing ever changes around here, does it? If a vampire does it, they can't help it. If a human does it, they're lunch meat."

Amelie said, "Is there anyone who will speak for him?" Claire knew it was a pro forma kind of question, like, *Speak now or forever hold your peace*, but she was thinking about Eve. About how she was ever going to tell her that she'd watched her brother die, and hadn't said a word . . .

But as it happened, she didn't have to.

"I will," Michael said.

There was a collective intake of breath. Nobody—Claire included—could quite believe he'd spoken up. It even made Oliver turn and lose his bitch face.

"Don't do me no favors, Glass Ass," Jason snapped.

"I'm not." Michael turned to Amelie. "He's a pathetic little worm, but he's just a criminal. He deserves to be punished. Not killed like some rabid dog."

"He's a killer," she said.

"Well, if he is, he's not the only one in this room, is he?"

Amelie showed her teeth briefly in a smile. "Will you take his parole, Michael? Will you put him into your own household and shelter him with those you love?"

Michael didn't answer. He wanted to—Claire could see it—but he just . . . couldn't.

Finally, he shook his head.

"If you won't trust him with those you love, how can I trust him with anyone else's family?" Amelie said, and nodded to Oliver.

Claire blurted, "Wait!"

"May we *please* have done with interruptions from the children's section?" Oliver said.

"Why is he here?" Claire asked, talking so fast that she stumbled over the words. "Why is he *here*? Who brought him *here*?"

"Who cares?"

Amelie held up a warning hand. "It's a reasonable question. Who brought him to us?"

"Nobody," one of the guards said from the door. "He came through the portal."

"*What?*" Amelie crossed to Jason in a flash, knocked Oliver out of the way, and slammed the boy back against the closest wall. "Tell me how you came to work the portals."

"Somebody showed me," Jason said. "He showed me a lot of things. He showed me how to kill. How to hide. How to get around town without anybody knowing."

"*Who?*"

Jason laughed. "No way, lady. I'm not telling. That's all I've got left to bargain with, right?"

Amelie's face twisted with anger, and she was about two seconds from snapping some bones for him. "Then you have nothing, because I will have it out of you one way or another."

Sam Glass, who hadn't said a thing, slowly rose to his feet. "Amelie. Amelie, stop."

"Not until this worm tells me who showed him the portals!"

"Then I'll tell you," Sam said. "I showed him. I showed him everything you showed me."

Silence. Even Oliver looked as if he didn't quite understand what he'd just heard. Amelie stood there like an ivory statue, holding Jason in place with one flattened hand on his chest.

"Why?" she whispered. "Sam, why would you do such a thing?"

It felt, to Claire, like suddenly the room was empty and they'd all turned to ghosts, except for Amelie and Sam. There was something so powerful in the stare between them that it just vaporized the rest of the world. "I did the best I could," he said softly. "You left me no choice. You wouldn't see me. You wouldn't speak to me, all those years. I was alone, and I—I wanted to do something good." He took in a deep breath and walked toward her, coming close enough to touch, although he didn't reach out. "Jason was a victim. Brandon brutalized him, and no one did anything to stop it. So yes, I taught the boy to fight, to defend himself from Brandon. I taught him to use the portals to help him escape when he needed to get away. I couldn't stop Brandon, not without you, but I could try to save his victims. I thought I was helping."

"Don't worry, man; I wasn't going to throw you under the bus." Jason laughed. "Fuck it. You were the only one who was ever good to me. Why should I?"

"The boy rewarded you by showing my father everything you taught him," Amelie said softly. She broke the stare with Sam and looked at Jason's face. "Didn't you?"

"It was what I had to trade. You set up the rules, lady. I just followed them."

Amelie grabbed Jason by the hair and shoved him at Sam, who caught him in surprise, and then held him when Jason tried to break free. "He's yours," she snapped at Sam. "You created this. Deal with it." She spun to Oliver. "You were right. Bishop does know how to use the network."

"Then we can take advantage of that," Oliver said. "Since he assumes we do *not* know that he does."

They'd effectively dismissed Sam and Jason. Sam stared at Amelie with so much pain in his face that it made Claire hurt to look at it, then shook his head. "Let's go," he said, and nodded to Michael and Claire. "All of us. Now."

No one tried to stop them. When Jason tried to make one last clever little comment, Sam slapped a hand over his mouth and dragged him out. "Shut up," he said. "You're still alive. That's a better outcome than you deserve."

Claire portaled them directly into the Glass House. She breathed an involuntary sigh of relief at finding Shane sitting on the couch, staring at a flickering TV screen like it held the secrets of the universe, and Eve pacing the hallway in her clumpy boots.

Eve spotted them first, screamed, and threw herself on Claire like a warm Goth blanket. "Oh *God*, everybody thought you were dead! Or, you know, Bishoped, which would have been worse, right? What happened? Where did you go?"

Over Eve's shoulder, Claire saw that Shane had gotten to his feet. "You all right?" he asked. She nodded, and he closed his eyes in sudden relief. Claire patted Eve's back, in thanks, love, and a little bit of get-the-hell-off-me. Eve got the message. She backed up, sniffling a little, and couldn't keep a smile from ruining her sad-clown makeup.

"Sorry about that," Claire said. "I . . . well. It wasn't exactly my idea, and I can't really explain. . . ."

"But you're okay. No fang marks or . . ." Eve's gaze darted past Claire, and she stopped talking. Stopped moving, too.

Shane, on the other hand, moved fast, putting himself between Claire and Jason. "What the hell is he doing here?"

"Fuck you too, Collins."

"Shut up," Sam said, and gave Jason a warning shake that must have rattled his bones. "He's here because I didn't want to kill him. Any other questions?"

Eve still wasn't saying anything. Claire couldn't blame her; she had the same kind of conflicted emotions passing over her face that Shane had when he thought about his dad. Love/hate/loss. That sucked, when Jason was standing right there. She hadn't really lost him. Not yet.

Michael went to her, the same way Shane had gone to Claire—to get between her and her brother. "He's not welcome here," Michael said, and that put the force of the Founder House behind it. Claire felt a pressure building, getting ready to evict Jason and—presumably—Sam, if Sam didn't let go of him.

"Wait," Sam said. "You send him out there, he's dead from all sides, and you know it. Bishop has no use for him, hasn't since Jason's assassination attempt failed. Amelie would kill him without blinking. You really want to do that to your girlfriend's brother?"

"Michael, don't," Eve said. "He won't hurt us." And *everyone* rolled their eyes at that. Even Jason, which was borderline hilarious.

"Look," Jason said, "all I want is a way out of this stupid town. You arrange that, and I'll never show my face around here again. You can keep your stupid hero lifestyle. I just want out."

"Too late," Shane said. "Last bus already left, man. And we're thirty minutes away from Bishop's big town hall meeting. You can run, but you can't hide. Anybody who isn't there is dead. He's going to send out hunters. It'll be open season."

"I could stay here," Jason said quickly. "Upstairs. In the secret room, right?"

They all looked at one another.

"Oh, come *on*, it's not like I'm going to run up your phone bill and watch pay-per-view. Besides, if I was going to kill you in your sleep, I would have already done it." He made a kissy-face at Shane. "Even you, asswipe."

"Jesus, Jason." Eve sighed. "Do you *want* to end up in the landfill, or what?" She touched Michael on the arm, and he glanced back at her and took her hand. "Can you tell if he lies to us?"

"Uh, no. Drinking blood doesn't make me a lie detector."

Sam spoke up somberly. "I can." He shrugged when Michael gave him an odd look. "It's just a skill. You pick it up, over time. People can't control their bodies the way vampires can. I can usually tell when they're lying."

"No offense, but you've been wrong plenty of times, Sam. Like, deciding that you could trust this little weasel as far as you can throw him," Michael said, then caught a devastating pleading look from Eve. "All right. Go ahead. Ask him whatever you want."

Eve took in a deep breath, looked her brother in the eyes, and said, "Please tell me the truth. Did you kill those girls?"

Because that had been Jason's rep. Murdered girls, dumped all over town, a string of killings that had begun right after Jason had gotten out of jail, just about the time Claire had moved to Morganville. One body had been put here in their own house, in an attempt to implicate Shane and Michael.

Jason blinked, as if he somehow hadn't really expected her to ask. "The truth?"

"Of course, the truth, idiot."

"I've done bad things," he said. "I've hurt people. I need help."

Eve's face fell. "You really did do it."

"It wasn't my fault, Eve."

"Never is, is it? I really thought—"

"He's lying," Michael said. He sounded as surprised as Claire felt. "Right, Sam?" Sam nodded. "My God. You really didn't do it, did you?"

Jason looked away from them. "Might as well have."

"What the hell does *that* mean?" Eve snapped. "Either you did, or you didn't!"

"No," her brother said. "Either I did, I didn't, or I was there when it happened and didn't stop it. Figure it out."

"Then who—"

"I'm not saying. People think I'm a killer; they leave me the fuck alone. They think I'm just some sad-ass ride-along clown. They'll kill me quick." Jason looked up now, right at Eve, and for the first time, Claire thought he looked sincere. "I never killed anybody. Not on my own, any-way. Well, I came close with you, Collins."

"But you won't tell us who did kill them?"

He shook his head.

"Are you afraid?" Eve asked, very gently.

Silence.

"You know what?" Shane said. "Don't care. Street him before we wake up with our throats cut by him *or* his imaginary playmate."

And they might have, except that the doorbell rang. Michael flashed to the window and looked out. "Crap. Our ride's here. We don't have time for this."

"Michael," Eve said. "Please. Let him stay, at least for now. *Please.*"

"All right. Get him upstairs and lock him in. Sam, can you stay with him?

"No," Sam said. "I have to go back to Amelie."

"We have to leave. Claire, can you shut down the portal that leads here?"

"I can try, sure."

As Sam hustled Jason up the stairs to the second floor, Claire touched the bare wall at the back of the living room, and felt the slightly pliable surface of the portal lying on top of it. It was invisible, but definitely active.

"Ada," she whispered, and felt the surface ripple.

Her phone rang. Claire answered it. No incoming caller ID had appeared on the display, just random numbers and letters. She answered.

"What?" the computer snapped. "I'm busy, you know. I can't just be at your constant beck and call."

"Shut down the portal to the Glass House."

"Oh, bother. Do it yourself."

"I don't know how!"

"I hardly have time to school you," Ada said primly. God, she reminded Claire of Myrnin—not in a good way. "Very well. I shall do it for you this one time. But you'll have to turn it on again yourself. And stop calling me!"

The phone clicked off, and under Claire's fingers, the surface turned cold and still, like glass.

Blocked. *Quantum stasis*, she thought, fascinated, and wondered how that worked, for about the millionth time. She wanted to take Ada apart and figure it out. *Yeah, if you live long enough.* It had taken Myrnin three hundred years to put Ada together; it might take her that long just to figure out the basic principles he'd used.

Michael came back into the living room, leading two other vampires— Ysandre, that smug little witch, and her occasional partner François, an equally nasty reject from some Eurotrash vampire melodrama.

They were walking clichés, but they were also deadly. Claire couldn't even look at François without remembering how he'd ripped the cross off of her neck and bitten her. She still had the scars—faint, but they'd always be there. And she couldn't forget how that had felt, either.

A hot flood of emotion came over her when she saw him smirking at her—hate, fear, loathing, and fury. She knew he could feel it coming off of her in sick waves.

She also knew he enjoyed it.

François gave her an elaborate bow and blew her a kiss. "*Chérie,*" he said. "The exquisite taste of you still lingers in my mouth."

Shane's hands closed into fists. François saw that, too. Claire touched Shane's arm; his muscles were tensed and hard. "Don't let him bait you," she whispered. "I was a snack. Not a date."

François closed his eyes and made a point of sniffing the air. "Ah, but you smell so different now," he said, with elaborate disappointment. "Rich and complex, not simple and pure anymore. Still, I was the first to taste your blood, wasn't I, little Claire? And you never forget your first."

"Don't!" she hissed to Shane, and dug her fingernails in as deep as she could. It was all she could do. If Shane decided to go for him, she knew how it would end.

Luckily, so did Shane. He slowly relaxed, and Claire saw Michael's tension ease as well. "We talking, or are we walking?" Shane asked. "I thought we had someplace to be."

Claire felt a sunburst of pride in him, and a longing that came with it—she wanted all of this to just *stop*; she wanted to go back to the night, the silence, the touch of his skin and the sound of his whispers. That was real. That was important.

It was a reason to live through all this.

She took Shane's hand and squeezed it. He sent her a look. "What?"

She whispered, "You're just full of awesome; did you know that?"

François made a face. "Full of something. In the car, fools."

Founder's Square at twilight was full of people—rock-concert full. Claire didn't even know this many people lived in Morganville. "Did they grab the students, too?" she asked Michael.

"Bishop's not quite that stupid. It's residents only. University gates were closed. The place is under lockdown."

"What, again? Even the stoners are going to figure out something's going on." Claire certainly would have, and she knew most of the students weren't that gullible. Then again, knowing and wanting to push the status quo were two very different things. "You think they'll stay on campus?"

"I think if they don't, the problem's going to solve itself," Michael said somberly. "Amelie will try to protect them, but we've got a much bigger issue tonight."

Technically, that challenge was saving Morganville, and everybody in it.

There were no chairs down on the grassy area, but Bishop's vampires were out and about, and they were separating people at the entrances to the park and sending them to special holding areas. Or, Claire, thought, *pens*. Like sorting cattle. "What are they doing?"

"Dividing people according to their Protectors," François said. "What else?"

Bishop had kept the Protection system, then—or at least, he hadn't bothered to really dismantle it. People were being questioned at the gate. If they didn't name a Protector, they got slapped with a big yellow sticker and herded into a big open area in the middle. "What if their Protector is one of Amelie's rebels?" She knew the answer to that one. "Then they're no longer Protected. They go in the middle, too?"

Michael looked pallid—not just vampire-pale, really stressed and upset, as if he knew what was coming before she did. Claire didn't get it until François said, "Just like your friends," and he grabbed Shane. Ysandre took hold of Eve. They both fought and cursed and tried to get free, but it was no use—they were shoved apart from Michael and Claire.

They were both dragged away to the big cordoned-off area in the center of the square. Claire tried to follow them, but Michael held her back. "Don't," he said. "Bishop may not know you're out of his control yet. Tell him you were drugged by Hannah to keep you out of the way. It's the truth; he'll probably sense that."

"What about Shane? Eve? God, how can you just *stand there*?"

"I don't know," he admitted. "But I know I have to. Claire, don't screw this up. You won't help them, and you'll only get yourself killed." He gave her a grim smile. "And me, because I'd have to get in the middle."

Claire stopped fighting him, but she still couldn't accept it. She saw why Richard had wanted people out of town who were at the highest risk; Bishop intended this to be a public spectacle.

His final act to make himself the undisputed ruler of Morganville. In the bad old days, that meant executing lots of people.

François took Claire's arm and marched her up to the front, past angry, scared men and women she knew by sight, and some she'd never seen before. That section had a symbol taped to the barrier that surrounded it—she vaguely recognized it as the symbol for a vampire named Valerie, who'd joined Bishop in the first round of fighting. And yes, there was Valerie, standing inside the barricade with her humans, but looking very much as if she wished she was somewhere else. Anywhere else.

Past Valerie's barricades was a big raised stage, at least twenty feet off the ground, with steps leading up to it. There were plush chairs, and carpet, and a red velvet backdrop behind it. Spotlights turned the sunset pale in contrast. The stage was empty, but there was a knot of people standing at the foot of the steps.

Richard Morrell was there, dressed in a spotless dark blue suit, with a sky blue tie. He looked like he was running for office, not about to fight for his life; apparently, he and Amelie had the same philosophy on looking good for the Apocalypse. Next to him, Hannah still wore her police uniform, but no belt—and no gun, handcuffs, baton, stakes, or pepper spray. They'd taken away the human cops' weapons. There were other people, too—mostly vampires, but Claire recognized Dean Wallace, the head of TPU, and a few of the other prominent humans in town, including Mr. Janes, who was the CEO of the biggest bank in town. Mr. Janes had decided to stay. She'd seen his name on Richard's evac list, and she'd seen him driving away from the warehouse instead of getting on the bus.

She wondered how Mr. Janes was feeling about that decision right now. Not too good, she was guessing. He kept looking out at the crowd, probably trying to find friends and family.

She knew how he felt.

Richard Morrell nodded to her. "You okay?"

Why did everybody always ask that? "Sure," she lied. "What's going to happen?"

"Wish I knew," Richard said. "Stay close to Michael, whatever happens."

She was going to do that regardless, but she appreciated that he cared. He patted her on the back, and under cover of shaking her hand, he pressed something into her hand.

It was a silver knife, no bigger than her finger. Razor-sharp, too. She tried not to cut herself—the last thing she wanted was for the vamps around her to smell blood—and managed to get it in the pocket of her hoodie without stabbing herself. From Richard's warning look, she got that it was a weapon of last resort.

She nodded to let him know she understood.

A cordon of vampires closed in around them, including the tall, thin, sexless dude whom she'd last seen with the Goldmans. What was his name? Pennywell. Ugh. He had a thin smile, like he knew what was going to happen, and it wasn't going to be pretty.

"Up," he said, and jerked his chin to indicate that they were supposed to climb the steps. Richard went first—trying to set a good example, Claire supposed—and she followed, along with Hannah and Michael. It seemed like a long climb, and it reminded her of nothing else than those old stories about people getting hanged, or walking the last mile to the electric chair.

Up on the stage, it was a whole lot worse. There were hisses and boos from the crowd, quickly hushed, and Claire was blinded by the white spotlights, but she could feel thousands of people staring at her. *I'm nobody*, she wanted to shout. *I don't want to be up here!*

They wouldn't care about her motives, or her choices, or anything else. She was working for Bishop. That made her the enemy.

Richard took one of the chairs, and Dean Wallace sat next to him. Hannah stayed standing next to Richard's chair, arms folded. Claire didn't quite know what to do, so she stuck close to Michael as Mr. Janes claimed the last plush chair.

Two vampires came up the steps carrying Bishop's massive carved throne, which they set right in the exact center of the carpeted stage.

Mr. Pennywell—if he was a he; Claire still couldn't really tell—stood next to the throne, along with Ysandre and François. The old friends, Claire thought. The clique.

Bishop came through the curtains at the back of the stage. He was wearing a black suit, white shirt, black tie, and a colorful red pocket square. In fact, he was dressed better than Mr. Janes. No ornate medieval robes, which was kind of what Claire had expected. He didn't even have a crown.

But he had a throne, and he settled into it. His three favorite hench-persons knelt in front of him, and he gave them a lazy blessing.

Then he said, "I will speak with the town's mayor."

Claire didn't know how it was possible, but Bishop's voice echoed from every corner of the square—a pocket microphone, she guessed, broadcasting to amplified speakers hidden in the trees. It was eerie, though. She squinted. Out behind the lights, she saw that Shane and Eve had squeezed their way through the crowd and were standing at the front of the group in the center of the square. Shane had his arm around Eve, but not in a boyfriend way—just for comfort.

The way Michael had his arm around Claire.

Richard Morrell got up and walked over to stand in front of Bishop.

"I demanded loyalty," Bishop said. "I received defiance. Not just from my daughter and her misguided followers, but from *humans*. Humans under your control, Mayor Morrell. This is not acceptable. It cannot continue, this blatant defiance of my rule."

Richard didn't say anything, but then, Claire had no idea what he really *could* say. Bishop was just stating the obvious.

And it was just a warm-up to what was coming.

"Today, I learned that you personally authorized the removal from our town of several of our most valued citizens," Bishop said. "Many members of your own town council, for instance. Leaders of industry. People of social standing. Tell me, Mayor Morrell, why did you spirit these people away, and leave so many of your common citizens here to bear the punishment? Were you thinking only of the rich and powerful?"

Clever. He was trying to make the town think that Richard was like his dad—corrupt, in it for his own sake.

It would probably work, too. People liked to believe that sort of thing.

Richard said, "I don't know what you're talking about. If anyone left town, I'm sure they must have had your permission, sir. How could they have left if you didn't authorize it?"

Which was a direct slap in the face for Bishop on the subject of his authority. And his power.

Bishop stood up.

"I will find out the secrets of this town if I have to rip them bloody from every one of you," he said, "and when I do have my answers, you will pay a price, Richard. But to ensure that we have a loyal and stable government, I must ask you to appoint a new town council now. Since you so carelessly allowed the last one to slip away."

"Let me guess. All vampires," Richard said.

Bishop smiled. "No, of course not. But if they are not vampires, I will, of course, *make* them vampires . . . simply to ensure fairness. . . ."

His voice trailed off, because someone was coming up the steps. Someone Bishop hadn't summoned.

Myrnin.

He looked half-dead, worse than Claire had ever seen him; his eyes were milky white, and he felt blindly for each slow step as he climbed. He looked thinner, too. Frail.

She felt sick when she saw the manic smile on his face, so out of touch with the exhaustion of his body.

"So sorry, my lord," he said, and tried to make one of his usual elaborate bows. He staggered, off balance, and settled for a vague wave. "I was detained. I would never miss a good party. Is there catering? Or are we dining buffet?"

Bishop didn't look at him with any favor. "You might have dressed for the occasion," he said. "You're filthy."

"I dress as nature wills me. Oh, Claire, good. So glad to see you, my dear." Myrnin grabbed Claire and dragged her away from Michael, wrapped her in a tight embrace, and waltzed her in an unsteady circle around the stage while she struggled.

There was nothing vague about his voice when he whispered, *"Do nothing. Something is about to happen. Keep your wits, girl."*

She nodded. He kissed her playfully on the throat—not quite as innocently as she would have liked—and reeled away to lean on the back of Bishop's chair. "Beg pardon," he said. "Dizzy."

"You're drunk," Bishop said.

"That's what happens when you are what you eat," Myrnin agreed. "I stopped off for a bite. Unfortunately, all that was left in town were pathetic alcoholics, and criminals too fast for me to catch."

Bishop ignored him. He turned his attention back to Richard. "Will you name your town council, Mayor? Or must I name them for you?"

"You'll do what you want." Richard shrugged. "I'm not going to enable you."

"Then I'll have to remove those of your appointees who remain." Bishop snapped his fingers, and Ysandre and François moved to grab Mr. Janes and Dean Wallace. When Hannah Moses tried to interfere, she ended up facedown on the carpet, held there by Pennywell. "And I'll allow my hunters to relieve us of any of your citizens who remain unclaimed, or are loyal to my enemy. There. That should clear the air a great deal."

The screaming started down in the crowd as the people in the center of the square realized they'd been put there to die.

Shane and Eve . . .

Claire grabbed the silver knife in her pocket and tried to get to Bishop. Michael tackled her, probably for her own good.

Myrnin lunged for Bishop. Bishop caught him easily, laughing at Myrnin's flailing attempts to fight, and snapped his fingers at Ysandre. She reached in her pocket and took something out that Claire recognized.

A syringe. From the color of the liquid, it was Dr. Mills's cure.

Bishop plunged the needle into Myrnin's heart and emptied the contents, then dropped Myrnin to lie on the carpet, writhing, as the cure raced through his body.

When he opened his eyes, the white film was gone from them.

He was healing.

But he was also in horrible pain.

"I know your plans," Bishop said, and smiled down at him. "I know you filled yourself with poison before coming here. I know you planned to have me drain you and cripple myself so your mistress could finish me off. Unfortunately, it's wasted effort, my dear old friend."

He gestured, and the curtain at the back opened.

Amelie was dragged out, bound in silver chains. She was still wearing her perfect pink suit, but it wasn't so perfect now—filthy, ripped, bloody. Her pale crown of hair had come down in straggles all around her face.

She had a silver leash around her neck, and Oliver was holding it.

Oliver.

Claire felt hot, then cold, then very still inside. She'd come to believe he wasn't as bad as she'd thought; she'd actually started to think he really was almost . . . trustworthy.

Obviously, Amelie had thought so, too. And Michael, because he went for Oliver in a big way, and was brought down by Pennywell and two others.

Worse, though, was the next prisoner, also wrapped in silver chains, and suffering a lot worse than Amelie from the touch of the poisonous metal. His skin smoked and blackened where it touched him, because he was younger and more fragile than she was.

Sam Glass.

Amelie cried out when she saw him, and closed her eyes. She'd lost her careful detachment, and now Claire could see in her how much she cared. How much she wanted Sam.

How much she loved him.

Bishop smiled, and in that smile, Claire saw everything. He didn't want to just destroy Morganville; he wanted to destroy life, and hope, and reasons for living at all. He could win only if he was the last vampire standing, no matter how many people that meant he had to kill along the way.

"You couldn't have won, Amelie," he said, and the tattoo on Claire's arm flared back into view, weaving its way up from a single spot of indigo on her wrist until it covered her arm. Then her chest. She felt it spreading like poison through her whole body, burning, and then it flared out like a brush fire. Gone for real, this time. "There, you can have your little pet back now. I no longer have need for her. She helped me learn everything I needed to know."

"I doubt that," Amelie said. Her voice was ragged with emotion, but she held her father's stare. "I was careful to keep things from her."

"Not so careful to keep them from Oliver, though. And that was a mistake." He tipped her chin up to meet her eyes. "Morganville is mine. You are mine. Again."

"Then take what's yours," Amelie said. She seemed weak now. Defeated. "Kill, if you wish. Burn. Destroy. When it's over, what do you have, Father? Nothing. Exactly what you've always had. We came here to build. To *live*. It's not something you would ever understand."

"Oh, I do understand. I just despise it. And here," Bishop said, "is where you die."

He yanked Amelie's head to the side, and for a horrible second Claire thought she was going to see him kill her, right there, but then he laughed and kissed her on the throat.

"Though, of course, not at my hands," he said. "It wouldn't be moral, after all. We must set a good example, or so you like to tell me, child. I'll let your humans kill you, eventually. Once you've begged for the privilege."

He shoved Amelie aside, into Pennywell's hands, and instead, he grabbed Sam Glass.

"No!" Michael shouted, and leaped to his feet to stop it.

He couldn't. Claire caught sight of Sam's pale, set face, of a determination she couldn't understand, and of Michael being brought down ten feet away, as Bishop exposed Sam's throat and bit him.

Amelie's scream tore through the air. Myrnin—still shaking and weak—crawled toward her. Ysandre kicked him aside, laughing.

Oliver just *stood there*, like an ice sculpture. Only his eyes were alive, and even they didn't show Claire anything she understood.

Michael wasn't there to hold Claire down anymore. She scrambled to her feet, clutched the silver knife, and plunged it into Ysandre's back as deeply as she could. It dug into bone.

"Oh," Ysandre said, annoyed. She tried to get at the knife, but it was out of her reach. She turned on Claire with a snarl, then staggered. Shock blanked her pretty face, and then worry.

Then fear, as the burning started.

She fell, screaming for help. Claire vaulted over her to kneel next to Myrnin. He was fighting his way back through the pain, panting, and his eyes were bright crimson from the stress, and probably hunger.

He wasn't out of control, though. Not anymore. "Get me up," he demanded. *"Do it now!"*

She offered him a hand, and he used it to haul himself to his feet—unsteady, but stronger than she'd ever seen him. This was a different Myrnin . . . sleek, glossy, dark, and dangerous, with his glowing, angry eyes fixed on Bishop.

"Stop him!" Claire yelled at Myrnin, as he just *stood* there. Sam was dying. Myrnin was letting it happen. "It's Sam! You have to stop him!"

Instead, Myrnin turned and attacked Pennywell.

"No! Myrnin, no! *Sam!*"

Oliver still wasn't moving. He was staring at Bishop.

Waiting.

They were all waiting.

Down in the crowd, screaming had started, and as Claire looked out she saw that people were trying to run. There were vampires moving through the crowd—hunters, taking victims. The Morganville humans were fighting for their lives. A lot of people had shown up armed to their own funerals, including Shane and Eve; Claire caught glimpses of them down there, and all she could do was pray they'd be okay. They had each other for protection, at least.

She had to help Michael. Claire didn't dare grab the knife from Ysandre's back—it was the only thing keeping her out of the fight—but she couldn't just stand there, either.

Luckily, she didn't have to. Hannah Moses shouted her name, and as Claire turned, she saw Hannah throwing something at her. She instinctively reached up to catch it.

It was a sharp wooden stake. Hannah didn't wait to see what she was going to do with it; she was already heading for François, who was trying to get hold of Richard Morrell. Hannah leaped on the nasty little vampire, pinned him with an expert shift of her weight, and plunged her own wooden stake through his heart. It wouldn't kill him, probably, but he was out of the struggle until somebody removed it.

Michael had already won his fight by the time Claire got there; he was bloodied and a little unsteady, but he grabbed her arm and yelled, "Get out of here!"

"We have to save Sam!" she protested.

But it was too late for that.

Bishop dropped Sam limply to the carpeted floor, and Claire could see that if Sam was still alive, he wouldn't be for long. The holes in his throat were barely leaking at all, and he wasn't moving.

Fury whited out her good sense.

Claire ran at Bishop as he turned, and rammed the stake at his chest, right on target for where his heart would be, if he had one at all.

He caught her wrist.

"No," he said gently, like someone with a pet who'd piddled on the good furniture. "I'll not be taken by the likes of you, little girl."

She tried to get away, but she knew it was over; there was just no way she was getting out of this. Michael had gotten into a fight along the way to reach Sam. Amelie was down on her knees, still bound by all the silver chains. Hannah and Richard were back-to-back, defending themselves against three vampire guards.

Myrnin was fighting Pennywell, and destroying half the stage along the way. There was some old hate there. History.

Oliver had drifted closer to Amelie, although Claire couldn't see any change in him at all. He still wasn't fighting, for or against, and he certainly wasn't making any heroic effort to save *her*.

"Claire!"

Shane. She heard him scream her name, but he was too far away—twenty feet down, at the foot of the stage, looking up.

He had a knife in his hand. As she looked down to meet his eyes, he flipped it, grabbed it by the blade, and threw it.

The knife grazed her cheek, but it hit Mr. Bishop right in the center of his chest.

He laughed. "Your young man has quite the throwing arm," he said, and pulled the knife out as casually as a splinter. Not silver. It wouldn't do a thing to him. "Your friends like to think they still have a chance, but they don't. There's no . . . "

Then the oddest thing happened. . . . Bishop seemed to hesitate. His eyes went blank and distant, and for a second Claire thought he was just savoring his victory.

"There's no chance," he started again, and then stopped. Then he took an unsteady step to the side, like he'd lost his balance.

Then he let her go altogether, to brace himself on the arm of his throne. Bishop looked down at the knife in his hand—Shane's knife—in disbelief. He couldn't hold on to it. It slipped out of his fist, hit the seat of the chair, and bounced off to the floor.

Bishop staggered backward. As he did, his coat flapped open, and Claire saw that the wound was bleeding.

Bleeding a *lot.*

"Get the book!" Amelie suddenly screamed, and Claire saw it, tucked in the breast pocket of Bishop's jacket. Amelie's book, Myrnin's book. The book of Morganville, with all the secrets and power.

Seemed only right that it ought to be the thing he lost tonight, even if he won everything else.

Claire darted in, grabbed the book, and somehow ducked his clutching hands.

Bishop lunged after her as she danced backward, but he seemed confused now. Slower.

Sicker?

As if sensing some signal, Oliver finally moved. He took a pair of leather gloves from his pocket, calmly put them on, and snapped the silver chains holding Amelie prisoner. He picked up the end of the silver leash and held it for a second, looking into her eyes.

He smiled.

Then he took that off her neck and dropped it to the floor.

Amelie surged to her feet—wounded, bloodied, messy, and angrier than Claire had ever seen her. She hissed at Oliver, fangs out, and then darted around him to kneel next to Sam.

His eyes opened and fixed on her face. Neither of them spoke.

She took his hand in hers for a moment, then lifted it to touch the back of it to her face.

"You were right," she said. "You were always right, about everything. And I will always love you, Sam. Forever."

He smiled, and then he closed his eyes . . .

. . . and he was gone. Claire could see his life—or whatever it was that animated a vampire—slip away.

Her eyes blurred with hot tears. *No. Oh, Sam . . .*

Amelie put his hand gently back on his chest, touched her lips to his forehead, and stood up. Oliver helped her, with one hand under her arm—that was the only way Claire could tell that Amelie wasn't herself, because she seemed to be more alive than ever.

More motivated, anyway.

Bishop was seriously hurt, although Claire couldn't figure out how; Shane's knife couldn't have really injured him. The old man was barely staying on his feet now, as he backed away from Amelie and Oliver.

That put him to moving toward Myrnin, who picked up Pennywell and threw him like a rag doll way out into the distance—all the way to the spotlight, where Pennywell slammed into the glass and smashed the machine into wreckage.

Then Myrnin turned toward Bishop, blocking him from that side.

The three vampires fighting Hannah and Richard suddenly realized that the tide was turning against them, and moved away. As a parting shot, though, one of them yanked the stake out of François's chest, and the vampire yelled and rolled around for a second, then jumped to his feet, snarling.

Oliver, annoyed, reached down and picked up the silver leash he'd removed from Amelie's neck. In a single, smooth motion, he wrapped it around François's throat and tied him to the arm of Bishop's heavy throne. "Stay," he snapped, and, just to be sure, wrapped another length of heavy silver chain around his ankle. François howled in pain.

Oliver plucked the wooden stake out of Claire's hand, removed the silver knife from Ysandre's back, and drove the stake all the way through her to nail her to the stage. It went through her heart. She shuddered and stopped moving, frozen in place.

"There, that should keep them for a while," Oliver said. "Claire. Take this." He tossed the knife to her, and she caught it, still numb and not entirely understanding what had just happened.

"You're . . . you're not—"

"On Bishop's side?" He smiled thinly. "He certainly has thought so, since I sold myself to him the night he came to Morganville. But no. I am not his beast. I've always been my own."

Amelie took a step toward her father. "It's over," she said. "You've done your worst. You'll do no more."

He looked desperate, confused, and—for the first time—really afraid. "How? How did you do this?"

"The key was not in guessing whom you would choose to kill," she said, and her voice was light and calm and ice cold. "You taught me end-games, my father. The key to winning is that no matter what move your opponent makes, it will be the wrong one. I knew you'd kill at least one of us personally; you enjoy it far too much. You couldn't resist."

Like Bishop, she lost her balance. Oliver caught her and held her upright.

Bishop's face went blank. "You . . . you poisoned me. Through Myrnin. But I didn't drink."

"I poisoned Myrnin," she said. "And myself. And Sam. The only one who didn't take poison was Oliver, because I needed him in reserve. You see, we knew about Claire after all. We counted on your knowing where we would be, and what we'd planned, at least insofar as she witnessed it." A pawn. Claire had always been a pawn.

And Sam—Sam had been a *sacrifice*.

Amelie looked unsteady now, and Oliver put an arm around her shoulders. It looked like comfort, but it wasn't; he took a syringe from his pocket, uncapped it with a flick of his thumb, and drove it into the side of Amelie's neck. He emptied the contents in, and she shuddered and sagged against him for just a moment, then drew in a deep breath and straightened.

She nodded to Oliver, who took out another syringe, which he pitched to Claire. "Give it to him."

For a second she thought he meant to Bishop, but then she realized, as Myrnin's strength failed and he went to his knees, whom it was really meant to help. She swallowed hard, looking at Myrnin uncertainly, and he moved his hair aside to bare the side of his pale neck. "Hurry," he said. "Not much time."

She did it, somehow, and helped him back to his feet.

When he looked up, she could see that he was better. *Much* better.

Amelie said, "In case you have any doubt, Father, that was an antidote to the poison that is taking hold inside you. Without the antidote, the poison won't kill you, but it will disable you. You can't win against us. Not now."

Down among the crowds, the fights were dying down. There were casualties, but many of them were Bishop's people; the humans of Morganville weren't quite as easy to lead to slaughter as he'd expected. All their anger and vampire-slaying attitude had helped, after all.

And now, pounding up the steps on the side of the stage, came Shane and Eve, backed by a party of grim-looking humans, including Detective Hess and several other cops. All held weapons. Eve had a crossbow that she aimed at Bishop's chest.

Michael took an extra stake from Hannah.

All of Morganville on one side, and Bishop alone on the other.

He backed up, toward the back of the stage.

Behind him, the curtain took on a silvery shimmer.

"Portal!" Claire yelled, but it was too late; Bishop had activated an escape hatch, and in the next second he stumbled through it and was gone. Amelie was too far away, and too weak to go after him anyway.

Claire didn't think; she just jumped forward, put her hand on the portal's surface, and yelled Ada's name.

"What?" the computer asked. The sound this time boomed out of the portal.

"I need to track Bishop!" Claire said.

"I don't work for you anymore, human," Ada said, and shut down the portal with a snap. Claire turned to look at Myrnin, who was watching a few feet away, eyes fading back to his normal black. He walked toward her, bare feet gliding over the carpet, and studied the empty space where the portal had been.

Then he reached out and drew a wide circle with a sweep of his arm, and the silver shimmer flickered back into view.

"Don't be rude, Ada," he said. "Now, I know you can hear me. Where did our dear Mr. Bishop take himself off to?"

"I can't tell you," Ada said primly. "I don't work for you, either."

Myrnin placed his palm flat on the surface of the shimmer and looked at Claire. "He's reprogrammed her," he said. "He must have gone to her and given her his blood while we were making our own plans. I didn't expect him to move so quickly. I wasn't thinking as clearly as I should have been." He removed his palm, and Claire realized he'd done it as a kind of mute button, so Ada wouldn't hear what they had to say. "Ada, my darling, I put you together from scraps and my own blood. Are you really going to say you don't love me anymore?" Claire had never heard him sound that way before—so in control of himself, so assured and darkly clever. It made her shiver somewhere deep inside. "Let me come to you. I really want to see you, my love."

Ada was silent for a moment, and then her ghostly image appeared on the surface of the portal—a Victorian woman, dressed in the big skirts and high collar of the times. She smoothed her pale hands over the fabric of her dress. "Very well," she said. "You may call on me, Myrnin."

"Excellent." He grabbed Claire by the hand and stepped through the portal.

Her foot came down on something soft that ran off with a shrill squeak, and she jumped and gave out a squeal of her own. *Rats.* She hated rats. It was too dark to see, but in the next second the lights flickered on around the cavern, and there was the monster tangle of pipes and elaborate bracing that was Ada.

Her ghost stood in front of the clumsy giant typewriter-style keyboard, smiling at Myrnin like a lovesick girl, but the smile faltered when she saw Claire. "Oh," she said, through the tinny speakers of the computer. "You brought *her*."

"Don't be jealous, love. You're the only girl for me." Myrnin strode up to the keyboard, *through* Ada's two-dimensional form, and Claire saw Ada make a startled face and turn toward him.

"What are you doing?" she demanded. "Myrnin!"

"Fixing you, hopefully," he said. "Claire."

She headed for his side, but Ada turned on her, and the prim Victorian image turned into . . . something else. Something dark and corrupt and horrible, snarling at her.

She flinched and veered off, but Myrnin's hand reached out and grabbed her to drag her in, past Ada. "Ignore her," he said. "She's in a mood." Myrnin tapped symbols, then uncovered the sharp needle on the control panel, and slammed his hand down on the point. "Ada. You will no longer accept commands from Mr. Bishop; do you understand me?"

"He was nicer to me," Ada said sulkily. "He gave me better blood."

"Better than mine? I believe I'm offended."

Ada's giggle sounded like a rattle of tinfoil. "Well, you haven't been yourself, you know. But you taste *much* better now, Myrnin. Almost like your old self."

"Imagine that. Well, then, I promise that you'll get all the lovely sweet blood you'd like from me, if you will block Bishop from access, my sweet."

Ada made a long, drawn-out humming sound, as if she was thinking, and then she finally said, "Well . . . all right. But you have to give me a full pint."

"I haven't moved my hand at all, my dear. Drink away." He let almost a minute go by, then gestured to Claire to come closer. "Nearly done, Ada?"

"Mmmmmm." Ada sighed. "Yes. Delicious. I feel ever so much— What are you doing?"

He yanked his hand off the panel, grabbed Claire's, and slammed it down on the needle. She knew better than to try to fight him this time, just winced and bit her lip and tried not to wonder if, say, having Myrnin's blood infecting hers would have any nasty side effects, like a sudden craving for blood and an allergy to the sun.

"Sorry," he said, not as if he was, and altered his voice again to that velvety, dark, seductive tone. "Ada, my love?"

No answer.

"Ada, Claire is my very good friend, and I really must insist that she have the same access I do."

Ada made a retching sound.

"Ada."

"No."

He sighed. "List for me who has access to the system, please."

Ada said, "There are currently six individuals with full access to the portals, not including you. I have removed Mr. Bishop, because you asked so very nicely. That leaves Amelie, Oliver, Michael, *Claire*, Jason, and Dean. Although Claire is no good for you, Myrnin. You should eat her immediately."

"Thank you, I shall think that over." He frowned down at the console. "Jason. Jason Rosser? Why did I not know this? And who is *Dean*?"

"That's for me to know and you to find out," Ada said, and laughed. Myrnin blinked.

"She's not supposed to do that, right?" Claire asked.

"Right. Oh dear. I think that my blood might have carried an infection deep into her systems. This may be a very bad thing."

"Can't you give her the cure?"

"It's not quite that simple," Myrnin said, and shifted his focus again. "Ada, my love? Can you tell me how Jason and Dean have access to the system?"

"Sam Glass gave it to Jason," she said. "But not full access, of course. Just to use open portals. Dean is Jason's friend. I revoked Sam's access, obviously. Because he's no longer functional."

Claire fidgeted uncomfortably. The white-hot pain in her hand was starting to eat away at her calm. "Um—Myrnin, can I please stop now?" She figured that Ada must have drained at least a pint by now.

"Please," Ada said. "I don't like your blood anyway." She made a computerized spitting sound. Claire yanked her hand away in relief and cradled it against her chest, squeezing her fist tight to stop the bleeding. "Disgusting. Too sweet."

Claire stuck her tongue out at the computer.

"I saw that."

"Good," she snapped. "Where did Bishop go?"

"Why should I—"

"Ada!" Myrnin's voice cracked across the computer's sulky response, and she went quiet. "I want you to block access to the portals for anyone except me, Amelie, Oliver, Michael, and Claire. Do you understand?"

"I'm not your slave." Ada's image flickered, then went out completely.

"I'm sorry," Myrnin said, and put his hands on the machine, almost like a caress. "My dear, I will come back and talk to you soon, and we'll work all this out. But you must promise me this. It's important."

Ada's sigh echoed through the speakers. "I can never say no to you," she said. "All right. I've locked out Dean and Jason, too."

"I guess that's it," Claire said, and felt a little bubble of relief that quickly popped when Myrnin shook his head.

"One more thing. I need to know where Bishop went when he traveled the last portal. Ada, love, can you do that for me?"

Behind them, Claire felt the subtle warping of a portal forming. She and Myrnin both turned to look. Ada's ghost reappeared, and then drifted off to the side, hands clasped behind her back. Definitely sulking.

Michael stepped through, holding Eve's hand. Behind him came Shane.

"Really." Ada sighed. "There's just no getting rid of *any* of you, is there?"

"Ada! Tell me where Bishop is!" Myrnin was out of patience, and she must have heard it in his voice. She shrugged.

"The university," she said. "I expect he can hide there for some time without detection. Plenty of snacks, after all."

If by *snacks* she meant *students*, then Claire supposed she was right. And the university was full of cavernous buildings, many of which were deserted at night. She was right. It was the perfect hiding place for Bishop, if he wanted to regain his strength and regroup.

They had to get him before that happened.

Myrnin was already on it. He stepped up to the portal Michael and the others had come through, tapped the surface, and listened. Claire heard it, too, faintly—a kind of ringing sound. A frequency. *Of course.* The portal worked on frequencies, like a radio—tune in to the right one, and you arrived at the correct destination. She'd been doing it without understanding consciously how, but now that she focused, she could hear the tone clearly.

"Here," Myrnin said, and stepped through. Claire reached back for Shane's hand, and walked into the unknown with him.

TEN

They came out in the Administration Building, in a deserted room that Claire remembered. Myrnin was already gone, but the door was still swinging on its hinges from where he'd headed through it. Claire made sure everybody was through, then took a second to look at the other three.

"You guys sure you want to do this?" she asked them. Michael looked more adult than she'd ever seen him—and more like Sam. He'd lost his grandfather, she realized—someone who wasn't supposed to be lost, ever. And that had fired up something in him that made him different.

More like Sam than ever.

Eve was still unmistakably Eve. She twirled the stake in her fingers, lifted the crossbow in her right hand. "How often do I get to go vamp stalking?" she asked, and smiled. "Let's do it."

"Shane?"

He'd been uncharacteristically quiet. Now he just nodded. "Watch yourself," he said, and brushed the back of his hand gently across her cheek. "You scare me."

She burst out laughing, shakily. "You're insane."

There was a short hallway outside of the room, deserted and dark; at the end of the hallway was a fire door, and one of the doors was still open a little. Myrnin had gone that way, Claire figured.

She set out after him.

As she stepped outside into the cool evening air, something grabbed her. Not Myrnin.

Bishop.

He looked bad—unsteady, but still stronger than a mere human. He fumbled at her clothes; for a second she thought, *Oh my God, he's going to rape me,* and then his flailing hand brushed the book she'd shoved into her pocket. She'd forgotten about it.

Now, as he tried to pull it away from her, she fought back. Hard. Bishop was weaker than he'd ever been, and she was panicked. Bishop heard Shane calling her name, and pulled her farther into the darkness— then he headed for a nearby building, and dragged her *up* as he climbed. They ended up on the flat roof of the maintenance shed.

"Over there!" she heard Michael shout, and then he was heading toward them in a blur, with Shane and Eve in hot pursuit.

Bishop had his fingers on the book. *No!* She couldn't let it happen. Claire didn't fully understand what was in those pages, but she'd seen how he could use it. She felt it, in that tattoo.

She wasn't going to take the chance there was more he could do with it.

Bishop screamed something at her, and his fangs came down. Claire planted both feet in his chest and heaved with all her strength.

Bishop tumbled away from her, skidding on the loose roof gravel. Claire flipped over and scrambled to her feet, running for the edge. She had no idea what she'd do when she got there. Fly, maybe. Or take the fall, no matter how hard it was.

She didn't have to. Michael swooped in, grabbed her by the waist, and jumped with her. He landed lightly on the ground, let her slide down him, and looked up.

Bishop was leaning over, breathing hard. His fangs and crazy eyes caught the moonlight.

"Oh, crap," Eve said. "He's still not exactly Mr. Fluffy."

Shane summed it up. "Run!"

They did. Shane took Claire's hand; she had the shortest legs, but the most motivation, and she kept up with them as they raced out into the open green soccer field in front of the Admin Building.

Bishop landed on the grass behind them and began to chase them.

"He's going to catch us!" Eve yelled. "Head for the library!"

The TPU library was a big, columned building catty-corner to the Administration Building. It had its lights on, and there were still students coming and going up the steps, oblivious to what was coming their way. "Get out of here!" Claire shouted, and ran full speed to the top of the stairs. Shane was just ahead of her, Eve somewhere behind.

Michael had stopped at the foot of the steps, and was turning to face Bishop. When Claire hesitated, Eve grabbed her by the collar of her T-shirt and yanked her forward. "Don't stop!" she said, panting. "Damn, I need more exercise. Head into the stacks. Don't stop for anything, Claire!"

As they blew through the metal detectors, sirens went off. Students popped out of study carrels and up from tables like prairie dogs, then yelped and scattered as they realized something bad was heading their way, leaving a trail of notebooks and open computers. As they flashed past rows of library books, Shane skidded to a halt, grabbed two volumes with black covers, and tossed one to Eve. She nodded and shoved it in the waistband of her pants.

There was a crash somewhere behind them, and the glass doors blew into a million jagged pieces that flew across the marble floor. Students scrambled for cover. Somebody yelled to call the campus cops; somebody smarter yelled to shut up and hide.

Michael hit the marble floor and rolled, leaving trails of blood. He landed on his hands and knees, facing Claire, Shane, and Eve, who'd paused halfway down the stacks. "Go!" he told them, and got to his feet as Bishop stepped inside. He didn't seem as unsteady now.

The poison was wearing off, way too fast.

Shane pushed Claire into a run. Eve stumbled after them, looking over her shoulder to see if Michael was going to follow.

He didn't.

The aisle ended in a brick wall, with windows way up high, but there was an exit sign pointing to the left. The three of them turned the corner and headed for it, dodging past students wearing headphones, oblivious to the trouble in the stacks.

Shane hit the fire door first, setting off another alarm, and they raced down another flight of concrete steps.

This side of the library faced the big fountain—only the fountain was gone, and had been for a couple of months. What was in its place, at the center of six converging sidewalks, was the big concrete rim of what had been the pool, and in the center, a bronze statue of Mr. Bishop, holding a book in his hand.

There was one of those eternal flames burning in front of his statue—the light of knowledge, or something stupid like that. Claire had been revolted by the statue when it went up.

Now she had an idea.

"Split up!" she yelled. "Make sure he sees that you have the books!"

Shane and Eve peeled off, heading right and left.

Claire went straight for the statue.

When Bishop emerged from the library, there was no sign of Michael. He paused on the steps, and he must have realized that two of the three of them were obvious decoys—but which two? Claire was betting that he'd assume she'd switched books with Shane.

She guessed right. Bishop jumped off of the stairs to the grass, and headed at a run after Shane. That gave Claire precious time to reach the stone rim of the fountain, climb over, and get to the eternal flame of knowledge—which was just a gas jet, really.

That was all she needed.

Claire pulled the book from her pocket and held it over the flame. *Yes. Finally.*

"Hey!" she distantly heard Eve shouting. "Hey, Bishop! Tag!" When she looked up, Eve was jumping up and down, waving her leather-bound book like a demented Goth cheerleader.

Bishop ignored her.

Shane zigzagged, doing the best broken field running Claire had seen outside of a football field, but Bishop was faster and more agile, and he cut him off and bowled Shane over.

Claire looked at the book in her hand.

It wasn't burning. She frantically turned it, trying the side with the gilded pages. "You've *got* to be kidding me!" she yelped, and kept trying.

It wouldn't even scorch.

Bishop took the book from Shane, examined it, and flung it away in disgust. He headed straight for Claire. Eve saw him coming, and got to Claire first, leaping over the rim of the fountain and skidding to a halt. "What are you waiting for?" she asked, panting. "Burn the damn thing already!"

"Trying!" Claire gritted out, and out of desperation, grabbed a handful of paper in the middle of the book and twisted.

The pages ripped out. When she held them out over the flames, they immediately caught like flash paper.

"Yes!" Eve cheered and jumped up and down, pumping her fists. "Go!"

Claire tore loose more pages and flung them into the fire.

Bishop landed flat-footed in front of her, red-eyed and growling, and backhanded Eve as she tried to get between him and Claire.

Claire ripped more pages and burned them. She'd done about half the book.

"You evil little beast," Bishop said, and held out his hand. "Give it to me."

She ripped pages and backed away, dodging around the other side of the brazier. Most of the paper made it to the fire. What didn't drifted lazily around her feet in the breeze. Sparks drifted on the wind and landed on her clothes.

Bishop lunged for her as she tore more pages free. She thrust the handful into the fire a second before he hit her, driving her back against his bronze statue. She landed hard enough to make the metal ring, not to mention her ears.

Bishop reached out to take the ragged remains of his book.

A shadow flashed by them, barely visible in the moonlight, and then Claire felt the statue shake as something leaped on top.

Myrnin, sitting on the shoulders of Bishop's statue, reached down and plucked the book from Claire's hand an instant before Bishop grabbed it. "Ah, ah, ah," he said. "Don't be rude, old man. This was never yours in the first place." He ripped loose a page, balled it up, and pitched it neatly into the brazier, where it burst into flame and was consumed. "Leave the girl alone. You're finished now."

Bishop grabbed Claire and pulled her against his chest, claws out and at her throat. "Give me the book or I kill her!"

"Oh, go ahead, then," Myrnin said, and ripped loose the last handful of pages. He studied the writing on them and smiled. "I remember this. Good times. Ah, well." He flung them toward the fire. Bishop desperately grabbed at one of the fluttering leaves and managed to pluck it out of the air before it caught fire. "Oh, dear. Now you have a memoir of my secret relationship with Queen Elizabeth. The first one. I hope it does you a lot of good, Bishop. If you're seeking spells and magic, you won't find it on that page. Now, *this one* . . ." Myrnin produced, by sleight of hand, another sheet, neatly folded. "This one could easily give you rule of Morganville. Maybe even the entire human world. I promised Amelie I would never let it fall into evil hands, but then again, it's in mine already, isn't it? So that might already be a moot point." He lost his smile. "Let the girl go, and you shall have it."

"Myrnin, don't," she whispered.

"I'm not doing it for you," he said. He quickly folded the paper into a toy airplane and sailed it toward Bishop, who snatched it out of the air with a greedy cry.

Myrnin's eyes flickered bright red. "Oh dear," he said. "I might have given you the wrong page. *Ardentia verba!*"

The page burst into purple fire, and it traveled from the page through Bishop's skin, over his hand, onto his clothes. The paper was ash in seconds. Bishop staggered back, engulfed in fire.

Myrnin reached down and grabbed Claire. He pulled her up and settled her safely on the metal arm of Bishop's statue—the one holding the open book.

"The goal of the wise," Myrnin said softly, "is good works. Here endeth your lesson, old man."

Claire swallowed. She couldn't stand to watch him burn, and shut her eyes. "I thought . . . I thought we needed his blood for the cure," she said. She didn't want to save him. She just hated to see anyone suffer.

"Why, you're right—we do." Myrnin snapped his fingers, and the purple fire went out. Bishop toppled to the stone floor of the empty fountain, too weak to escape.

Myrnin jumped down from the statue, pinned Bishop to the ground, and bit him. He didn't drain him—not quite—and rose, wiping blood from his lips. "I've got all his blood I need," he said. "Now I have something for you, Bishop. Don't worry—I won't kill you. I won't even allow you to die." He reached into his pocket and pulled out another syringe, this one filled with blood. He injected Bishop with it, straight into the heart. "My blood," Myrnin said. "Before you cured me. Now I hope you can enjoy a long, slow decline into madness, just like mine. I wish you the joy of it."

Bishop didn't move. He blinked up at the moon, the cold stars, and finally closed his eyes.

Not dead, though.

Claire wasn't sure *that* was a great idea.

"Hey," Eve said, and sat up, holding her head. "Ow. What is that smell— Oh. Is he—"

"No," Michael said, and stepped over the rim to help Eve to her feet. "He's alive." He looked up at Claire and smiled, and it was a full-on Michael Glass special smile, one that turned on the sun and made the stars dance. "We're all alive."

"Relatively speaking," Myrnin said. "Ah. Your white knight has arrived. A bit dinged, but intact."

Shane. He was more than a little dinged, but Claire knew he'd be okay with that. They'd all given up hope of coming out of this alive, at some point; she could see in his smile, like Michael's, the joy of being wrong.

"Wish I had a camera," Shane said, staring up at her. "Is this some kind of college thing? Like flagpole sitting or something?"

"Shut up," she said, and jumped.

He caught her.

The kiss was worth the fall.

Two days passed in a blur. Claire spent most of it sleeping; she'd never felt so exhausted, or so glad to simply be alive.

On the third day, when she came down for dinner, she found the others sharing a massive platter of chili dogs and looking somber. Shane stood up when he saw her, which made her heart turn cartwheels, and he pulled out her chair. Eve and Michael shared an amused look.

"So cute," Eve said. When Shane glared, she smiled. "No, really. It is. Dude, chill."

There was something forced about it, and Claire didn't know why; she didn't get the sense that she'd walked in on an argument or anything like that. "What's going on?" she asked as she loaded her plate with a couple of hot dogs. She wasn't sure she really wanted to know. She'd just gotten used to the idea of not being marked for death. *Please don't let it be about Bishop escaping, or something horrible like that . . .*

It wasn't. Michael took a shallow sip of whatever was in his coffee mug and said, "Sam's funeral is tonight."

Oh *God.* Somehow, she hadn't expected that, and she really didn't even know why. The chili dog lost its taste, and she had to work to swallow it.

"They haven't had one before," Eve put in. "A funeral, I mean. For a vampire. At least, not one that's been open to the public. But this one was posted in the newspaper, and they ran it on the nightly news, too. Everybody's invited."

Most people would come out of curiosity, but for the four of them, it would be real loss. Under the table, Claire saw that Eve was holding Michael's hand. He was taking care not to look at any of them.

"It's in a couple of hours," Eve continued. "The three of us were going to go . . ."

"Sure," Claire said. "I want to go." She didn't, because it already hurt to think about it, but she thought they ought to be there for Michael. "I should find something to wear."

"You should finish your dinner first," Eve said. "One bite does not equal a balanced meal."

"Neither does a whole chili dog," Claire said.

"Do not diss the dog," Shane said. "It's right up there with mom and apple pie when it comes to cultural icons."

"You forgot Chevrolets," Eve said.

"Never been a Chevy man, myself."

"Heretic." Eve broke off to give Claire a fierce look. "Eat. I'm not kidding."

Claire managed to choke down the rest of her chili dog, but one was all she could manage. Despite Shane and Eve's bantering, there was a sadness that hung around Michael like a second skin. He didn't say much, except, "My parents are here. They flew in to El Paso and drove from there."

Wow. Claire had never heard much about Michael's parents, except that they'd moved away, and he'd never expected to see them back in town again. She finally said tentatively, "I guess that's good . . . ?"

"Sure," he said, and got up from the table. "I'm going to get ready." He walked out, and the rest of them watched him leave. Eve looked very sad, suddenly. And very adult.

"His mom had cancer, you know," she said. "That's why they got to leave Morganville. Because she needed serious treatments. Sam made sure she got them. This is the first time they've been back."

"Oh," Claire said. "Is Michael okay?"

"He just won't let it out," she said. "Guys. What is it with you and emotions, anyway?"

"They're like Kryptonite," Shane said. "He'll deal. Just give him time."

Claire wasn't too sure about that.

Michael drove, and nobody had much to say, really. It felt sad and uncomfortable.

As soon as the car stopped at the church, vampire escorts were at the doors to open them. The undead valet service. Under normal circumstances that might have been creepy, but there was something almost comforting about it tonight. Claire looked up and realized that the vam-

pire offering a hand to her was, of all people, Oliver. She froze, and his
eyebrows tilted sharply upward.

"Today, if you please," he said. "I'm here as a courtesy. Don't take it
personally."

"Oh, I don't," she promised, and accepted his strong, ice-cold touch to
help her out of the car. Shane quickly took her arm, giving Oliver a go-away
glare, which was a little funny, and then they fell in behind Michael and Eve.

It was bizarre, Claire thought. The church was full, standing room
only to the back, but the crowd parted as they walked in, led by Oliver.
And every head turned to follow them.

"Okay, this is weird," Claire whispered. She felt like she had a target
painted on her back at first, but then she realized that most of the people
looking at them weren't angry—they were interested. Or sympathetic. Or
even proud.

"Very weird," Shane whispered back.

The front row held Amelie, sitting alone, dressed in a white suit so cold
and perfect that it made her look like an ice sculpture, head to toe. Behind
her sat a man and woman in their late forties, and as soon as she saw them,
Claire saw the family resemblance. The woman must have been really beautiful when she was younger; she was now very handsome, the way older
women got, and her hair was a faded shade of gold with red highlights.
They both stood up as Michael let go of Eve and came toward them.

"Honey," Michael's mother said, and Michael fell into a three-way
embrace with both of his parents. "Oh, honey—"

"Mom, I'm so sorry, I couldn't—I couldn't do anything . . ." Michael's voice failed, and Claire saw his shoulders shake. His mother
smoothed his hair gently, and the smile she offered him was kind and full
of understanding.

"Just like him," she said. "Just like your grandfather. Don't you apologize, Michael. Don't you dare. I know you did everything you could. He'd
never blame you, not for a second."

Claire hadn't realized that Michael felt guilty, but looking back on it
now, she couldn't imagine he wouldn't. His mom was right—he was just
like Sam, really.

He'd feel responsible.

Mrs. Glass looked past Michael, and her eyes focused on the rest of them. Claire first, then Shane, then Eve. She took a deep breath, moved toward them, and held out her hands to Eve for a hug. "I haven't seen you in years, Eve. You look wonderful. And Shane . . ." She moved on to him. Shane wasn't a hugger, not like Eve, but he tried his best. "I'm so glad you're here for Michael."

He looked down. Claire knew he was thinking about how angry he'd been with Michael over the past few months—too angry, sometimes. "He's my best friend," Shane said, and finally met Michael's eyes. "Vampire or not. He always will be."

Michael nodded.

Mrs. Glass hugged Claire, too. "And you're Claire. I've heard so much about you. Thank you for all you've done for my son."

Claire blinked. All *she'd* done? "I think it's the other way around," she said softly. "Michael's a hero. He's always been there for me."

"Then you've been there for each other," Mrs. Glass said. "True friends."

The crowd was parting again, letting more people pass, and as Claire looked around, she saw her own mother and father. "Oh no," she whispered. "I didn't know they were back yet."

"Your parents?" Michael's mom asked, and Claire nodded. Mrs. Glass quickly moved to greet them, gracious and sad, and then they closed in on Claire.

And Shane.

She winced at the icy stares her parents gave Shane, but they knew better than to start that here, now. They took seats to Claire's right, with Shane, Eve, Michael and his parents stretching out to her left.

And directly ahead, Amelie.

At the front of the church, surrounded by a blizzard of flowers of all colors, was a shiny black coffin with silver trim. The lid was closed. The discreet sound of organ music got louder, and the whispering buzz of the crowd in the church quieted as the door opened off to the side, and Father Joe came out, dressed in a blinding white cassock and a purple stole.

He mounted the steps and looked out at the crowd with quiet authority. For a young priest, he had a lot of presence, but then Claire expected he'd have to, to serve a Morganville congregation that was composed equally of vampires and humans.

"We come to celebrate a life," he said. "The life of Samuel Glass, a son of Morganville."

Claire's eyes blurred under a wash of tears. She couldn't imagine Sam would have wanted to be remembered any other way, really. She barely heard the rest of what Father Joe said about Sam—she found that she was watching Amelie, or at least the very still back of Amelie's head. Not a hair out of place, not a whisper of motion.

So quiet.

And then, suddenly, Amelie was getting up, in absolute silence, and walking up the steps. She stopped not at the podium, but at the coffin, and opened the hinged cover. It clicked into place, and Amelie stayed there for a moment, staring down at Sam's face.

Then she turned and faced the hundreds of people gathered in the church.

"I met Samuel Glass here in this church," Amelie said. Her tone was soft, but it carried. No one moved. No one coughed. As far as Claire could tell, no one breathed. "He came here to demand—*demand*—that I right some wrong he imagined I had done. He was like an angel with a flaming sword, full of fury and righteousness, with absolutely no fear of the consequences. No fear of me." She smiled, but there was something broken in it. "I think I fell in love with him in that moment, when he was so angry with me. I fell in love with his fearlessness first, and then I realized that it was more than mere courage. It was a conviction that life must be made fair. That *we* must be better. And for a time . . . for a time I think we were."

She paused, and looked again at Sam's pale, still face.

"But I was weak," she said. "Weak and afraid. And I let him slip away from me, because I didn't have his courage, or his conviction. This moment, this loss, is my fault. Sam gave himself, again, to save lives. To save *me*. And I have never deserved it."

There were tears running down her cheeks now, and her voice was trembling. Claire couldn't breathe because of the weight of emotion in her chest.

"Someone else recently demanded that I change the rules of Morganville," Amelie continued. "Just as Sam demanded it fifty years ago, and continued to demand it of me at every opportunity."

Claire realized, with a shock, that Amelie was talking about *her*. As if what she'd said was somehow brave.

Amelie reached up and pulled pins from her hair, one after another. Her icy crown of pale hair began to unravel and fall loose around her shoulders.

"I have decided," she said, "that changes must be made. Changes will be made. Sam earned the right for humans to stand as equals in this town, and it will be done. It will be painful, it will be dangerous for us all, but it *will* be done. In Sam's memory, I make it so."

She leaned over, and very gently, placed a kiss on Sam's lips, then closed the coffin. No one spoke as she walked away, down the steps and out through the side door. Oliver and a few of the other vampires exchanged silent looks, then moved to follow her.

Father Joe spoke over the rising tide of whispers. "Let us pray."

Claire clasped her hands and looked down. Next to her, Shane was doing the same, but he whispered, "Am I crazy, or did we just win?"

"No," Claire whispered back. "But I think we just got a chance to."

Four weeks later

"Chaos, disorder, mayhem," Shane said. "Situation normal in Morganville." He took a drink of his coffee and pushed the other one across to Claire.

Common Grounds was holding a grand reopening, with half-priced coffee, and the place was packed. Everybody loved a bargain. It wasn't exactly normal for the two of them to be sitting in Oliver's territory like this; Claire never thought Shane would do it voluntarily, but the lure of cheap caffeine proved powerful.

He'd further surprised her by exchanging some semicivil words with

Oliver himself as he'd claimed the coffee. Speaking of which . . . "What did Oliver say to you?" Claire asked.

Shane shrugged.

"I asked Oliver if they'd found my father, but he was his usual douchey self. Told me to forget about my dad. I don't know if that means they found him, they killed him, or they just don't care. Dammit, I just want someone to tell me."

Claire looked up at him, struck into silence. *I need to tell him*, she thought. *I really do.*

She just couldn't quite think of the words.

Life was getting back to normal in Morganville. Amelie had declared an absolute ban on hunting. The blood banks had reopened, and the people of Morganville had been given a choice—start over, or start running. Plenty had taken the second option. Claire figured that half the town had decided to seize the chance to leave . . . but she also knew that some of them would come back. After all, some of their families had never been out of town at all. It was a whole new world out there. For some, it would be too much.

Common Grounds had renovated in record time, and was open to students once more. Oliver was behind the bar, wearing his nice-guy face and pulling espresso shots like nothing had ever changed.

The bronze statue of Bishop was gone from the university. In fact, all traces of Bishop were gone. Claire didn't know where François and Ysandre had ended up, but Myrnin assured her, with a perfectly straight face, that she didn't *want* to know. Sometimes, she was content to be ignorant. Not often, true. But sometimes.

Shane, however, needed to know about his father. Frank Collins, as far as Claire knew, had just vanished into thin air. If Amelie knew, she wasn't saying.

This was a moment that Claire actually had wanted to avoid, in a way. She'd put it off as long as she could, but Shane was getting more aggressive about asking people if there was any sign of Frank Collins in Morganville, and she really couldn't put it off any longer.

"I have something to tell you about that," she said, and cleared her throat. "Your dad—I . . . I saw him."

He froze, coffee cup halfway to his lips. "When?"

"A while ago." She didn't want to be too specific. She hated that she'd hidden it from him for so long. "He . . . ah . . . he could have killed me, but he didn't. He said to tell you that . . . that he loved you. And he was sorry."

Shane blinked at her, as if he couldn't quite believe what she was saying. "Where did you see him?"

"In the cells where the sick vampires were being kept. He's not there anymore. I looked. He's just . . . gone." She swallowed hard. "I didn't want to tell you, but I think . . . I think he was going to kill himself, Shane."

Something changed inside of Shane for a long second—she didn't recognize the look in his eyes or on his face. And then she did. It was his dad's look, the one that came before he lashed out at someone.

Shane closed his eyes, took a deep breath, and bowed his head. She didn't dare move for a few seconds, then carefully reached out and put her hand on the table, just a few inches from his.

His fingers twined with hers.

"Dammit," he whispered. "No, I'm not mad. I just feel . . . I guess I feel relieved. I wanted to know. Nobody would talk to me."

"I should have said something," she said. "I know. I'm so sorry. I just didn't know how. But I didn't want you to hear it from Oliver or something, because that would just . . . bite."

"No kidding." He took another deep breath, then raised his head. His dark eyes were glittering with unshed tears, but he blinked them back. "He wouldn't have wanted to go on like that. He made a choice. I guess that's something."

She nodded. "That's something."

She'd ripped off the bandage, and now at least he could start healing.

It was the same everywhere. Healing. All over Morganville, burned buildings were being demolished and rebuilt. City Hall, destroyed by a tornado, was getting a municipal makeover, with plenty of marble and fancy new furniture. All of the surviving Founder Houses—even the Glass House—were getting repaired and repainted. The ones that hadn't survived were being rebuilt from the ground up.

In an amazingly short time, Morganville life had gone back to normal. As normal as it ever was, anyway. And if the vampires weren't happy about things changing, well, they were—so far—keeping their objections on their side of the fence.

Shane sipped his coffee—plain coffee, not the fancy milky stuff she liked—and watched people go by outside the front windows. She let him sit in silence and come to terms with what she'd said; he was still holding her hand, and she figured that had to be a good sign.

"Oh, great," Shane said, and nodded to the door. "Trouble, twelve o'clock. Just what we needed."

Monica Morrell posed in the doorway, making sure the light caught her best side. She'd returned to town, along with her BFFs, and slipped right back into her role as Morganville's queen bitch without a pause. It helped that Richard Morrell was still mayor, of course, and that Monica's family had always been rich.

Monica surveyed the busy room disdainfully, snapped her fingers, and sent Gina to stand in the coffee line. Then she and Jennifer made a beeline for the table where Claire and Shane sat.

Nobody spoke. It was a war of stares.

"Bitch, please," Shane said finally. "You can't be serious. Out of all the people in here, you pick us to evict? Really not in the mood today."

"I'm not evicting you," Monica said, and slid into the chair next to him. Jennifer looked deeply shocked, then put out, but she bullied some poor freshman out of his chair at the next table, and yanked it over to plop down as well. "I thought since you had extra chairs, you wouldn't be a complete dick about it. Should have known you'd be a bad winner or something."

He blinked.

"Not that you *won*," she said quickly. "Just that you're, you know, still here. Which is a form of winning. Not the best one."

Shane and Claire exchanged looks. Claire shrugged. "Oliver take you back?" she asked. Monica traced some old carving on the tabletop with a perfectly manicured fingernail, and then flipped her still-dark hair over her shoulders.

"Of course," she said. "What would Morganville be without the Morrell family?"

"Wouldn't I like to know?" Shane muttered. Monica sent him a freezing glare. "Kidding." Not.

"I heard you're working," she said. "Wow. Good for you. Shane Collins, actually earning a paycheck. Somebody should alert the press."

He flipped her off, then checked his watch. "Speaking of the job, damn," he said. "Claire—"

"I know. Time to go."

He leaned over and kissed her. He made it extra-special good, with Monica watching, which made Claire warm all the way down to her toes; he took his time, to the extent that people at other tables started clapping and hooting.

"Watch your back," he murmured, his lips still against hers. "Love you."

"Watch yours," she said. "Love you, too."

She watched him walk away with an expression she was sure made her look like a total fool, and she didn't care. Other girls watched him go, too—they always did, and he rarely noticed these days.

Monica made a retching noise into the coffee that Gina thumped down in front of her. "God, you two are disgusting. You know it's not going to last, right?"

"Why, because you're going to take him away?" Claire asked, and smiled slowly. "Too much car for you, rich girl."

"Is that a challenge?"

"Sure. Knock yourself out. No, really. Hammer to the head, works every time." Claire drained the rest of her mocha as Gina settled into Shane's vacated chair. "Hey, kid. Here." Claire scooted her chair back over to the bewildered freshman Jennifer had bullied out of a seat; he settled gratefully into it, nodded, and put his headphones back on. Studying.

Claire had a stack of that to do, too. She'd aced the semester, but that was just the beginning of her challenges. Ada had a lot to teach her, although the computer still hated her and probably always would. Myrnin . . . Myrnin had absorbed so much of Bishop's blood that he was a walking serum factory, to Dr. Mills's delight; the vampires of Morgan-ville were being cured, one by one.

All except Sam. Sam's absence was a hole in everyone's life. Amelie hadn't left her home except for official appearances; she'd become a her-mit again, dressed in formal white, back to being the ice queen Claire had first met. If she grieved, she didn't show it to the unwashed public.

But Claire knew she did.

She knew Amelie always would.

As Claire headed for the door, someone caught the strap on her back-pack. "Hey, Claire!" The voice wasn't familiar, but it seemed cheerful and happy to see her. She turned. It took her a few seconds to place the face barely visible over a pile of books.

It was the awkward boy with the emo haircut—the one she and Eve had met at the University Center before everything had blown up in Mor-ganville. The one who'd once been friends with Shane.

"It's Dean, remember? Do you have a minute?"

She wasn't too sure it was a good idea. There was something odd about him, something she'd filed away in her memory . . . Oh yeah. "Be-fore we get into that, how do you know Jason Rosser?" she asked.

Dean froze in the act of clearing his backpack from the chair next to him. "Oh. Uh . . . busted, I guess. When I moved here, me and Jason hung out when he got out of jail. I mean, my theory was his sister was living in the house with Shane, so he'd be a way to keep track. Only he was kind of nuts, you know?"

Claire kept watching him. He seemed honest enough. "He must have shown you some things. Secrets, I mean. About the town."

Dean's ears turned red. "You mean—yeah. The shortcuts? The ones that take you from one place to another? Honestly, I never used them except that once. Scared the holy crap out of me."

He sounded ashamed of himself, but Claire could fully get behind the concept of finding Morganville terrifying. Granted she thought it was kind of fascinating, but then, she was a freak of nature.

Dean looked pathetic. "Let me guess. I blew it, right? You'll never talk to me again."

"No, it's okay." She sighed and slid into the chair. "It's just that Jason's not what I would call a great character reference."

"I hear you. But then, I was working for Frank Collins, and my brother was a crazy biker dude, so it really wasn't that much of a stretch." He shrugged. "Thanks for cutting me some slack, Claire."

"Everybody deserves a second chance. Hey, did you see Shane? I thought you wanted to talk to him."

"I did. Where is he?"

"Gone to work. He just left."

"I missed him?" Dean looked around, as if Shane would just materialize out of thin air. He looked disappointed when that didn't happen. "Damn."

"Well, it's pretty busy in here. If you didn't see him, he probably didn't see you, either. It's not like he's avoiding you or anything."

"Yeah, probably. So. You're, ah, staying on? In Morganville?"

"Yes." She left it at that. Between her new, completely amazing relationship with Shane, and the fact that Myrnin was teaching her physics so advanced that most Nobel Prize winners would weep, no way was she leaving now. "You?"

He shrugged. "Got no place else to be. You still living at the Glass House?"

"Uh, no. I made a deal with my parents. I have to live at home with them until I'm eighteen, and then I can move back. Eve promised that they'd keep my room for me, though." The truth was, she pretty much still lived there, and she looked forward to the time she spent with her friends—shared dinners, board games, zombie-smashing video games, and Wii tennis . . . And Eve doing dramatic readings from her favorite vampire books as Michael squirmed in embarrassment.

She looked forward to everything.

Morganville wasn't perfect. It would never be perfect. But Amelie had kept her promise, and humans were starting to feel like equal citizens, not possessions. Not walking blood banks.

It was a start. Claire had plans for more, in time.

"Hey," she said. "Maybe you could come over tonight, to the Glass

House? Have dinner with us? I'm sure Shane would love to see you. It'd be a great surprise."

"It would," Dean said, and gave her a matching grin. "Yeah, okay. Seven o'clock?"

"Fine," she said. "Listen, I have to get to work. See you then!"

He hastily stood up and shoveled his books and papers into his backpack. "I'm going too," he said. "Just a sec."

Is he hitting on me? Claire wondered. She knew what Eve would say, but she couldn't quite believe it. Dean seemed like a nice guy—but there was a glint in his eye when he looked at her.

She wondered if she should just take off, but that seemed rude.

Oliver was watching her from his place at the bar. She nodded to him, and he gave her a cool look that told her just what he thought of her. No, they were never going to be friends. And that was fine with Claire. She still thought he was a creep.

Dean stumbled over his own feet getting up, jostled the arm of a jock at the next table, and had to apologize his way out of trouble, backing into Claire as he did so. She sighed, grabbed his backpack, and towed him toward the door.

She was surprised he didn't fall over the cracks in the sidewalk, but once he was out of public view, he seemed to straighten up and be a little more coordinated. Huh. He was taller than she'd thought. Broader, too. Not Shane-broad, but solid, after all. It was the hair that fooled her— emo hair always made guys look kind of wimpy.

"Where are you heading?" she asked Dean. He adjusted the weight of his backpack on his shoulder.

"Oh, you know," he said vaguely, and pointed down the street. She was starting to think that he really was trying to hit on her. The going-my-way routine must have been old when Rome was still building roads. "You all done with classes and stuff?"

"Mostly. I have a couple of labs still to finish out, extra credit stuff, really. You looked like you were studying hard."

"Not really," Dean said. "I mostly carry the books around just to make stupid girls like you think I'm safe to be around."

She blinked, not sure she'd heard that right. He'd said it exactly the same way he'd said everything else. Like a nice, normal guy.

They were just passing an alley between the buildings. Nobody in sight.

"What—"

She turned her head toward him, and the last thing she saw was his backpack, full of books, heading at full speed toward her head.

Claire woke up not really sure she was waking up at all—everything seemed weird, smeared, dreamlike. She couldn't move, and her head hurt so bad she started to cry.

She heard voices.

". . . can't believe you brought her here," one said—she knew the voice, but she couldn't place it; the headache was too huge to think around. "Are you mental? That's not just *anybody*. She's going to be missed, Dean!"

"That's the point." Dean. That was Dean's voice. "I want them to miss her. I want them to look all over. They won't find her until I want them to. Come on, Jason. Man up, already."

"Dude, I knew you were crazy. I didn't know you were stupid, too. We have to let her go."

Sound of scuffling. Feet on wood. Grunts. Two men fighting.

One went down.

"Shut up," Dean snapped. "You're always whining. All you ever had to do was carry the bodies. I'm not even asking you to get your hands dirty."

"No! Look, I *know* her. You can't—"

"That's why she's perfect. *Everybody* knows her. C'mon, man, get it together. She's just a girl. Worse, she's a vamp lover. We're making the world a better place, and having fun while we do it." Dean laughed. It was the worst sound she'd ever heard from a human—and a good match for the worst sound she'd ever heard, period.

Jason must be Jason Rosser, Eve's brother. The one Dean said he barely knew. Maybe this was some horrible dream. It made sense that she'd put Jason's brother in a dream about being abducted and tied up, right? Because Jason had been accused of those murders . . .

Claire opened her eyes and stared at the ceiling of what looked like an old, abandoned house. Spackle was peeling off in sad sheets, hanging down, waving in a slight breeze through a broken window.

Jason had been accused of those murders. But he'd told Amelie, straight up, that he hadn't killed anybody.

He'd just seen it happen. He'd never said who was behind it. *Dean.*

Claire felt short of breath. *This is bad; this is really, really bad.* . . . Her head felt like it had been smashed with a brick. She felt sick enough to barf, and when she tried to move, the pain got worse. She couldn't do much, anyway. She was tied up, ankles and wrists.

There was sunlight coming in the window, but it was at a low angle. She'd been out for hours, and there was a bitter, nasty taste in her mouth. They'd given her something, on top of knocking her in the head. Maybe chloroform.

By twisting her wrist, she could see her watch.

Five o'clock.

The sun would be down soon. Nobody would have missed her yet; it wasn't dinnertime, and she'd been casually intending to drop in at Myrnin's lab to see how far he'd gotten with setting it back up. But he hadn't been expecting her.

Nobody had been expecting her. Shane had gone to work, and wouldn't be home until dark.

Phone.

It wasn't in her pocket. They'd taken it.

She blinked, and she must have lost time, because when she opened her eyes again, Dean Simms was sitting next to her, staring down. In the doorway of the decaying room stood Jason Rosser, looking sick and ill at ease.

Dean was smiling like he owned the world.

"Hey," he said. "So, you're up and around, right? Good. I thought you'd be tougher. I mean, they all talk about you like you're something special, but you went down just like the others. No problem at all."

"I . . . " Nausea boiled up inside when she tried to talk, and she stopped and swallowed helplessly until she could talk again. "My friends will look for me."

"Yeah, that's what I figured. So when they find you drained like some sad little vamp quickie outside of Oliver's back door . . . well. They won't be real happy, will they?" Dean's eyes practically glowed. "Man, you were so *easy*. Frank thought you had backbone. Guess not."

"Why?" she whispered. "Why are you doing this?" She really wanted to know. Somehow, if she had to die, she felt like she wanted to understand. She wanted it to make sense.

"Look, it's not personal." Dean dragged a fingernail down her cheek, scratching her. "Well, maybe a little personal, because, you know, fun. But this is about setting this town free. Fighting evil. It's what Frank Collins wanted. It's what I want. It's what you want, right, Claire? I know it's what Shane wants, too. So you're doing everybody a favor by dying."

Dean hadn't come to Morganville just to have Shane's back; he'd come to have his fun. If he even knew Frank Collins at all, he'd just been using Frank. Once he'd come to Morganville, he'd realized it was open season, and he could do whatever he wanted.

Still could, Claire realized sickly. Nobody suspected him at all.

She certainly hadn't.

"What?" he asked her. "You're not going to tell me I'm making a mistake? Beg me not to do it?"

"Why bother?" she whispered. "You'll do what you want, right?"

"Always do." Dean leaned back. "Jase. Hold her feet. I don't want her kicking me."

"It's not right. This isn't right, man."

"Shut up or I'll make it two bodies tonight. It just makes my point better."

Claire kicked out, but it was no use; Jason leaned on her ankles and held them down. Dean forced her arm down and opened up a rusting medical kit. He took out one of those hollow needles doctors used to draw blood, but instead of connecting it to a sample tube, he stuck on some rubber tubing.

The rubber tubing ended in a big empty gallon jug that had once held milk.

"Little stick." He smirked and slid the needle into her vein.

Claire screamed. Jason looked away, guilt written all over his face, but

Dean just kept on smiling. Red flooded out into the tube, ran along the coils, and began pumping out into the milk jug.

"How's it feel?" he asked her. "You like vampires. How's it feel to have your life drained out of you, just like they do it? I hate vampires. I really, really do. And if I can get this town to rise up and kill even one more by doing you, it's a bargain."

She squeezed her eyes shut and tried to think of something she could do.

Blood.

A black-and-white ghost flickered into view at the far end of the room. Ada's image looked quiet and composed, and just a little bit pleased. She'd come to watch Claire die.

"Get help," Claire whispered. "Please, go get help!"

Jason and Dean, at least, had no idea whom she was talking to, since Ada had manifested behind them. "Who are you talking to, idiot? Jason's not on your side. Jesus, Jason, hold her feet! Come on, man! I'm not asking you for much, here!"

Ada raised thin eyebrows. Her image flickered. Claire didn't want to look at the red line rising in the milk jug; she could feel herself getting weaker, her heart pounding harder to keep up.

"Myrnin," Claire panted. "I need Myrnin."

Ada flickered out. Claire had no idea whether or not she'd even make the effort.

Outside, the sun settled below the window.

Twilight.

Jason jumped up at a sound from outside. "What the hell is that?"

"Nothing," Dean said. He was watching Claire's face. She was breathing too fast, and she tried to slow down; her heart was racing, and she was losing too much blood. *Ada, please. Please.* "Don't worry about it. It's the wind."

Jason let go of Claire's feet. She was too weak to move much anyway. "No, it's not. There's somebody out there. Dude, leave her. Let's go!"

"No frickin' way. We're almost done here. Five more minutes. Keep it together, bro."

"I'm not your bro!" Jason snarled. "You're on your own, asshole!"

He took off. *No—please wait.* Claire tried not to cry, but she was losing track of why she ought to be strong. Was somebody coming? No, she had to save herself. Nobody was coming to save her.

"Dean," she said. "You know about the portals, don't you?"

That got his attention. Full on.

"I can tell you something about them you don't know. If you stop this."

His dark eyes took on a strangely stubborn look; he didn't like being robbed of his pleasure. "What kind of something? Because it'd have to be really good."

"Oh, it is," she said. "I can tell you how to make your own portals. How to go anywhere. Do anything. Imagine what you could do with that, Dean."

He was imagining it, all right, and she could see color rising in his cheeks. He liked it.

He liked it a *lot.*

Dean glanced over at the milk jug, which was shimmering with her blood. A steady stream flowed out of the tube to patter down inside. "Start talking," he said. "If I like what you say, I'll turn it off."

He was lying to her; she could feel it. "You can stop pretending you're killing me for a cause. You're not. You're killing me because you like it, Dean. You're not a vampire; you're worse. They're like tigers. You're a cannibal."

His eyes flickered, and he leaned forward. "Maybe I'll try that, too," he said. "Maybe I'll start on you."

She blinked, light-headed. The world seemed to shift in front of her. She had a vision, and it was so *real.*

She was looking past him into the living room at home, just like through a tunnel. The TV was on. Eve was singing along to some obnoxious commercial, shimmying her hips as she put a plate full of hot dogs on the table. It was Eve's night to cook. Michael was tuning his guitar, intent on frets and strings and sounds.

Shane walked in from the front hall, dropped his keys on the table, and said, "Where's Claire?"

"Not here yet," Eve said. "Probably on her way."

I'm not. I'm not coming. I'm sorry.

Shane dug his cell phone out and dialed.

Somewhere in another part of the abandoned house, Claire heard her ring tone echoing. The odd thing was, Shane seemed to hear it, too. He looked around, raised his eyebrows at Eve, and Eve shrugged. "Maybe she left it."

They could hear the phone. But the phone was here.

Claire pulled in a breath to scream, but she didn't have to.

Shane looked right at her, and for a second, she realized what that tunnel was, that silvery shimmer at the edges.

She realized that Ada hadn't let her down after all. It was a portal, and Shane was going to save her.

He saw her.

His eyes widened.

"Claire!" he screamed, and lunged at the portal.

It closed right before he got there.

"Oh, man," Dean breathed. "Close. You can do that thing, too? The portal thing? Comes in handy; am I right?" He waved his arm, and the portal shimmered back into existence—but in place of the tunnel that had led to the Glass House, there was one leading into darkness. No— not quite darkness. It was the old prison, the one where the sick vampires had been kept. "Ada locked me out for a while, and man, I was starting to sweat. But I promised her some fresh blood if she'd just let me have it for a couple more days."

He'd been using the network to kill, and Jason had helped him— probably just because Jason was a joiner, and lonely, and Dean knew how to make people feel wanted. Even Claire had felt it, and she should have known better.

Her heart was racing so fast now.

"See?" he said. "I can do it from anywhere. Just like you. Guess that makes us special."

He was smart, she realized. Clever and cold. Like Myrnin.

Only Myrnin had a conscience.

Something moved on the other side of the portal. A ghost. Ada?

No, although Claire saw the flicker of her black-and-white image for a second standing in the portal, facing away from her. Beckoning to someone else on the other side.

Then misting out of the way.

Ada had brought help after all, but it wasn't Myrnin.

It was Frank Collins.

Shane's dad stood on the other side of the portal, staring through at them, looking more like a ghost than Ada had. Claire must have made some sound, because Dean turned to look, and his face went completely slack with surprise. "Frank?" he asked. "Frank, wait—let me explain . . ."

Frank Collins reached through, grabbed Dean, and dragged him through the portal.

Dean screamed, once, and then there was silence. Just . . . nothing.

Claire felt herself getting cold. *This is how it feels*, she thought. *Becoming a vampire. Except I won't wake up.*

Frank stepped through the portal.

"Keep breathing," he told her, and crouched next to her as he took the tube out of her arm and tossed it away. He wadded up a piece of bandage and stuck it in the bend of her arm, then bent it back to add pressure. "Sorry about Dean. I always knew he wasn't good in the head, but I never thought he'd go this crazy."

He looked at her for a few seconds, then pushed to his feet and headed for the portal.

Along the way, he grabbed the milk jug, and then he was gone.

Ada's ghost misted back into view, staring at Claire. She was smiling.

"Help," Claire whispered.

"I did." Ada's prim voice came out of the distant, tinny speaker of the cell phone. "He promised me blood, but I don't want *yours*. I don't like it."

Ada disappeared.

She was alone, and cold. For a little while, that was all there was.

Then hands were lifting her, and she felt a tiny sting in her numb arm, and there were voices.

Light.

Then a different kind of nothing.

The hospital room was dark in the middle of the day, out of courtesy to the visitors. The overhead fluorescent lights bleached everybody, but at least nobody burst into flame.

That was Morganville in a nutshell. Compromise.

"I'm told that you're doing well," Amelie said, and pulled up a chair at Claire's bedside. Her bodyguards had taken up posts at the door. One of them winked at Claire, and she smiled back. "I feel I must apologize for my lack of care for your safety."

"You couldn't have known I was in trouble," Claire said.

"You wear my mark on your bracelet, and that makes you my dependent." That seemed to settle everything for Amelie. "That does not reflect well upon my stewardship. Luckily, Dr. Mills believes you will make a complete recovery. You may thank your friends for being so quick to act on your behalf."

Claire felt pleasantly warm, safe, and a little drugged. "Yeah, about the rescue," she said. "What happened?"

"Several things. First, Eve called me and demanded my help." Amelie nodded to Eve, who managed to look simultaneously smug and embarrassed as she leaned against the wall. "Although Eve presumed a great deal about my willingness to help, I decided to speak with Ada." Claire bet that had been an interesting, scary conversation. "She admitted that she knew where you were. From there, it was a simple enough matter to open a portal to you and bring you help."

"Who was it?" she asked. Her eyelids felt heavy. "Shane?"

"In fact, no," Oliver said, from the darkest corner of the room. "I carried you. Don't get sentimental; the doctors saved you, not me. I simply moved you from one place to another." He sounded as if he deeply wished to be out of the round of thanks at all costs. Claire was happy to oblige him.

"The blood bank came in handy," Dr. Mills said cheerfully, leaning over her to check her tubes and wires. "About time it did humans some good, too." He didn't seem shy about saying it in front of Amelie and Oliver, either. "You owe us about four pints, kiddo. But later, I promise. No rush at all."

"Thanks," she said, and gave him a drowsy thumbs-up.

"Just doing my job," he said. "Of course, some days it's a pleasure. Rest. You're going to be here for a few days. Oh, and I hope you enjoy off-brand flavors of Jell-O."

She thought he was kidding about that last part, but she absolutely couldn't be sure. Before she could ask, he scribbled something on her chart and hurried off to the next patient. Jell-O victim.

Amelie's cool fingers adjusted the covers minutely—for Amelie, that was positively fussy. "I am pleased you'll be working with us a while longer, Claire," she said. "Sleep now."

Claire badly wanted to, but she had another question. "Did you get him?" Claire asked, and opened her eyes again. "Did you find Dean?"

"Yes," Amelie said. Her expression was absolutely unreadable. "We found Dean." She rose, nodded to her bodyguards, and left without an explanation or a backward glance. Oliver pushed off and followed, but he made it look like it was his own idea.

Oh, that was going to be trouble, if Oliver kept up with the attitude. But it was trouble that Claire didn't have to worry about. The only thing she had to worry about, in fact, was choking down horrible, weird flavors of gelatin.

About a minute after the departure of the vampires, the door opened again, and Shane came in juggling a handful of drinks. Coffee, it smelled like. The sight of him made Claire feel like a sun had exploded inside her—so much happiness she was surprised it wasn't leaking out of her skin, like light.

His smile was *amazing.*

"Hope you brought some for me," Claire said as he handed Eve and Michael their cups. There was one left over.

"You're kidding, right?" Shane asked. "You don't need caffeine. You need sleep." He held out the last cup, and Claire realized she'd been wrong; there was someone else in the shadows. Deeper in the shadows even than Oliver had been.

Myrnin.

He looked completely different to her now, and not just because he wasn't crazy anymore. He'd remembered how to dress himself, for one thing; gone were the costume coats and Mardi Gras beads and flip-flops. He had on a gray knit shirt, black pants, and a jacket that looked a bit out of period, but not as much as before.

All clean. He even had shoes on.

"Yes, you must sleep," he agreed as he accepted the cup and tried the coffee. "I've gone to far too much trouble to train up another apprentice at this late date. We have work to do, Claire. Good, hard work. Some of it may even earn you accolades, once you leave Morganville."

She smiled slowly. "You'll never let me leave."

Myrnin's dark eyes fixed on hers. "Maybe I will," he said. "But you must give me at least a few more years, my friend. I have a great deal to learn from you, and I am a *very* slow learner."

Claire laughed at that, because it was just silly. At least, she thought she did. She felt pleasantly floaty, and so very tired.

Her parents dropped in and evicted everyone, for a while. Even Myrnin. She supposed that was all right, in her dreamy haze. It was nice, being loved like that.

When she opened her eyes again, it was night. Her parents were gone, and Eve was asleep in one of those uncomfortable hospital chairs, curled up with her head on her arms and a hospital blanket covering up her pink Goth bowling shirt. Michael had his guitar, and he was playing very quietly—something slow and sweet and peaceful. When he saw Claire's eyes flutter open, he stopped, looking guilty.

"No, go on," she murmured. "It's really beautiful."

"I'm supposed to play at Common Grounds later," he said. "I can blow it off if you need me to stay, though."

"No, you go. Don't rob Morganville of the amazing Michael Glass comeback tour."

"Yeah, like anybody will care," Michael said, but he smiled in that way that meant he was kind of embarrassed about it. And delighted. "I wouldn't leave, but it looks like you've got a permanent bodyguard already."

Shane was asleep, too, head down on the edge of her bed. She longed to run her fingers through his hair, but she didn't want to wake him up.

She didn't have to. Shane's breathing changed, and he sat up, blinking, as if he'd gotten some invisible signal. He focused on her instantly. "Hey," he said, and she saw him relax as relief rolled through him. "Sleepyhead." He reached out and took her hand in his, then leaned forward and kissed her. It felt warm and drowsy and sweet, like a promise. "Welcome back."

She felt like she'd never take her life for granted again. "Did you talk to my parents?"

"I did. Man, my ears are still burning. It's all my fault, apparently." Shane smiled, but she could see he really did feel that way, about his guilt. "I can't believe I wasn't there for you, Claire. I can't believe I couldn't get to you—"

She put a finger on his lips. "You've always been there when I needed you," she said. "You're here now, right?"

"You know what I mean."

She thought about telling him about Frank, about how he'd saved her. But she wasn't sure, really sure, that she hadn't just imagined it.

And if Frank Collins was around, he could show up and tell his son himself.

"I know," she said. Something Monica said back at Common Grounds haunted her, especially in this weakened state: *You know it's not going to last, right?* Things changed. People changed. Even Morganville changed. "Don't go." She hadn't meant to say it out loud. *Needy much, Claire?*

Shane took her hand and raised it to his lips in an old-fashioned kiss worthy of Myrnin at his best. "I'm not going anywhere," he said. "Not even to take a shower. And you're really going to regret that, by the way."

"Dude," Michael said. "I already regret it."

"Shut up, man."

Michael threw a box of tissues at him. Shane fielded it and fired it back, which wasn't much of a challenge to Michael's vampire reflexes.

Eve woke up, wiped drool from her chin, and yawned. "You jerks want to take the Super Bowl outside? Some of us need our beauty rest— *don't say it, Collins.*"

Shane caught the tissue box. "Say what?" he asked, and tossed the box underhanded in Eve's direction. "Fetch!"

She came out of the chair, picked up the tissue box, and whacked him over the head with it. Several times.

Claire couldn't stop laughing. Tears burned in her eyes, and she loved them so much.

She loved them all so much.

Michael rescued Eve from a tissue paper war and towed her toward the door with his guitar case in the other hand. "I'm calling a truce," he said, and looked back at Claire from the door. "We'll come back after the show."

None of them were letting her stay the night alone; she got that. She supposed later, that might annoy her, but tonight, it just felt . . . great. She loved being looked after.

Then the door shut, and it was just her and Shane.

"So," she said. "What's on TV tonight?"

"Hockey."

"I'm pretty sure there's something other than hockey."

"Nope. Just hockey. It's on every channel. Better complain to the cable company." He kicked back in the chair and settled in with the remote.

"Jerk." She sighed. "I'm the one with low blood pressure, here. Shouldn't I get the remote?"

"I'm thoughtful. Look, I brought you a present." He pulled a wooden stake out of his pocket and put it next to her hand, on top of the blankets.

"What's this for?"

"Emergencies," he said. "Morganville emergencies."

She examined the stake. It looked like it might have been one of Eve's, at least originally. "I hate to break it to you, but Dean wasn't a vampire."

"Bet it would have worked good on him, too."

She spotted some writing on the side. "You put my name on it!" Hand-carved. That must have taken a while.

"I had time, sitting around here waiting for you to wake up. Anyway,

Amelie just issued a new law. All humans are allowed to carry stakes for self-defense. See? Progress."

"Or mutually assured destruction."

"Well, whatever works."

Claire held up the stake. "Some girls get jewelry. But they're such losers."

He reached in his pocket, came out with a small velvet box, and set it next to her pillow. She took a deep, sudden breath, and felt her whole body go a little bit woozy around the edges.

"What is it?" she asked softly.

"It's . . . kind of for later," he said. "I just didn't want you to think I'm not well-rounded or anything."

He kissed her, and she felt everything melt away. All the pain, the fear, the worry. It was all just going to be . . . okay.

Somewhere, Michael Glass was playing to a packed house at Common Grounds.

Amelie was sitting alone in her study.

Myrnin was writing down secrets in a leather-bound book.

Monica Morrell was sneering at a blushing freshman girl.

And Claire Danvers was . . . happy.

At least for tonight.

TRACK LIST

In celebration of reaching book six, I'd like to share with you a list of some songs that have kept me going through the writing process! As always, if you've got suggestions, I'd love to hear them (rachel@rachelcaine. com).

"Bridge to Better Days"	Joe Bonamassa
"Believe"	The Bravery
"Danger Is Here"	Elliot Scott
"The Geeks Were Right"	The Faint
"Sister Self Doubt"	Get Shakes
"Caravan" (DJ Smash's Smashish Remix)	Dizzy Gillespie
"Video"	India.Arie
"Hole in the Middle"	Emily Jane White
"Black Is the Color of My True Love's Hair" (Jaffa Remix)	Nina Simone
"Hell Yeah"	Rev Theory
"Count to Ten"	Tina Dico
"Silence" (DJ Tiesto's In Search of Sunrise Edit)	Delerium and Sarah McLachlan
"Let It Die"	Foo Fighters
"Get Free"	The Vines
"Violet Hill"	Coldplay
"Could've Had Me"	Lex Land
"Mercy"	Duffy
"Feeling Good"	Nina Simone
"Not Dead Yet"	Ralph Covert and The Bad Examples

"Burnin' Up"   Jonas Brothers
"Let It Rock"   Kevin Rudolf and Lil Wayne
"Disturbia"   Rihanna
"Hot N Cold"   Katy Perry
"Heavy on My Mind"   Back Door Slam
"Guess Who"   Nekta
"Now You Know"   We Are The Fury
"What You Want"   Neva Dinova
"Get Back"   Demi Lovato
"Sacre Couer" (Live)   Tina Dico
"Ghost Town"   Shiny Toy Guns

Read on for an exciting excerpt from
the next Morganville Vampires novel,

BITE CLUB

Coming in hardcover from
New American Library in May 2011.

Looking back on it later, Claire thought she should have known trouble was coming, but really, in Morganville, *anything* could be trouble. Your college professor doesn't show for class? Probably got fanged by vampires. Takeout forgets to put onions on your hamburger? The regular onion delivery guy disappeared—again, probably due to vampires. And so on. For a college town, Morganville had a remarkable lot of vampires.

Claire was an authority on all those subjects: Texas Prairie University and, of course, the vampires. And mysterious disappearances. She'd almost been one of those, more often than she wanted to admit.

But this problem wasn't a disappearance at all. It was an appearance . . . something new, something different, and something cool, at least in her boyfriend Shane's opinion, because as Claire was sorting the mail for their weird little fraternity of four into the "junk" and "keep" piles, Shane grabbed the flyer she'd put in "junk" and read it with the most elated expression she'd ever seen on his face. Scary. Shane didn't get excited about much; he was guarded about his feelings, mostly, except with her.

Now he looked as delighted as a little kid at Christmas.

"Mike!" he bellowed, and Claire winced and put her hands over her ears. When Shane yelled, he really belted it out. "Yo, Dead Man, get your ass down here!"

Michael, their third housemate here at the Glass House, must have assumed that there was an emergency under way . . . not an unreasonable assumption, because hey, Morganville. So he arrived at a run, slamming the door back, looking paler than usual, and more dangerous than normal, too. When he was acting like a regular guy, he seemed quiet and sweet, maybe a little *too* practical sometimes, but Vampire Michael was a whole different, spicy deal.

Yeah, she was living in a house with a vampire. And strangely, that was not the weirdest part of her life.

Michael blinked the tinges of red away from his blue eyes, ran both hands through his wavy blond hair, and frowned at Shane. "What the hell is your problem?" He didn't wait to hear, though; he walked over to the counter and got down one of their mismatched battered coffee mugs. This one was black with purple Gothic lettering that spelled out POISON. It was their fourth housemate Eve's cup, but she still hadn't made an appearance this morning.

When you slept later than a vampire, Claire thought, that was probably taking it a little too far.

As he filled the mug with coffee, Michael waited for Shane to make some sense. Which Shane finally did, holding up the cheaply printed white flyer. It curled around the edges from where it had been rolled up to fit in the mailbox. "What have I always wanted in this town?" he asked.

"A strip club that would let in fifteen-year-olds?" Michael said.

"When I was *fifteen*. No, seriously, what?"

"Guns 'R Us?"

Shane made a harsh buzzer sound. "Okay, to be fair, yeah, that's a good alternate answer. But no. I always wanted a place to seriously train to fight, right? Someplace that didn't think aerobics was a martial art? And look!"

Claire took the paper from Shane's hand and smoothed it out on the table. She'd only glanced at it when sorting mail; she'd thought it was some kind of gym. Which it was, in a way, but it wasn't teaching spin and yoga and all that stuff.

This one was a gym and martial arts studio, and it was teaching self-defense. Or at least that was what Claire took from the graphic of some guy in a white jacket and pants kicking the crap out of the air, and the words DEFEND YOURSELF in big, bold letters at the bottom.

Michael leaned over her shoulder, slurping coffee. "Huh," he said. "Weird."

"Nothing weird about people wanting to learn a few life-preserving skills, man. Especially around here. Not like we're all looking forward to a peaceful old age," Shane said.

"I mean it's weird who's teaching," Michael said. "Being that this guy"—he tapped the name at the bottom of the page—"is a vampire."

Vassily was the name, which Claire made out only when she squinted at it. Small type. "A vampire's teaching self-defense," she said. "To us. Humans."

Shane was thrown for just about a minute, and then he said, "Well, who better? Amelie put out a decree that humans were free to learn this stuff, right? Sooner or later, some vamp was bound to make some cash off of it."

"You mean, off of us," Claire said. But she could see his point. A vampire martial arts instructor? That would have to be all kinds of scary, or awesome, or both. She wouldn't have gone for it, personally; she doubted she had half as much muscle or body mass as it was going to require. But Shane . . . Well, it was a natural for Shane, really. He was competitive, and he didn't mind taking some punishment as long as he enjoyed the fight. He'd been complaining about the lack of a real gym for a while now.

Claire handed the flyer back to him, and Shane carefully folded it up and put it in his back pocket. "Watch yourself," she said. "Get out of there if anything's weird." Although in Morganville, Texas, home of everything weird, that was a pretty high bar to pass. After all, there was a vampire teaching self-defense. That, in itself, was the strangest thing she'd seen in a while.

"Yes, Mom," Shane said, but he whispered it, intimately close to her ear, and then kissed that spot on the neck that always made her blush and shiver, every time. "Eat your breakfast."

She turned and kissed him full-on, just a sweet, swift brush of lips, because he was already moving . . . and then he did a double take, and came back to kiss her again, slower, hotter, *better*.

Michael, sliding into a seat at the kitchen table with his coffee cup, flipped open the thin four-page Morganville newspaper, and said, "One of you is supposed to be somewhere right about now. I'm just saying that, not in a Dad kind of way."

He was right, and Claire broke off the kiss with a frustrated growl, low in her throat. Shane grinned. "You're so cute when you do that," he said. "You sound like a really fierce kitten."

"Bite me, Collins."

"Whoops, wrong housemate. I think you meant that for the one who drinks plasma."

Michael gave him a one-fingered salute without looking up from his study of the latest Morganville high school sports disaster. Claire doubted he was actually interested in that, but Michael had to have reading material around; she didn't think he slept much these days, and reading was how he passed the time. And he probably got something out of it, even if it was just something to impress Eve with on his local knowledge of football.

Claire grabbed her breakfast—a Pop-Tart just ringing up out of the toaster—and wrapped it in a napkin so she could take it with her. Book bag acquired, she blew Shane (and Michael) an air kiss as she hit the back door, heading out into a cold Morganville fall.

Fall, in other parts of the world, was a beautiful season, filled with leaves in brown, orange, yellow. . . . Here, the leaves had been brown for a day, and then dropped off the trees to rattle around the streets and yards like bones. Another depressing season, to add to all the others that were depressing in this town. But at least it was cooler than the blazing summer; that was something. Claire had actually dug out a long-sleeved tee and layered another shirt over it, because the wind gusts carried the sharp whip of approaching winter now. Pretty soon, she'd need a coat, and gloves, and a hat, and maybe boots if the snow fell hard enough.

Morganville in summer was dull green at best, but now all the grass was burned dry, and most of the bushes had lost their leaves, leaving black skeletons to shiver in the cold. Not a pretty place, not at all, although a few house-proud people had tried some landscaping, and Mrs. Hennessey on the corner liked those weird concrete animals. This year, she had a gray deer fake-sipping from an empty stone fountain, and a couple of concrete squirrels that looked more menacing than cute.

Claire checked her watch, took a bite of her Pop-Tart, and almost choked as she realized how little time she had. She broke into a jog, which was tough considering the weight of the bag on her shoulder, and then kicked it to a full run as she passed the big iron gates of Texas Prairie University. Fall semester was a busy time; lots of new, stupid freshmen wandering around confused with maps, or still unpacking their cars with boxes. She had two or three near-collisions, but reached the steps of the Science Building without much incident, and with two whole minutes to spare. Good, she needed them to get her breath back.

As she munched the rest of her breakfast, wishing she had a bottle of water, others she knew by sight filtered past her . . . Bruce from Computational Physics, who was almost as out of place here as she felt; Ilaara from one of the math classes she was in, but Claire couldn't really sort out which one. She didn't make close friends at TPU, which was a shame, but it wasn't that sort of a school—especially if you were in the know about the inner workings of Morganville. Most of the just-passing-through students passed the year or two they were here with the usual on-campus partying; except for specific college-friendly stores that were located within a couple of blocks, they hardly ever bothered to leave the gates of the university. And that was probably for the best.

It was dangerous out there, after all.

Claire found her classroom—a small one, nothing at her level of study had big groups—and took her usual seat in the middle of the room, next to a smelly grad student named Doug, who apparently hated personal hygiene. She thought about moving, but the fact was there weren't many other places, and Doug's aura was tangible at ten feet away anyway. Better to get an intense dose close-up so your nose could adjust quickly.

Doug smiled at her. He seemed to like her, which was scary, but at least he wasn't a big chatterbox or one of those guys who came on with the cheesy innuendos—at least, not usually. She'd certainly sat next to worse. Well, maybe not in terms of body odor, though. "Hey," he said, bending closer. Claire resisted the urge to bend the other way. "I hear he's springing a new lab experiment on us today. Something mind-blowing."

Given that she worked for the smartest guy in Morganville, maybe the entire world, and given that he was at least a few hundred years old and drank blood, Claire suspected her scale of mind-blowing might be a little bigger than Doug's. It wasn't unusual to go to Myrnin's secret lair/underground lab (yes, he actually had one) and find he'd invented edible hats, or an iPod that ran on sweat. And considering that her boss built blood-drinking computers that controlled dimensional portals, Claire didn't really anticipate any problems understanding a mere university professor's assignments. Half of what Myrnin gave her to read wasn't even in a living language, anyway. It was amazing what she'd learned—whether she wanted to or not.

"Good luck," she said to Stinky Doug, trying not to breathe too deeply. She glanced over at him, the way you do, and was startled to see that he was sporting two spectacular black eyes—healing up, she realized after the first shock, but he'd gotten smacked pretty hard. "Wow. Nice bruises. What happened?"

Doug shrugged. "Got in a fight. No big deal."

Someone, Claire thought, had disliked his body odor a whole lot more than usual. "Did you win?"

He smiled, but it was a private, almost cynical kind of smile—a joke she couldn't share. "Oh, I will," he said. "Big-time."

The door banged open at the far end of the room, and the prof stalked in. He was a short, round little man, with mean close-set eyes, and he liked Hawaiian shirts in obnoxiously loud colors—in fact, she was relatively sure that he and Myrnin might have shopped at the same store. The Obnoxious Store.

"Settle down!" he said, even though they weren't exactly the rowdiest class at TPU. In fact, they were perfectly quiet. But Professor Larkin always said that. Claire suspected he was actually deaf, so he just said it to be on the safe side. "Right. I hope you've all done your reading, because today you get to do some applications of principles you should already know. Everybody, stand up, shake it off, and follow me. Bring your stuff."

Claire hadn't bothered to unpack anything yet, so she just swung her backpack to her shoulder and headed out in Professor Larkin's wake, happy to be temporarily out of the Doug Fug. Not that Larkin was any treat, either. . . . He smelled like old sweat and bacon, but at least he'd bathed in recent memory.

She glanced down at his wrist. On it was a braided leather band with a metal plate incised with a symbol—not the Founder symbol that Claire wore as a pin on the collar of her jacket, but another vampire's symbol. Oliver's, apparently. That was a little unusual; Oliver didn't personally oversee a lot of humans. He was above all that. He was the Don in the local Morganville Mafia.

Larkin saw her looking, and sent her a stern frown. "Something to say, Miss Danvers?"

"Nice bracelet," she said. "I've only seen one other like it." The one she'd seen had been around the wrist of her own personal nemesis, Monica Morrell, crown princess (she wished!) of Morganville. Once the daughter of the mayor, now the sister of the *new* mayor, she thought she could do whatever she wanted . . . and with Oliver's Protection, she probably could, still, even if her brother Richard wasn't quite as indulgent as Daddy had been.

Larkin just . . . didn't seem the type Oliver would bother with, unless he wasn't what he seemed.

Larkin clasped his hands behind his back as they walked down the almost-empty wide hallway, the rest of the class trailing behind. "I ought to give you a pass from today's experiment," he said. "Confidentially, I'm pretty sure it's child's play for you, given your . . . part-time occupation."

He knew about Myrnin, or at least he'd been told *something*. There weren't many people who actually knew Myrnin, and fewer still who'd been to the lab and had any understanding of what went on in there. She'd never seen Larkin, or heard his name mentioned by anybody with clout.

So she was careful with her reply.

"I don't mind. I like experiments," she said, "provided they're not the kind that try to eat me or blow me up." Both of which, unfortunately, she'd come across at her job at the lab.

"Oh, nothing that dramatic," Larkin said. "But I think you might enjoy it."

That scared her, a bit.

When they arrived at the generic lab room, though, there didn't seem to be anything worth breaking a sweat over: some full-spectrum incandescent lights, like you'd use for indoor reptiles; some small ranked vials on each table of what looked like . . .

Blood.

Oh, crap, that was never a good sign in Morganville (or, Claire thought, anywhere else, either). She came to a sudden stop, and sent Larkin a wide-eyed look. The rest of the class was piling in behind her, talking in low tones; she knew Doug had arrived because of the blanket of body-smog that settled in around her. Of course, Doug took the lab stool beside her. Dammit. That blew, as Shane would have said; Claire covered it by sending him a small, not very enthusiastic smile as she dropped her backpack to the ground, careful of the laptop inside. She hated sitting on lab stools; they only emphasized how short she was. She felt like she was back in second grade again and unable to touch the floor in her chair.

Larkin assumed his position in the center of the lab tables, and grabbed a small stack of paper from his black bag. He passed out the instructions, and Claire read them, frowning. They were simple enough—place a sample of the "fluid" on a slide, turn on the full-spectrum lighting, observe and record results. Once a reaction was observed, mix the identified reactive blood with control blood until a nonreaction was achieved. Then work out the equations explaining the initial reaction, and the nonreaction, to chart the energy release.

No doubt at all what this was about, Claire thought. The vamps were using students to do their research for them. Free worker bees. But why?

Larkin had a smooth patter, she had to admit; he joked around, said that with the popularity of vampires in entertainment it might be fun to apply some physics to the problem. Part of the blood had been "altered" to allow for a reaction; part had not. He made it all seem very scientific and logical, for the benefit of the eight out of ten non-Morganville residents in the room.

Claire caught the eye of Malinda, the other one in the room who was wearing a vampire symbol, and Malinda's pretty face was set in a worried, haunted expression. She opened her eyes wide and held up her hands in a silent *What do we do?*

It'll be okay, Claire mouthed. She hoped she wasn't lying.

"Cool," said Stinky Doug, leaning over to look at the paper. Claire's eyes watered a little, and she felt an urge to sneeze. "Vampires. *I vant to drink your bloot!*" He made a mock bite at her neck, which creeped her out so much, she nearly fell off the stool.

"Don't *ever* do that again," she said. Doug looked a little surprised at her reaction. "And by the way, showers. Look into them, Doug!"

That was a little too much snark for Claire's usual style, but he'd scared her, and it just came out. Doug looked wounded, and Claire immediately felt bad. "I'm sorry," she said, very sincerely. "It's just— You don't smell so great."

It was his turn now to look ashamed. "Yeah," he said, looking down at the paper. "I know. Sorry." He got that look again, that secret, smug look. "Guess I need to get rich enough nobody cares what I smell like."

"That or, you know, showering. That works better."

"Fine. Next time I'll smell just like a birthday bouquet."

"No fair just throwing on deodorant and aftershave or something. Real washing. It's a must."

"You're a tough sell." He flashed her a movie-star grin that looked truly strange with the discoloration around his mouth and nose. "Speaking of that, once I take that shower, you interested in going out for dinner?"

"I'm spoken for," she said. "And we have work to do."

She prepped the slide, and Doug fired up the lamp. The instant the full-spectrum lighting hit it, there was a noticeable reaction—bubbling under the glass, as if the blood had been carbonated. It took about thirty seconds for the reaction to run its course; once it had, all that was left was a black residue of ash.

"So freaking cool," Doug said. "Seriously. Where do you think they get this stuff? Squeeze real vampires?" There was something odd about the way he said it—as if he actually knew something. Which he shouldn't, Claire knew. Definitely, he shouldn't.

"It's probably just a light-sensitive chemical additive," Claire said. "Not sure how it works, though." That was true. As much as she'd studied it, she really didn't understand the nature of the vampire transformation. It wasn't a virus—exactly. And it wasn't a contaminant, either, although it had elements of that. There were things about it she suspected that all of their scientific approaches couldn't capture, try as they might. Maybe they were just measuring the wrong things.

Doug dropped the uncomfortable speculation. He wasn't so bad as a lab partner, if you forgot the stinky part; he was a good observer, and not half bad with calculations. She let him do most of the work, because she'd already done most of this with Myrnin; interesting that Doug came up with a slightly different formula, in the end, than she had on her own, because she thought his was a little more elegant. They were the first to come up with a stable mixture of the blood, and the second to come up with calculations—but Doug's, Claire was confident, were better than the other team's. You didn't have to finish first to win, not in science. You just had to be more right than the other guys.

All was going okay until she caught Doug trying to pocket a sample of the blood. "Hey," she said, and caught his wrist, "don't do that."

"Why not? It would be awesome at parties."

Again, there was that unsettling tone, a little too smug, a little too *knowing*. Whatever it was he intended to do with it, she doubted he was going to show off at parties with it.

"Just don't." Claire met his eyes. "I mean it. Leave it alone. It might be—toxic." Fatal, she meant, because if the vamps found out Doug was sneaking out samples . . . Well, accidents happened, even on the TPU campus. Stupidity wasn't covered by the general Protection agreement, and Doug seemed to have caught a little bit too much of a clue.

Doug grudgingly dropped it back to the table. Professor Larkin came around, checked out the sample bottles, and recorded them against a master sheet. As he walked away, and she and Doug packed their bags, Claire said, "See? I told you they'd be auditing."

"Yeah," Doug whispered back. "But he already checked us out."

And before she could stop him, he grabbed a couple of the vials, stuck them in his bag, and took off.

Claire swallowed the impulse to yell, and a second one to kick the table in frustration. She didn't dare tell Larkin; he was Protected, and Doug had no idea what he was getting into. She had to get him to give the vial back. Dumb ass wouldn't have any idea what to do with it, anyway.

She hoped.

Photo by Sharon Sams-Adams

Rachel Caine is the *New York Times* bestselling author of more than thirty novels, including the Weather Warden series, the Outcast Season series, and the Morganville Vampires series. She was born at White Sands Missile Range, which people who know her say explains a lot. She has been an accountant, a professional musician, an insurance investigator, and, until recently, still carried on a secret identity in the corporate world. She and her husband, fantasy artist R. Cat Conrad, live in Texas with their iguanas, Popeye and Darwin. Visit her Web site at www.rachelcaine.com, and find her on Twitter, Livejournal, Myspace, and Facebook.